A RIVER MOVES FORWARD

Selena Haskins

Calidream Publishing
Capitol Heights, Maryland

A River Moves Forward

Published by:
Calidream Publishing
P.O. Box 4201
Capitol Heights, MD 20791
Email: selena@calidreampub.com
Website: http://www.booksbyselena.com/
Selena Haskins, Publisher

QualityPress.info-Cover Design

Michelle Patricia Browne- Magpie Editing Services
Karen Perkins, LionheART Publishing House

ACKNOWLEDGEMENTS

I thank my Heavenly Father, Jehovah and his son, Jesus Christ for the gift of storytelling. I thank my supportive husband Ken, and my son, who gave Mommy the space and time to write. I love you guys! I thank my mother Celeste for her love and support through the years. You are part of the reason I wrote this book. You always said I have an "old soul." I love you very much, Mom! Thanks to my stepfather Patrick for stepping into the role as "Dad"; always my hero! Much love to my siblings- Terrence "T.J.", Yvette, Melvin, Calvin, Crystal, Michael, and Ricky. Thanks to my grandmother, the first storyteller in the family, and my paternal grandparents for their support. I thank my in-laws for accepting me as part of the family-Vernell and Jerron. My Uncle Tony who asked me to write the storyline for his comic strip back in '88, and now here I am writing novels. Who would have thought? I thank my cousin Tish, who is like my big sister. Tish is a true cheerleader for my writing, and is always supportive and encouraging, not just with writing, but personally. If we weren't related, we would be BFFs! Uncle Stevie, who has supported my stories since day one! Thanks to Toni, my adopted cousin, for telling me to never give up! I thank my nieces and nephews who keep me young and "in-the-know", especially Dominique and Maurice. Special thanks to my "Hoorah Corner"- Barbara, Lauren, Henry, Veria, Michelle, Pat, Pam, Susan, Stacy, Mike, the twins Glenda and Belinda, Edwina, Klaudette, Michelle, Tangie, Trina, Serena, Steve "Dink", Malanka "Seedie", and Calvin. Most of all, I thank my readers. Hug yourselves for me, because I really appreciate you supporting a first-time author. Much love!

Special thanks to Michelle P. Browne, Magpie Editing Services. She was very helpful with revising this book. She is the most tactful and patient editor that I have ever met! I look forward to working with her again.

Many thanks also to Karen Perkins, LionheART Publishing House, for formatting this book and giving great publishing advice and suggestions.

Much respect to the starving artists—we are the mavericks, the innovators, and the mirrors of humanity and sometimes the insanity. We are the abstract thinkers and the perfectionists. Our sacrifices help us to carry the torch of those who came before us, and at the end of the day, we are exhausted geniuses staring at our masterpieces!

AUTHOR BIO

Selena Haskins is a native Washingtonian, who enjoys music, reading, movies, and spending quality time with her family. Her first book, *A River Moves Forward*, evokes every human emotion as it addresses issues of poverty, abuse, race, and relationships. The mix of uncertainty and the infusion of events come together like a well-pieced puzzle. Throughout the book are messages of hope, love and forgiveness. Her upcoming project is the sequel, *Riding the Waves*.

Please connect with Selena through her website and join her social network of friends:

Author website: http://www.booksbyselena.com/
Facebook: https://www.facebook.com/authorselena.haskins
Twitter: https://twitter.com/BooksbySelena
Goodreads:
https://www.goodreads.com/author/show/6949131.Selena_Haskins

A RIVER MOVES FORWARD

"A River Moves Forward"

Dance with me waves flowing down the stream with ease

Dip and dive you river from the wind of the Chicago breeze

Sing me a new song that I can read in the sky

No matter my troubles, a river keeps flowing by . . .

I see you ol' river staring back at me

Sometimes I wonder what you see in me

You are a swimmer's dream

a beauty for a sailor at sea

A reflection of my soul bringing me clarity

You ol' river give me a natural high

You are my relaxation as you keep on flowing by

"Be quiet ol' river," Jesus said, "Peace, be still"

If I should die tomorrow, take my ashes if you will

I wish to be buried in the bed of the sea

so I can swim with the fishes for all eternity

No troubles, no worries, leave Cabrini Green behind

No matter what happens, a river will keep flowing by.

-Gina "Baby" Morris

Selena Haskins

PROLOGUE

1954

Mason Morris had just received an honorable discharge and returned home to Newburg, South Carolina. His first stop was the community hospital to visit his wife, Frieda Morris who had just given birth to his second child. He hoped for a boy this time, so he could teach him to play ball, make paper planes, and skip rocks across the river. "It's another girl, Mason," said Frieda. "I hope you're not disappointed."

"Oh that's all right." Mason wiped his sweaty forehead. "I just want to see my baby." He freed his shoulder of the weight from his big army bag and let it drop to the floor.

"Man, she's so light she can almost pass for White folk," Mason said. His southern accent was still heavy despite his military travels. He cuddled his infant in his arms and said, "Why, looky-here Frieda, she got blue eyes."

"Aren't they gorgeous?"

"Well, Frieda, I . . . I ain't never seen no colored baby with blue eyes before," he chuckled nervously.

"My great-grandmother had blue eyes."

"Well I ain't never seen your great-grandmother. You sure this here baby is mine?" he asked with one raised brow. He laughed. "Never mind. I knows she's mine. She's all mine. Got me two girls now, Donna and . . . what we calling this one here?"

"Connie Marie Morris."

"Hmm . . . I kinda like the sound of that. It's got a nice flow to it."

"I read in a baby book that Connie means independent and stable."

"Good, 'cause I don't want my girls to be dependent on nobody, especially no man," Mason replied firmly. He had seen his mother running after his father all his life, and all he did was abuse her. Mason wanted his girls to rely on themselves, and if they needed help, he wanted his girls to be able to rely on him. Serving in the army gave him a good feeling of authority, power, and pride. He felt the army had made him into a man, and he was determined to raise his girls with the same mental toughness it would take to survive in the world. As he held his newborn, he felt more than prepared to not only care for his family, but protect them too.

Everywhere the Morris's took their girls, everyone asked them about their daughter. The neighbors would say, "What'cha doin' with that blue-eyed baby? You watchin' her for somebody?"

It didn't stop there. "Looks like your wife done slept with the milkman," his coworkers would tease him. Finally, Mason insisted Frieda tell him the truth about Connie.

"I'm sorry Mason, but Connie ain't your baby," Frieda confessed.

"You a snake and a liar!" screamed Mason. He chased Frieda around the small room of their one-level house with a belt in his hand. "I'll kill you, woman!"

"No, Mason, no! Please . . . don't!" Frieda ducked and dodged as Mason swung his belt. When he caught her in the corner of the room, he whipped her down to the floor until she started crying.

"You had me looking like a damn fool!" Mason tossed his belt on the bed when he was done and walked away from her. "Can't believe you hurt me like this Frieda, you know how much I love you. You got some nerve sleeping with that white man!"

"If you wanna gets a divorce, I understand," Frieda cried. She slowly got up off the floor and inched her way cautiously towards him.

"No, you is mines woman. What done happen between you and that cracker boy Scott McKenzie is over with now," he barked. "Damage already done. Now I gots to raise this here white baby."

"I'm so sorry, Mason. When you was gone I felt all alone, but nothing like this here will ever happen again. I promise."

"Save your tears and apology, woman. Now we just gotta pack it up and move up north." Mason turned his back to her and looked out the window at his pickup truck. He wondered if his truck would last the long ride.

"Where we going?" Frieda sniffed, gently resting her hand against his back.

"Gonna move to Chicago. Can't stay here much longer. Won't be long before folks find out Connie is Scott's baby. Harm may come to us then," Mason snapped. "An ole buddy told me about housing they done built for veterans. All we gots to do is go up there and they gonna put us up in one of them apartments, dirt-cheap. Now you go on and pack our things. We're heading out at the crack of dawn."

While Frieda packed up their belongings, Mason took a long hot bath to wash off the dirt and grind from a hard day's work. He stared at the scars on his arms that reminded him of when Charlie hazed him while he was in the army. He hated Scott McKenzie for impregnating his wife, and even more because he was a white man like Charlie. He knew he had to hurry and get out of South Carolina before the hurt and anger festered to the point of killing Scott McKenzie, and then he would really be in trouble!

CHAPTER ONE

CABRINI GREEN

Mason moved his family to the Cabrini Green Housing projects, located on the North side of Chicago, blocks away from downtown. Cabrini Green was a newly developed housing project for low-income soldiers like Mason, who were returning home from the war. The Italians dominated Cabrini Green in the sixties, and the community was very family friendly, no matter what color you were. The Italians looked out for the Blacks and the Blacks looked out for the Italians, because the one thing the two races had in common at that time was being poor. As the years progressed, the Italians started moving out of the projects as better job opportunities became available to them, and more Black people started moving in because of fewer jobs for them.

To avoid overcrowding, the city built more housing projects to accommodate the poor. The Morris family moved into the brick building called "The Reds". The Morris family lived on the tenth floor and shared a three-bedroom apartment on North Sedgwick in The Reds.

Mason, who had gotten a job in sanitization, would often collect bulk pieces of furniture during his trash pickups and refurbish it for the family's home. Mama Frieda would sew tablecloths and make cushion seats to dress up the furniture. As time moved on, their family expanded to three girls, and by 1965, "Peaches" (Donna) was thirteen, Connie was eleven, and "Baby" (Gina) was six.

Mama used all the help she could from her girls during those days, but most of her help around the house came from Connie. She never had to ask Connie to help; she volunteered, whereas getting Peaches to help her was like pulling teeth. Baby would only help because she wanted to feel like a big girl. She would mimic whatever Connie did around the house.

Other times, Baby was hot on the trails of her Dad, who spoiled her with small toys from the five-and-dime store, and would let her tag along with him when he made errands. Baby didn't have a care in the world and was too young to realize how poor they were, but her father did everything he could to help his family.

To make more money to help the family, Mason and his friend would buy fish from the fish truck and have Mama to cook it so they could have more income coming into the house. Every Friday became Fish Friday, and Mama became known in the Projects as the "Fish Lady." Connie would open the kitchen window so everyone could smell the aroma of the fish and come running to get some. Neighbors would line up outside her door for a fish sandwich or plate. While Mama cooked, the girls would collect the money and bag the fish for the customers. Baby loved to hand out the bags, and she would say, "Thank you. Come again," just as her big sister Connie had taught her.

To outsiders, the Morris family seemed perfect. They helped their neighbors, spoke to everyone, and went to church every Sunday. The girls never got into any trouble, and they obeyed their parents.

For young Connie, she never felt normal, at home or in her neighborhood. At school, the children teased her and called her a "white girl" or "zebra." In the neighborhood, some of the kids would tease her just the same and say she was adopted. At home, Papa Mason would make Connie do all the chores. Meanwhile, her sisters could go outside and play or watch TV unless their mother asked them to help her in the kitchen.

"Get up, drop down and give me fifty!" Mason shouted at Connie. It was early in the morning, and Mason woke Connie up out of her sleep. "When you're done, I need you to spit shine my shoes and iron my shirts," he shouted. Connie was used to Mason's demands, but it didn't mean she liked them. She turned up her nose, frowned, and performed each task grudgingly. Later in the day while having dinner, Mason went to check the closet and found the shoes were not put in order. While the family was sitting at the table eating, Mason stormed over to the dining table with his nostrils flared. "You didn't do what I asked you to do!" he shouted at Connie, and right before he swung at her, Mama Frieda jumped in between them.

"No Mason! Stop it! You will not lay another hand on *my* child!" Mama came to Connie's defense. Connie felt thankful that her mother stood up for her, but Mason would not stop his abuse. He looked for reasons to scold Connie and even wanted her to be the blame for her sisters' shenanigans. Connie would go to school with bruises and could barely sit down, but she would always tell her teachers she had gotten into a fight with someone in her neighborhood.

Sometime later, Mason bought an old record player and tossed it in the closet. When Connie found it, she fixed it and would track down every old record in the house and play it. After a while, when Mason came home from work, he would demand Connie to stop playing music so he could watch TV, but Connie knew he was upset that she had fixed it and he couldn't. She also knew that he hated to see her having fun. Mason also tried to cause a division between Connie and her sisters. He didn't like seeing them talking and laughing together or outside jumping rope. He felt Connie should stay in the house, so he whenever he felt like it; he would make her do just that. Connie would watch her sisters from the window as they played with other girls in the neighborhood while she was stuck in her room, crying most of the time because she wanted to go outside with them.

"Connie honey, come into the room with me," Mama Frieda rested her hands gently on Connie's shoulder. "I'm going to teach you how to sew these brand new beautiful buttons I bought for your coat. It'll make your coat look brand new." During those moments, her mother would try to comfort her by teaching her how to sew and cook. Sometimes they would sing popular songs together, and put together beautiful nature puzzles. Other times, nothing could stop Connie from feeling lonely. Connie would secretly go into the bathroom and cry in front of the mirror. She would ask herself why her father didn't love her and why she didn't look like her sisters.

One day, Connie bluntly asked her mother, "Why don't I look like my sisters, and why does Daddy hate me so much? What did I ever do wrong?"

"Your father was raised tough, so he just raising ya'll girls the same, is all." Mama explained to Connie. She and the girls were in the kitchen, cleaning and peeling fresh kale greens.

"How come I don't look like my sisters?" Connie tossed a handful of greens into a pot of water on the stove. "People are saying I look like

I'm white. I'm not white! I'm black! Why can't they see that I'm black Mama?"

"Come here, child, let me show you something." She dried her hands off on the dishtowel. "Girls, keep washing those greens, 'cause I don't wanna taste no grit on 'em, and watch that pot on the stove too."

"Why can't we just wait 'til ya'll come back?" Peaches snapped. "This is too many damn greens to be cleaning by ourselves. Daddy wouldn't make us clean no greens anyway, especially not Baby," Peaches griped.

"Girl, don't you sass me. Do as I say, or else you gets a good licking!" Mama shouted. No sooner than her back was turned, Peaches was talking bad about her mother to Baby in a hush tone. She hated the private talks her mother was spending with Connie. She thought to herself, *Connie is nobody special.*

"Wow, I didn't know you had so many pictures, Mama." Connie's hazel green eyes flickered when her mother opened a grey box she had kept locked away in her closet.

"Pictures keep your memories alive, child," Mama smiled.

". . . and who is she, Mama?" Connie asked, flipping through the photos.

"This your grandmother Ida from Newburg, South Carolina."

"She looks white. Is she?" Connie questioned, admiring the woman who was wearing a pretty fur coat with a matching hat. Her features were soft like her own, and her eyes were a gentle dreamy blue, like hers during the winter. In the summers, Connie's changed to green.

"Yes, your Grandma Ida was white, and that's the reason you looks the way you do," Mama told her. She quickly put the picture back in the box, locked it and put it back in the closet. "You gets your looks from your Grandmother, and ain't no shame in that 'cause you beautiful."

"But Mama, I don't understand. Why do *I* look like Grandma, and Peaches and Baby don't? And neither do you."

"Child, what difference does it make it? You still beautiful all the same, and don't let nobody tell you different."

Mama's reassurance of where Connie came from still didn't stop her from being teased and feeling inadequate. It surely didn't stop her father from abusing her.

As the years went by, Connie noticed that her father became more abusive with *everyone* in the household except Baby. Baby had the habit of knocking his dentures in the toilet whenever she used the bathroom, and Connie would end up cleaning them so that Baby wouldn't get in trouble. She knew Baby was Mason's favorite, but even with Baby, he had his limits. The last time Baby dropped his dentures in the toilet, Mason whipped Baby's behind so bad it bled.

One day, when Baby knocked the dentures in the toilet out of her usual habit, her father caught Connie cleaning them.

"Whatcha' doing with my teeth?!"

"I'm—I'm—I'm cleaning your dentures . . . sir."

"Why?"

"Uhm . . . uhm . . . ."

Mason didn't let her get her words out. He charged at her and smacked her so hard across the face he left a hand print. Her lip started bleeding.

"Get outta here! If I catch you in here again, I'mma' punch you with my fist like you was a man!" he yelled, mouth slobbering spit everywhere.

Connie told her mother what happened to Mason's dentures. "And he blamed me Mama! I didn't even do it!"

Frieda approached Mason who was sitting on the sofa in the living room. "You know good and well Baby likes to play with your dentures, so why would you take it out on Connie?"

"Woman, don't you stand over me like I ain't a man," he warned.

"I know you's a man Mason, but you need to start treating these girls fair, starting with Connie!"

Mason sat down his beer on the table, stood up from the sofa, and then punched Mama in the nose. The girls' mouth dropped in shocked, as they watched at a distance, holding each others' hands in fear. Mason stood still for a moment and stared down at his fists, startled at the progression of his own escalated anger. His eyes shifted from mama to the girls who were shivering in fear, hoping they wouldn't be next.

"See what you made me do!" He shouted at Frieda, then abruptly grabbed his coat and headed out the door to nearby bar to drink away his guilt . . .

CHAPTER TWO

A CHANGE IS GONNA COME

The Black Riots that took place after Dr. Martin Luther King Jr.'s assassination resulted in many businesses laying off workers. Some were simply not able to recover financially from their losses. The White-owned sanitization company where Mason worked started laying off Black workers in fear of retaliation, and Mason was one of the black men who was laid off.

Feeling defeated, Mason began to abuse alcohol and his family more than ever before. He was arrested several times for domestic violence. Neighbors or one of his children would call the police on the manic Mason. Yet Frieda always refused to press charges against him, and allow him to come back home.

After a while, Peaches was the only one who mustered up the courage to fight Mason back, and he eventually backed off her.

One night, her mother suffered another brutal beating from him simply because his dinner wasn't ready when he got home from job hunting.

"If you kick him in the nuts, Mama, he'll stop!" Peaches told her mother.

"Peaches, don't speak that street talk in my house!" Mama shouted, upset. A part of her resented Peaches for her courage to stand up to Mason. "I just need to get a job and help out, that's all," Mama told the girls.

When Mama found a job as a waitress and was earning good tips, she told Mason and the girls. The girls were happy, but Mason stood up from the sofa, looked her in the eye. Then he spit straight in her face and walked out the door to the bar. Mama was left standing in the middle of the living room, feeling humiliated in front of her daughters. They insisted it was time for her to fight back. The girls weren't the only ones . . .

Frieda did a poor job of trying to hide the bruises with the cheap make-up she bought. Her coworker at the Southside Diner noticed.

"You don't have to take that type of abuse, Frieda," said Pat.

"Mason just having a hard time is all. Things will look up," Frieda replied uncertainly.

Pat rested her hand on top of Frieda's, looked her friend in the eyes and said sincerely, "Frieda, I love you and I love your girls. I'm only saying this because I don't want something awful to happen."

Mama snapped. "What am I supposed to do? He's my husband, Pat!"

"Frieda, the only excuse an abuser has is the ones we give them, do you hear me? Now, you better get out while you still have a chance!"

"I can't just leave him. He always was on his own. His Daddy done left him, and then his Mama. We all he got."

"For now, until he kills you. Then he just gonna be by himself again, and I'm gonna be without a friend," Pat said. "Frieda, you can do it, girl. Get out. Please get out."

Six Years Later . . .

"We on our own now," Mama said to her daughters. Mason had punched Frieda in the jaw that previous day for opening his mail. She found out Mason had applied for a personal loan that was approved and that he owed the bank. Frieda figured out the money was going towards his alcohol and gambling debts. When she asked him about it, that was when a fight broke out, but it was over now. Frieda was done!

"Anybody step foot through this door without permission gonna get their head bashed in! That's all it is to it!"

Connie was proud that her mother finally defended herself and stood up for the family. Even she had started fighting Mason back, but Mama had been too afraid. Connie had been upset with her mother's passiveness and the way she would make excuses for her father's behavior, but now she was proud her mother found her own strength.

That night, Mama gave orders to her daughters. "Ya'll girls gonna have to stick together and always defend each other. Now, Peaches, you keep this here in your purse, 'cause a woman's fist ain't nothing against these thugs out here, but a knife will slice them like bologna. You got it?"

Mama handed Peaches the same switchblade she'd ended up using on Mason just the night before to defend herself. It was enough damage to make him stop, but not kill him.

Peaches clicked the switch and her eyes flickered in admiration from its shine. She couldn't wait to use it on the first person who tried her.

"One other thing, I ain't raising no babies in this here house. Peaches, I know you nineteen now and you done finished school, but your little job at Hot Wings and Fries won't be enough to take care of no baby if you get pregnant. And Connie, you just a junior at Lakeview High, and got one more year after this, so don't screw up," Mama warned as she finally sat down on the sofa. She lit up a cigarette. Smoking was a new habit she had developed to calm her nerves. She glanced at Baby, who sat across from her in a chair, watching TV. "And Baby, you make sure you in this house on time. Don't you be running around here with Jackie all hours of the night like your father allowed you to do. I'm not having it. A twelve-year-old like you got no business in them streets, especially around here," she paused to blow smoke into the air. "One day, we'll make it out of these projects. We just need to stick together as a family, and we can make it."

"We'll make it out of here Mama. I know we will," Connie rested her head on her mother's shoulder.

Peaches smirked. "We can't make it out of here on me and Mama's salary."

"Well, after I graduate I'm going to college. I'm not sure what I will be, but I'll get a job and make sure I save enough money for all of us to make it out of here," Connie replied.

"Oh yeah?" Peaches crossed her arms. "And how you think you getting into college? Mama can't afford no college."

"If I keep my grades up then maybe I will get a scholarship."

"Humph, a scholarship? Girl you dreaming," Peaches walked away laughing.

Mama shifted her gave from Peaches to Connie. "You keep following your dreams baby, you hear me?"

Connie's concerning expression turned into a glowing smile. "Yes Mama. I will. I promise I won't let you down."

"I know you won't baby. I know you won't."

CHAPTER THREE

FREEDOM

Connie tried hard to grow an Afro. She cut her hair and used several cans of Afro Sheen to try to get her hair to stay airborne, but it never worked, since the texture of her hair was too fine. She ended up buying wigs.

Connie father was out of the picture. She was glad her parents officially divorced. The peace and quiet around the house felt foreign at first, but gradually the Morris family began to experience normalcy. Their mother allowed them to go to decent parties, as long as they were home before midnight. Mama wanted them to feel human again and be teenagers who enjoyed life. She still had her rules, and the children had to obey them. However, being the teens that they were, sometimes they snuck and broke the rules, like having boys over the house when Mama wasn't home or staying out past curfew. It was easy to get by on breaking the rules since Mama worked three jobs now, including the one at the Southside diner at night.

At school, Connie became friends with May and Ray Brown, a pair of twins. May and Ray used to live in Cabrini as kids, but their mother married a man who had enough cash to move them out the projects to a middle-class neighborhood. He had also financed their mother's nursing school, and Mrs. Brown became the school nurse at Lakeview High.

May always wanted to make the kind of money her twin brother did from deejaying parties, so she would help spread the word about his deejaying skills and get him gigs. When May formally introduced Ray to Connie, they clicked because of their love for music. May was trying to help Connie to break out of her shell and loosen up. Connie wasn't sued to having any friends. She was a loner who would usually go to school and straight home afterwards.

Eventually, Lakeview's star running back on the football team, Vernon "Jet" Michaels, took Connie out on her first date. Gradually,

Connie came out of her shell. At parties, Connie would cut a rug on the dance floor with Jet. Peaches would also go to the parties with her new boyfriend Barry Johnson. Like Peaches, Barry had graduated from Cooley High Vocational School two years prior. Barry was working as a mail carrier, but when he wasn't working, he partied or was busy hanging out with his biker boys. Peaches loved to watch Barry and his friends race their motorcycles, but she enjoyed riding on the back of it more. "Be careful, those things are dangerous!" Mama would warn her whenever Peaches would tell her they were going riding.

Connie and Peaches were enjoying their new freedom without Mason around, but Baby felt all alone, since her sisters had boyfriends and she didn't. They also had jobs. Connie worked part-time at the record store and Peaches worked full-time at Hot Wings. She felt more and more distant from her sisters the older they got and the more independent they became. She wanted to be like them, and she definitely wanted to know what it was like to have a boyfriend.

"What's it like to kiss a boy?" Baby dropped her pencil, after finishing her homework.

Connie looked over top of her reading glasses at Baby and said, "You don't need to know that."

"Jackie says her sisters tongue kiss their boyfriends. Do you and Peaches do that too?" Baby wanted to know. Peaches, who was sitting in the corner of their room reading a *Right On* magazine, wanted to see how Connie was going to respond.

"Like I said, you don't need to know that," Connie insisted. Peaches sucked her teeth. She didn't see what the big deal was about telling Baby about kissing.

"Oh Connie, tell the girl the truth," Peaches chimed in, tossing her magazine on the dresser.

"No, Mama would never approve of that."

"Well Mama ain't here. So we're in charge!" Peaches reminded her. "Now, Baby, the answer to your question is 'yes', we do. Matter of fact, that's all Connie does is kiss Jet, 'cause she too chicken to do it to him."

"I'm not chicken. I just don't move fast like you."

"Well, if you don't let Jet pop that cherry, he just gonna get it from somebody else."

"I ain't afraid of him leaving me if that's all he's about. Anyway, you shouldn't talk like this in front of Baby."

"If we don't tell her the truth, she'll get lied to in the streets."

"Mama will tell her."

Peaches sucked her teeth. "Mama ain't never told us!"

"Well, Baby will learn at school like we did."

"Can ya'll just tell me everything I need to know about boys? Geez!" Baby shook her head. She knew her sisters were always arguing with each other, yet they always did everything together. Sometimes she found their relationship confusing, and hated being caught in the middle.

"Look, baby sis, let me give it to you straight, all right? Your first time gonna hurt like hell 'cause ain't nothing ever been inside you except a tampon. You ain't gonna like it at first, but a few more times, you'll get used to it," Peaches explained.

Baby was surprised to hear that everything was so simple. "Well, I been meaning to tell ya'll something." Baby walked in front of the mirror on her dresser and unfastened her short ponytail.

"Please don't say you're pregnant." Connie sat up abruptly on the bed.

Baby shook her head. "Nope, I'm not pregnant."

"Then what is it?" Peaches was anxious to know.

"I don't want ya'll calling me Baby no more," she said, combing out her hair and looking at herself in the mirror. She noticed she looked older than twelve with her hair down to her shoulders. "Call me Gina."

Peaches was thrilled. "My little sister is growing up. Look at you!" she said as she put her arm around her neck. The two stood in front of the mirror. Both had smooth brown skin and full cheeks like their father, and collar-length hair, like their mother. Connie thought about their resemblance. Inside, she still wished she looked like them, but quickly blew off the thought.

"For a minute you scared me, Baby. I'm glad you're not pregnant," Connie told her.

"No, I'm still a virgin, can't you tell?" Baby sat her comb down and grabbed her house key off the dresser. "I'm going over to Jackie's house."

"Finish your homework first." Connie pointed with her pencil.

"I already did it."

Connie knew Baby was telling the truth. When it came to school, Baby was the first kid she ever met who enjoyed it. In fact, Baby was part of the start-up program for the talented and gifted. Baby was selected to attend Harvey Elementary School on the other side of town, where her talents could be enhanced in advanced educational classes. Although she was only in the sixth grade, the curriculum was junior-high-school level.

The family was very proud of Baby, and Mama worked extra hard to make sure she made enough money to pay for Baby's uniform, books, and supplies for special projects. It also cost money for her to ride the bus and the train everyday to school. Mama felt the expense was worth it.

"Just make sure you come back before nine o'clock. That's the curfew, and you better not listen to the crazy stuff Jackie tells you to do," Connie warned her. Jackie was Baby's "so-called" best friend who lived in "The Reds" too, but in another building. Jackie was selected to Harvey too, but with her behavior, Connie never understood why.

"What stuff?" Baby raised a brow.

"Like the time you were caught stealing candy out the store because Jackie said no one would catch you. Or the other time you came home smelling like cigarettes because Jackie told you it's cool to smoke."

"That was a long time ago!"

"It was just last winter. And what's with Jackie's crazy fascination with killing stray cats and birds?"

Baby laughed.

"That's not funny. Something is not right with that girl. What child walks around with dead animals inside a cage, and brags that she killed them? That girl is crazy, and I'm telling you to be careful around her. And if I hear about you getting into trouble with her again, I'm telling Mama."

"All right, leave the girl alone. She needs to learn some stuff on her own," Peaches interrupted. "I'm going to work. See you chicks later. I need to go make my *little bit* of money, as Mama put it," Peaches chuckled, donned her red "Hot Wings and Fries" hat, and pinned her name badge to her red uniform shirt.

Mama always loved the fall and the beautiful colors of the leaves on the trees, but as she headed home one day, she was distracted when she overheard two young men speaking about Connie and Peaches, and the vulgar things they said they wanted to do them sexually when they saw them at the next party. She feared saying anything to them because they looked like gangbangers. Never did she want anyone to view her girls as loose partygoers. The young men described Connie and Peaches wearing short skirts and go-go boots with heels, and Mama knew she would never allow them to dress that way.

Mama confirmed with a few neighbors, including Ms. Knight who lived next door, if her daughters had been partying and how they were dressing at these parties. She didn't mind her girls going out, but from what she heard, she didn't like the *type* of parties, or the way her girls dressed for them. Each neighbor confirmed that when they had seen Connie and Peaches they were surprised to see their provocative style of dress and make-up, knowing they were supposed to be decent girls, the way their Mama raised them. Mama said nothing to them that evening as she thought about what she was going to do.

That next day, Mama whisked the three of them on the public bus and headed in another direction from their schools, and opposite of Peaches' job.

"Mama, where are we going?" Baby protested. Once they got off the bus, they were facing the Southside Community Clinic.

"Come on here!" Mama snatched Baby by the hand as if she was still a baby. Peaches and Connie followed her inside the clinic, wondering what was going on. Mama rushed her girls inside as if they had just caught chicken pox. She asked the doctor to check out each one of her girls, and then sat in the lobby until he was finished examining them.

She was nervous and felt embarrassed just being there, seeing so many pregnant teenage girls. She was one of those girls herself at one time when she got pregnant with Peaches at only eighteen, but she didn't want her daughters to repeat the same mistakes. Her father had had a shotgun wedding for her and Mason, but part of her heart was always with Scott McKenzie. At any rate, Mama felt like she was losing control of her household, and had to find out from the doctors what was going on with her girls.

She picked up an *Essence* magazine with Diahann Carroll on the cover and flipped through the pages, admiring all the beautiful Black models. She wished she had more time to tend to herself and look as beautiful as the models did. She barely had time to put on lipstick or curl her hair. She always pinned it up in a bun, since it was easier to care for.

Her mother had been a plain Jane just like her before she died. She never wore a lot of make-up or anything. She was just a hardworking woman, but she loved her daughter. Unfortunately, she had died in her sleep.

Frieda was heartbroken, but it was Mason who cheered her up. She leaned on him, since she didn't have Scott anymore. Their parents had made her and Scott break up, since he was white and she was black. So she got with Mason. They were connected through that same emotional pain, but unfortunately, a similar pain would be the cause of their divorce.

"Say, Miss?" A woman sitting next to Frieda tapped her shoulder.

"Yes?"

"Are those your girls that went back there to see the doctor?"

"Yes."

"Hope they ain't pregnant. I gots me five girls, and four pregnant and the other one got syphilis."

Mama nearly panicked, and started flipping through the pages of the *Essence* magazine like a mad woman. When the nurse called her back to the doctor's office, she felt rescued from the strange woman.

"Mrs. Morris, everything is fine with your girls. No diseases," the doctor said, as he sat behind his desk. "I know you wanted to put your daughters on birth control, but I can only do that with Connie, and I am not sure if want to do that with Gina, since she's a minor."

"That's fine. Gina should be okay, but I want Connie taking those pills. I know how it is to be young, so I don't want her to get pregnant at no seventeen. No sir!"

"I understand."

"Now why can't you give pills for Donna?"

"Donna has a right to say if she wants to take pills or not. She's nineteen, so it's up to her, but I am afraid it may be too late for birth control for Donna anyway."

Peaches slouched down in her seat and hung her head low. Peaches didn't have to say a word; her mother knew.

"So how many months are you, Peaches?"

Peaches mumbled, "Four."

"Come again?"

"Four months."

"Who's the daddy? Is it that Barry fella?"

"Yes ma'am, its Barry's" Peaches couldn't look her mother in the eyes. She wished she could run away and hide as feelings of shame came over her.

"Well, you gonna have to go and live with Barry, then. He knocked you up, so he's gonna be responsible for you and the baby. That's all is to it!" Mama was upset. "Now when we get home, you call him and tell him come get'cha'."

Connie was angry with her mother for kicking Peaches out of the house. As she watched Peaches pack her bags in her room, she also felt a little upset that Peaches didn't tell her that she was pregnant. So she asked her why.

"I don't know," Peaches shrugged, still upset with herself. "I never can do right in Mama's eyes anyhow. I'm just a failure."

"You didn't fail, Peaches. Everybody makes mistakes. Mama mad because you kept it a secret. Maybe things would be different if you told the truth, you know?" Connie hugged her big sister, tried to console her.

"*Me*, tell the truth?" Peaches stepped back. "Shoot, Mama got her own secrets that she ain't telling ya'll the truth about. One day, you will know what I mean."

"I beg your pardon?" Mama popped her head in the room as she was walking by she overheard Peaches mention her.

"Nothing, I was talking to Connie," Peaches and Mama stared at each other for a moment, then Mama walked away . . .

Connie missed Peaches not being home, so she started hanging out more often over May's house. She would meet Baby at the bus stop after school, and walk three blocks to take a different bus to May's house. May's three-bedroom house in a middle-class area felt like an escape from the Projects. Inside May's house was a color TV, wall-to-wall carpet, nice furniture, and new stereo equipment. Sometimes Mrs. Brown would be home, and sometimes she wouldn't.

When Mrs. Brown was home, she loved to brag to Connie and Baby. "See, ya'll can have this kind of stuff if ya'll get out them Projects," Mrs. Brown would say. "See, ya mother shouldn't have got rid of her husband. He would have eventually drunk himself to death and she could have collected his social security and veteran's pension."

Connie and Baby would feel bad when they returned home. The comparisons between May and Connie's house were visible from the moment Connie's feet entered into their apartment building. Graffiti now graced the walls with gang tags, and the elevators often smelled like strong urine. Connie felt like the Cabrini she knew and grew up around had turned from a clean, beautiful and friendly environment to a dirty, disgraceful, criminal-infested prison. To make matters worse, they struggled without their father around. True, he was in and out of work, but without an additional income, it was hard on Mama, especially since she had been laid off from her day job as a maid for being accused of stealing. Although her boss eventually found her ring and tried to hire Mama back, she didn't like being wrongly accused, so she turned the family down.

No sooner than Mama lost the maid job, she lost her job at the Cleaners.

"They hired an Asian woman. They said they needed somebody who could sew faster than me," Mama told the girls. It meant she only had one job now--the waitressing job at night at the Southside Diner. With so many bills to pay, caring for her growing daughters, and trying to save money to get out of Cabrini, Mama had no choice but to contact an old friend of hers from Newburg. He was delighted to help her.

When the check arrived in the mail days later, Mama tucked it away in her purse and made a mental note to cash it at the liquor the next day. The check was in a larger amount than what she expected, and it was enough to last the family for a few months. Mama was going to call and thank her friend, but Connie was around. Mama turned the TV to the *Flip Wilson Show*, her favorite, and sat back on the sofa. She thought about the fact that Peaches knew the truth about her *friend* and could have told Connie, but she was glad that she didn't. For a moment, she thought about telling Connie the truth as she lit up a cigarette. She took a few puffs, but then decided against it. Too much time had passed, she thought. Once again, she buried her guilt as she joined Connie and Baby at the table for dinner.

CHAPTER FOUR

FIRST LOVE

*T*he passion intensified between Connie and Jet while the song *"Just My Imagination"* by *The Temptations* played from the record player. Jet had been waiting to have Connie for months, but she would always tell him no. Tonight was different. Connie allowed Jet to have her right there on her couch as the snow began to fall outside.

She was thinking how right Peaches was about it hurting at first, but once she and Jet caught a good rhythm, she began to enjoy it. Just as she felt an orgasm coming on, Jet's body jolted like an electric shock, and then it was over. Jet cuddled her in his arms and kissed her.

"Thank you for letting me hit it," he whispered.

"Hit it?"

"You know what I mean."

"No." Connie sat up and put on her blouse. "What do you mean?"

"I mean thanks for letting me have you, baby." Jet gently rubbed her back. Suddenly, they heard the sound of keys outside the door.

"Oh shoot! It's my Mama!" Connie hissed. She quickly helped Jet to get his shirt and pants on. When the door opened, the music was still playing and the only lights on were from the kitchen.

"Hey Mama . . . y-y-y-you're home early. Me and Jet was just playing records, right Jet?" Connie wiped her sweaty palms on the front of her skirt.

"Um . . . yeah, just listening to *The Temptations*. You know they sure can sing, Mrs. Morris," Jet replied nervously. Mama stood at the door with an angry expression on her face as she folded her arms and held her purse to her chest. She hadn't even taken off her coat, she was so upset.

"Jet, turn that record player off," Mama watched Jet walk over to the record player with his fly open, and shirt backwards with the tag in the front of the neck. She looked over at Connie and got even more upset when she saw her blouse wasn't fastened properly, and the sofa pillows were out of place.

"Bid Connie goodnight, Jet."

"Oh yes ma'am. Goodnight, Connie." Jet rushed to the front door.

"Jet, zip up your fly before you go out," Mama told him. Jet felt even more uncomfortable. He zipped his fly, grabbed his coat, and rushed out the door. He sprinted down all ten flights of stairs; never mind the elevators, he ran all the way home. What would have been a fifteen-minute walk to West Oak Street where he lived in the Cabrini Green row houses turned into a nine-minute run for Jet, the star running back.

"Mama, let me warm dinner up for you."

"I can warm up my own dinner tonight, Connie, so don't bother," Mama rolled her eyes. "Now sit your hot tail down!"

"Yes Ma'am."

"Tell me why the hell did Jet just leave here with his fly open and shirt on backwards, and you just sitting there with your blouse barely fastened?" Mama was so angry she could spit fire. "How far did you and Jet go tonight?"

Connie wiped her sweaty palms on the front of her skirt, and bit down on her bottom lip. "Nothing happened, Mama, I swear."

"You take them birth control pills?"

"Yes Ma'am," She lied. The pill had been making her sick.

"Connie, if you get pregnant like your sister, you are out. You hear me? There are no favorites in this here house, and when I said I am not raising any babies, that meant you too."

"I'm sorry for having Jet over, Mama."

"Sorry is as sorry does. You just make sure you don't carry on in my house like that ever again. Most guys just want to slam, bam, and say 'thank you ma'am'!"

Connie twisted her lips and rolled her eyes to the ceiling when her mother turned her back. She felt her mother didn't know what she was talking about.

"Where is Baby?" Mama turned to sit down in the chair across from the sofa. .

"Don't you mean Gina?"

"Girl don't you play with me. She gon' always be "Baby" to me, regardless if she wants folk to call her by her birth name."

Connie folded her arms and shrugged. "I don't know where she is." Just then, Baby walked in. Baby was also shocked to see her mother home early, since she normally didn't get in until midnight. It was just eleven o'clock, and Baby thought she had beaten her home.

"Where have you been? Your curfew is ten o'clock on the weekends."

"I . . . um . . .I was over Jackie's house. She was showing me her dead goldfish and how to dissect them," Baby explained, nervously, not wanting to get into trouble."

"What?" Mama placed one hand on her hip. "Is that part of some science project or something?"

"No ma'am."

"Well, don't you be playing around with dead animals n' things. Besides, your curfew is ten o'clock. Now, I don't know what has gotten into you and Connie with disobeying me," She shook her head, then puffed her cigarette. "But since ya'll can't obey my rules ya' both punished for a month," Mama blew the smoke from her mouth. "No TV, radio, outside activities, no phone calls, no company, and especially no boys!" She glared at Connie who was sitting across from her on the sofa.

"But Mooom!"

Peaches took her new baby boy, Barry "BJ" Johnson Jr. to visit her family back in Cabrini. Connie, Baby, and Mama were excited to see BJ. He was the first baby boy to the family. A boy Mason always wanted to have, but now he wasn't around to see it. Mama draped him in a baby blanket that she hand knit for him with a pair of matching blue booties. Mama was happy to see her new grandbaby and Peaches doing well. She tried to bury her financial worries and not trouble Peaches by asking for money until her public assistance kicked in, but she knew she needed it. About a week after Peaches' visit, Mama sent Connie to ask Peaches for money. Connie took the bus to Peaches' house on her last dollar. She would have to miss school the next day or hitch a ride with a classmate from the neighborhood. It wouldn't be her first time doing that.

Connie arrived at Peaches house and explained everything to her. She hoped Peaches would help the family's desperate situation.

"Tell Mama I can't help her."

"Well, why not? You still working, and Barry has a good job at the post office."

"So!"

"*So* you can help."

"Why should I help Mama when she kicked *me* out?"

"But this ain't just about Mama. What about me and Baby?"

"So what, you're working, ain't you?"

"I don't make that kind of money and you know that. Look, all we need is a hundred dollars, and we'll pay you back. The rent is almost two months behind, and if we don't pay, they're going to kick us out."

"I need my money for BJ. Besides, Mama never could budget her money right. Why she go and buy ya'll clothes knowing rent was due? That was dumb. Daddy wouldn't have ever done that!"

"How can you say no to your own Mama?"

"She always was *your* Mama, more than she was mine."

"Oh don't start that mess, Peaches." Connie folded her arms.

"You just think Mama is a saint, don't you? Mama got her secrets."

"What does this have to do with you helping us out?"

"Tell Mama to ask Scott for the money."

"Scott? Who is he?"

Peaches smirked and stated, "Girl you ain't my real sister. Scott McKenzie is your daddy. We're half-sisters."

Connie's mouth dropped. "What are you talking about?"

"Have you stopped looking in that mirror? You used to look all the time." Peaches raised a brow. "I promised Mama I would never say anything, but I checked that box in her closet one day and found out Scott McKenzie is your daddy. He's a white man from New Burg, South Carolina. Mason is me and Baby's daddy, but not yours. Why you think Mama and Daddy left there to move here to Chicago? It's because of you."

"LIAR!" Connie charged at Peaches and grabbed her by the neck to choke her.

"Stop it! Get off me, girl!" Peaches fought off Connie's hands around her throat.

"Gonna find out the truth from Mama," Connie abruptly headed towards the front door.

"Go ahead and ask her, White girl!"

Connie left Peaches' house feeling devastated. When she got off the bus at the front entrance of Cabrini, she saw Jet standing around, talking to his friends, and walked right pass him.

"Hey, hold on, Mama, where you going?" he ran to catch up with her. "How you been? I haven't seen you around?"

Connie quickly answered. "I been busy."

"What's wrong with you? You still on punishment for that time I was at your house?"

"Nope!" Connie sped up, but Jet caught up and walked beside her.

"Yo' dig, I got tickets to see James Brown. You down?"

"No. You can take somebody else."

"I guess I'll see you later then."

"Yeah, much later."

"What does that mean?"

"I don't have time right now, Jet!" she kept walking.

"Forget you, then!"

Connie looked over her shoulder. "Forget you too!"

Mama was laughing at the *Flip Wilson Show* when Connie came back from Peaches' house. She looked up when Connie walked in. Connie knew she would have to ask someone else other than Jet for a ride to school tomorrow.

"So what did Peaches say? Could she help us out?" Mama asked. Connie ignored her, walked straight to her room, and slammed the door. Mama turned to Baby who was sitting next to her on the couch. "What's the matter with your sister?"

Baby shrugged. "I don't know." Mama put out her cigarette in the ashtray and walked back to Connie's room.

"What's going on?" Mama's heart raced with worry.

"I don't want to talk right now, Mama," Connie rolled over on her bed, turning her back to her mother.

"Connie, did something happen at Peaches' house?"

"No!"

"Are you . . . are you pregnant?"

Connie sucked her teeth. "No, Mama, I'm not *pregnant!*" That was the least of her worries, and she was sick of her mother being worried about her and Baby being the next to get pregnant.

"Well, what is it?"

"Just leave me alone!"

"Connie, I can't help you if you don't talk to me. You're always bottling up your feelings about stuff. Sit up right now and tell me what's going on, right this minute!" Mama was losing her patience.

Connie slowly sat up in bed and asked, "Mama, is Mason Morris my real father, or is it Scott McKenzie?"

Mama froze. She wasn't expecting her daughter to ask that question. "Have you been in my room, too? You been snooping like your sister Peaches used to snoop in my room!"

"No, I haven't been sneaking in your room, Mama," Connie angrily replied. "Why did you lie to me? Now my sisters who I thought were my whole sisters are my half-sisters, and the man I thought was my Dad is not my father, and the grandmother I thought was your mother is really Scott's mother—my real grandmother. It's all lies!"

Baby who had been eavesdropping on the conversation, peeped her head through the bedroom door, and asked, "I'm your half-sister?"

Mama looked over her shoulder. "Baby, you go on outside, but be back here by your curfew."

"Oh all right," Baby pouted, and went outside. She would normally take off running, but she really wanted to know what was going on.

Mama's whole mood changed. "Connie, baby . . ." she approached her daughter and tried to give her a comforting hug, but Connie pushed her away for the first time. Connie slid towards the end of the bed away from her. "I was trying to protect you, baby."

"All these years, I knew I looked different from my sisters and different from my father. I knew I favored you some, but I always felt different. Now I know why daddy hated me so much. It's because I was never his!"

"Nobody hated you, sweetie," Mama slid in closer to her. "I'm the one made the mistake of cheating while your father was on another tour of duty. I was lonely. I been left alone, and old feelings came up for a boy I used to love- Scott. His name was Scott McKenzie," she began to explain. "Our folks had made us break up when they found out about us. Colored folks had no business messing with White folks, or vice-versa, not during those days. When I saw Scott later on, we took our feelings too far, and ended up with you. Of course, I didn't know I was pregnant by him. I thought you were Mason's baby. I'm not proud to say I messed around with two mens. I told your daddy the truth, but kept it from you. Thought I was protecting you. I guess I was really protecting your daddy, Mason."

"The truth would have been better, Mama," Connie sniffed, wiping the tears that escaped her eyes. "All those beatings and all those nights I spent crying because I didn't know why my daddy didn't love me. This hurts, Mama. This hurts more than you'll ever know!"

"I'm sorry, Connie. I swear I never meant to hurt you, baby. I swear."

"Were you ever planning on telling me if Peaches hadn't told me?" Connie asked, curiously. Mama bit down on her bottom lip as her mind searched for another excuse to console her daughter, but now the truth was hitting her like a ton of bricks.

"No, baby," Mama confessed. "I'm afraid I was never gonna tell you the truth, but I'm sorry. I really am." Connie buried her face in her pillow and kept sobbing. Mama found herself wiping a couple of tears from her own eyes. She got up and went into her bedroom and grabbed the gray box from the top of her closet, then returned to Connie.

"Everything you need to know about your real father is in this here box, and if you have more questions, I have his phone number and address. You can talk to him if you like," Mama offered. "Maybe it's time you do."

"Mama," Connie called.

"Yes baby?"

"Did you kick Peaches out because she learned the truth about me?"

"No, I kicked Peaches out because she needs to be her own woman and raise her own child the way I had to raise her. We all got secrets in this family, and one thing you never knew about *her* was this was not her first time being pregnant. I found out from Barry. He said to me on the phone, "I'm glad she decided to keep this one," as if I knew about the first time she was pregnant."

Connie was shocked. "Does that mean that she . . . ?"

"Yep, she got rid of that baby and Barry paid for it," Mama explained. "You know, Connie, you's beautiful, smart, mature, and Peaches always been jealous of you."

"You think so?"

"I know so. I'm your Mama," she winked. "We all is still family no matter what, though. We all make mistakes, including me. I just hope one day you can forgive me."

Baby came rushing back inside the apartment, hoping they were finished talking. Connie told Baby everything and she sat and listened. Connie cried when she explained it, and showed her the pictures from the box.

"Don't be sad," Baby said. She placed her hand on top of Connie's as they sat next to each other on the bed. "I don't care that we're half-sisters. You always felt whole to me anyway." Baby wrapped her arms around Connie's shoulders.

Thanks to Scott McKenzie, Mama's *friend* and Connie's father, the rent was paid for another three months. Mama gave Connie permission to call and thank him. Connie called Scott collect, and he accepted the charges. When the operator connected them, Connie's heart pounded heavily and her palms began to sweat. She didn't know what to say to the man who she'd never known was her father.

"Hello?" answered a man with a heavy southern accent. Connie could hear dogs barking in the background.

"Hello. May I speak with Mr. Scott McKenzie, please?"

"This here is Scott, and you must be Connie."

"I am. My mother said to call and thank you for helping us out again."

"You're welcome. Any time you need anything, I'm just a phone call away, is all."

Silence lingered for a few seconds between them until Scott spoke again.

"So I reckon ya Mama done finally told you about me and who I am."

"She said you're my real father."

"She's right. I've been waiting to talk to you a mighty long time now. I bet you have to be about sixteen or seventeen right now, am I right?"

"Seventeen."

"Well I wish things been different and all, and maybe you and I could've known each other better, but it ain't too late now, you know." Connie was surprised by Scott's excited interest in her. The longer they talked on the phone, the more relaxed she felt.

She sat down on the sofa holding the phone to her ear as Scott talked about life in the South, his favorite things to do, and about how he grew up. Connie learned that she had a younger half-brother named Willie. Scott had also fathered him by a Black woman he'd married and later divorced due to racial pressures in the South. He was now living with his girlfriend Margaret, a White woman. She was several years his junior but very kind, Scott said.

Connie also discovered she had a lot in common with him; they both loved music and dancing. She admitted that the only White men she knew who could dance were in the movies. From that day forward, Connie and Scott would talk by phone once a week. Talking with Scott everyday helped her to learn more about her roots and where she came from. Connie felt good to finally know her true identity and feel a connected to her paternal family.

CHAPTER FIVE

BABY

*B*y the spring of 1972, things seemed to be looking up for the Morris Family. Mama had found two more jobs. She used the money to pay the rent and other household bills, and the bills that had mounted when she didn't have the three jobs.

As for Connie and Jet, they got back together. Jet easily forgave Connie, mostly because he didn't want anyone else to have her. Connie was the most attractive girl in the neighborhood and in school. He was very attracted to Connie's physical beauty, from her long flowing hair to her beautiful eyes that changed colors by the seasons, and her smile that could brighten anyone's day. Jet's mother also loved her, and his brothers thought that Connie would be the girl he married one day, but Connie always wanted Jet to see *her*, and not just her outer appearance.

"Jet can be so shallow and selfish. I don't know why I took him back," Connie was saying to May, who was sitting on her bed, watching her fix Baby's hair for the school dance.

"But he's cute. I just love his sleepy puppyish-eyes, and that sandy brown hair, it blends so well with reddish undertone. Besides being cute, he's going to be football superstar girl. And when you get married, you guys will be rich!"

"That's all you think about is money! What about love and happiness?"

"Who cares?" May shrugged her shoulders. "We're too young to be thinking serious like that right now anyway."

"I hope I meet a guy like Jet. He's cute with muscles," Baby smiled, watching Connie hot curl her hair before the mirror.

"Baby, you're too young to be thinking about boys. You're going to be a successful writer first. Speaking of which, how is that poem coming along for the poetry contest?"

"Mrs. Bradford said she thinks I'll win first place this year, but Jackie said I'll just come in second, like always."

"Don't worry about Jackie; she's just jealous. I told you that."

"Maybe you're right, but I still want to win. Mrs. Bradford said if I win I will get one thousand dollars."

"If you do win, what will you do with all that cash?" May asked.

"I'll buy my favorite sister, Connie, a new record player so she won't have to use quarters to hold the needle down to play records anymore." Baby flashed a quick smile at Connie. "And then I'll buy my Mama a nice dress and a pair of shoes, and a typewriter for myself."

"That's sweet of you, Baby." Connie sprayed her hair as a final touch.

"What about me?" May wanted some of the prize money too.

"I'll buy you something special too, since you're like my family."

"Thank you, Baby!" May smiled, hoping Baby would win and keep her promise.

"You're all set, Kiddo. Let me take your picture." Connie snapped the old Polaroid camera, happy that it still worked so she could show her mother how beautiful Baby looked tonight.

The three of them rode the bus and train to Harvey Elementary. Connie and May waited for Baby to go inside.

"Don't forget I'll be back to get you at ten!" Connie shouted. Baby quickly waved her off, not wanting Connie to embarrass her. She joined her friends who were standing outside waiting for her, and then they all walked inside the building together.

Back at Connie's house, Connie and May caught the last few minutes of *Sanford and Son,* while eating hotdogs and drinking Kool-Aid.

"Hi, Mrs. Morris," May said as Mama walked in from work.

"Hi, May." Mama sat her purse down on the small dining table that was on its last leg. She made a mental note to visit a yard sale over the weekend so she could replace it.

"How come every time you're at my house you gots to be eating? Tell your Mama I'm gonna send her a grocery list, since she's the one bragging about all the cash she got."

May laughed, but Mama was serious when she said it. She knew Mrs. Brown had forgotten that she came from Cabrini Green. Mama used to sell her fish sandwiches, and when Mrs. Brown was short on laundry detergent, she borrowed it from Mama.

"Mama, you're off early tonight." Connie looked at the clock on the wall above the TV; it was just after eight.

"Slow night, child," she yawned. "My boss let some of us go home early, and I'm glad he did. These three jobs are wearing me out, but I have to get us out of these projects if it's the last thing I do."

"How much money do you have to save now, Mama?" Connie asked.

"I hate to think about it, child. I had to spend some of it, and every time I dip in it, I have to put it back." Mama shook her head, feeling a little discouraged. She had groceries, the phone bill, utilities, rent, two growing girls who needed clothes, food, and money to get to school, and she had her own needs. She also had credit cards she had to pay off. She had to use the cards to buy herself a new waitress uniform, maid uniform, and new shoes for each job. Connie's part-time job at the record store contributed very little, so she let Connie keep that for her and Baby to have a little fun—to see a movie or go to a show. She didn't want them feeling deprived because they didn't have much.

"The P.A. should kick in soon though right Mama?"

"Child those people at the Health and Human Services are driving me crazy. They told me I need to stop working in order to get food stamps. Those folks are working my last nerves."

"Things will look up soon Mama," Connie hated to see her mother working so hard and still barely making it.

"Mrs. Morris, Gina looked so pretty for the spring dance." May skipped the subject as she gulped down the last bit of Kool-Aid that Connie had given to her. The Morris' troubles didn't bother her one bit.

"She sure did Mama. Take a look at these." Connie showed her mother the pictures she took from the old camera.

"My, my, my! Baby girl is growing up." Mama smiled at the picture. "She is beautiful. Connie, you did her hair?"

"Yes, Ma'am."

"Oh, she is beautiful." Mama kept smiling in awe. Baby favored a young version of Mason with her full brown cheeks and wide smile, but she had Mama's slightly slanted eyes and lashes that curled in tight, making her eyes stand out brightly. Seeing the pictures of Baby made her night. It felt if all her hard work was paying off with her girls.

Mama scratched the side of her temple as she tried to remember what time the dance was over. Her tired brain gave up, and she asked Connie, "What time did she say the dance was over with?"

"Ten o'clock."

"Okay, well, you girls be safe. Make sure you pick her up on time. I can't wait up another minute. I'm taking my butt to bed."

"I understand, Mama. Have a good night."

Two hours later . . .

May took a bus and went home, while Connie took a different bus and then the L Train to go get Baby. The L Train was late, so by the time Connie arrived at Harvey Elementary School, it was about ten-thirty. Connie walked inside the school and didn't see anyone she recognized. There were a few teachers and a couple of straggling students with their parents, who looked like they had stuck around to help clean up the school gym. She turned around to leave when someone tapped her on her shoulder.

"Are you looking for your sister Gina?" said Mrs. Bradford, Baby's teacher. She was putting on her jacket and heading out. "You're her sister Connie, right?"

"Yes, have you seen her?"

"She left about ten fifteen. She said she thought you were running late, and didn't want to get into trouble for being out too late."

"Oh, shoot! I gotta go, Mrs. Bradford. Have a good night," she hurried towards the exit.

"Wait, Connie, wait! I can give you a ride!" Mrs. Bradford offered.

"But I don't live in the best of neighborhoods."

"I'm familiar with Cabrini Green. Your sister writes about where you live all the time."

On the way to Connie's house, Mrs. Bradford talked about how well Baby was doing in school, and had hopes about her winning the poetry contest this year.

". . . and she looked so pretty tonight," Mrs. Bradford was saying. "But that Jacqueline spilled punch on the beautiful dress your mother sewed for Gina."

"What? Why did she do that?" Connie jolted in shock.

"Well, Jerry Winslow asked Gina to dance with him. He chose her out of all the other girls. He's supposed to be the cutest little boy in the school, and Jacqueline got upset that he asked Gina and not her," Mrs. Bradford explained. "I saw the two of them tussling at the punch bowl, and then Jacqueline maliciously threw punch on that pretty dress. So tell your mother it was not Gina's fault."

"I will."

"I sent Jacqueline home early because of what happened."

"Good!"

"I never understood why Gina wanted to be friends with Jacqueline. It's obvious that Jacqueline is a bad influence. She has had so many behavioral problems, that if it wasn't for her excelling grades, she would have been kicked out of Harvey by now."

"I agree," Connie nodded. "Hey, isn't that Jackie?"

Jackie was walking so fast down Larrabee Street that she started to skip along. Mrs. Bradford pulled over to the curb and waited for Jackie to catch up to them. "Why is Jackie out this time of night when I sent her home over an hour ago?" Mrs. Bradford wondered.

"She's always running the streets. Her mother doesn't care, but I'm going to ask her if she's seen Baby." Connie stepped out of the car and yelled, "Jackie!" Jackie jumped in shock when she saw Connie.

"Have you seen Baby? Mrs. Bradford said she . . ."

"No, nope, I ain't seen Baby. No," she replied, cutting Connie off. Her eyes darted in every other direction.

"What's the matter with you? Look like you seen a ghost or something?"

"Look get outta my face, all right! I said I ain't seen her!"

"You don't have to get nasty, you little brat!"

"So!" Jackie taunted with her tongue.

"Well, if you see Baby, tell her—"

"I ain't telling her nothing! What I look like, a messenger? Get outta my face!"

"Girl I oughta choke you!" Connie snatched Jackie up by the collar of her dress.

"Get off me!" Jackie broke free and took off running down the street, and Connie went back to the car.

"That girl has one attitude problem. I saw what happened," Mrs. Bradford stated.

"Jackie is a mess, and so is her family. All of them are on drugs, and they let her do whatever she wants to do," Connie said. "She must be a natural when it comes to academics, because I don't know how she even has the time to learn and study."

"She is a very bright young lady and all her tests have high scores, but if this wasn't her last year at Harvey, she would have been expelled. I think Principal Matthews keeps her around to help us continue to rank high in state-wide tests, but you keep that between us."

"Maybe you're right, but look, Mrs. Bradford, just drop me off at the next corner. I'll be okay from that point."

"Okay, if you insist."

"Thanks for the ride." Connie waved good-bye and walked the remaining two blocks home. As she approached her building, she saw two of her neighbors, Tony and Leroy, hanging out front.

"Wassup, Connie? You know the Vice Lords and the Cobra Stones had a big shootout tonight," said Tony, drinking a Colt 45 with his friend Leroy. "Word on the streets is that they coming back through here later tonight, so you best stay away from your windows," he warned. Whenever there was a shootout, Connie and her family slept on the floor in their bedrooms like most neighbors did. Sometimes, if it was really bad, they slept in the bathroom. There were some nights when it seemed like they were in the middle of a warzone because the shooting wouldn't stop. Police were often late arriving, and sometimes they were too scared to show up at all.

"Thanks for the heads up. By chance, have you guys seen Baby?"

"Nah, we ain't seen her today."

"Tell her I was looking for her."

"Yeah, all right," Tony said. As Connie walked by, he and Leroy talked about how good-looking she was and admired her figure.

As soon as Connie walked in the house, her mother jumped up from the sofa. "Connie, where on earth you been? Where is Baby?" Mama demanded. "I woke up from my sleep to the sound of them shooting outside and it scared me to death. Now, where is Baby? Where is she?" Mama shook Connie with both hands. Connie stood there with her mouth open for a moment, not knowing what to say. She wished her mother would calm down.

"Well, where she at?"

"I . . . I don't know, Mama." Connie was hoping Baby would have beaten her home.

"Did you go to the school to get her?"

"Yes I did, but when I got there Mrs. Bradford said she left. I got there too late."

"Too late?" Mama asked angrily, with one hand on her hip.

"The L train was late, Mama. I didn't get there until ten thirty."

"Maybe she'll be here in a minute, then," Mama began to pace the room.

"I'mma call over to Jackie's, see if Baby over there."

"She's not there, Mama."

"How you know?"

"I just saw Jackie walking home and she said she ain't seen her," Connie answered, taking off her jacket and sitting down on the couch.

"By the way, Jackie messed up Baby's dress," Connie mentioned. "Mrs. Bradford told me that she threw punch on her dress, so don't give her a beating when she come home, 'cause it wasn't her fault."

"I keep telling Baby to stay away from that girl. She just as rotten as she can be, and her family ain't no better."

"I keep telling her too, Mama, but she won't listen. She just sneaks off to her house anyway."

"From now on she won't be sneaking out, 'cause if I find out, she's punished for a month!" Mama continued to pace the room, and then decided she had waited around for Baby long enough. She snatched her jacket out the tiny coat closet near the front door. "Let's go out here and see if we can catch Baby getting off the bus."

Connie and her mother walked to the bus stop and asked a few people they knew walking by if they saw Baby, and they had not. They waited at the bus stop for nearly an hour before heading back home. Once they got inside, they sat down on the couch next to each other trying to figure out what they should do next.

"It's so late. Where is she?" Mama asked as she gripped Connie's hand while they sat next to each other on the couch. "I gots a bad feeling right now. I'm telling you, I can feel it in my stomach," Mama moaned, loosening her hand from Connie's grip. "Something ain't right. I know it."

The same troubled feeling of anxiety came over Connie. Her palms began to sweat and her heart pounded fast and hard. "I'm calling the cops." she abruptly got up from the sofa and rushed over to the rotary phone and dialed 911.

"Well, it's about time somebody answered the phone!" Connie shouted. "I'm calling to report a missing person."

"Oh all right, so, uhm . . . where do you live?" the officer drawled. Connie could hear him slurping a beverage through a straw, and crunching on food in the background.

"812 North Sedgwick."

"Cabrini Green?"

"Yeah, Cabrini Green. So, you got a problem with that?"

"I'm just asking." He continued to eat and drink in her ear.

"Well, my sister is missing, and we need help now!"

"How long has she been missing?"

"Well, she was supposed to be here by now, it's almost midnight."

"What time were you expecting her?"

"I don't know, at least by eleven."

"Technically, we can't do anything unless she's been missing for twenty-four hours."

"You can't patrol the streets for her?"

"Like I said, she's not considered missing just because she's an hour late," the officer reiterated. "For all we know she could show up as soon as we hang up the phone."

"All right, we'll call back." Connie hung up the phone.

As Connie was explaining to her mother what the officer told her, suddenly they heard the sound of gunshots going off outside, and she and her mother did a nosedive towards the floor. They held on tight to each other and prayed that God would keep them safe. When the shooting stopped, they heard the loud sirens, and could see the red and white lights of the ambulance flashing throughout their apartment. Mama jumped to her feet. "They shot my baby, they done killed her!"

"Mama, wait!"

Connie caught up with her Mom at the elevator down the hall, and waited to ride down with her because some of the lights in the hallway had blown out. As soon as the elevator doors opened, there were two people inside having standup sex. They took the stairs instead. Once they were outside, they found an ambulance and police everywhere.

"They killed my baby!" a neighbor cried. "They killed my baby! He had nothing to do with the Vice Lords; he was just coming from work!"

Officers started questioning the people who were standing around wondering what had happened. One by one, they departed back to their homes, stating they hadn't seen anything. Mama turned to one of the officers.

"Look, my baby is missing. With all this shooting and carrying on, ya'll need to find my baby. She could be shot up somewhere out here too!"

"Right now, we need to find out who killed this boy," the officer told Mama, as if her daughter didn't matter. Mama shook her head in frustration. Chicago had always been a place of neighborly love, and what was happening now seemed foreign to her. The passing of time had changed the people in her community. No one seemed to care about each other anymore. Most of all, nobody seemed to care about her daughter, Baby.

"Mama, maybe wherever Baby is, she will find her way home soon." Connie gently rested her hands on her mother's shoulders. "Let's go inside, Mama, it's too dangerous standing out here."

Connie escorted her mother back inside their building, but there was no way that Mama was going to sleep without knowing where her child was.

The Next Day . . .

Connie called Peaches and Ms. Pat the next morning to let them know that Baby was missing. All of them searched the streets for Baby, but came up empty. Mama and Connie went to the police station to report her missing. Mama didn't care if it wasn't quite twenty-four hours; somebody was going to find her baby, or at least start searching for her . . .

Just hours after Mama and Connie had left the police station, Detectives Hughes and Brown responded to a frantic phone call by a woman who said her name was Loretta Harris. Loretta Harris, who lived on Greenbelt Avenue, just blocks from where Connie lived, had said she went in the basement of her apartment building to wash clothes when she found a child lying on the laundry room floor.

Senior Detective Gary White and his partners Hughes and Brown immediately went to Greenbelt Avenue. He walked around to the back of the three-story apartment building, searching for evidence and clues as to what may have happened to the girl. Just as he was headed back inside the building, his foot struck a piece of metal that was sticking out of the soil near the dumpsters.

"What is this?" he asked himself, kneeling down to see what the object was. He withdrew his pocketknife and started to dig around the object. The more he dug, the more he noticed the object resembled a broken piece of pipe.

"Hey, I think I got something here. Meet me out back, and bring Susan from forensics," White said to the other detectives on his walkie-talkie. Detective Hughes and Brown, along with Susan from forensics, rushed outside of the building. Inside, they had been questioning neighbors and finger printing the laundry room.

"Before I pull this out, I wanted you guys to see it." White put on his protective gloves while Hughes and Brown held their flashlights over the area so White could see it better. Slowly, White removed a small pole from the dirt. The pole had fresh blood all over it.

"Looks like you found the weapon," Hughes said. "Here, check this for fingerprints." White handed Susan the pole, which she dropped into a plastic evidence bag. Hours later, close to midnight, Detective White received a call from dispatch.

"Yeah?" Detective White answered. "What'cha got for me?"

"It's her," Susan said to Detective White. "It's Gina "Baby" Morris."

"Dammit!" White shouted. "Hey guys, it's Gina."

"Oh no!" they each shook their heads, upset.

"Her mother was just at the station this morning," Detective Hughes said. He shook his head in bitter disappointment. He was the one who had taken down the information about Baby.

Detective White gritted his teeth, took a spit and said, "I want every Black kid on this block who even looks like a purse-snatcher to be stripped, searched, and questioned about the murder of this girl."

"As a matter of fact, get that rookie cop Wilson in on this. He likes browbeating these people, it gets the truth out of them."

"You mean Dean Wilson or Patrick Wilson, sir?" Detective Brown wanted to clarify.

"Dean Wilson, the Black cop."

"Gary, you can't be serious. Dean is a cocky jerk, is what he is!" Detective Hughes replied. He couldn't believe White wanted him on the case. Detective White rarely ever worked with a cop, let alone a black cop. Hughes couldn't stand Dean's guts.

"Yeah, he may be cocky, but I know he's good, and we need him. These Black kids around here are scared of him, so they'll talk, but not to us," White said. "You saw how far those other officers got last night with that kid who was shot in that gang shootout, don't'cha? They got nowhere. No leads, no nothing, they don't talk to white guys like us, so we need Dean."

Detective Brown chimed in and asked, "So when do we tell Mrs. Morris about her daughter?"

"Don't worry about it, Hughes and I'll go there first thing in the morning. I say we call it a night, for now. Besides, I'm in no shape to deal with Cabrini Green this time of night," Detective White replied.

CHAPTER SIX

WHAT LIES BENEATH

*B*ill Wither's *"Lean On Me"* played from the record player. Mama sat on the couch smoking her second pack of cigarettes within the last few hours, and stared at the TV with the volume turned low. Mama had reported her daughter missing on Saturday. Now it was Sunday, and she still hadn't heard back from the Chicago PD.

Mrs. Bradford, Baby's teacher, had called to see if Mama had heard anything. Connie had informed all the neighbors about what was going on so they could be on the lookout for Baby in case they saw her. Meanwhile, Mama had spent all night pondering over all the possibilities of where Baby could be. She didn't fit the stereotype of a runaway, so she knew Baby wouldn't do that. She questioned Connie a hundred times, almost accusing her about the timeframe when she went to pick up Baby. She knew the train was late, but still wondered. If Connie had had the money to take a cab, then maybe she would have been able to pick Baby up on time. Connie had her own wandering thoughts. Since Baby was missing, where was she? Where did she go after the dance? Did one of the gang members kidnap her? If they did, where did they take her? Was she still alive or was she dead? She thought about calling her friend Pat again and Peaches and Barry to see if they heard anything. The three of them, along with Connie had searched the streets all day yesterday looking for Baby, but to no avail.

Suddenly, there was a knock at the door, and Mama quickly snapped out of her thoughts. She snuffed out her cigarette and hurried to the door.

"Hello, ma'am, I'm Detective White. Are you Mrs. Morris?"

"Yes I am."

"I believe you met my partner, Detective Hughes, yesterday morning. May we come in? We have some news about your daughter, Gina Morris."

"Of course, come on in." Mama stepped aside.

Connie came out of her room when she heard someone at the door. She sat down in the chair next to her mother. The two detectives greeted Connie, and removed their hats.

"Would you like a cup of coffee?" Mama offered.

"No thank you, Mrs. Morris," Detective White answered. He was tall, about six feet six inches with white hair, and looked like he was in his late sixties. His partner Hughes had red hair and freckles, and appeared to be in his mid-forties.

"Mrs. Morris, we won't take up too much of your time, but we have some news about your daughter," Detective White said.

"Please, ma'am, why don't you have you a seat?" suggested Detective Hughes. He and White both stood up from the sofa and let Mama and Connie sit down next to each other. Connie held her mother's hand.

"The police received a call yesterday morning shortly after you had reported Gina missing. We investigated to the wee hours of the morning regarding that report we received," Detective White gently explained.

"What report was that?"

"A woman reported that she had found the body of a girl in the basement laundry room of her apartment on Greenbelt Avenue. I must warn you, the pictures I have are graphic, but I need you to tell us if this is your daughter, Gina?" Detective White handed her the photographs from the scene.

Mama gasped. Her chest shivered up and down as tears streamed down her cheeks. "Y-y-yes this is . . . this my baby!"

"We're awfully sorry Mrs. Morris," Detective White said, placing the pictures back into an envelope.

Connie wrapped her arms around her mother, and squeezed back tears of her own.

Detective White held his head down and pressed his hat against his chest. "I'm afraid Gina is dead. I'm so sorry."

"What happened to her?" Connie asked while her mother sobbed uncontrollably.

"Looks like someone hit her with a pole and she died. Maybe they were trying to rob her, but we don't know for sure yet," Detective Hughes stated. "We promise, we will find her killer."

"I don't understand!" Mama cried. "Why would someone do this to my baby? Why?"

"We're still putting together all the details and we're still investigating, so that's all we have for now. If I were you, I wouldn't tell anyone what you know so far. We don't want this to get out to the neighborhood. They will start speculating, and it could possibly ruin our investigation process," Detective White suggested.

"So what should we do?" Connie asked. At this point her mother was crying so loud and so hard, she could barely hear what else the detectives were saying.

"We know people will hear on the news that Gina was found dead, but we're not sharing any details with the media right now. It could ruin the case, so only tell closest family."

"We'll do our best," Connie replied, trying to keep her emotions together and be strong for her mother.

"If you hear of anything that may help us out, here is my card. Give me a call," Detective White said.

"One last thing; you will need to come down to the morgue to officially identify the body and sign the paperwork. No rush, we understand what you're going through right now," Hughes told them. When the detectives left, Mama screamed as tears raced down her cheeks. "WHY? WHY? WHY MY BABY!"

Connie sat on the sofa crying uncontrollable. She cried for Baby, her mother, and she cried for her family.

"I can't believe they killed my baby! Why did they kill my baby! Take me! Take me instead!" Mama pulled at the sides of her hair. "Oh Lord somebody help me! They done killed my baby!"

Ms. Knight, the neighborhood knocked on door to see what was going on. Connie got up to let her in and explained what happened.

"I'm so sorry Frieda," Ms. Knight hugged her. "Connie, help me get your mother to bed."

Connie helped her mother to the bedroom. She was crying hysterically as Mrs. Knight and Connie stroked her hair, and sat a cool wash cloth on her forehead.

While Ms. Knight stayed at Frieda's side, Connie called her family and friends to break the news. Peaches arrived in what seemed like seconds. She raced to her mother's side. Her face was beet red from crying and her eyes were swollen.

"I just can't believe they took my baby!" Mama cried.

Peaches cried as she held her mother. "I'm sorry Mama. I'm so sorry this happened."

"We need to get out of this place before they take another one my children or even me!" Mama cried.

"We will make it out of here, I'll see to it," Connie said, she was sitting on the opposite side of her mother on the bed.

Later that day, the Morris family went to the morgue. When Mama saw the body of her daughter Baby, she fainted and was rushed to the hospital . . .

CHAPTER SEVEN

DEAN WILSON

Dean Wilson was a uniformed Chicago police officer called to serve on the case for Gina "Baby" Morris. As he entered the diner, he had to duck down a little so his head wouldn't hit the Easter decorations hanging above the door. His dark, piercing eyes searched for White and Hughes as he stood in the corridor for a moment. Some women who were having lunch together noticed Dean when he walked in. They whispered about how handsome his dark bronze looked, and how sexy his bowed legs moved when he walked. Dean caught their eyes, tossed off a 'hello', flashed a dimpled smile, and made his way towards the back of the diner where he spotted White and Hughes. After a few cups of coffee and small talk, the detectives filled Dean in on what they knew so far about the case.

"While it's a good idea for me to chase down the knuckleheaded gangsters for information, I still think we shouldn't fall asleep on the possibilities that something may have happened at Harvey Elementary School before Gina Baby ever left. Those are the people we need to talk to first," Dean stated.

"We can't talk to the kids!" Detective Hughes snapped

"We'll get their parents' permission, and we will talk to the teachers at the school as well," White interjected, cutting his eyes at Hughes. He thought Dean had made a good suggestion.

Dean was perking up after having a little coffee. He had pulled an all-nighter, and here it was mid-day, and he was still working when he was supposed to be home with his wife Phyllis, and his four-year old son, Dean Jr. The caffeine made Dean fully alert to what was going on, including Hughes' looks of envy. He knew how some detectives felt about cops, and with him being a rookie, Hughes' every smirk and frown indicated to Dean how he felt about him, and his remarks. Hughes insisted that Dean arrange for them to speak to the students, assuming this would be an easier task for a rookie.

"No. How about you make the arrangements, Hughes?" Senior Detective White told him, reminding him who was boss.

"Me?" Hughes felt insulted.

"Yes you!" White pointed his finger. "Dean and I'll investigate from there. We're gonna need more than just my brain on this one."

"Good day, gentlemen. Looking forward to working with you guys." Dean got up from the table and left the diner. He couldn't wait to get started on the case. He knew this was going to be special, because usually detectives and uniformed officers in Chicago didn't get along, especially the Black officers and the White detectives. Dean knew he was building his credentials on the force. Despite his race, he didn't expect to be chosen for a high profile case like Gina's, but he was ready to take on the challenge.

Dean and Detective White were able to interview the teachers and the students at Harvey Elementary School. Since Jackie wasn't in school that day, they went to her house.

"Do you mind if we ask your daughter some questions about the disappearance of Gina "Baby" Morris?" Dean asked Jackie's mother Ms. Jones.

"How long you gonna be?" she stood in the doorway, the smell of beer and cigarettes wafting toward them.

"About twenty minutes."

"She don't have nothing to do with that girl being missing, I'm just letting ya'll know right now."

Dean simply nodded and asked, "Is she around?"

"Come in." Ms. Jones stepped aside to let them in and stared Dean up and down. She thought he was a handsome young guy, but she didn't like his straightforwardness with her. As Dean and White sat down at the dining room table, a young man walked out the back room with a smashed Afro, as if he had just woken up. He was wearing cut-off jean shorts, and a raggedy T-shirt.

"Say, what'chall niggas and crackers want with my sister?" he asked.

Dean looked to his left and then to his right. "I don't see any niggers in here, or crackers."

"Yeah, whatever, chump!"

"You need to go take a shower and put some clothes on, and then comb your nappy hair while you're at it."

"This is my house!"

"Then I suggest if you want it to stay that way, you will go back to your room. This business is about your sister." Dean gave him a hard stare. He meant business, and he didn't look away until the young man turned away.

"Go on back to the room, Leroy." Ms. Jones told her fifteen-year-old son.

"Jackie!" Ms. Jones called. "They waiting for you!"

"I said I'm coming!"

"Hurry up, 'cause I don't like having cops in my house," She looked at Dean and White, rolling her eyes as she flopped down on the couch.

Within a few minutes, Jackie came out of her room. She was wearing a purple T-shirt with a yellow flower on the front. Her hair was braided back from her big forehead, and her cheeks were covered with preteen acne. She looked at the officers nervously with her small, sneaky-looking eyes. She pulled up the chair and slouched down in the seat with her legs stretched out in front of her. She was tall for a twelve-year-old, and could pass for fourteen. Her knees showed scars from rough child's play and her arms had old chicken pox bumps. Dean and White introduced themselves to Jackie and got straight to the point about their visit.

"Jacqueline, we have some questions to ask you about your best friend, Gina. Now, all you have to do is tell the truth, okay?" Detective White asked, speaking gently. Jackie nodded her head.

"You need to answer yes or no," Dean told her. He turned on the tape recorder.

"Now hold up; you can't tape her!" Ms. Jones rushed over to the table where they were sitting.

"Now wait a minute, Ms. Jones, all she has to do is answer yes or no," Dean said to her firmly.

"I don't want her recorded!"

"What's going on now?" Leroy came from the back, this time fully dressed, hair combed. He looked much better. Dean was glad he had listened to him, and assumed the young man simply needed a good father figure in his life. It was obvious to Dean that he didn't have one.

"Part of our investigation is to ask questions, and we need this tape as part of the investigation. Now we can do it here, or at the police station, it's your choice," Dean responded impatiently.

"What do you think we should do?" Ms. Jones turned to her son Leroy.

"Well I don't want nobody seeing Jackie in their squad car like she did something wrong. So if she innocent, just let her go ahead and say what she gots to say and get it over with."

"She ain't done nothing, no way," Ms. Jones said, blowing her cigarette smoke in the air. She went back to sit on the couch.

"Jackie, don't you admit nothing you ain't do, you hear me?" Leroy pointed his finger at her. "I'm steppin' out. See ya'll later."

The detectives asked Jackie some questions and she answered a nervous "no" to all of them. Detective White knew he would have to dig deeper to get answers from her, so he turned it up a notch. Dean watched in admiration.

"What time did you leave the dance?" Detective White asked.

"She got in about eleven o'clock," her mother yelled from the couch.

"Did you come home at eleven o'clock like your Mom just said?"

Jackie hunched her shoulders.

"Mrs. Bradford said she sent you home about nine o'clock. Is that true?"

Jackie nodded, and Dean gave her a firm look. She nervously replied, "Yes."

"So does it usually take you two hours to get home?"

"The train was late."

"Mrs. Bradford said she sent you home because you threw punch on Gina and got into a scuffle, is that true? Yes or no?" Dean chimed in.

"Gina was trying to get me in trouble, but she shouldn't have hit me. That's the only reason I threw the punch," Jackie answered darkly.

"So because she hit you first, you naturally defended yourself, right?" Dean asked.

"Yes I did!" Jackie blurted out. "She kept saying her dress was prettier than mine and bragging in my face that she danced with Jerry Winslow!"

"So that's why you *threw* the punch on her? Because her dress was prettier and she danced with Jerry?" White asked for emphasis.

"That's right!"

"So then," Detective White continued, "you threw punch on Gina's dress and got sent home. Did you actually go home?"

"Yeah, I came home by myself."

"Your classmates said they saw you with Gina on Greenbelt Avenue."

Jackie sucked her teeth. "So!"

"What were you doing on Greenbelt Avenue?"

"I don't know. I heard somebody was shooting on our block, so I told Baby, let's go hide in the apartment building."

"How is it that Baby was with you when you said you went home alone?"

"Well . . . I waited for Baby so we could ride home together."

"Why would you do that after a fight?" White asked, puzzled.

"Because we squashed it!"

"What apartment building did you hide out in?" Dean asked.

"The one with the door always open. It sits on the corner by the liquor store."

"How do you know the door is always open?" White asked.

"Because my sister and her friends smoke reefer there sometimes."

"How long did you hide there?" Dean followed up.

"I don't know. I left, but Baby stayed." "Why would Baby stay in a place she doesn't know? And why would you leave her there?"

"I don't know."

"You know Jackie, I'm sorry to tell you this, but Gina is dead," Dean told her. Detective White was furious that he had let the cat out the bag. He just knew the investigation was blown. He looked at Dean and rolled his eyes.

Jackie put her hands over her face in shock. "She died?"

"Baby Gina is dead?" Ms. Jones asked from the couch.

"Why didn't ya'll say that at first? Ya'll coming in here saying she was missing. So on the news, that body of the child they said they found over there was Gina's?"

"She died because your daughter Jackie hit her in the head with a broken piece of pipe, didn't you, Jackie?" Dean said to her.

Jackie burst into tears. "It was an accident! I told her to get up, but she wouldn't. I told her to get up!"

"What are you saying, Jackie?" her mother approached her.

"Oh, Ma, shut up. Just be quiet!"

"No you shut up! Did you kill that girl?"

"It was an accident! I didn't mean it! I swear!"

Dean read Jackie her rights and then handcuffed her. Detective White was happy that Dean had solved the case after all.

Trial . . .

Of course, there is always a twist of events when it comes to crimes. Jackie had admitted her confession on tape, but during her arraignment before the judge, she pled "not guilty". Jackie's defense lawyer claimed the interrogation was coerced, which resulted in the case going to a full trial in court before a jury. Mama Frieda had a nervous breakdown and had to be hospitalized, so every day Peaches and Connie attended the trial. After a week's long trial, the Morris family sat and listened to the closing-argument, starting with the prosecution.

"Jackie is not an innocent kid the way the defense tried to point out. She's not the sick kid who needs mental and emotional help. In spite of the psychological examination of Jackie that she is delusional and demonstrates fits of rage. The evidence is not pointed enough to say she was out of her mind when she maliciously killed Gina. There is more evidence that Jackie was intelligent, kind, and witty, but on the other hand she is spiteful, mean, controlling, and manipulative. Before the spring dance, Gina was Jackie's best friend. In fact, Gina was always Jackie's best friend because Gina always did what Jackie wanted her to do. On the night of spring dance, Jackie became so jealous of Baby that she intentionally threw punch on Baby's dress. The two got into a scuffle, which Mrs. Bradford broke them up. Mrs. Bradford sent Jackie home, but Jackie waited for Baby outside on the schoolyard, where she found a broken pipe and put it in her purse. Jackie apologized to Baby while she was waiting for Connie to come and pick her up. Jackie was plotting, just the way she plotted when she saw birds and cats in her neighborhood. She watched and waited, then went in for the kill, except Gina was no animal. She wasn't some bird or cat. Gina was a human being who deserved to live, but Jackie in her conscious controlling and manipulative mind didn't see Gina as a human being that night. Jackie saw Gina as a girl who did not listen to her. A girl who wouldn't stay away from the cute boy she wanted to be with. So what did she do? She convinced Gina to follow her. She got inside Gina's head and made her believe her sister Connie was not coming to pick her up. Let's walk through the night's event play-by-play . . ." as the prosecution talked Connie began to visualize the moment as if it were playing out right before her eyes . . .

"If you don't wanna miss your curfew, we better leave now," Jackie said to Baby. Baby then told Mrs. Bradford she was leaving, since she didn't want to miss curfew. Unbeknownst to Mrs. Bradford, Jackie was waiting outside, and Baby left with her. They rode the L Train, and then took the bus afterwards. Jackie told Baby that she needed to pick up something from her mother's boyfriend Bobby and asked Baby to come with her. They got off the bus six blocks or so before Sedgwick and walked down Greenbelt Avenue.

The two walked inside the apartment building. Jackie told Baby to go down in the basement and knock on the door to ask for her mother's boyfriend (which was really the laundry room door), but Jackie lied and said it was her mother's boyfriend's apartment.

"Go ahead, Bobby lives down there he will let us in," Jackie had urged Baby to walk down into the basement.

"But it's dark down there."

"Go ahead, don't be a chicken. Go on," Jackie urged. Baby turned to walk down the stairs and Jackie reached in her purse for the short pole, and hit Baby in the back of the head. Baby tumbled down the stairs after the hit. Delirious, she tried to stand up and make her way through the laundry door, believing she was going into Bobby's apartment for help. "Why did you do this to me, Jackie?" Baby cried, as blood started to pour down her face, she crawled inside the laundry room. "Help me Jackie please! Call 911!" Baby started to lose sight, as she was going in and out of consciousness. "Jackie I can't see . . .I can't breathe." Jackie stood over Baby with

an evil look on her face, as she watched life leave Baby. When Baby took her last breath, Jackie said, "That'll teach you not to mess with me!" Jackie ran to the back of the building-buried the weapon and then rushed home.

When Connie saw the judge approaching the bench with the jurors' verdict an hour later, she snapped out her daze.

"The jury finds the defendant, Jacqueline Jones guilty for first degree murder . . ."

The people in the public galley jumped up and down and started cheering with excitement over the verdict. Most of them were from Cabrini Green and the surrounding communities.

"Order in the court!" the Judge slammed his gavel. "Will the people in the galley remain seated and silent until the sentence is read or be dismissed," the Judge ordered, and slowly the crowd started to hush. "As a result of the guilty verdict, Jacqueline Jones shall serve a mandatory sentence of twenty-five years in prison, with eligibility for parole in ten years. The first six years shall be served in a juvenile detention facility until Jacqueline turns eighteen. The six years shall be applied as time served toward her sentence. She shall serve the remaining nineteen years in Cook County Prison for Women. Case dismissed."

There were crowds of people waiting outside of the court building. News reporters were waiting for the Morris family and their public attorney to make a statement. Before the attorney could speak, Peaches shouted in front of the cameras, "Justice has been served!"

"And how do you feel?" one reporter asked Connie.

"My sister is gone. For me, there is no justice in that. She's not coming back, and I'm really sad about it."

The attorney went on to speak to reporters using the law jargon and formalities, and then he escorted the girls to a taxi where they went to visit Connie's mother in the hospital.

Connie went to pay her mother a visit after the trial was over, and she looked frail and weak. Mama didn't want to eat or drink, and she was spaced out most of the time. She spoke few words. She would only nod her head yes or no to doctors and nurses when they asked her questions. Connie told her mother that Jackie was going to serve twenty-five years in prison for murdering Baby, but it didn't matter,

Baby was gone. After sitting with her mother for quite some time, Connie grew tired and decided to head home. She leaned over and kissed her mother's forehead. "I love you Mama. Get better soon." Her mother mumbled words that Connie could barely hear. "What did you say Mama?"

"It's time."

"It's time?"

"Time for . . . you . . ."

"Huh?"

"It's time for . . . for you to live."

"Mama, I don't understand what you're saying."

Mama took a deep breath to say what she needed to say. She said in a low tone. "It's time for you to live your life, child. Live for you," she squeezed her daughter's hand tight, and then slowly eased her grip until her hand fell back down at her side.

"But Mama I am living."

"I don't have much longer, Connie."

"Mama don't talk that way everything will be all right."

"Remember everything I taught you, and use what you done learned to get out them projects."

"Well, after I graduate next year I'm going to college. I'll make it out Mama. I promise I'll make you proud, okay?"

Mama reached out for her, and Connie leaned in enough so that her mother could stroke her cheeks.

"I'm already proud of you, Connie. Now you go on . . . and live. Live the life I never had. Be better than me and your Daddy, and be . . . happy," Mama was short of breath, as tears fell from her eyes.

"Don't cry Mama. Everything will be okay."

Mama closed her eyes, feeling her time to rest was approaching.

"Mama? Mama?"

The nurse walked in. "Maybe she needs to rest honey. Come on back tomorrow," the nurse told Connie. Connie was hesitant, but felt that maybe her mother did need to rest, so she left but promised to return tomorrow.

Later that night, Connie got a call that woke her up out her sleep. "Your mother's soul has gone to rest honey. She is resting in peace now. Her poor heart held on as long as it could, but all she been through and then to lose your sister on top of that was just too much," the doctor told Connie. She dropped the phone and burst into tears.

Baby's poem, *A River Moves Forward,* won the national and local poetry contests which prizes totaled a thousand dollars. Connie had to use the money to pay the rent and the bills. Connie's biological father Scott flew in to attend Frieda's funeral, which he had paid for everything. It was the first time Connie had seen her real father in person. She had only seen him in pictures and spoke with him by phone. When the funeral and repast was over, Scott and his now wife, Margaret, left Connie with some money and told her to think about coming to live with them in South Carolina because she was still a minor. Peaches overheard the conversation and insisted that she and her boyfriend Barry would lookout for Connie. The funeral was standing room only, and Peaches was upset that her own father was nowhere in sight at her mother's funeral, and he didn't even show up for Baby's. She and Connie knew that Mason had to have heard about everything that had gone on, especially with Baby since it was national news. It was the seventies, and no one had heard of a child murdering another child in those days- not frequently. In truth, Mason had heard, but he knew if he went to the funerals that Beth-Ann would find out he hid his other family from her. He had tried to bury the memories of his family by starting his new life with Beth-Ann. He still hallucinated about being hazed in the army, and would sometimes act out on the family by physically abusing them. He didn't drink as much as he used to, but he was still a very sick man who refused to get help despite Beth-Ann's urging. Like Mama, Beth-Ann continued to take his abuse both verbally and physically, hoping Mason would one day change.

CHAPTER EIGHT

TRAPPED

Dean Wilson was happy that he had helped Detective Gary White solve the Gina "Baby" Morris case. Following Gina's death, the community put a lot of pressure on city officials, especially the Mayor, who was up for re-election. The Mayor knew he had to do something about the increase of crime and violence, particularly the Cabrini Green Housing Projects., which at the time was one of the worse housing projects in the country. As a result, the Mayor put a heavy hand on police Chief Jeff Blake, who in turn, blasted his officers for lackadaisical work. Chief Blake demanded double-duty for all uniformed officers like Dean. Dean was exhausted, and today was a day he didn't feel like working. He missed spending time with his son, and having fun with his cousin Henry, whom every called "Hank." Dean and Hank used to go to many house parties, shoot pool at the pool hall, bowl, and just hang out at the bar and watch sports. Due to his double shifts lately, they hadn't hung out in a while, and he missed his cousin. Hank was like the older brother that Dean never had. He was twenty-nine, and was five years older than Dean was. Hank lived in Chicago since birth while Dean came to Chicago when he was fourteen. Dean's father, Reverend Thaddeus Wilson moved his family up north after the death of his young son, Johnny. He became the assistant Pastor to his brother-Hank Sr. In time, Rev. Wilson established his own church on the Southside with a congregation that was steadily growing in large numbers. Rev. Wilson did not like the ways of his nephew Hank and the influence he had on his son Dean as they were growing up. He felt that Dean was a wet behind the ears country boy when he first moved to Chicago, but Dean proved to hold his own to some degree even when it came to his career choice of becoming a cop, when college didn't work out. Dean and his father had an estranged relationship since Johnny died, and their move to Chicago didn't change that, it only made them more distant with each other, so Dean grew very close to his mother and Hank. In spite of what Dean's father thought of Hank, Dean felt, his cousin wasn't a bad person. Hank personally had no interest in law enforcement or working hard at anything, except at being a gigolo, but he taught Dean about the streets and it helped him once he became a cop. Rev. Wilson despised Hank Jr. for using women the way he did. He couldn't understand why the son of a preacher would be interested in modeling for Sears, and shaking his behind on stage as a male dancer, and getting women to buy whatever he wanted in exchange for sex. Hank felt his uncle was jealous of him for his easygoing living. Hank had a nice luxury home in the Highland Park suburbs of Chicago, drove a white Cadillac and wore expensive suits and jewelry. Hank could be easily mistaken for a hustler or a pimp, but he was just a guy who had it going on materially speaking. As Dean ruminated in thought about these things, he looked over his shoulder at Phyllis who was still sleep next to him in bed. It bothered him that after four years of marriage, he still was not happy. He had married Phyllis at the urging of his father during his sophomore year at Loyola University. Phyllis was a freshman at Loyola when she became pregnant with Dean's son, knowing his pastor father would force them to marry or face humiliation from his congregation. Dean learned from Phyllis' roommate, shortly after they were married that Phyllis had been flushing her birth control pills down the toilet, but it was too late. Dean and Phyllis were already married.

Despite trust being broken, Phyllis showed no ambition to work and no goals about bettering herself. In fact, Dean learned from her friends that Phyllis went to college just to find a husband. Dean being the track star that he was, made him a target for opportunist like Phyllis. Phyllis believed Dean would continue his track pursuits and become rich and famous. That didn't happen for Dean. He ended up dropping out due to the pressures of becoming a family man before he was ready. It was moments like these when Dean missed his dreams in track and field, because he had to work in order to take care of his family. The only thing Dean had left to remember from those days was his Olympic recognitions, where he competed for the gold in the U.S. Olympics, but didn't win. He lost because he was not focused. A week before that race, Phyllis had announced she was pregnant, but Phyllis didn't think

Dean would stop pursuing his career. When Dean's parents said they weren't going to raise a baby, her plans backfired and Dean quit school to care for her and the baby. Dean pushed aside the bed covers and rose to his feet. He felt totally off balance about going in to work today. He had only slept four hours after pulling a double shift, and was starting to feel drained. He walked over to his bedroom window to check the weather, when he spotted his neighbor pulling into an empty parking space outside. He could hear the music from his car playing an old 1968 classic from *The Dells*, *"Stay in My Corner."*

"Mmmm," Phyllis woke up to the sound of the music vibrating outside of her house in their middle-class suburb. She stretched her arms to the ceiling and yawned, and opened her eyes to see her handsome hubby looking out the window. He was half-naked in his boxers. His long chocolate-coated legs looked tanned under his baby blue boxers. A silver chain hung around his neck, with a medallion piece of a scorpion. "Remember that used to be our song?" she asked Dean, rubbing the sleep from her eyes.

"I remember," Dean sulked, as he closed the blinds, and tried not to dwell on the past. He looked at his wife who had dry slobber at the corners of her mouth, turned up his nose at her, and then walked into the bathroom to get ready for work.

"Hi Daddy!" Little Dean was still in his superhero pajamas, and his curly Afro was wildly sprawled all over his head from last night's sleep as he rushed into his parent's room. Dean easily scooped his four-year old into his arms and spun him around. Phyllis looked on from the bedside wishing Dean still had affection for her. Lately, he barely even looked at her. He used to care about her feelings, but the tenderness and intimacy of their marriage was gone.

"Daddy's got a present for you, just let me get dressed for work first, and then I'll give it to you."

"Okay Daddy."

"Go on in your room and I'll bring it in there shortly." Little Dean ran away excited.

"You know, Dean, your son misses you. He needs *you* more than gifts."

"You think I don't know that?" he snapped. Phyllis had a habit of nagging him and complaining. Dean felt he was doing the best he could.

"*I* need you too, Dean. I'm your wife and you're my husband." Hearing Phyllis call him her *husband* made Dean's skin crawl. He asked himself quite often, what he ever saw in her. She was still cute in the face with big eyes, long thick hair, smooth chocolate skin, and a nice big-boned body. Yet, she was spoiled, deceitful, and lacked the ambition Dean felt she should have. She also stopped wearing sexy clothes that enhanced the curviness of her body, and settled for sweatpants and T-shirts. She never looked for a job and preferred to be a Housewife. Dean saw things differently; she was always on the phone gossiping with her friends, eating take-out food and watching TV, and meddling in other peoples' business. Dean did all the work around the house. He would come home from work and wash the dishes, clean, and cook after a hard day's work. He wished he had a cooked meal when he got home, but that wasn't the case. If Dean didn't cook, Phyllis would order out for the family. Dean's mother offered to teach Phyllis how to cook, but she was too lazy to put forth an effort to learn.

"Dean, are you hearing me? I miss you baby," she walked over to him and stroked his back with her hands, and he flinched, as he buttoned his uniform shirt.

"What's the matter with you?"

"Just don't touch me like that, all right?"

"Is there someone else? Dean, please don't make me beg for your affection."

"I have to go to work," Dean was no longer going to allow himself to be suckered into her sappy emotions. Phyllis trailed behind as Dean walked down the hall to Little Dean's room with his present.

"Do you still love me? Do you?" Phyllis tugged on Dean's shirt.

"Stop it!" Dean shouted. "Dean doesn't need to hear all of this whining!"

"Then when are you going to listen to me? When will you make love to me again?"

"Phyllis," Dean sharply turned around and pointed his finger in her face. "I said, stop it! I mean it. I have to go to work. I don't have time for this right now." Phyllis stormed back into their bedroom down the opposite end of the hallway. Dean could hear her crying but he ignored her as he opened the door to little Dean's room. He was watching *Scooby Doo*.

"Hey Dean, I have your present."

"Yaaay, what did you get me Daddy?"

"Open it." Dean kneeled down in front of him and watched him open the box.

"Yaaay, it's Evel Knievel toy!"

"What are you supposed to say?"

"Thank you."

"You're welcome son. Daddy's going to work now. I'll see you later."

"Okay. Bye, daddy."

"One thing about this job is that it's the best education on Earth," Stuckey, Dean's new partner was saying to him as they patrolled the Cabrini Green area. Dean was driving while Stuckey decided to cruise control from the passenger seat, with his belly hanging over his belt.

"Is that so?"

"Yep. If you keep at this long enough, you'll learn there's not a lot of difference among people, regardless of their educational or economic status," Stuckey said. "You see, son, people sit in classrooms for years trying to learn why people do the things they do, but in the end, their education is all based on theory and hearsay."

"I can dig it."

"You better *dig* it," Stuckey told him. "I heard you got compassion for this work, and that's good, but that will only get you so far. You still need to know the difference between your compassion for the job and knowing how to do your job. It's like basketball. People may love it, but it doesn't mean they know how to play it."

"Stuckey, no disrespect, man, but I'm sick and tired of you old heads on the force acting like we young cats don't know anything," Dean interjected. "I work investigations sometimes with Detective White, so I think I know a little something."

"Wise guy," Stuckey chuckled. "You're just another rookie cop acting like because you investigate cases, that you can call all the shots."

"I'm the wise guy? You must be jiving," Dean countered, pulling into the 7-Eleven. "If you want donuts or coffee, you need to pay for it yourself," Dean extended his hand for the cash. He had seen rookie cops pay for veteran cops all the time, but he wasn't one of them. Dean was earning his stripes, and the last thing he was going to do was get punked by a veteran cop for social acceptance.

"Oh, so it's like that?" Stuckey questioned.

"On my beat it is, Jack."

After Dean and Stuckey ate their donuts and drank their coffee, they patrolled the beat of North Larrabee Street near the Cabrini Green Projects. When Dean made a left onto West Division Street, he spotted a drug transaction on the corner of North Michigan Avenue near a corner liquor store. When he stopped the patrol car at a distance, Stuckey raised his brow in wonder.

"Wilson, you better keep driving, it ain't worth the paperwork today."

"He's doing the crime, so he's gonna do the time."

Stuckey shook his head, lamented, "Rookie, rookie, rookie."

While Stuckey was trying to win an argument with Dean, someone spotted their patrol car, and the guy making the drug transaction took off running.

"Now see there!" Dean shouted.

"Fooling with you, he's running away."

Dean jumped out of the car and gave chase. The young man ran down an alley, but Dean caught him just as he tried to hop a fence and get away. Stuckey was behind, trying to catch his breath. He was amazed at how fast Dean could run.

"Show off," Stuckey panted.

"Just doing my job man," Dean escorted the young man back to the patrol car.

"Stop killing your own people, young fella, do you hear me?" Dean shoved the man into the back of the patrol car.

"I'm just trying to feed my family, man, that's all," the young man protested.

"I am too, but you don't see me selling poison to my own people, do you?"

"Man, whatever. I'll be out this joint in the morning."

"Yeah? Well I'll be out here in the morning to lock you right back up."

"You take your job too seriously. Why don't you let me pay you a little something on the side and let me keep working this corner?"

"Don't try to hustle me. I'm not that type of cop."

The man twisted his lips, frowned. "Yeah I see, tell me something I don't know. I'm gonna remember you when I get out."

"Don't you go making threats you jive turkey!" Dean shoved him into the back of the police car. He felt satisfied catching a bad guy today. It made him feel like his job was worth it after all.

CHAPTER NINE

DOWN SOUTH

Despite not doing as well on her finals, Connie's teachers gave her passing grades, since she had been maintaining a very good GPA throughout the year before the recent tragedies in her family. In September, she would be a senior at Lakeview High. Her father had been paying the rent until Connie could decide where she wanted to move. She was still grieving, and although her mother urged her to leave Cabrini, their apartment still held memories of times they shared together.

Peaches moved back that summer in June after breaking up with Barry. Barry wanted to settle down, have another baby, and get married, but Peaches was not ready for the mature lifestyle that Barry wanted. Only a few weeks after Peaches moved back home, Barry was killed in a hit-and-run motorcycle accident. Although Peaches was very sad when Barry died, what troubled her more was the fact that she had to be a full-time mother to BJ. Being a mother didn't fit into her young lifestyle. She was used to partying, getting high, and coming and going as she pleased. Barry was stuck with watching the baby, but he was gone now.

Peaches applied for public assistance after she was fired from Hot Wings and Fries. She was fired for being late all the time and calling out sick. She told the Department of Human Services that she was taking care of Connie and her son. Since Connie was not eighteen yet, they allowed her to claim Connie as well.

Still, Peaches did not use the money wisely; she used it to party and get high and drunk with her friends, and buy whatever else she wanted. She and Connie would argue often about cut-off notices for bills and the rent being past due. She was tired of calling her father to save them. "This is my money, so I'm in charge," Peaches would argue with Connie. The most she ever saw of Peaches was her backside.

Connie fed BJ, changed his diapers, played with him, and gave him all the attention he needed. Peaches took advantage of her sister's kindness. When Connie's friends stopped by to visit, she couldn't leave the house because Peaches would stick her with BJ.

When Connie's father called her out of routine of checking on her, he could sense that Connie was deeply depressed. She normally engaged more in the conversation, but now she was giving him terse responses. He insisted she needed to get away to clear her head. The more Connie thought about it, the more she felt he was right. She asked Peaches to join her in traveling to Newburg, South Carolina. "Hell no! And if I was you, I wouldn't go either. You don't wanna end up like Emmett Till." With May, the response was more of a gentle let down. "I don't think I'll like it down there. The people talk so slow, and I don't like rural areas." Connie didn't have a choice but to take the trip alone. Before she left, she gave Peaches the rundown of how to care for BJ in her absence. Peaches didn't know what his feeding times were, or when he took his naps. Connie feared leaving him, but the thought of being away felt like a good idea.

Scott paid for Connie's flight, and he picked her up from the airport. Scott reintroduced Connie to Margaret, who was now his wife. Connie thought her stepmother Margaret could pass for Lucille Ball, only heavier. She was tall, big-boned with red hair, and wore bright red lipstick. She was loud when she said *hello* to Connie, as if she was hard of hearing, and talked at length about the country on the way to their house from the airport.

Connie tuned her out by watching the city streets turn into dirt roads. She saw fields of green and houses that seemed to be more than ten minutes apart from each other. The pickup truck pulled into a reddish brown dirt driveway, and parked in front of a huge ranch-style black and white house with a walk-around porch. It was a two-level home with five bedrooms, a basement, and three bathrooms. Most of the rooms were all on the first level of the house. On the porch was a US flag that was blowing back and forth in the summer breeze. Connie thought about what Peaches had said—'*Remember what happened to Emmett Till*'—and became a little nervous. She realized she was a long way from Chicago, and she thought about the segregation stories her mother used to tell her about the South. She said a silent prayer to God that nothing bad would happen to her during her visit.

Scott and Margaret showed Connie the farm and the horses inside of the barn, and then escorted her inside the house.

". . . and this here is your room," Margaret said, she showed her the final parts of the enormous house.

"You go on and get settled, Connie. Margaret and I gonna prepare supper, okay?" Scott smiled, happy to have his daughter visiting him for the first time.

Connie walked to the back of the house and sat down on her queen-sized bed. The bed felt soft and cozy. She didn't feel any springs poking her like her bed back in Chicago. She noticed how quiet her surroundings were, she didn't hear people arguing, ambulances or police car sirens sounding off, or shotguns. It was so quiet she could hear her own thoughts. She decided to write letters, and quickly whipped out her writing pad from her suitcase. Before she knew it, she had written letters to everyone, including Peaches, May, and a letter apologizing to Jet for leaving without saying goodbye.

"Supper is ready, Connie!" yelled Scott.

Connie hoped and prayed that whatever he and Margaret put together would taste good. She had a taste for a good ole' Chicago dog . . .

CHAPTER TEN

BACK IN CHICAGO

Peaches was busy partying and getting high on her new boyfriend Poncho's supply. At every party, Peaches wanted to take her high to the next level. She wanted to take her mind off losing Barry, her mother, and Baby. She went from smoking weed and Angel Dust to snorting cocaine, and then . . .

"You sure you ready for this?" Poncho asked Peaches. She was sitting in the bathroom of the apartment, squeezing her arm until a thick green vein appeared.

"Yeah, you said it's good, right?"

"It's what I hear, but I don't even mess with this stuff myself. Now I'm gonna ask you one more time."

"Nigga, shoot me up!" Peaches snapped.

"All right, let me get my boy Doug in here, 'cause I don't even know if I'm doing this right." Doug came into the bathroom, tied a rubber strap around Peaches' arm until he could see her vein, and then he shot heroin into her arm. Peaches eyes rolled into the back of head, and her mind escaped into another world. Freed her from all the pain she no longer wanted to feel. The death of her mother didn't hurt anymore, the loss of her sister didn't hurt anymore, and the death of Barry Johnson no longer hurt either. Peaches felt nothing but ecstasy and she wanted to be taken to that place of *feel good* over and over again. From then on, Peaches partied and shot heroin in her veins. In a matter of days she was hooked, and would shoot dope several times a day. When Poncho wasn't around to give her some of his supply, she would sell her food stamps for cash and buy it from another drug dealer.

"Tell you what, you like this stuff a lot. Let me set up shop here," Poncho said to Peaches one day. "I'll pay your rent, and you get your dope for free, deal?" Poncho offered Peaches.

Peaches agreed to let him set up shop in the apartment where her own mother and father raised her. BJ was left without food, a clean diaper, and smelled awful. The stench was so bad that her neighbor, Ms. Knight, could smell it next door. She knocked on the door and asked what was going on and found out that Peaches was neglecting BJ. She took BJ with her and quickly cleaned him up and fed him.

From then on, Peaches would throw BJ on Ms. Knight. "Watch him for a minute," she would say, and then disappear for days or not answer her door. Eventually, Ms. Knight had had enough. Social Services showed up and tried to take BJ from Peaches, but Peaches put up a fight. The women threatened to return later on with the cops, but Peaches didn't care.

Connie grew worried because she hadn't heard from Peaches in weeks. Each time she called the house, she got the operator saying the phone had been disconnected. She wrote letters and never heard back. Connie decided to ask May to go by to make sure everything was okay. May promised that she would, but instead, she went out partying with Jet and his new girlfriend, and she took along her new boyfriend Levi. When Connie didn't hear back from May, she called her house again.

"May is out partying. I doubt if she's been to your crib. If you want, I can check out things for you," Ray told Connie.

"Would you, please?"

"Sure, no problem."

Ray hurried to Cabrini Green. He had a car, but he knew better than to park it anywhere near Cabrini and risk it being stolen.

Peaches opened the door. "What do you want? Connie ain't here!"

"I know. She asked me to check on things," Ray replied, as he stood at the door. Peaches looked a mess, and a strong stench was coming from inside the apartment.

"I have to get myself cleaned up," Peaches sniffed. She left the door open for Ray to come in, and walked away, scratching her arms as if something bit her. She was wearing a dingy bathrobe, her hair looked like she had been in a catfight, and there were dark circles around her eyes.

"Ray, you do know that Connie is not my mother, don't you?" Peaches grabbed a rolled-up joint off the table and started smoking it. He noticed how huge her hands were. They were the size of turtles. Ray knew people who looked like that.

"I know Connie is not your mother, but she was worried about you. I see you on that junk."

"Don't judge me, nigga! You think 'cause you a hot DJ that you better than everybody else?"

"I'm no junkie, that's for sure."

"Yeah, well you tell my sister I ain't dead . . . yet," Peaches blew smoke circles into the air.

"Where is uh—um—BJ?"

"Sleep."

"Can I see him?"

Peaches hunched her shoulders. "Go ahead. He's in the back."

Ray walked to the back and as he walked down the hallway, the bedroom that used to be Mrs. Morris's room had a naked couple lying in the bed. Ray knew if Mrs. Morris were alive, she would never allow what was going on in her house right now. He remembered how strict she was. Even when he would come over to show Connie how to spin records, he had to speak when he walked in, wipe his feet at the door, and take off his hat. Mrs. Morris didn't allow anyone to disrespect her household.

BJ's eyes lit up and he smiled and cooed at the giant person looking down at him in his crib.

"Aw, look at you," Ray smiled. "You want me to pick you up, don't you?" Ray picked up BJ and he noticed he was wet. He looked around the room for a diaper, but there weren't any.

"Hey Peaches, where are the diapers?" he shouted from the room.

"I just bought diapers, he pees too much!"

"So what are you going to do?" Ray walked out of the room, holding BJ in his arms.

"I don't know. If you buy him some, I'll pay you back."

Ray decided to help. When he returned, the door to the apartment was wide open. His eyes popped in shock as police officers handcuffed Peaches and the naked couple that was in Mrs. Morris' old bedroom. On their way out the door, one of the officers draped the couple with a blanket they had grabbed from the bedroom.

"What's going on?" Ray reached his hand out to stop one of the officers.

"Are you affiliated with these drug dealers and users?" the officer questioned him.

"No sir. I saw the baby needed some diapers, so I went to buy some."

"You do know me! You know me!" Peaches shouted as the other officer escorted her out the door.

"I know Peaches, but I don't do drugs, and I don't know those other people. I'm just a friend of her sister's." The officer nodded and moved on his way, while two White women who were social workers approached Ray. They were next door talking with Mrs. Knight, who'd initially reported Peaches to CPS. While one of the social workers held baby BJ, the other one questioned Ray, starting with whether or not he was the daddy. Ray explained to the social worker that he wasn't the father, but BJ's aunt's best friend.

"Well, you just tell Connie we couldn't leave her nephew under these conditions," the social worker told Ray. "He won't be returned to his mother until she can prove she deserves him." The social workers left their business cards with Ray, and Ray used Mrs. Knight's phone to call Connie collect. Connie accepted the charges, and Ray told Connie everything.

"I'm sorry about what happened to Peaches and BJ," Scott said to Connie over dinner. "Make this your new home. Me and Margaret can find you a new school," he assured her.

Connie immediately shook her head. "Chi-town *is* my home. I can't stay here. This place is too slow and too quiet for me. I'm a city girl, you know?"

"Well, I can't have you living in Cabrini Green no mo'. If you wanna go back to Chicago, that's fine, but you're a minor until you turn eighteen. Any place you live will need a guardian unless I co-sign on a place for you."

Connie shook her head again. "I can't take any more money from you. I'm not some charity case."

"Sugar, we respect how you feel, and we don't view you that way, but honey you're still young. You can't make it out here on your own. You got no family left except us," Margaret said gently.

"Then I'll pay you guys back every penny."

"You don't have to pay us back, Connie. I swear, you just as stubborn as me."

"Connie, why don't you stay here another week or so to let things cool off up there in Chicago?" said Margaret.

"Then my nephew may get put up for adoption!"

"Connie, you too young to be taking on so much, you know. You're seventeen and ought to be living ya life. You got to live ya life, child, you really do," Scott told her. Connie paused in the middle of her train of thought, dazing off a minute as she recalled her mother saying, '*live your life, child.*' There she was, sitting at her father's dinner table, and he was telling her the same thing.

"I bet you don't even have a driver's license yet, now do ya?" Scott asked.

"No sir, I don't."

"See, you got to live. If you don't live for you, Connie, you can't take care of nobody else. Not even BJ."

"Connie, try to enjoy yourself while ya still here with us. You haven't even had a chance to enjoy yourself without worrying about the goings on back in Chicago," Margaret suggested. "Look around, honey. Somewhere in this town, being around all this nature will give you peace of mind. I promise you."

Connie decided to give the town of Newburg a chance. She tried hard to take her mind off what could be happening in Chicago. The next day Connie received a reply letter from Jet. He talked about how much fun he was having at the different parties, going swimming, training for football for the next season, and when he concluded, he told her he loved her. The letter was very short, but she felt satisfied. She wasn't sure if she loved him, and didn't trust that he really loved her, but she did miss his companionship. As she placed the letter it back in the envelope, she realized what her mother and her father was trying to say. Jet was living life. He was being a teenager. He was having fun. Connie had to figure out how she could do that. For starters, Scott took Connie for driving lessons each morning. Margaret showed her how to pick fresh vegetables out the garden, how to knit a quilt, and her father taught her how to ride a horse, which Connie thought was a lot of fun.

Scott invited over some of his family, including his parents, whom Connie had never met. Initially, the visit was awkward. They looked at her closely, as if she were from out of space. Connie, in turn, looked at them as if they were crazy for acting like they had never seen a Black person with green eyes before. Scott then took Connie to see her ailing maternal grandfather. She had a chance to go through photo albums, and hear stories about the family she never knew. She was in awe at how much her mother and she looked alike when her mother was a young girl. Both of them had the same pug nose, thin lips, and pointy chin. She could see that she had her father's big round ears and green eyes. She knew if she ever cut her long hair that she would look like a chipmunk with those ears.

One lazy afternoon after lunch, Connie ran with the dogs out in the fields until she was tired and lay down in the grass. She looked up at the blue sky, and felt engulfed in the arms of the earth. Her father had everything, she thought. He grew his own food, had his own farm, and house. She learned that Scott and his Dad used to own a construction company called McKenzie Construction. They would build properties in the inner cities of the South. Connie's grandfather eventually sold the company to a group of New York investors. Connie wondered what it would feel like if she owned her own business one day, and she thought about what type of business she would want to start up in Chicago. With her last year of high school approaching, Connie was determined to do whatever she needed in order to get out of the projects of Cabrini Green. As she laid there in the middle of the grassy field, feeling like a small dot in the middle of the earth, she closed her eyes and prayed to God that one day her life would be better than what it was. When she opened them, she saw a young pair of blue eyes staring back at her. She blinked twice to make sure she wasn't dreaming and quickly sat up.

"Hi," the young boy said with a smile. He was wearing blue overalls without a shirt and a straw hat. He stood about four feet tall, and walked around her a few times in circles, checking her out.

"Hello," Connie wondering who he was. He didn't look white and he didn't look black. His skin was fair, his hair was reddish brown and curly, and he had the prettiest dreamy blue eyes.

"Papa says you my sister, is that true?" he asked, taking a spit.

"You must be Willie."

"Yep, that's me." He pounded his chest with his little fist.

"It's nice to meet you. Yes, I'm your big sister, Connie." They shook hands.

"I figured that. See, my Mama said to me, Willie, you got yourself a half- sister, but I ain't seen you 'til now. Where ya been?"

"Well, I live in Chicago."

"Where Chicago is?"

"It's in the Midwest; it's a city in Illinois."

"What's Illinois?"

"A State."

"What's a state?"

"A place in the United States."

"I wanna go to the United States. Can my horse take me there?"

Connie laughed. "You're already here. How about we go inside and get some lemonade?" Connie stood up, dusted the grass and dirt off her cropped pants, and they went inside. Connie spent the day getting to know her little brother.

The remainder of her time in Newburg was filled with fun. She even went to a concert to see the Doobie Brothers. Finally, it was time to head back to Chicago. Connie was so glad she was able to learn how to drive, milk a cow, pick the right chicken eggs for breakfast, ride a horse, and cook on a wooden stove. She was actually going to miss Newburg, but she was still anxious to get back home . . .

CHAPTER ELEVEN

TRUTH HURTS

*I*t was amazing how summers always made Dean appreciate Chicago more. It must have been something about the heat or the smell of chlorine from the public pools, the fresh cut smell of grass by Lake Michigan, or the asphalt sizzling after a late afternoon thunderstorm. Whatever it was about summer, Dean enjoyed taking it all in on slow days like this. Dean was on foot patrol and decided to rest a minute in Washington Park. He was watching the young boys play basketball.

"Hey, Dean, come get some of this," the youngsters on the basketball court challenged.

"Oh, you don't want none of this, youngblood," Dean laughed them off.

"Why not? Go change your uniform and we'll sock it to you."

"You guys go ahead. Make me proud and keep up the hustle. You never know where your talents may take you," Dean told them. He glanced at his watch, and it was time to head back to the station. He drove back, clocked out, and stepped into his spotless red Dodge Charger.

He looked at himself in the front-view mirror, and decided that once he got home he would trim his short afro and mustache. He hated for any strand of hair to be out of place or signs of his mustache growing unevenly. He wished his wife would take more pride in the way she cared for herself. She barely visited the beauty salon, and walked around the house barefoot so much that the bottom of her feet were hard and crusty.

When he arrived at home and parked outside of his three-bedroom home in the Oak Forest community, he could predict what she was wearing and doing before he entered. Sure enough, his thoughts were right. Phyllis was wearing jogging pants, a T-shirt, and watching TV. She held the phone to her ear, stuffed her mouth with potato chips and seemed to be gossiping to one of her friends. The fun and the peace of a relatively easy workday quickly faded into a cloud of darkness for Dean. He searched the kitchen for something to cook. She had left a pot on the stove with a hotdog floating in stale water, and that wasn't Dean's idea of a meal. He put the top back on the pot, and opened the fridge to see what he could cook for himself. Everything he wanted to prepare would take at least an hour, and he was too hungry to wait that long. He wanted to have a meal.

"Phyllis, how come you didn't fix any dinner?" Dean asked.

"Hold on Barbara . . . what did you say Dean?" Phyllis held the phone from her ear.

"I said," Dean appeared in the living room. "What's for dinner?"

"There's plenty of food in there."

"Yes, I can see that, but everything is frozen."

"There's a hotdog on the stove, warm it up."

"Phyllis, I worked a double-shift!" he complained. "The least you could do is fix me a meal."

"Well I was busy Dean."

"Doing what? Besides gossiping on the phone? Did you even take my shirts to the Cleaners for me?"

"I forgot. I'll take them tomorrow."

Dean shook his head and walked away. When Phyllis got off the phone, he picked up the phone from the kitchen and dialed his cousin.

"What's cooking, youngblood? What'cha know no good?" Hank greeted Dean. Dean could hear The OJay's *"Love Train"* playing in the background, and voices of women in the background, sounding like they were having a party.

"Man, what's happening tonight? I need to go get out of here," Dean said.

"Brother, I got three fine foxes at my place, and all I'm gonna say is I can entertain 'em all, but I am willing to share. Are you down or what?"

Although the thought intrigued Dean a bit, he glanced at his wedding band and decided against it.

"You go ahead and have your fun. I'll catch'cha later."

Sensing a little desperation in Dean's voice, Hank thought it over.

"All right, I'll tell you what. It's about six now. Let me handle this here business with these chicks, and I can meet you at the Rico's Restaurant and Lounge by eight o'clock."

"Cool," Dean was glad to hear it. He went upstairs and saw his son watching TV. Dean Jr. complained about being inside all day, so Dean took him outside to ride his bike and play with him for awhile. Afterwards, he went inside to shower and noticed rings around the tub. He heaved a long sigh of frustration as he kneeled down to clean it first before he took a shower. Once he was showered up he went into the room to change clothes and saw he only had one pair of clean underwear left in the drawer. The dirty clothes basket was full, and Phyllis had not done the laundry like she said she would.

"See you later. Don't wait up," he said to Phyllis, who was eating popcorn and watching TV in the living room with her feet propped up on the table before her.

"Where are you going? I thought you were going to spend the evening with me."

"In this messy house? I'm going out!"

"I can clean the house tomorrow Dean, but Fridays are supposed to be our date nights, remember? You promised."

"Well you made promises too like keeping the house clean from now on, and having my dinner cooked, but haven't kept your end of the deal in months," he argued.

"Fine! Go ahead out with your cousin Hank, but you better not come back here smelling like another woman's perfume!"

Dean waved her off, and left out the door.

After small talk, Dean vented about what was going on with he and Phyllis with Hank.

". . . and I just feel like I'm trapped, man," Dean said, eating barbeque ribs. It was Dean and Hank's favorite spot on the Southside.

"You *are* trapped. I told you not to marry Phyllis, but you listened to your folks."

"Well, they wanted me to do the right thing since she was pregnant."

Hank twisted his lips. "Sure ya right, youngblood? Your pops cared more about his reputation at his church than your happiness."

"Yeah, well, what's done is done."

"You don't *have* to stay. You can get a divorce."

"It's not that simple."

"Youngblood, if you're not happy, quit it and split it."

"I can't just think about myself. What about my son?"

"What about him? You take better care of little Dean more than his mama does anyway."

"I don't have grounds for a divorce, man."

"You going by what the Good Book say, but I say what man's law says. "Irreconcilable differences and that *is* good enough for a divorce."

Dean shook his head, feeling unsure. "I don't know, Hank, I just don't know."

"Dean, I never seen you this unhappy, bro, and you should just tell Phyllis how unhappy you are. Do it now or spend the rest of your life being miserable."

"It'll hurt her."

"Truth hurts sometimes, but the longer you wait the more painful it's going to be."

Dean slept until noon the next day, which was a Saturday, until Phyllis woke him up to remind him that their son was invited to his cousin's birthday party. Phyllis had a fear of driving, so Dean had to take them to the party.

"You know, Dean, I really didn't appreciate you coming home so late last night," Phyllis mentioned during the drive.

"Not now, Phyllis. We can talk about it later," Dean said. He continued to sing along to the radio.

"We need to talk, Dean, and we need to talk as soon as we drop little Dean off."

"Yeah, okay, we'll see what's up," Dean brushed her off.

Once they pulled up in front of the house, Dean stayed in the car this time. He was sick of making appearances. Phyllis treated him more like a trophy than a husband. He knew she wanted to make her girl cousins and aunts jealous. *"Don't my man look handsome? Look at his muscles,"* she would say. *"Look at his haircut and mustache."* She put him on display, but not once did she ever say, *my husband works hard, and he comes home and cook and clean. I don't have to lift a finger.*

"You're not coming in?" Phyllis stepped out of the car.

"Nope," Dean replied bluntly. Phyllis rolled her eyes and slammed the car door, then hurried little Dean inside his cousin's house on the Southside. She called her cousins and aunts to the front door, and pointed to the new car that Dean had bought. Dean caught them looking and smiling at it, and could only shake his head in frustration from Phyllis' bragging.

Dean drove off after he and Phyllis dropped off little Dean. He turned the music up louder because he didn't want to talk. Phyllis was no dummy; she quickly reached over and turned off the music.

"It's time to talk," Phyllis said. Dean heaved a long sigh, and then pulled over into a gas station off the highway. Phyllis just couldn't wait until they got home, and Dean hated having deep discussions while driving.

"Dean, do you still want to be married to me?" Phyllis placed her hand on his.

Dean quickly withdrew his hand from hers. "I think you know the answer to that, Phyllis."

"How long are you going to punish me for what happened in the past? We have been married for four years now, and each year, our relationship grows further apart. We don't do anything together as a couple like we used to. All you do is work, and lately, whenever I try to have sex with you, you give me the cold shoulder. I don't know what to do anymore, Dean." She started to cry. "Is there someone else?"

Dean shook his head. Nothing she said sounded believable. Even as she started crying, he could not bring himself to comfort her. She had cried when she found out she was pregnant, and told Dean and his parents that she was afraid he was going to abandon her and the baby, so he'd married her. She had cried when they lived in an apartment, claiming a house provided more space for their son to grow, so he bought a house. It was Phyllis' same sappy emotions that he felt kept him trapped in their loveless marriage. Dean tried to think about his choice of words without hurting her more, but he was tired of protecting her feelings. He recalled what Hank had said the night before: *'just tell her the truth.'*

"Phyllis, you know we were both too young for marriage. You knew I never wanted any kids at that age or any serious commitment, but you trapped me. How would you feel if you were me?"

"Are you saying you never loved me?"

"Stop making this about you and answer the question, Phyllis. How would you feel?"

Tears streamed down her cheeks. She sobbed, "I don't know. I would have forgiven you."

"I don't trust you anymore. I tried to build up my trust in you again, and I tried to make this work, but we're not compatible, and I'm miserable!" Phyllis could hear the anger and the pain in Dean's voice and she could see it written all over his face. She knew no matter how hard she pressed, she would never be able to make him love her the way he used to.

"Let's get a divorce." Phyllis had heard enough. "Once we divorce, I can move to California to be with Craig."

Dean snapped. "Craig? California? What are you talking about?"

"Little Dean is coming with us."

"Us?" Dean couldn't believe what he was hearing. "So you were having an affair all this time? You were screwing somebody else behind my back?"

"What was I supposed to do, Dean? You haven't made love to me in months!"

"That's no excuse!" Dean shouted. "I never cheated on you!"

"Well what have you been doing for sex these days? Because you sure haven't been getting any from me! Is that why you take so many long showers instead of just being with me, your wife?"

"Maybe," Dean replied, bitterly. "But I never cheated on you, although I had plenty of opportunities to do so, believe me!"

"Well, Craig is a good friend. I told him that if you refused to be with me and work things out, Dean and I would move out to California with him. He just moved from Chicago to LA to start his own record company, and he says the only missing piece in his life is me and Dean."

Dean couldn't believe what he was hearing. He wasn't sure if this was one of Phyllis' tricks again to try to make him feel like the failure of their marriage was his fault. He questioned if she was making this whole thing up to make him jealous.

"Fine, let's file for a divorce first thing Monday morning," Dean casually said, not giving into the game he felt Phyllis was playing.

"So you don't care about us moving to California?"

"Dean can spend his summers with me, and we can rotate holidays every other year, and you can go ahead and be with this *Craig* person."

"You sound like you don't even believe me. In fact, you seem to have this all planned out."

"I rolled over lots of scenarios in my mind lately," he admitted. "Truth is, I only stayed married to you for little Dean's sake."

"How could you be so heartless? What happened to the Dean I fell in love with in college?" she cried.

"He grew up. I waited for you to do the same, but it never happened."

Within a few weeks after processing the paperwork, the divorce was final. Dean was to pay alimony and child support until Dean Jr. turned eighteen. Dean and Phyllis had to rotate summers and holidays with Dean Jr. by court order. After the divorce proceedings, Phyllis asked Dean for a ride to the airport, and Dean drove her only because he wanted to spend more time with his son before he left. Dean didn't know that Craig had flown out from California to meet them. Phyllis ran up to a tall, light-skinned man with an afro and freckles around his nose.

"Hey little Dean, come here, man," Craig called. When little Dean ran up to Craig and hugged him, Dean knew that his son was too familiar with Craig, and he just lost it. He couldn't believe that Phyllis would expose his son to a man she had been having an affair with.

"Look here, Jack." Dean snatched Craig by the shirt collar. The two stood toe to toe; both of them were over six feet tall. "Dean is *my* son. He will never be your son, and if I hear about you laying a hand on him, I'll fly out to California and kick your ass. You got it?"

"Daddy, stop it!" Little Dean cried.

"Nigga, who do you think you are?!" Craig shoved Dean, and they started tussling.

"Stop it! Just stop it!" Phyllis pulled Craig away from Dean with a slight grin on her face. She felt as though the two of them were fighting over her.

"I meant what I said!" Dean pointed his finger in Craig's face.

"Yeah, whatever! Come see me then, chump!" He grabbed Phyllis' and little Dean's hands.

Airport security rushed over when they saw the commotion. "Is everything okay?" one of the security officers asked.

"I'm fine. I just need to say goodbye to my son," Dean snatched little Dean's hand away from Craig, and pulled him to the side to speak with him privately. Dean quickly turned off his anger and hugged him. "I love you son. I'll always love you."

"I love you too, daddy," Little Dean replied, feeling afraid and confused.

"You call me any time, all right?" Dean stared his son in the eyes. He hugged him. "Don't worry okay? If anything happens, I'll come and get you. Do you remember our password for you to use when you're in danger?" He asked, and little Dean nodded his head.

"Good. I love you, son. Don't ever let anybody tell you anything different. Not Craig, not your mother, nobody. You understand. Just because Mommy and I are not together anymore, doesn't mean I don't love you, because I do."

"Come on, Dean, they're calling for our flight." Phyllis walked over and took Dean by the hand. As they turned and walked away, little Dean looked over his shoulder and waved goodbye to his father.

When Dean returned home and sat down on the sofa, it finally hit him that it was all over with, just that fast. He felt heartbroken at the thought of not being able to see his son every day. Little Dean was across the country now, with his mother and Craig, a man he felt didn't deserve to be anywhere near his son. A man who had been sleeping with his wife and he didn't even know it. Dean leaned forward on his forearms, let out a long sigh, and muttered into the space of the nearly empty room, "I hope I made the right decision this time."

CHAPTER TWELVE

I KNOW A PLACE

Sweat dripped from the side of Connie's temples as she lugged her suitcase for three blocks under the hot July sun. The taxi dropped her off blocks from where she lived because he was too afraid to drive in closer. When Connie entered the building's courtyard, she saw swarms of people hanging around, talking, laughing, eating, drinking, and having a good time. As she walked through the gates of Cabrini, she noticed a banner that said, *"Give Back to Cabrini Green."* Connie would later learn that the Mayor, who was up for re-election, put the block party together and that he'd paid CBS-TV Broadcasting, and WLSR-radio station to sponsor it.

"Hi Connie, where you been, girl?"

"Hey Connie, what's happening, Mama?"

"Connie, come get you something to eat and drink, baby."

Everyone on the block was being exceptionally kind, and had been since her mother and sister died. Connie accepted a hotdog and a nice cold cup of lemonade from one of the neighbors. Connie hadn't seen the people of Cabrini having such a good time like this since she was a little girl. It was good to see everyone having wholesome fun.

"Connie!" she heard a familiar voice from the crowd calling her. "Connie! Over here!" the voice shouted again. Through the crowd appeared Mr. James, her boss from the record store. He was a middle-aged man who was going bald and had a potbelly. He always wore paisley butterfly shirts and bellbottoms.

When Connie spotted him, she smiled and rushed over to him. "How have you been?" Mr. James smiled as they embraced.

"I'm holding up. How are things at the store? I can start back to work tomorrow. I didn't think I would be gone for so long, but . . ."

"Connie, Connie, Connie, don't worry about the store. You take your time and get settled. As long as I'm the owner, you will always have a job, okay?"

Connie nodded. "Mr. James, thank you so much."

She and Mr. James talked for a little while, and then she headed across the courtyard to her apartment building. Connie was happy that the elevator was working, and that the hallways were surprisingly clean. The whole building smelled like Pine-Sol, but she knew it was temporary because of the event today. As she approached the door to her apartment, she saw a sign that said, "EVICTION NOTICE", and the deadline date at the bottom said *August 1st*. It was July 25th.

Connie gasped and quickly removed her key from her purse to open the door, but as soon as she stuck her key in the lock, the door slid open. Connie stood in the doorway, facing an almost completely vacant and trashy apartment that smelled like waste. She cautiously treaded inside, stepping over trash and dodging giant cockroaches that were eating waste from food left behind. She kicked empty bottles of liquor out of the way so she wouldn't trip and fall. She immediately noticed that the TV and the stereo were gone, and the sofa didn't have any pillows. In a panic, she dropped her suitcase on the dining room table and rushed throughout the apartment, hoping her valuables hadn't been taken. In her bedroom, she noticed her bed and dresser were gone and autograph posters were taken off the walls. Her heart raced with fear and anxiety. She opened her closet door, and it was completely empty. No clothes, no shoes, no coats; it was empty.

"No, no, no!" she was in shock. "They even took my record collection!" Anger and hopelessness consumed her as she rushed into her mother's old room. All her mother's clothes and jewelry were gone. The dresser was gone, too, but the bed was still there. The room was in shambles. She discovered the gray box that her mother kept in the closet. It had been tossed behind the bed, and pictures that were inside were scattered between the bed railings. Connie quickly salvaged the pictures, placing them back in the box, before she went into Peaches' room. The first thing she noticed was that BJ's crib was gone and the dresser was gone. The floor was trashed with old diapers, baby socks, mismatched shoes, and stale food.

"Why, God? Why? Why do you hate me? How could you allow this to happen? Now I have nothing!" she cried. "I'm sorry, God, forgive me. I didn't mean what I said, but what am I going to do? Where can I go? Please help me. Please!"

Connie rushed next door to see if Ms. Knight was home so she could use her phone to call her father, but there was no answer when she knocked. As Connie headed outside the building, it started to rain, and the people outside having the event started packing up everything as quickly as they could. Connie tried to see if she saw Mr. James still hanging around, and thought maybe she could go to his place to use his phone, but he was gone. People started running for shelter as the rain came down heavier. Drenched, with her suitcase in hand, she ran down the street to try to find a payphone.

Connie looked over her shoulder as a burnt orange Plymouth Roadrunner pulled up to the curb, just as she was about to call her father collect on a payphone. With the rain coming down so heavy, Connie couldn't see who was inside honking the horn at her.

The window rolled down. "Hey, Connie, it's me, Ray. Need a ride?"

"Yes!" Connie felt relieved. She could barely see with so much rain pouring down her face. The suitcase she used as coverage wasn't helping, because the wind just blew the rain in her face. She got in the car and noticed Ray's backseat was filled with stacks of records and Deejay equipment.

"Looks like you got a gig," she said, wiping rain from her face. "I hope I'm not putting you out of your way or nothing."

"Nah, it's cool. I just picked up the rest of my stuff from my mom's pad. Got my own place now. This cat I know bought a house, and he rents it out like a duplex. I stay up top. Someone else lives in the basement."

"Wow, that's cool to have your own place when you're not even eighteen yet."

"I told him I'll be eighteen in six months, and he wasn't sweating it. As long as I had the cash, he took it." His big brown eyes lit up with excitement. Connie always felt he had a cartoonish face and lanky build.

"I bought this car just last month, too. I used my deejay money to get it. I'm telling you, Connie, being a deejay will help you make some real cash if you really get into this."

"That's good Ray, I'm really happy for you," Connie said. Inside, she was worried sick about her own situation. She was homeless now, and had to make a decision if she was going to stay in Chicago or move to South Carolina with her father after all.

"Thanks. So um . . . what'cha doing out here in the rain? Are you just getting back? I see you gotcha suitcase and all."

"Just got back and found out the city is evicting me and Peaches. The notice said the rent hadn't been paid, and drugs had been found on the premises."

"WHAT?!"

"Yeah. I don't know where she is, they ransacked our crib . . ." Connie paused as she fought back her tears, taking in what she remembered seeing at her apartment. She shook her head. "I got nothing left, man."

"I'm sorry, Connie. I was so stupid not to ask how you were at first. I started talking about myself. I'm so sorry. How can I help you out right now?"

"I need to call my dad. We had plans to move me out of Cabrini anyways. I just wasn't expecting it to be so soon, you know? It's either that or I move to South Carolina, but I would rather stay here in the Chi."

"You can crash at my place as long as you like."

"Are you sure?"

"Yeah, it's cool. I don't mind."

Ray lived on the Southside in the Englewood Community. It was nothing like the middle-class Kenwood Community he had moved from and where their school was located, but it wasn't as bad as Cabrini was. Ray took Connie's suitcase inside, and he let her into his place. He went back to unload his deejay equipment with a big blanket to cover it from the rain. Connie called her father collect from Ray's phone and explained what had happened.

"My dad will be here in the morning, so I won't be any more trouble," she said to Ray. She hung up the phone just as he was walking into the living room with his final pieces of equipment.

Ray chuckled. "You don't bother me. Stay as long as you need to. Just so you know, I don't cook, but I got enough cash to order us some Chinese. You hungry?"

"Sure am, but I can contribute," she offered. "Here, my dad gave me some money." She pulled a few wet dollar bills from her pocket.

"Nah, I don't need it. You keep it."

"Sure?"

His light brown eyes widened. "Look. Just relax, it's my treat. No strings attached. No nothing."

"Okay, you got any towels or soap? I could really use a shower and I need to get out of these wet clothes before I catch a cold."

"Sure, everything is in the bathroom. It's just down the hall. Help yourself," Ray said, setting up his deejay equipment in the corner of the living room so he could play some music.

Connie took a long, hot shower, and when she was done, she walked into the living room with the towel wrapped around her.

"Do you have something I can sleep in? I had to hang my clothes in your bathroom to dry. My cheap suitcase is drenched and my clothes got wet. Where should I sleep?"

Ray looked up from his set of turntables and spotted Connie standing in front of him, half-naked.

"WOW!" his mouth nearly dropped to the floor.

"Wow what?"

"Oh nothing, um . . . you can, um . . ." he cleared his throat. "You can sleep in the sleeping bag I have. I know it's somewhere around here." he searched through his packed closet. "Oh, here it is." He shook it out good to make sure no bugs had gotten in it. "I have a clean T-shirt that, um . . ." he swallowed hard. ". . . that you can sleep in." He was amazed by how beautiful Connie was. *Calm down, boy, she's like your sister. Don't go there,* he told himself.

"The food will be here in a minute. You want to check out some sounds in the meantime?"

"Sure." Connie slipped into the T-shirt with her back turned to him so he wouldn't see her breasts.

"I got something that will cheer you up. Now dig, this here is going to be a hot hit. Ain't nobody even heard it yet. It's a sample single."

"How'd you get it?"

"I got connections with people at WCHI-93.3 Soul. When I graduate, I'm going to radio school and will start interning for them."

"Get outta here! That's great, Ray!"

"Yep, And when I make it big, I'm putting *you* on." Connie twisted her lips. "You may not believe me now, but I will. You have a nice voice, you can spin records, and people will like you."

"Yeah, whatever! Just play the record you wanted me to hear."

As soon as the beat started to the song, Connie recognized the tune, and when the voices started singing, she knew right away who the group was.

"Sound like The Staple Singers to me."

"How did you guess that?"

"I recognize their voices. What's the name of this song?"

"The name of this one is called *I'll Take You There.*"

"That's a hit. I know a hit record when I hear one."

"See, that's what I'm saying, Connie. You got a good ear for music. You'll make it big if you really take it serious."

"I don't know if deejaying is for me. Not sure what I want to do, really."

"You'll figure it out sooner or later," Ray was certain of it. "Let me get the door. I think that's our Chinese food delivery."

The next morning, Connie's father came to pick her up, and they went apartment hunting all day long until they found a duplex similar to Ray's place. The owners were renting the basement. Scott had to sign the lease since Connie was a minor, and put down an extra amount of money for the security deposit. The couple agreed with Scott to keep an eye on Connie, and she had to agree to follow their strict rules of no loud music, parties, drugs, or pets. It was six blocks from her school Lakeview High. When she lived in Cabrini, she'd had to take a bus to school, but now she could walk there.

Scott stayed the night at Connie's new place and slept on the new sofa he bought her, while she slept in her new room on her new bed. The next day, Scott took Connie to take her driver's test so she could get her license, and she passed. Afterwards, he bought Connie a used brown Chevy, and left her with four hundred dollars to get started with buying clothes, food, and other necessities.

It was amazing to Connie how quickly her prayer was answered. "Thank you God!" she shouted. She was excited that she had her own place and her first car. She was so happy that her homelessness was temporary. She was thankful she had a friend in Ray and a father who loved and cared for her. Her celebration was short-lived, however. Connie became overwhelmed with sadness and guilt again. She worried about her sister, and felt guilty about her nephew being up for adoption. She also felt sad that her mother and sister Baby couldn't be there to see her now and how she had finally got out of Cabrini. Evicted or not, she got out. She missed them dearly, and she felt lonely without her family.

With her father on his way back to South Carolina, Connie quickly found herself at the Department of Human Services. "Connie, Barry Johnson Jr. is expected to be adopted within a few weeks," Ms. Carter, the Social Worker explained. "The papers have already been signed. We're just waiting to hear back from the court for final approval."

"I'm his aunt, so you can't put him up for adoption if he still has family."

"Connie, you are not old enough to adopt your nephew."

"No offense, miss, but teenage mothers take care of babies all the time. The only difference is, I got my own place, car, I work, and I'm an honor student."

"So tell me." Ms. Carter removed her glasses and sat them down on the desk before her. "Why on earth would you want to hinder your growth process to raise a child that's not even yours?"

"He's still my family."

"You know," Ms. Carter exhaled as she leaned forward on her desk, looking at Connie, "the Smiths have been on our waiting list for a baby for the past three years. You are causing trouble here. This will just break their hearts."

"And you are breaking mine," Connie retorted. Ms. Carter began to tap her ink pen on the desk in deep thought. Connie had a point, and she felt caught in the middle.

"I need to contact the Smiths. Can you step out for a few minutes, please?"

Connie returned within a few minutes, and Ms. Carter explained to Connie that the Smiths wanted to setup a mediation to discuss the wrench that was thrown into their plans. They had already prepared a room for BJ and told their families about him.

"So what happens at mediation?"

"They want to try to make an agreement with you."

"No disrespect, but I'm his aunt. They can't have him. It's as simple as that."

Ms. Carter bit down on her lip, trying to restrain herself, but she couldn't. "Connie, you cannot handle a baby. You're only seventeen!"

"Ms. Carter, I'm not trying to be disrespectful towards you, but I grew up in Cabrini Green, and if anybody can survive Cabrini Green, they can surely take care of a gentle baby."

Ms. Carter stood up from her desk and looked out the window. "Give me some time to think this over."

"So I should come back in five minutes?"

Ms. Carter turned around sharply. "No Connie, I need a few days, so don't call me. I'll call you."

Meanwhile, Connie was doing all she could to bring her family back together again. She started searching for her sister Peaches. "I know she got out of jail, but no soon as they let her out, she went back to them streets," Ms. Knight explained to Connie. "By the way, Ms. Pat asked about you girls. She wanted to say goodbye to ya'll before she moved to Georgia. She said she done got married." Connie was going to miss Ms. Pat. She knew Ms. Pat and her mother were very close. As she continued to drive around, searching the streets for her sister, she finally found out from old friends that Peaches lived in the Robert Taylor Homes. The Robert Taylor Homes were on 39th Street. It was a housing project about fifteen minutes from Cabrini, over the North Lakeshore Drive Bridge.

When Connie knocked on the door to Peaches' apartment, Poncho answered. He was wearing a tank top and had a big pick sticking out the back of his afro.

"Is Peaches here?"

"Who are you?" Poncho asked, revealing a gold tooth in the front of his mouth.

"I'm her sister, Connie."

"Oh yeah, dig, I think I remember you. Come on in." Connie stepped inside and immediately felt sick to her stomach. The place smelled awful. Heavy drapes hung from the windows phasing out the sunlight, and the apartment felt hot and muggy. That's when she spotted Peaches in the corner of the living room, looking like she was high. She was nodding off and fighting to keep her eyes open. Connie couldn't bear seeing her sister like that, and there was no way to try to talk to her with her head in the clouds.

"Look," Connie turned to Poncho. "Just tell her I stopped by."

"All right, but if you ever need a favor, I got'chu." Poncho pulled out a tiny plastic bag from his front pocket. "Your first time is free."

"I don't do drugs."

He griped, "That's what they all say."

"Yeah, well, you can keep that."

Connie returned about a week later and Peaches answered the door. She kept scratching her arms as she offered Connie a seat, but Connie didn't want to touch anything in the room. It still looked dark and dingy, and smelled disgusting. Peaches wasn't high, but still heroin sick. Her arms had track marks from the needles, and her hands were still swollen.

"I can't believe you're up here doping up while I'm trying not to let your son get adopted!"

Peaches looked up at her sister from the raggedy sofa she was sitting on. "Connie, I can't feel the pain when I shoot, and I don't want to."

"What pain?"

"Losing Mama and Baby, then Barry and now BJ," Peaches slowly uttered.

"So you think it's easy for me? What happens if I lose you? Then I won't have anybody!" Connie grabbed Peaches and started shaking her.

"You have to stop using this stuff. It's killing you, dammit!"

"Get off me!" Peaches shoved her. "Poncho will be back in a minute. He got what I need. You should try it. I'm telling you, it feels so good, Connie."

"This is not my big sister talking, it's not!" Connie rubbed her temples in frustration. "You know, Mama and Daddy would be so disappointed in you."

"Daddy got another family. He don't care about us."

"What other family? Are you high?"

Peaches shook her head no, and continued. "Mama found out about Daddy's other family and she wrote him a letter about it. Lots of letters to try to get him to pay child support, but he wouldn't."

"How come you didn't tell me this before?"

Peaches hunched her shoulders. "I wanted to have one up on you. You always thought you was all that."

"Peaches don't go there," Connie stated. "Besides, you're always talking about what you don't know."

"Well, I was right about your real father."

Connie knew Peaches had a point.

"Connie, what I got? Look at me, nobody cares about me. Daddy doesn't care."

Connie looked at Peaches, who looked like death.

"I care! That's why I'm here."

"My man back yet? I need my fix." Peaches started to twitch more.

"Peaches, I love you. I don't want you to die. Please stop using drugs." Connie searched her eyes, and hoped somewhere inside Peaches' soul, she understood what she was saying.

"I can't stop, Connie. I need it. Here," Peaches reached in her pocket for money. "Go get some for me so I won't get sick."

Connie fought back her tears. "I'm not going to help you kill yourself, and I won't stay here seeing you like this."

"You can leave. I don't need you!" Peaches snapped.

"Then I guess this is goodbye."

The Mediation . . .

"We found out about Barry Jr. after being on the waiting list for the past five years," Mrs. Smith explained with tears in her eyes, as she sat across the conference table from Connie.

"And when we learned that the adoption was almost final, we started decorating the extra bedroom," Mr. Smith added, with his arm around his wife.

"We understand that Barry is your nephew, but we beg you to please consider allowing us to care for him. We promise we will love him and give him the best care possible," Mrs. Smith said sincerely.

"And if you ever want to come and visit, our doors will always be open to you. We will make sure that Barry knows you and his real mother," Mr. Smith promised.

Connie suddenly realized just how stubborn and selfish she had been. Although she knew she really could take care of BJ, she finally understood what everyone had been telling her, including her mother before she died. She still wasn't living her own life, but trying to save everyone else's. She was young and should have been having fun, not trying to take on the burdens of the world. While she loved her nephew BJ, the reality of it was she would have been cutting her own life short. Her father was right, too; it was time to be a teenager and have fun. Connie agreed to let the Smiths adopt BJ. "I'll see you around, buddy." Connie kissed BJ goodbye, and he smiled coyly. Connie knew the Smith family would take good care of BJ.

CHAPTER THIRTEEN

CASANOVA

Mr. Big Stuff by Jean Knight became Dean's anthem as he quickly threw himself into the dating scene with full gusto. He enjoyed sexual stunts with all the gorgeous women he laid eyes on, including the women who had flirted with him in the past while he was married. He and his cousin Hank were back to hanging out together whenever Dean was off-duty.

"We own the night," they would boast, while toasting their glasses, puffing cigars, and walking the streets of Chicago with fine women on their arms. Dean loved every minute of it. He was having so much fun that it made him more easygoing with his job. He became less formidable and more laid-back. These days, when he would catch a man smoking weed on the corner instead of instantly arresting him, Dean would simply say, "Hey, if you're going to smoke that, do it in private." Prostitutes that he used to scorn, before cuffing them and shoving them into the back of the squad car like men were told, "Hey sisters, come on, you're too beautiful for this. Keep it moving."

"Hi, Dean, I got something for you, sugar," they would flirt.

"That's okay. Ladies, move along. Let's keep everything peaceful tonight." People on the streets saw Dean change. Most of the hustlers hated when Dean patrolled their areas, and wanted the opportunity to beat him up. Dean became the coolest cop on the beat. Even his partner Stuckey was shocked by his sudden change of attitude.

"What in the world brought all this on?"

"Brought what on?"

"You used to bust people with no questions asked, just to try to build up your resume, but now you giving people breaks? Not you," Stuckey said. "What gives?"

"I'm in a better place in my life, that's all."

"Oh, finally divorced, and getting some trim now, huh?" Stuckey chuckled.

"If you weren't so old, I would hook you up with a nice lady."

"Youngblood, I don't need a *hookup*, I can pull any woman I want."
Dean laughed. He knew better.

"Laugh all you want to, but I got more game than you ever will have."

A few months later . . .

"I'm afraid you have gonorrhea, Mr. Wilson," Dr. Schwartz told Dean.

"How could this happen to me?" Dean asked. "Who did this?"

"That's a question you ought to ask yourself, Mr. Wilson; but if you don't use a condom from now on, you will be seeing me more often," Dr. Schwartz warned him. "The good news is that we caught it in time enough to cure you." he handed Dean a prescription slip after giving him instructions on how to take it.

Dean left the doctor's office feeling upset with himself and angry towards all the women he had slept with. As soon as he healed, however, he jumped right back into the dating scene, albeit with more caution.

While playing the field, Dean started to forget some of his other obligations such as calling Dean Jr. on the regular basis, accepting his mother's regular invitation to have Sunday dinner, or sometimes helping out a friend in need. "I'm sorry I forgot," he would say so often that it was a part of his regular vocabulary. Today as parked his car outside of his parents' house, he thought about what excuse he would give for his absence.

Dean always felt like he was walking into an eye-stinging fog of disinfectant whenever he visited his parents. He was dressed in his uniform and planned on leaving from their house to go to work afterwards. Later that night he was going out with Belinda to the club, and Sunday he had plans to do with Jenny. Like Hank, he had a woman for each day of the week.

As usual, Mama Wilson greeted him with a big hug, as if she hadn't seen him in years. She was wearing her usual housedress with an apron. Dean figured she had probably been cleaning all morning long, then prepping Sunday's dinner, the way she normally did. After that, she would invite the women over from the church to play Gin Rummy until dark. One thing about Dean's mother, she never changed her routine. Dean's father was quite the opposite. As a pastor, he was busy too. Whenever he wasn't doing something with his congregation, he would find something to do, usually either fishing or golf.

Dean took a seat at the dining room table, and his mother sat down across from him.

"You want something to drink, or a slice of the fresh apple pie that I made?"

"No, thank you. Is Dad around?"

"He's in the basement, practicing his sermon for tomorrow."

"Eva, who are you talking to up there?" Dean's father called from the basement.

"Dean is here, honey. Are you coming up to see him?"

"No, I am practicing my sermon. He can come back later on." Dean abruptly got up from the dining room table and rushed into the basement.

"Hey Pops," he called. "Look, I said I was sorry about not coming in time to paint the house. We can paint it next week."

"Boy, don't you see I'm practicing my sermon?"

"*Boy* plays on Tarzan."

"I don't have time to talk to you right now, Dean."

"Is that it?"

"Yes," his father said, looking at him sharply over top of his dark framed glasses. "You may leave now."

"All right, fine, have it your way." Dean stormed back up the stairs and joined his mother at the table in the dining room.

"Don't mind your father, honey," Dean's mom said to him. She slid a slice of pie in front of him. He started eating it and chased it down with a cold glass of milk. Dean ate the pie because he knew his mother wouldn't feel satisfied until he did.

"Dad only gets that way when I don't do things on his timetable," Dean said, wiping his mouth as he finished up. "I don't owe him, Mama."

"I know you don't, sweetie. One of these days, he'll get over what happened to your brother Johnny."

"Mama, I'm twenty-four. Johnny was killed when I was twelve," Dean said as he stood up from the table. "I don't think that day you're hoping for will ever come. Now look, thanks for the pie, but I gotta go. I'm running late for work."

"I love you, son, but be careful out there."

"I love you too, Mama. I'll be just fine."

CHAPTER FOURTEEN

LIVING

*F*amily was the most important thing to Connie. After realizing she'd done all she could to help Peaches and BJ, she made time to enjoy the last few weeks of summer before school started. Connie and Ray deejayed at backyard cookouts and house parties for money. Initially, they started playing music together, but once Connie got over her fear of crowds, she started deejaying on her own. Like today at May and Ray's back-to-school cookout in their backyard. Connie was spinning the wheels, keeping the people dancing while Ray admired Connie's mixing skills. He smiled and bopped his head feeling good that he taught her well. He keenly listened to her smooth transitions from one song to the next. Connie winked at him, and smiled, feeling happy she had his approval . . . until she spotted Jet walking into the backyard arm in arm with another girl.

"Who is she?" Connie stepped from behind the turntables and approached Jet.

"My girlfriend," Jet replied. "You didn't think that one night we had since you been back meant we were back together, did you?" Jet walked off with his new girl.

Connie nearly got into a fight with Jet and May for not telling her about his new girlfriend. "I thought you knew," May argued with Connie. Ray came to the rescue and helped calm Connie down.

"Connie what are you doing? Don't ever leave your set no matter what happens," Ray said to her, he had quickly changed the record to keep the party going.

"My boyfriend shows up with another girl and I'm supposed to worry about the music?" Connie angrily questioned Ray.

"Yes! Forget Jet! He's a jerk!" Ray barked. "He doesn't realize he has a good thing so it's his loss not yours."

Connie assumed that sleeping with Jet meant that they had gotten back together, but instead, he made her feel used.

Although the people at the party said Connie played good music, all she could think about was how Jet disrespected her by showing up with another girl. When school started, Connie befriended Smokey and Franco. She broke ties with anyone connected to Jet.

As for May, she had to work hard to earn Connie's friendship back. "Connie, I swear I thought you knew about Jet. I mean, you guys are always breaking up, and then you get back together, and half the time, I don't even know. You keep me in the dark, and I'm supposed to be your best friend," May had pleaded.

It was true that Connie had an on-and-off-again relationship with Jet. When they would have sex, Connie did it because she loved the feeling, but not because she was madly in love with him. She had never felt that type of emotional connection. Connie cared for Jet, but a part of her was always reticent.

Connie forgave May, but enjoyed her friendship with Smokey and Franco more. Smokey lived in the Robert Taylor Homes, where Peaches was staying, and Franco lived three blocks from Smokey in an apartment above the hair salon that his mother owned. Smokey was the cool cat out of the group, with plenty of street knowledge. He always had a hustle going on. Women's clothing, incense, perfumes; you name it, and Smokey sold it. When it came to school events, teachers used Smokey to help sell tickets to games and fundraisers.

Franco was more flamboyant and flashy. Because he was close to his mother, he always knew what looked good on women and what they liked and didn't like. Smokey and Connie couldn't tell if Franco actually liked the girls or if he wanted to be one of the girls, but they never questioned him directly about his preference. Although Smokey would joke with him about it, Franco never took offense. He would counter back with a joke of his own. Connie felt like she was around two brothers who always playfully cracked on each other. It was Smokey and Franco's idea that Connie should start showing off her deejay skill at the record store.

"You're good on the turntables. You should setup right outside the store and play all the latest hits," Smokey suggested to her. "That is, if you aren't afraid to do it. You know how you women are."

"We women? Humph! I'll show you what I can do."

While working at the record store one Saturday, Connie set up the turntables, and spoke over the microphone. People could hear her voice blocks away.

"Hey, my Black people, ya'll gon' dig this next record by my main man, Stevie Wonder, and I say if it makes you boogey, then we have plenty of copies for you to buy, right here up front, so don't be shy." As Connie was preparing to play her next record, she looked up and saw a familiar face. It was Don Cornelius! Connie's mouth dropped in shock. She had only seen Don on TV, hosting his music variety show, "Soul Train", on WCIU-TV.

"Mr. James and I are old friends, I was just telling him I like your style," Don said to Connie in his usual slow monotone voice.

"Here are tickets to the show. Be sure to bring your friends," Don handed Connie ten tickets.

"Thank you so much Mr. Cornelius! I love your show! I promise me and my friends will be there!"

Connie drove to May's house after work. May screamed when she saw the tickets, and immediately called to tell her boyfriend Levi. Connie only had ten tickets, but she gave them away to each of her friends, except Jet, who got upset when Connie didn't invite him.

"Now you know what it feels like to be left hanging, Jet," Connie said. She walked away, leaving him standing at her locker with his mouth open in shock that she would treat him that way.

Being on "Soul Train" made Connie and her friends popular at school. The day after the show aired, the students at Lakeview were asking them for their autographs. Shortly afterwards, Don called Connie and said if they wanted to be regulars on the show they could officially audition. Connie paired up with Smokey, May partnered with Levi, and Ray collaborated with his girlfriend, while the rest of Connie's friends did solo auditions. Unfortunately, none of them made the show as regulars.

Years later, Connie would learn that a few of those people they were up against would become famous stars—Jody Whatley, Damita Jo, and Jeffrey Daniel, to name a few. They would become regulars on the show, and Jody and Jeffrey would later form a group called *Shalamar*.

Despite not making the cut, Connie was happy for the opportunity. The experience inspired her so much that she wanted to entertain others more. She came up with the idea to form her own party promoting company where she would deejay, Franco would find the venues, and host, and Smokey would sell the tickets. She called the company Connie Morris Promotions.

Connie's popularity grew from her deejaying house parties and throwing parties of her own at rented recreational facilities. The three of them made pretty good money. Connie used her money to keep food in her house, buy clothes, and even buy her class ring and pay her senior fees at school. May saw how much money they were making and she was jealous. She stopped speaking to Connie for awhile until Connie gave her a piece of the action. She let May help with the promotions and paid her a few dollars on the side to draw up posters and spread the word about the parties through word-of-mouth.

Whenever people in the community would see 'A Party by CMP' on the top of the poster sign, they knew who put it together, and told everyone it was going to be a good party. Ray was proud of Connie, but he suggested to her, "Change your name from DJ Connie to something sexy. No disrespect, but you need something catchy, like people call me "Disco Ray" or "Soul Ray". It's catchier than DJ Ray, you dig?" Connie thought about it, and ran it by Franco and Smokey. Together, they came up with "Cat". All the promotional posters for the parties would say, *'A Party by CMP Promotions, with the best female in town, the DJ Diva— "Cat Morris."*

Jet broke his leg during the last game of the football season, and his new girlfriend broke up with him shortly afterwards. She couldn't deal with Jet sitting at home, depressed. She moved on to a basketball player. Jet called Connie on the phone, feeding her lots of sweet talk, but Connie would hang up the phone on him.

Jet didn't give up, though. Connie was the prettiest girl at Lakeview High, and he really didn't want any other guy to have her. Since Connie was hanging out with Smokey and Franco, Jet felt the need to compete for her affection. He didn't know that the three of them were just friends, but he followed her around the school and began to stalk her.

He would show up outside of her homeroom and insist on walking her to all her classes. He left apologetic letters and love notes in her locker, and he tried to get his mother to invite her over for dinner, but Connie kept turning him down.

Eventually, Jet's persistence paid off, and Connie agreed to take him back. It was a slow process at first, starting with studying together at the library or taking a walk in the park. Eventually, they started going out to the movies and concerts. When Jet's leg healed, they went bowling and roller-skating. Sometimes Connie would let Jet stay the night and sneak him out the back door during the early morning hours, so the owners of the house wouldn't see him. Since they were back together, it was hard to get Jet to fit in with Smokey and Franco. Smokey felt jealous, and Franco felt their friendship was divided. Jet didn't want the other guys around anymore at all, but Connie wouldn't allow Jet to make her stop hanging out with her friends.

By the time spring rolled around, it was 1973. Jet took Connie to the prom, where they were voted King and Queen of Lakeview High School. "One day I'm going to make you my wife," Jet said to Connie after they made love in the backseat of his car.

Connie had a good time, but she couldn't shut her brain off and stop worrying about her future, now that school was ending. She wondered, *what if I flunk out of college and end up on welfare and back in the Projects. What if I become a junkie like my sister?* She wondered as Jet stroked her hair and kissed her.

"Did you hear what I said?" Jet asked, noticing Connie's mind was somewhere else.

"What?"

"I said one day, you will be my wife."

She smiled. "That's nice."

"You don't believe me?"

"Jet, what do you think will happen after we graduate?"

"Well I don't plan to marry you that soon," he laughed.

"I know that, silly, but I'm wondering about the future for us individually. I mean, what if we don't make it?"

"Connie, why are you bringing up this kind of talk now?"

"I just don't want to end up failing, that's all."

"I know I'm going to end up playing in the NFL. Now, if you don't believe you will make it, that's your problem."

Connie shoved him. "You're so cocky, Jet!"

"Call it whatever you like, but I'm not worried. If you don't believe in yourself, then you can feel free to believe in me." He flashed a smile.

Connie grabbed her unfinished milkshake from the cup holder and poured it on Jet's head. "Now take me home!"

"Damn you, Connie! What the hell is wrong with you?" Jet reached over her and grabbed some napkins from the glove compartment to clean himself off. Connie cracked up, laughing.

"It's not funny. I look like a clown with all this milk on my face!"

"Now the surface fits the man!" Connie burst out laughing.

"Thanks for ruining my night!"

CHAPTER FIFTEEN

NOW WHAT?

Connie graduated from Lakeview High School with honors and received a full scholarship to Loyola University. She planned to major in Communication Arts to pursue a career in radio/TV. Jet received a football scholarship to Florida University, Smokey got a full-time sales job at Southwestern Bell Corporation, Franco worked full-time as a hairstylist at his mother's salon, and May was six months pregnant by Levi when she walked across the stage to accept her diploma. Levi went on to work as a mechanic in his father's shop to help support May, but her mother complained that May needed to find a man who was making more money so she could move out of her house.

That summer of '73, Connie, Franco, and Smokey continued to have parties and made good money. At one point, Smokey got caught stealing money, so Connie fired him. Smokey tried to host his own parties, but failed. He apologized and later rejoined CMP, but Connie had Franco watch the cashbox instead of Smokey.

When Connie didn't have gigs, she was spending as much time with Jet as she could before he was to leave for college in a few weeks. Since he would be playing football, the coaches wanted him in Florida by July for football camp. Jet's mother had Connie over for dinner more often, and she was around Jet's family to the point where she was a part of his family. The family was optimistic for Connie and Jet. Even Connie's father had met Jet when he came up to visit a few times, and he and Margaret had dinner with Jet and his family to celebrate their graduation. With the family setting high hopes for them, and things seemingly on the up and up, Connie was afraid to tell them that she was pregnant . . .

"Just tell him," May urged, but Connie dragged her feet, and Jet would now be leaving in a few days for college. May decided to call Jet on the phone and tell him for Connie.

"She's what?" Jet shouted over the phone.

"Yep, she pregnant. She probably got knocked up on purpose," May grinned deviously behind the phone before hanging up.

"I can't believe this, she set me up!" Jet griped.

"Of course she did, she wants some of that money you make it to the pros."

"If she's just trying to use me, she got the wrong one!"

"Besides, how do you know it's your baby Jet? It could be Smokey's. You know she hangs out with him a lot and he likes her. It's obvious."

Jet fumed at the thought of another guy sleeping with Connie.

"I gotta go! I'm headed over to Connie's now. I need to straighten this out!"

"You do that."

Jet hopped in his car and sped over to Connie's house, and when he got there, he banged on the door like a mad man. Connie opened the door. Before she could say hello, Jet nearly tackled her to the floor.

"Get off me, what the hell is wrong with you?" Connie tried to break free, but Jet pinned her hands down to the floor.

"Say it ain't true!"

"What are you talking about?"

"You know what I'm talking about!"

"Who told you?"

"May, that's who!"

"I told her not to say nothing!"

"So it's true?" Jet let her up from the floor.

"Jet, the last time we did it, the condom popped. Remember?"

"We've done it at least two other times since then, and those condoms never popped."

"Well, maybe I was already pregnant. I don't know." Connie made her way to the sofa and sat down, shaking her head in disappointment. Jet sat down next to her and buried his face in his hands. It was Saturday morning, and the *Jackson 5ive* cartoon was playing on TV, although Connie hadn't been watching it. It just happened to come on right after the early morning news. All Connie could think about was her dreams going down the drain. She stared at the cartoon, wishing she could recapture her days of innocence again. She'd lost her scholarship, and dreams of becoming a radio host seemed far-fetched.

Her worst fears were coming true. She thought. *I'm not going to make it.* Now she wondered how she was going to tell her father.

Jet turned to her, feeling frustrated and angry. "So, now what?" he asked, hoping she would have a solution they could both live with.

"I don't know."

"Well, think of something," Jet snapped. "You know we can't have this baby, you know that!"

"I don't believe in abortions."

"Well, neither do I . . . except just now."

"Boy, you talking crazy! God don't want us killing no baby!"

"God didn't want us having sex either, but we did it," he argued. "Don't try to pull no religious card on me now."

"I'm not getting rid of the baby, Jet, whether you like it or not!"

"You can't take care of no baby working at a record shop and deejaying parties, Connie."

"I'll find a way."

"Look, my brother told me if I ever got caught up in a situation like this, he would help me out. Now dig, once you get rid of this one, I'll give you all the babies you want when I make it to the NFL. I promise."

Jet searched her eyes for some type of response, but Connie sat with her arms folded, staring at the TV.

"Don't have this baby right now, Connie," Jet insisted. Connie rolled her eyes to the ceiling and sighed. Jet stood up from the sofa. "Well, say something, Connie!"

"Are you deaf? I already told you!"

"Fine! Just mess up both of our lives, then!" Jet headed for the door.

"All you think about is football and yourself!" Connie followed behind him.

"Look!" Jet turned to her sharply. "If you have this baby, we are over with. So you need to decide who's more important: me or a baby!"

"You are one selfish bastard!"

"Say what? I ought to knock you out, girl!"

"Do it! I dare you!" Connie challenged, ready to defend herself.

"It's over between us so don't ever call me again!"

"Don't worry, I only call people I know I can count on!"

When Jet left, Connie cried her eyes out and wished she had someone to comfort her. She and Jet were always fighting and then making up, but this time was different. She knew it was over. Later on that day, she broke down and told the news to her father.

"Connie, now why would ya go and get caught up like that? You had so much going for ya'self." To Connie, it was as if she was hearing her mother's voice. "You know the owners of that place don't want any kids. It's written in your lease," he reminded her.

"I saved up some money from deejaying gigs. I'll get my own place or find a roommate."

Connie tried to feel as confidant as the words coming out of her mouth, but a part of her was scared. Having a baby was going to be a challenge. She felt anxious, not knowing just how much it would affect her life.

When she called to tell Jet's mother, she was happy. "I always wanted me a grandbaby. My older sons have moved out and have no children. With Jet leaving for college, the baby can keep me company. Don't you worry about a thing honey. I'll help you take care of my grandbaby," Mrs. Michaels assured her, but these days it was hard for Connie to trust her, Jet, and even herself.

CHAPTER SIXTEEN

IT'S COLD OUTSIDE
(Three Years Later-1975)

*S*even-year-old Dean Jr. stood outside on the patio shivering as he watched his mother and Craig entertain their guests for another business party. Craig, a music producer, was always having celebrity guests at his house, but he never wanted little Dean around. Over the past few years, Craig grew to resent Dean. If Craig and Phyllis wanted to travel out of town or attend a party, they had to find a babysitter. If Craig wanted to be alone with Phyllis, they had to wait until Dean went to bed first. Craig felt that everything revolved around Dean, and he didn't like that.

This evening was no different, as Dean Jr. had been running around at the party showing off in front of their guests. Craig felt so embarrassed that he locked Dean outside of the house. He told Phyllis, "Let him play out by the pool. He will be all right."

By eight o'clock that evening, Dean Jr. was finished swimming. Although they lived in California, the temperatures dropped at night. Dean knocked on the patio door, but no one heard him knocking because the music inside was too loud to hear it. Dean walked around to the front of the house and rang the doorbell, and when no one answered, he began to cry. He decided to walk to a neighbor's house, still wearing his swim trunks and flip flops, but nothing else. He was freezing as he walked down the street because his body was still wet from being in the swimming pool. An elderly White woman with droopy, wrinkled cheeks answered the door. When she looked through the peephole, she didn't see anybody, so she cautiously, opened the door with the latch still on.

"I—I—gotta pee!" Dean shivered and his teeth chattered. The woman put on her glasses, which were hanging around her neck by a gold chain. She looked at him more closely through her aged eyes. She recognized him.

"Aren't you Phyllis and Craig's little boy?" Dean shook his head yes, and the woman let him inside.

"Go on upstairs. The bathroom is on the right," she pointed, and Dean took off running. When he came out of the bathroom, the woman had already grabbed clothes for him to put on.

"Here, my grandchildren left these behind," the woman said. "Anyway, what are you doing out this time of night by yourself?" the woman slid a slightly oversized shirt over Dean's shoulders and handed him a pair of near-perfectly fitting pants.

"Craig locked me out. He said I was acting a fool and embarrassing him."

"Don't call your father by his first name. Show some respect," she said, walking with her cane to the sofa to sit down.

"He's not my father. My father's name is Dean Wilson," Dean proudly stated.

"Well, anyway, what you're saying is nonsense. Craig fixed my car for me the other day. He's a nice fella." She picked up the phone to call him. "Hmmm, nobody is answering the phone."

"Call my Daddy, you can reach him."

"But I just called him."

"I told you Craig is not my father," Dean Jr. insisted, and then he told her the phone number to dial his father at.

"18th District, Chicago Police. How may I help you?" asked the male dispatcher.

"I think I misdialed."

"No, ask for Dean!"

"Uh . . . sir, wait a minute, please don't hang up," the woman said.

"Yes?"

"I'm looking for . . ."

"Officer Dean Wilson," Dean Jr. said in her ear.

"I'm looking for Officer Dean Wilson."

"Hold on a minute . . ."

Dean was just about to get into his squad car to start his night beat when the station door opened and the dispatcher yelled, "Ay Wilson, there's a call for you!" Dean thought it was strange, since nobody ever called him at work, so he hurried back inside.

"This is Officer Wilson."

"Um . . . Officer Wilson, your son Dean is looking for you, this is his neighbor. Hold on a minute." The woman put little Dean on the phone.

"Daddy, come get me, please!"

"What's wrong, son?"

Dean Jr. looked at the woman, who looked back at him, afraid. She didn't want to get Craig into any trouble.

"Craig kicked me out, and he won't let me back in the house!"

"He did what?"

The woman quickly snatched the phone from Dean Jr.

"Sir, I'm a good neighbor of Craig's, and I think your son just wandered off when he wasn't supposed to. We didn't mean to trouble you at work."

"Who are you?"

"A neighbor." Her hands trembled nervously as she held the phone. Dean's demanding voice intimated her.

"Yeah, I know you're a neighbor, but you got a name, right?"

"My name is Anna Mae Cunningham, and I don't want any trouble, officer."

"Daddy, 'the jack is in the box!'" Dean Jr. shouted in the background. Dean heard his son and immediately hung up the phone. He knew he had to get to California, and fast!

In the meantime, Mrs. Cunningham called Craig again, and finally he answered the phone. He and Phyllis went to pick up Dean. "Kids are always lying. Thanks for calling us, Mrs. Cunningham," Craig said to her. "This is for your troubles." he slipped her a fifty dollar bill, and they left.

The Next Day . . .

"My Daddy's coming, and he's going to kick your butt!" Dean Jr. said to Craig, who was making him clean all the bathrooms in the mansion that next morning.

"Let him come. Your Dad is not the only one with a gun, chump," Craig said, withdrawing his pistol and making sure Dean Jr. saw it. His young boy eyes widened at the sight of it, and his mouth dropped. "Yeah, I'm not scared of your Daddy!"

Ding Dong . . .

Craig looked over his shoulder. "Is that him? I got something for that nigga!" Craig stepped out of the first-level bathroom and started towards the front door. Phyllis was in the living room.

"Craig, no! It's not that serious!" Phyllis ran behind Craig as he rushed to the front door. Craig shoved Phyllis aside, and Dean Jr. dropped the bucket and sponge and rushed to the door to see if it was his father. Craig swung the door open, and Dean Sr. was standing there with a small duffle bag over his shoulder. He stared Craig up and down with an evil look on his face.

"Nigga, what do you want?" Craig asked as he held the gun behind his back.

"I came here for my son." Dean shoved Craig out of his way and stepped inside.

"Dad!" Dean Jr. rushed towards his father with open arms.

"Hey son, are you all right?" Dean dropped his duffel bag, embraced him in his arms, and spun him around. When Dean spun him, he saw Craig withdraw his pistol and his eyes lit up in horror.

"Dad, Craig's got a gun!"

"Don't Craig!" Phyllis shouted. Craig aimed and cocked the gun at the back of Dean's head.

"Son, run upstairs and hide! Phyllis you go upstairs, too!"

"But Dad!"

"Run upstairs now and hide! Do it!"

"Craig, please put the gun down!" Phyllis cried. Dean Jr. ran upstairs and hid in the guest room, underneath the bed.

Dean slowly rose to his feet and turned around to face the barrel of Craig's gun.

"You think I'm scared of you because you're a cop? Well I ain't!" Craig shouted, smelling like liquor and sweating profusely.

"Now, Craig, you don't want to shoot me, man. I just want my son, that's all." Dean spoke calmly.

"He is *my* son!"

"Look, I know you help take care of him and you do a good job at it, man, but come on, this is not the way you want to handle this situation right here." Dean held his hands in the air to show he wasn't a threat. Phyllis tried to ease her way to the phone to dial the police, keeping an eye on the situation.

"You don't tell me what to do! I can handle this however I want!"

"Come on Craig, don't do this, man, don't."

"I'm through talking!" Craig held the gun with both hands and he aimed it at Dean's forehead. Phyllis decided against calling the cops, and eased her way close to Craig to see if she could grab the gun. Craig shut his eyes and slowly moved his finger . . .

"NOOOOO!" Phyllis shouted, as she rushed towards Craig.

POW! POW! POW! The entire room went silent for a few seconds.

Craig dropped the gun to the floor and began to sob uncontrollably. He dropped to his knees, and tried to pick Phyllis up off the floor. She was covered in blood.

"Step away from her right now!" Dean ordered Craig. He withdrew his gun and ran for the phone to dial 911.

Craig cried. "I didn't mean it, man, I didn't mean it!"

"Step away from her now!"

Craig began to cry. He reached over to pick up his gun off the floor. It was lying a few feet away from Phyllis' body.

"Don't think about it, Craig. I'm warning you!" Craig picked up the gun anyway. "Put the gun down Craig or I'll shoot!"

"I didn't mean to do it, man. I didn't." Craig slowly moved the gun towards his own head.

"I need an ambulance and police!" Dean shouted into the phone, letting it drop to the floor. He knew everything happening was being recorded.

"Craig, you don't want to do that, man. Come on, put the gun down."

"I'm going to jail anyway." Craig started crying and sounding like a small child.

Dean slowly moved in towards him. "Come on, hand me the gun."

"I can't."

"Yes you can. You want to live. You're one of the best producers on the west coast. They need you. They need good records and good music." Dean stepped in closer. He knew his timing was everything. He'd rehearsed these kinds of scenes in the police academy. Craig's hand shook nervously as he held the gun to his temple.

"Come on, Craig, you want to live. I know you do."

"No I don't," Craig cried. Dean had inched his way in to get close enough to grab Craig's wrist. He harshly swung his arm back and the gun went off behind him, shooting a picture off the wall making it fall to the floor shattering to pieces. Dean wrestled Craig to the floor and finally pried the gun out his hands, and aimed his own gun at Craig's head.

"Shoot me! You know you want to! Shoot me you, sorry nigga. Shoot me!" Craig yelled.

LAPD rushed in the house. Dean held up his Chicago PD badge, still aiming the gun at Craig's head, until LAPD took over. The paramedics trailed in behind the cops and tried to revive Phyllis, but she was already dead. LAPD arrested Craig, who kept crying that he didn't mean to kill Phyllis.

Before the ambulance covered Phyllis' body, Dean kissed her forehead and said, "I'm sorry this happened to you, Phyllis. I'm so sorry," He wiped a tear that fell from his eyes. He quickly collected himself, remembering that Dean Jr. was still upstairs. He knew he would have to be strong for his son. "I tried to save you, I really tried."

"Sorry for your loss," said one of the EMS, and then he rushed Phyllis out the house on a gurney.

Craig ended up going to jail for second-degree murder after confessing that he killed Phyllis by mistake. Craig had a prior criminal history, so the judge sentenced him to life without parole.

Dean felt hurt to his heart over Phyllis's death, and for weeks, her family blamed him for Phyllis' death. They believed Dean acted out of jealousy. Meanwhile, Dean's mother was supportive. She would stop by the house to clean and cook and help care for little Dean. Dean Jr. missed his mother and cried for her every day. On the contrary, Dean's father gave Dean a stoic "I'm sorry", - no hug or pat on the back and rarely asked how things were going or if he was holding up okay.

Inside, Dean knew what his father was thinking, because every time someone died, it brought back memories of Dean's brother Johnny. Dean still blamed himself for his Johnny's death, mostly because his father wouldn't let him forget it. A part of Dean blamed himself for Phyllis's death, too. He wished he could have pushed her out the way and taken the three bullets that Craig shot, just so his son would have a mother. Dean was filled with internal agony, sorrow, and self-blame. The judge gave Dean full-custody of his son, and he gave Dean Jr.'s maternal Grandmother Visitation rights. Dean knew that raising a son as a single parent would be hard, and the race he had been running with different women had to stop. He realized he had to set a better example for Dean Jr., especially when it came to how he treated women, because Dean Jr. would be watching . . .

CHAPTER SEVENTEEN

PILLOW TALK

Connie gave birth to Tracey Gina Michaels on April 21, 1974. In the beginning, Connie felt very lonely when she had Tracey. She thought about her mother often, and wished she were there to give her advice on how to care for her newborn. All she had were baby books and limited experience from when she took care of her nephew BJ. She wished she could share Tracey's milestones and other new developments with someone in her family besides her father and May (who was now her roommate in a bungalow style house that they rented). She also wished Peaches was there to see her niece, but she hadn't seen Peaches since her senior year in high school.

As for Jet, he did very little to show support or concern for Tracey. Whenever Jet came home for the holidays from college, he ran the streets with his old friends from Lakeview High. He left everything up to his mother, and it was through Mrs. Michaels that Tracey received extra clothes, diapers, and toys from time to time. Mrs. Michaels also watched Tracey when Connie attended Chicago's School of Broadcasting until she graduated.

When she graduated a few years later, she a hard time finding a job in radio. She ended up working for Mr. James at his record store as a full-time employee and assistant manager. By 1977, Tracey was three years old. Mrs. Michaels would watch Tracey during the day while Connie was at work. For a while, May worked with Connie at the record store, but complained that Connie was making more money than her, so she quit and decided she could get more money being on welfare. May only watched Tracey if Mrs. Michaels had an errand to make, needed a break, or was under the weather.

Overall, Connie received more support with raising Tracey than she realized. Smokey and Franco also pitched in to help and were Tracey's godfathers. Smokey and Franco competed with each other over who bought Tracey the cutest outfits or the best toys that she liked to play with. They fought for Tracey's attention as if they were her biological fathers. Sometimes they would stop by and play with Tracey when they had gotten off work or take her out for ice cream while Connie ran errands. May didn't like all the attention Tracey received from everyone, which was why she didn't want to watch Tracey full-time. She would tell Connie that watching her own daughter, Lydia (now four), was hard enough.

Living with May in their three-bedroom house sometimes felt crowded. It wasn't that it was literally crowded in a physical way, but mentally, Connie was feeling like she missed her privacy. She also saw how selfish and lazy May could be. She was also sneaky and dishonest. During tax season, May let her mother claim her and Lydia. She lied on her taxes and said she lived with her mother. The two of them would split thousands of dollars they received in tax refunds and go on shopping sprees, mostly for themselves.

"I don't know why you just can't get an honest job and stop stealing from the government. One day, your lies and deceit will come back and bite you in the butt!" Connie would tell May year after year.

"Everybody ain't like you, Connie. You think you are so much better than everybody else, but you don't have anything to show for being honest," May contended.

Connie wanted to kick May out, but she couldn't, since both of their names were on the lease to the house. She wish she had more money so she could afford to live on her own, but she was not about to defraud the government just to get ahead. She wasn't raised that way.

At any rate, there were days when Connie and May got along well, and did things together with their daughters. Today was one of them. Connie and May were taking their daughters out in their strollers at Lincoln Park. Connie was talking to May about all the parties she deejayed, and how she wanted Ray to guest spot some of her gigs, since he had gotten a job at WCHI-93.3 Soul. She knew his reputation as "Soul Ray" the deejay would help bring in more revenue at her gigs. Still, she was too apprehensive to ask him because she didn't want him to think she was mooching off his new popularity. She just wanted his help.

"If you ask Ray for anything, he would do it for *you*."

"What's that supposed to mean?"

"You know my brother has always liked you, Connie." Connie knew that Ray was attracted to her, but so were plenty of other guys. Besides, she viewed him like a brother, and nothing more.

"When I asked Ray to put me on at WCHI he told me I didn't have the experience, but if you ask him, he would do it for you. Besides, we could use more money to do things around the house," May said.

"I can't ask Ray. I want him to help, but I can't bring myself to ask. I just can't."

"I'll call him and I'll tell him to call you, because you acting all scared."

"I'm not scared. I just don't want him to think the wrong thing."

"He wouldn't. He said he was going to put you on at the station anyway, and I'm sure he wouldn't mind helping you with your gigs too."

"Well, that hasn't happened yet. Maybe he's forgotten about us little people."

"Girl, whatever!" May threw up her hand and continued to stroll throughout the park.

"Ooh, look at that there," May said as she eyed the officers walking towards them along the tidal basin.

"I know you don't mean that Sugar Daddy."

"Of course not," May popped her gum in her mouth. "I'm talking about that brother walking next to that Sugar Daddy cop. Look at him; he is fine, with his bow-legged self." She stared as they were walking towards them. They appeared to be on foot patrol throughout the park.

Connie took notice. "Hmmm . . . he *is* kind of cute," she admitted. "But you got Levi, and you know he would break your neck if he found out you were with another guy." Connie shoved May playfully with her elbow as they continued to push their daughters down the sidewalk in their strollers.

"Nothing is wrong with a little eye candy." May flirtatiously raised her brow.

"Hello ladies," the younger officer said, smiling with a set of pearly whites. His skin looked as smooth as chocolate.

"Good evening, ladies," the older officer tipped his hat. Connie and May said hello, but kept their eyes on the younger of the two.

"My buddy here, Stuckey, told me that you must think I'm cute by the way you keep staring at me," the younger officer said.

"Who? Me?" Connie asked. "You must mean her." She pointed to May.

"I mean *you.*" Connie blushed.

"I take it your name must be Beautiful, with a smile like that," he winked. "My name is Dean Wilson. What's yours?"

"Connie and this is my friend, May."

"Dean, I'm going to walk down and grab a Chicago dog from the hotdog stand," Stuckey said.

"You do that," Dean replied without even looking at Stuckey. He was busy admiring Connie. She was wearing an orange halter-top and bell-bottom pants, with beige sandals. He thought she looked like she was about to go out dancing instead of just walking in the park. He thought she was gorgeous, and there was something familiar about her face, but he couldn't place it. His dark, piercing eyes danced with hers, and he admired her long, flowing hair that fell below her shoulders. Connie noticed Dean's handsome set of muscles glistening under the Chicago sun. May saw the two of them staring gooey-eyed at each and took the hint.

"Me and Lydia will meet you at the end of the park," she said to Connie, leaving her and Dean standing alone in front of each other with Tracey in the stroller. Connie felt a bit awkward still, because May had seen Dean first, but it was obvious that Dean was choosing her.

"You have beautiful eyes, Miss Connie. What color are they?" Dean stared deeply at her.

"Right now, they're green, but they change colors by the season."

"That's amazing." He smiled ear to ear. "You know, you look familiar to me. Do I know you from somewhere?"

"I don't think so. I mean, you may have seen me at a party or something."

"Hmmm . . . maybe." He scratched the side of his temple, trying to pinpoint where. "So, who is this little one here?" Dean peeked down in front of the stroller.

"This is my daughter Tracey."

"She's a doll, just like you." Dean observed Tracey nodding off to sleep. "So where's her daddy, if you don't mind me asking?"

"Out of the picture."

"Sorry to hear that, but you know, I'm a single parent too."

"Oh yeah?"

"My son Dean Jr. just turned ten."

"And where is his mother?"

"Deceased."

"Sorry to hear that."

"Well . . . seems like we have at least one thing in common, though," Dean mentioned.

"What's that?"

"Kids."

Connie shrugged. "Perhaps."

"You know, if I could rearrange the alphabets, I would say that *U* and *I* should go out together," Dean stated with confidence.

Connie burst into laughter.

"What's so funny?"

"That's the corniest line I've ever heard." Connie shook her head, laughing. "You were doing fine until you said that."

"You didn't like it? It usually works," he chuckled, trying to laugh away his embarrassment. He quickly took out his small notepad and a pen from the front of his shirt pocket below his Chicago Police badge. "How about you put your phone number on here so I can call you and take you out?"

Connie looked away for a moment in thought.

"Is something wrong?"

"I'm sorry Dean, but I don't date cops."

Dean asked, "Well, why not?"

"It's not cool, that's all."

"Not cool to you or your friends?" Dean chuckled sarcastically.

"Listen sugar, I think you're funny and cute, but I have to be honest with you, I just wouldn't feel comfortable with the idea."

Dean folded his arms. "The only person who will know I'm a cop would be you. It's not like I'll take you out in uniform," he found himself explaining. He'd never had to before.

"I never care about what other people think, it's *me* who's not comfortable with it," Connie replied, visualizing Dean crashing the party just because he had the authority to do so.

"At least accept one date. If I'm a bad guy, you have a right to judge me. But now you don't know if dating a cop is fun or not."

Connie thought about it for a moment. She gave him a yes/no smile.

"Oh, come on, take a chance. What do you have to lose?"

"All right. Well listen, I'm throwing a party over at a hall on West Division Street. It starts at ten. You can meet me there. It's a small venue, and we sold out of tickets, but you can pay at the door." Connie jotted down her phone number on Dean's pad. "I have to go now, *Officer.*"

Dean grinned. "Just call me Dean. I'll see you at the party."

Dean sang along to KC and the Sunshine Band's *Get Down Tonight.* You could hear the rhythm of the cowbells down the street. There was a long line waiting to get inside the dancehall. He was dressed in a brown bellbottom suit with cream-colored snake-skinned shoes, and a butterfly-collar shirt with a brown paisley print. He'd had a shave. His short afro was trimmed, and he made sure he splashed some Blue Suede aftershave around his neck. The women always complimented him on how good he smelled, and he hoped Connie would like it as well.

Dean was anxious to see Connie, and had hopes of taking her out to a nice 24-hour breakfast spot afterwards or to his house for drinks, since Dean Jr. was staying the weekend with his maternal grandmother. After standing in line awhile, Dean excused himself as he brushed by people and made his way to the doorkeepers. He flashed his Chicago Police badge, then said, "You mind if I take a look inside?"

The two guys—one was Italian and skinny, and the other was brown-skinned and tall—weren't sure about letting him pass. Dean didn't know it, but the two guys were Franco and Smokey.

"It's just a party, officer. We ain't doing nothing wrong," Smokey protested.

"I know. Here you go." Dean handed him a ten-dollar bill and headed up the steps to the dancehall.

"Officer! You forgot your change!" Franco called, since it was only five dollars to get in.

Dean looked over his shoulder and said, "Keep it."

"Punk cops," Smokey sneered once Dean's back was turned. "Can't stand them!"

The hall was packed with people, and Dean knew they were probably over the maximum capacity. He also knew there was no way he would find Connie in a crowd like this. He noticed how young the crowd looked, too. Most of them looked high school age or barely twenty-one. He was used to crowds his age- near thirty and over. He was tempted to ask one young man for his ID when he saw him buying a beer, but didn't. He started to feel a bit uncomfortable and thought about making a B-line towards the exit until someone in the crowd said, "There's Cat!"

Dean saw Connie take the stage behind two turntables. She was wearing a blonde Afro wig, a short red skirt with white go-go boots. *So she is Cat,* Dean thought. He had seen posters around with her name on it, but not her picture. Connie faded the music out to greet everyone.

"Ya'll ready to get down tonight?" she asked the crowd, and they cheered and whistled. "Looks to me like you guys have been getting down already to *KC and the Sunshine Band.* Not bad for a group of funky White boys, right?" Everyone clapped. "We got some brothers up in that band, too. They know how to get down with them horns, don't they?" The crowd shouted back. "I want everybody to have a good time tonight and show some love for the cash bar in the back. And don't forget the ticket raffle booth, too. Our photographer Mr. "C" is ready to take your pictures over there to my right, so show him some love," Connie said over the mike.

Dean was amazed by her power over the crowd, and the fact that she was a female deejay. Connie continued to run her set, and the people danced up a sweat, including Dean. The songs kept coming because Connie knew how to keep the people on the dance floor.

"Hi Dean," a voice called from behind. Dean looked over his shoulder.

"Hey." he wasn't sure who the young lady was.

"How you doing tonight?" she asked, sipping a drink.

"I'm dynamite, baby," Dean said, snapping his fingers to the music. "So, Connie, I mean "Cat", deejays all the time, huh?" Dean asked.

"Yep."

"I can dig it."

"So did you come here tonight for Cat, or just to party?"

"I'm sorry, but do I know you?"

"I'm May, Cat's roommate. I was with her the day she stole you from me at the park."

Dean laughed and thought to himself, *how did she steal me when I stepped to her?*

"You know, Dean, we're all *good* at something. I may not deejay, but I like to have my own kind of fun, if you know what I mean." May unfastened her blouse and showed her cleavage. "It's a little warm in here? Wanna go outside?"

Dean stared at her breasts for moment. His body said, *yes!* But his mouth said, "Nah, that's all right."

"You don't know what you're missing," May said, walking away and swishing her hips from side to side. She turned to see if Dean was looking at her, but he wasn't.

Dean practically forced his way through the dance floor to make his way up to the front of the stage. He waved his hands to try to get Connie's attention.

"Hey!" he shouted. "How is it going?" Dean yelled overtop of the music as Connie blended in another record to play. She looked at him standing at the bottom of the stage and smiled. She was happy to see him, but still a little uneasy about him being a cop. Although he wasn't in uniform, *she* knew who he was, and had already learned from Smokey and Franco that he flashed his badge to beat the line out front.

"I see you found your way!" Connie replied, moving and trying to keep focused on her music.

"Just promise me that I can get one dance with you before the night is over with!"

"I'll see what I can do," Connie told him.

As time moved on, Dean felt he was being ignored. By midnight, Connie started to slow things down so people could do some bumping and grinding.

"Can I have this dance?" Dean asked, feeling like he had to beg. Connie walked down off the stage after putting on an extended version of New Birth's "Wild Flower". Dean escorted her by the hand onto the dance floor. The building engineer turned on the blue lights and dimmed them. Dean pulled Connie in close to him. She felt soft, and she smelled like sweet perfume.

"You look good tonight," he whispered in her ear. He loved her blonde wig, and thought she had the most beautiful eyes he ever saw.

"Look, I'm not in uniform." He opened his suit jacket, revealing his whole ensemble.

"Yeah, but you had no problems flashing your badge at the door."

"Oh," Dean had forgotten all about that. "Well see I can explain that. The line was long so I . . ." It was the truth, but he could see Connie wasn't buying it.

"Not cool, Dean. So not cool," she shook her head.

"Baby, I'm sorry. I only did that to get in. That line was around the corner, I swear!" he declared, raising his hand. "It won't happen again. I promise."

"You can't do that, Dean," Connie warned. "If you start doing that, then everyone will feel uncomfortable trying to party around a cop. No offense, but most people just don't like cops, and so far, you have not given me a reason to make you the exception."

"Look, I can't change what I do or who I am. I know what I did wasn't cool or fair, but I only did it so I could hurry up and get in here to see you."

Connie folded her arms, unsure of what to believe.

"Are we cool?" Dean wanted to make sure. He needed to look into her eyes and see it, but she kept looking away, so he gently lifted her chin to face him.

"Are we?"

"Yeah, we're cool."

"So, how about we split and go grab some drinks at this cool spot I like on the Southside?"

"Not tonight, maybe some other time."

"No strings attached."

"Not tonight, Dean. Maybe some other time."

"Tomorrow we can have lunch in the park at noon. How does that sound?"

Connie was turned off by his aggressiveness. "I'll call *you*, okay?"

Dean felt defeated. No woman had ever turned him down before. "All right. I guess this is good night then," he said, as the song was about to end.

"Goodnight."

Saturday Morning . . .

"Hello?" Connie answered as the phone awakened her the next morning.

"What's happening, Miss Lady?" The voice sounded familiar. "Who is this? Dean?" If so, she wasn't ready to talk to him just yet. She needed time to forgive him for what he had done and for being so aggressive.

"Whoever Dean is, I'm not him. This is your boy, Ray."

"Oh, hi, Ray!" she was excited to hear from him, as she sat up in bed.

"I've been hearing good things about you in the neighborhood. Heard you been keeping the party people on the dance floor almost every Friday and Saturday night.

"I do my best."

"Good. Well, May told me you need me to be a guest deejay for some of your parties so you can book bigger venues"

"Oh yeah, I almost forgot." Connie ran her fingers through her hair as she slowly rose to her feet.

"I'll do the first two gigs for free, and we can work out a price for future sets later," Ray said. "For now, I need you to come by the studio so I can show you some things."

"Now?"

"What do you mean, *now*? It's almost eleven o'clock. Can you be here by noon?"

"I'll try."

By noon, Connie got herself and Tracey cleaned up and dressed. She packed a small bag with toys and snacks. Gone were the days of toting baby bags with diapers and bottles. Tracey was a three-year-old toddler who was developing quickly. Connie hopped in her brown Chevy, which was on its last legs, and drove downtown to North Michigan Avenue near Pioneer Court.

Connie double-checked the address she had jotted down on a piece of paper and walked straight into the building, taking the elevator to the top floor. The entire top level of the building belonged to WCHI. The rest of the floors were law firms, doctor's offices, and other businesses. A receptionist greeted Connie and Tracey with a warm smile and escorted them down the hallway to the studio. They walked by walls of autographed pictures of celebrities, gold record plaques, and photographs that some celebrities had taken with the staff members there. They stopped outside of the studio, where Connie could see Ray through the soundproof booth. He was sitting behind an engineering board, and behind him was a big light that said, 'ON AIR'. Ray kept talking on the mike to his audience as he motioned his hands for Connie to come inside the booth.

"I can watch your daughter for you, Connie. I'm Cheryl, by the way." The nice receptionist extended her hand and Connie shook it.

"I can't stop you from doing your job. That's not right," Connie said.

"Oh, don't worry, I can answer the phone in the conference room, and if someone comes and rings the doorbell, I can just get up and go let them in. It'll only take a second."

"Okay, I just don't want to inconvenience you."

"You're fine, and she will be fine too," Cheryl said as she kneeled down in front of Tracey. "What's your name, doll?"

Tracey smiled coyly. She wanted to say it. She knew it, but she was shy in front of the giant woman she didn't know. She held on tight to her doll baby. She inherited Jet's sandy brown hair and honey coated complexion, but favored her mother more. They had the same long hair, pug nose, round ears, and hazel eyes.

"Do you want to go play with me in this conference room?" Cheryl asked, admiring Tracey's hazel eyes that took in the world around her. Tracey reluctantly took Cheryl's hand as they walked down the hall to the conference room.

"Ladies and gentlemen, we have a local guest visiting us this afternoon. You may know her, because she's a local deejay and party promoter throughout Chicago. Come on over. Don't be shy. Introduce yourself to Chi-town." Ray patted the empty seat next to him and handed Connie the extra headset. When she sat down, he pushed the microphone towards her mouth.

"Good . . . afternoon . . . Chicago," Connie nervously said into the mike. She was taken off-guard. She hadn't planned to be on the air and wasn't sure what to say. All her formal training went out the window and nerves took over.

Ray whispered, "Go on tell them who you are, and say something about your upcoming parties next week. Say it just like you do at your parties."

"My name is Connie . . . Connie Morris. Some people call me Deejay Cat or just Cat. I would love you guys to come party with CMP promotions."

"So Connie, these parties cost, right? What, three dollars or five dollars?"

"It's just five dollars to get in. Call 555-1100 and ask for Smokey or Franco to get tickets."

"So, Connie, what's it like being a female deejay?"

"Well, I don't think about gender when I spin records. I just play what people want to hear."

"So how did you get started with deejaying?"

Connie was ready to stop talking, but Ray kept coming with the questions.

"I always loved music, and I would play records all the time after school, and then of course, you taught me some techniques, and after high school I went to the Chicago School of Broadcasting."

"Cat has asked me to guest deejay for her at the Disco Lounge next Saturday at seven. So you guys make sure you're there. Do you want to say anything else to Chi-town?"

"Well . . . um . . . I'd like to give a shout-out to my party promoting team from CMP—Smokey and Franco—my best friend May, and . . . to my sister Peaches. If she's listening, I love you girl, and get better soon."

"Well, that about wraps it up for this afternoon. This is Discoooo Raaaay, and I'm gonna close out with the hit from the Brothers Johnson, "I'll Be Good to You", and you know I will be. Peeeeace!"

When Ray put down his headset, Connie put down hers.

"Don't ever do that again!" Connie punched him on the arm.

"Ouch! What did I do?"

"You put me on the spot, Ray. That wasn't cool."

"Oh come on, you did fine. The more questions I asked, the more relaxed you were."

"Just don't do me like that again."

"Okay, okay. I was only trying to help, geez."

Suddenly, the studio door burst open. Connie looked up and saw a tall man with an Afro so big she could barely see his face. He wore gold rings on each one of his fingers, including his thumbs, and wore a black suit with a white shirt that had butterfly collars. His glasses were so thick that his eyes looked like dots.

"Who in the hell told you to get on my station and self-promote?" the man shouted. "You don't put people on my show without asking me first!"

"Sorry, Billy," Ray said with a smirk on his face. It wasn't the first time he had done that.

"Young lady, what is your name?" Billy asked.

"Connie Morris, sir."

"Connie Morris, also known as DJ Cat the party promoter, huh?"

"Yes sir."

"Connie, I happen to think you have a pretty nice voice, despite what you just did to my show."

"Thank you, sir."

"Quit it with that 'sir' stuff. I'm only thirty-five, young lady."

"Okay. Sorry."

"My name is William Donovan. Folks call me Billy. I'm a program manager. Here's my card. We're actually looking to make some changes to spark up our night programming and give the Quiet Storm on WKJL some competition. I'd love it if you could step in my office for a few minutes for a few voice tests to see if you fit what we're looking for."

Connie and Ray went into Billy's office and he began to explain the type of program he wanted to start. He had her to speak over the backdrop to Donna Summers' instrumental version of *"Love to Love You Baby"*. It took a few tries for her to get it right, but when she finally got it, Billy thought she would be a perfect fit.

Billy decided to call the night show "Pillow Talk", and allowed Connie to have Smokey to be her partner, since he wanted the show to be about love and relationships. Ray trained Smokey on how to use the equipment. Billy thought it was the best to have both a female and a male perspective on the show. Connie put on her sexiest voice, while Smokey put on a heavy bass voice to try to sound like Barry White.

After weeks of training and rehearsing, the show went live by the end of the summer, and became an instant winner with listeners. They were able to attract both female and male listeners. Connie was hosting the show Monday through Friday from eight o'clock until midnight, and ended up quitting the record store job so that she could spend time with her daughter during the day and rest up before the show.

The show became so popular in the urban community that Connie and Smokey stopped hosting parties. Billy had them serving the community when they weren't in the studio. They were promoting the show throughout Chicago by speaking engagements, visiting colleges and universities, and Connie was offered to do commercials that advertised hair and cosmetic products over the radio. Franco, who was assisting them with parties, ended up moving to San Francisco with his partner and explored other business ventures. Connie's salary tripled from working at WCHI. She never would have seen that kind of money working at the record shop. She ended up buying the house that she and May rented, and a new car, too. She had everything put in her name. *"Pillow Talk" with Cat Morris and Smokey Jay* was on billboards throughout Chicago.

Soon, Connie was doing photo-shoots to advertise the latest clothing, especially tight-fitting, stylish jeans. Her beautiful face was on billboards and on the side of busses and taxicabs. She couldn't go anywhere without being recognized. People would either see Connie on TV or hear her on the radio. This also helped boost revenue for the radio station, who earned thirty-percent from each advertisement. Billy knew that turning Connie into a sex symbol would be the best way to market *Pillow Talk*, and Connie definitely attracted more male listeners than female.

While Connie climbed her way to success, Dean was promoted to detective, and working on Operation: Big Sting.

"This sting is going to be big!" Dean said to Hank over drinks one evening at a bar.

"Oh yeah?"

"Man, this is going to make the news. Now dig," Dean leaned in closer to Hank at the bar so no one would overhear the plan. "We're going to raid Cabrini Green, Robert Taylor Homes, and all the other projects on the South and North side of Chicago. This operation took three months to plan, and I can't wait to nail these bastards that are selling that poison to their own people."

Hank laughed at his cousin's enthusiasm. "I hope it goes down the way you plan," he said. "So uhm . . . what's with the foxy chick that does the radio thing? You still seeing her?"

Dean finished off his beer, sat the empty mug on the counter. "I've crossed paths with her a few times at nightclubs, but I can never talk to her at length the way I want.

"Why not?"

"She's always with an entourage and fans always surround her for autographs and pictures. I haven't forgotten about Connie, it's just hard trying to connect. I even called *Pillow Talk* one night and made a song request while I was on my beat, but she didn't know who I was since I said my name was "DW." I hope when things slow down a bit, our paths will cross long enough for me to ask her out again."

"Don't throw all your eggs in one basket youngblood. Connie's a hot chick, but there're plenty of other broads out there to roll in the hay with."

"I know that, but there's something about Connie that I actually dig, man. I have a gut feeling that she's more than just a roll in the hay."

"Sounds like she done gave you the "jones" already!" Hank laughed.

"Call it whatever you want, but if I ever get another opportunity with her, I won't blow it next time."

CHAPTER EIGHTEEN

MORE THAN A HOST

While working at WCHI, Connie and Smokey often hosted concerts, and would give away free tickets to callers who named the correct songs they played. Connie began to develop an interest in concert promoting, and frequently talked to promoters about what was involved. Her interest grew so much that after learning all there was to know, she turned her company, CMP, into a concert-promoting company instead of a party-promoting company. She started hosting small gigs locally throughout Chicago. Most of the artists were local musicians who were looking to catch a break, and Connie would work with their managers and set up venues for them to perform. She realized quickly that the fame of her name was powerful enough to get things done. However, when Smokey got wind of what Connie was doing, he became furious.

"You are going to ruin what we have if Billy finds out!" Smokey warned Connie one night after the program ended.

"What I do outside of the radio station is my business!"

Smokey folded his arms and griped. "Well what about me? You put me on, and now you're leaving me?"

"No, I wouldn't leave you hanging. I plan to make you my partner. I can't do this alone, but I wanted to get things off the ground first."

Smokey sucked his teeth. "Well, it doesn't look that way to me."

"You will see. Just be patient. I plan to have you work with me and help me out the same way you did with the parties. Since Franco is gone now, I'll need you to help me to check out venues, not just here in Chicago. When the company grows, I plan to get gigs for artists throughout the mid-west, then the east coast. Before long, we'll be booking gigs all over the country!"

Smokey shook his head. "You're dreaming. Nobody is going to give a woman promoter a chance."

"A few of them have already, and all I need is one big artist to put me on, and then go from there. Right now, this station has given me the connections I need." Smokey listened to Connie. He felt she was in over her head and would possibly mess things up for him, so he went to Billy and reported what she was doing. Billy called Connie into his office . . .

Days Later . . .

"It's a conflict of interest," Billy was arguing with Connie in his office.

"That's not written in my contract," Connie protested.

"We'll write an amended contract, and you will sign it, or be replaced."

"I won't sign it," Connie sternly said. "Besides, nobody said anything about Ray or that guy Vincent who started his talent agency, so why stop me from having side gigs?"

"Your job to host your radio show. Besides, you're already doing enough with commercials and modeling on the side. We need you to remain focused on hosting and nothing more."

"So you mean to tell me you didn't want Ray and Vincent to do the same?"

"Connie, things are a little different for Ray and Vincent."

"Why? Because they're men and I'm a woman?"

"You still need more experience and they don't."

"That's bull!" Connie contested. "I carry this station on my back. I helped build this station. I have plenty of experience Billy so don't patronize me."

"Connie, either you sign the new contract we're going to put together or else."

Connie folded her arms, as she paced the office. "Or else what? Are you going to fire me?"

"Connie, you have a job that most women do not have, but wish they could. Now if you're smart you will sign the contract and keep your job."

"I don't see what the big deal is. If you can let me do commercials and model, then why can't I be a concert promoter too?"

"You can, but we need fifty percent."

"You already get thirty percent from everything else I'm doing. Fifty percent is highway robbery!"

"Forty-percent is my final offer Connie. Concerts is big business and your name here carries a lot of weight. You are not WCHI, you're the *host* of WCHI don't forget. You're not bigger than the station, so you either sign the new deal or else," Billy refused to back down. "The contract will be ready by tomorrow, so sleep on it tonight."

Connie snatched up her purse. "I won't sign it Billy. You'll hear from my lawyer!" She stormed out of the office.

Connie hired a lawyer and things got ugly at the station. A riff ensued between Connie, Billy and upper management. Each morning that she came into work the revised contract was sitting on her desk for her to sign, but each time she refused per her lawyer's advice. Billy, the program manager started letting Smokey dictate how the show was going to go, including having full control over the song selections. Every night Connie tried to have some say so or play a song she wanted to play, but Smokey would take over, and then Connie would abruptly leave the set. Some nights Connie wouldn't show up at all. Listeners started complaining about repeats of the show, and the ratings that had once skyrocketed began to drop.

"See the mess you created!" Smokey argued with Connie. Neither of them was being paid for the rerun shows.

"Nobody told you to tell Billy, Smokey," Connie argued. "I asked you to be patient. I had planned on finishing our contract with them, but noooo, you had to go and run your mouth."

"Well you didn't say all of that at first!"

"You should trust me, Smokey. You've known me since high school!"

"Look I'm sorry for dropping a dime on you," Smokey thought. "But if you insist on fighting with Billy, they could fire us both and then I'll be out of a job. I'm not trying to move back into the projects Connie. I'm living too good to go backwards."

"I don't know what's going to happen with me and WCHI. My lawyers said I need to sign the amended contract, and be done with WCHI all together."

"So what about the show? What about me?"

"You rat me out and then expect me to hold your hand?"

"I'm sorry Connie, but please understand what will happen to me if you leave," Smokey begged. "I know we have our disagreements but we've always made a good team and you know that."

Connie thought about it and realized he was right.

"I didn't think things would get this ugly. It seems like all the guys who work at WCHI get better treatment than the women. If I start the concert promoting company I may consider you as a partner."

Smokey smiled.

"But you need to trust me, even if things don't look right. Just know I'm making moves."

"It's a deal."

Three Years Later- 1980

For the next three years, per the advice of her lawyers, Connie signed the contract with WCHI believing it was better to finish up her agreement with them and then start her own business. It was now 1980. Time was flying by, but not quickly enough for Connie, who still had six months to go before her contract would finally be complete with WCHI. Things were not the same since the ugly contract dispute and upper management continued to let Smokey call all the shots for the show's programming ideas. Although Smokey seemed concerned about Connie leaving before, to her it seemed like he shouldn't have a care in the world. He dominated the show. After a while, he got used to Connie leaving the set when the night didn't go her way. "Cat had to wrap things up due to an emergency, but we'll keep the show moving," Smokey would tell listeners. Tonight was no different. Connie got so upset by the way Smokey was dictating the conversation during the show, and she lied and said she was sick during a commercial break, and left the station. She got into her 1980 black Camaro and drove to the Southside Diner where her mother used to work.

"Hey Cat, aren't you supposed to be on the show tonight?" asked a man walking by as she headed towards the diner.

"Not tonight."

"Hi Cat, can we have your autograph?" asked a couple. Cat signed it for them and quickly rushed inside.

The owner of the Southside Diner always insisted Connie eat there for free since her mother had worked there for many years, and was respected as one of the best waitresses who ever worked there. A picture of Frieda hung near the front door in her honor. However, Connie always insisted on paying. If one of the chefs gave her extra food, she would ask for a doggie bag and give it to a homeless person on the street. In fact, one day when she thought no one was looking, she had given a homeless man a bag with a burger inside, and next thing she knew it was in the *Chicago Sun*, 'Cat Morris Feeds the Homeless'. Connie insisted it wasn't about her but helping other people in need, which made people in the urban community of Chicago love her that much more. She only wished the guys at the station respected and appreciated her as much as Chicago did.

Dean and Detective White were in the diner having coffee and discussing the "Big Sting" project when Dean spotted Connie taking a seat at a booth in a corner towards the front door. She looked depressed, and Dean wondered what was wrong with her. Although he hadn't had a chance to develop any romantic feelings for Connie, he was still attracted to her. Seeing her sitting by herself without an entourage was rare, and Dean knew he had to take advantage of the opportunity. In the few years that had passed by, they had only seen each other sporadically, but Dean could never get pass the basic *'hello, how are you?'* because there was always an interruption.

"Dean, I need your attention here." White tapped his hand on the table, trying to show him a map of where the drug dealers were making transactions and where their "connect" was hiding out.

"Hold that thought." Dean sat his coffee on the table. "I'll be right back. This won't take long," he said to White.

"Is this seat taken?"

Connie slowly raised her eyes from her bowl of soup.

"I'm Dean Wilson, but you probably don't remember me." He smiled, feeling a little nervous at first. Things were different now. Connie wasn't a young deejay and party promoter anymore. She was twenty-five and a local celebrity, and Dean was almost thirty-two.

She smiled, thought, *Of course, I remember you, sweetie, with your fine self. Too bad you're a cop.* "Wow! How have you been, Dean?" she asked as Dean took a seat across from her in the booth.

"I was waiting for you to call me back one of these days, but I figured after three years, I should stop waiting by the phone and get on with my life."

Connie burst out laughing. Dean started laughing too.

"Well who's keeping count?" She laughed, and so did he.

"I've seen you around, though."

"Oh really? I didn't think you noticed," Dean mentioned. "It's so hard to get your attention."

"You have it now," she replied with a flirty grin.

"Well um . . ." Dean paused and cleared his throat. "I think I owe you an apology for being a bit forward last time."

"A *bit* forward, huh?"

"Yeah just a bit," he grinned. "You know, I called your show once."

"So you listen to *Pillow Talk*'?" Connie asked.

"Around here, everyone knows "Cat", he chuckled. "We listen to you every night on my beat. It's a hot show."

Connie pushed her cold soup to the side, decided against finishing it. "No offense," she said tactfully. "But I get so many calls that I don't remember."

"Hey," Dean casually threw up his hands. "No offense taken."

"So why aren't you in uniform?" she asked, noticing he was dressed in a suit.

"I'm a detective now. Been promoted."

"Good for you."

"Say, aren't you supposed to be on the show right now?" Dean pointed to his watch.

"I decided to let Smokey finish the program for tonight."

"Excuse me," Detective White interrupted. "I hate to be rude, but I need to have a word with Dean here."

"Listen, baby, I gotta go. But when you get home, play number three on *Shalamar's* new album."

"Number three?"

"Number three."

Connie nodded. "Okay. I will. And you just happen to know I have their new album?"

"You can't be a deejay and not have the latest records."

She smiled. "You're right. I have everything that's out right now: Shalamar, the S.O.S. Band, The Whispers, Rufus and Chaka Khan, and a collection of classic soul records. You name it and I'm sure I have it."

"Maybe one day I'll get a chance to listen to your collections." Dean jotted down his phone number and slid it across the table to her. "The ball is in your court." He winked and walked off with Detective White.

When Connie got home, May had already fed and put the girls to bed. She was more helpful since Connie was bringing in more money, and sharing it with her. By now, Lydia was going on seven, and Tracey was six. Connie paid May to babysit Tracey while she worked at night. Mrs. Michaels had moved to Buffalo, New York a few years ago when the Buffalo Bills drafted Jet. Jet claimed he would send for Tracey to visit him once he was settled. Up to this point in Tracey's life, he hadn't been involved, except to send her gifts for her birthday and Christmas presents. He rarely called to talk to her and didn't spend any time with her when he was in town when the Bills played the Chicago Bears, so Connie wasn't holding her breath. At any rate, May had become Tracey's new babysitter.

"You will never guess who I saw tonight." Connie was grinning ear to ear as she hung up her coat in the closet near the front door.

"Who? Kool and the Gang? George Benson? Tom Browne?" May tried to guess, as she stuffed her mouth with popcorn as she sat in front of the TV watching *Kojak*. She knew Connie was always meeting celebrities at the station.

"No, not this time," Connie shook her head. "Do you remember that cop named Dean?" Connie asked, heading towards her record collection in the corner of the living room. She thumbed through her collection until she found Shalamar.

"How could I forget? You took him from me and then let him get away."

"What? I didn't take him. He showed more interest in me than in you."

"Anyway, so now that you ran into him, when you gonna jump his bones?"

"MAY!"

"I'm being honest. He is a sexy brown thing!" May recalled. "Does he still have that muscular physique?"

"Hard to tell, since he was wearing a suit and trench coat, but he was just so smooth, you know? He wasn't pushy like he was when we first met. I like that."

"Just let me know when you guys need some privacy."

"Girl, you know, ever since you and Levi been over with, you been hitting the sack with every good-looking brother with two legs."

May shrugged, admitted, "I'm young and single, and just like to have fun. It's time you do the same."

"Anyway, Dean wants me to play number three from Shalamar's new album." Connie put on the record. As soon as the beat started playing, they both recognized the song.

May jumped up from the sofa. "Yes, that's my song, *Second Time Around!*"

"Girl, he wants you, he wants a second chance, and if I were you, I would give him some!"

Connie tilted her head, sucked her teeth. "Is that all you think about?"

"These days? YES!"

Connie loved Dean's choice of song, and made a mental note to call him.

"You know you like him, Connie. Quit playing games and get'cha some. All these men hit on you, and you turn them all down. But now here is a cat that really digs you, and you need to go for it before you miss out!" May expressed. "Besides, you ain't been laid since Jet anyhow."

"Just because I don't broadcast my business like you doesn't mean I haven't."

"Yeah, right!" May frowned. She knew better.

"I'll be in touch with Dean. Put him on my schedule."

"Listen at you, already sounding like he's one of your business projects."

"No, it's just that I'm very busy these days."

"Yeah well you have to learn how to have fun sometimes. That's how you and Jet broke up years ago. He felt you were too serious all the time."

"Is that what he told you?" Connie chuckled in disbelief.

"Yes, that's what he said. Besides," May sat down her popcorn, "I know you, Connie. I've known you for years. You need to lighten up. Have some fun sometimes."

"What I do is fun."

"You know what I mean." May cut her a look. "If you don't go out with Dean this time, somebody else may take him. People don't usually get a second chance to get things right. If you don't I will."

"You better back off girl! He's mine!"

"Then start acting like you want him."

CHAPTER NINETEEN

KISS ME

Dean was in a deep sleep when his phone started ringing. He and Detective White had spent all night on the plans for The Big Sting operation. Dean opened one eye and looked at the clock- it was twelve noon on Saturday. He reached for the phone and accidentally knocked it on the floor.

"Shoot!" he griped, shoving the covers off his body as he leaned over the bed to pick it up.

"What'cha got for me, White?"

"Hello, Dean," spoke a sexy familiar voice.

"Who is this?" he snapped, hoping it wasn't an old fling calling to hook up.

"Cat Morris, but you can call me Connie. It's more personable."

"Oh . . . hey . . . wassup?" Dean remembered, smiling behind the phone.

"I was hoping that if you weren't too busy, we could meet for a cup of coffee this afternoon."

"I'm supposed to take my son to karate lessons at two o'clock, but maybe we can get together for dinner this evening."

"Hmm . . . I have an early morning flight to L.A., but what time are you talking about?"

"How does six o'clock sound?"

"Groovy."

"So what's in L.A.?" Dean asked, sitting up in bed, wiping the sleep from his eyes.

"I booked the Doobie Brothers for Soul Train."

"Wow, the Doobie Brothers! I like them. Those cats are pretty good."

"Yes, and I'm so excited."

"I thought you just hosted the radio station. You manage groups too?"

"No, I'm a concert promoter. I'm just building up my clientele so by the time my contract expires at the station; my company will be well established."

"That's pretty cool."

"So, should I dress up for dinner tonight?"

"That'll be perfect. I have a very classy place in mind."

"Okay, I'll see you at six." Connie gave him her address before they said goodbye.

"I'm taking you to your grandmother's house this evening," Dean Sr. said to his son while they were headed home, after karate lessons.

"I don't feel like going over there. I thought today was our day. This is our weekend together, remember?"

"I know you're upset, Dean, but I have a meeting this evening. It just came up."

"What time are you picking me up?"

"I'll pick you up about nine thirty."

"Then the rest of the day is gone."

"I'll make it up to you tomorrow. We'll go bowling, all right?"

Dean Jr. was disappointed for a brief moment, but the thought of going bowling did seem fun.

"All right," Dean Jr. sighed. "But can my friend Danny come with us?"

"Sure."

"By the way, you did a good job today in class. Your kicks are much better."

"Dad, you know I don't really like karate class."

"Why? It'll make you into a man."

"Dad, I really just want to play the violin."

Dean turned up his nose. "The violin?"

"Yes. Mom used to play the violin, and she used to show me how I could play too. I want to play the violin, Dad. Can I take lessons? Can I?"

"I don't know about the violin, son. Why not play the drums or the sax?"

"Dad, I want to play the violin."

"I tell you what." Dean glanced over at him, as he kept his hands on the steering wheel. "If you earn a black belt in this karate class first, then you can play the violin."

"Okay."

Dean walked up Connie's porch steps, carefully stepping over icy patches and remnants of snow. He rang the doorbell and saw a shadow walk past the window behind the curtains. He was dressed to impress in a nice pinstriped gray suit with a white shirt and shiny burgundy shoes. He was draped in his long black leather trench coat to keep the chill off. He had also taken his yellow *"deuce and a quarter"* to the carwash. Cars were Dean's hobby, and he loved driving the classics.

"Hello Dean," May she said as she opened the door in a see-through blouse.

"Hi, is Connie home?"

"You don't remember me? I'm May, Connie's best friend. Come on in." Dean remembered her and the way she had flirted with him that night at Connie's party. *Some best friend you are,* he thought to himself as he stepped inside and the smell of incense drifted by his nose. He hated incense, and was suspicious of it, because most people he investigated used incense to cover up their marijuana smoke.

"Have a seat," May offered. "Connie will be down in a minute." Dean sat down on the plush brown sofa, holding the roses he had bought for Connie in his hands. He noticed Connie's stacked collection of 45's, albums, and cassettes next to her record player with the waist-high speakers.

"Hiiiii," waved a cute little light-skinned girl with curly braids in her hair, and the other little girl, with cute bushy ponytails and a cute dimpled smile, waved too.

"Hi girls," Dean waved hello.

"This is my daughter Lydia," May said about the one with the cute dimples, ". . . and this is Connie's daughter, Tracey. They were toddlers the last time you saw them."

Dean nodded. "Amazing how time flies. Look at them. They're school-age little girls now."

"Yep, that's how it is. You got kids?"

Dean looked at his watch. "I have a son," Dean answered. "Would you mind asking Connie how much longer she will be?"

"I'm ready!" Connie came walking down the stairs in her heels, wearing a short black dress with spaghetti straps. She was busy trying to fluff out her curls. She grabbed her long faux fur coat out of the closet. She wanted to be sexy with her dress, but not cold once she got outside. The Chicago winters could be a monster, and she wanted to wrap up tight.

"You look amazing." Dean smiled and handed Connie a dozen red roses. "These are for you."

"Thank you."

"I'll put those in water for you," May offered.

"Thanks. We'll see you later."

"Take your time. You have *all* night," May grinned, and Connie knew clearly what May was thinking.

On the way to dinner, Stevie Wonder's *Send One Your Love* was playing from the car radio as Connie and Dean had small talk. They arrived at a nice Italian restaurant on the corner of East Grand Avenue in downtown Chicago. Connie was impressed with the restaurant that Dean chose. He ordered a bottle of wine for both of them. Connie chose the lasagna, and Dean selected the leg of lamb.

"So, how long will you be in L.A.?" Dean asked. His only memory of California now was the death of his ex-wife.

"Probably a week. I'm using my vacation time."

"So you mentioned you were under contract with the station. It doesn't sound like you plan to renew it."

"No, I don't, actually. I have ideas that are out of this world, and all I need are artists. I want to promote concerts for all types of artists. I just hired a realtor to help me find a decent location where I can set up shop to run my business," Connie explained.

Dean listened to Connie's ambitions. He admired the fact that she was so driven and determined. "So besides your career, what do you enjoy doing personally?" he asked, taking his next bite into the piece of lamb.

"I love spending time with my daughter. I just signed her up for ballet lessons."

"That's good. She may grow up to appreciate the arts."

"Whatever she's willing to do, I'll always support her."

"Anything else you like doing?"

"Well, I love listening to music, and I definitely love to party and meet new people," she answered, then took a sip of her wine. "What about you?"

"Like you, I like to spend time with my son when I can. Other times, a long jog through the park gives me a chance to think and clear my head," he expressed. "I know that may sound selfish, but the type of work I do makes me enjoy a little bit of solitude whenever I can get it. Sometimes these cases will drive you nuts if you don't have some sort of an outlet."

"So do you like to party? I mean, I've seen you a few times at some of the clubs. I just assumed you would be an outgoing type, not an introvert."

"Oh, I do like to party, but it's not as often anymore. I work longer hours now, so whenever I can get some rest, I just try to take advantage of that more than partying."

"So besides jogging, do you lift weights?" She could see some of his muscular physique was still there. His biceps protruded each time he moved his arm to bring his fork to his mouth.

Dean blushed. "I'm a bit of a health buff, yeah. It started back in high school when I used to run track, and then later on, I competed in the Olympics, so yes, you can say I'm athletic, too."

"The Olympics? Wow! That's something special."

"I didn't win though. I came a few seconds short of winning the bronze."

"Have you ever thought about competing again?"

"I have thought about it, but I don't have time to train."

"Well, I happen to think that if you really want to do it, you should go for it. I think people should do what they love, or they risk the rest of their lives being miserable doing something they don't. My mother worked three jobs, but she told me she always wanted to be a clothing designer," Connie said. The wine had loosened her up, and she felt at ease with Dean.

Dean smiled in amazement, and his eyes sparkled. "Are you always this energetic and passionate?"

"Well, I wasn't always this way, but my mother told me before she died to live my life. I just try to appreciate each day, because tomorrow is not promised to us. And since my mother didn't live to see her dreams, I want to make sure I live mine."

"Sorry to hear about your Mom, but I do think she was right about living one's life to the fullest," Dean agreed. "May I ask you a question that I know a man shouldn't ask? You're so intelligent and mature; I'm just curious about your age."

"I'm twenty-five. And how old are you?"

"I just turned thirty-two last month."

"You don't look like it."

"Is that a compliment, or do I look older?" Dean asked.

"You look a few years younger. I'm not going to boost your head up." Dean laughed. "So what made you become a cop?"

"I like helping people and keeping our community safe."

"That's it?"

"For the most part."

Connie finished her wine and gazed around a moment at the beautiful ambiance of the restaurant. She knew it was expensive to eat there, and mentally gave Dean brownie points for having good taste. He was definitely making a good first impression.

"So why aren't you married? You have a good career. You're nice looking. What gives?"

Dean folded his arms. "I could say the same about you."

"Don't avoid the question."

"I *was* married."

"So what happened, if you don't mind me asking?"

"Why do I feel like I'm being interrogated?"

"Ha! Some nerve!"

"It's awkward for me to be the one answering questions."

"Well you don't say!" The two shared a laugh.

"Maybe we can talk about that part some other time."

"Just tell me you're divorced and not separated, because I don't date married men."

"I am divorced. Actually, Phyllis and I divorced before she died."

"I'm sorry. So Phyllis was Dean Jr.'s mother?"

"Yes."

"I think I remember you telling me that his mother passed away. I'm sorry."

"That's okay. You didn't know," Dean paused to wipe his mouth with a napkin. He'd finished with his meal before Connie finished hers.

"Well, now I'm posing that same question to you," Dean stated, discreetly glancing at his watch. He saw that it was almost ten o'clock. He had to wrap things up quickly, but didn't want to end things by talking about death, that's for sure.

"I'm not married, and I have never been married. I just happen to be one busy lady."

"I see. Not much time for dating?"

"I wouldn't say that. I mean, I'm here with you, right?"

Dean smiled and extended his hand. "Would you like to dance?"

"I would."

The restaurant had a live band, and as Dean listened, they were playing the violins. It was beautiful. He glanced over Connie's shoulders as they danced, and noticed the men playing the violins from the stage. The men were professionals, and they sounded good. He imagined this was what his son meant about playing the violin—it was classic!

"You're a beautiful woman, Connie," Dean whispered. He leaned down and placed a tender kiss on her cheek as they danced to the music.

"Now I feel self-conscious."

"You shouldn't. It's a compliment."

"Thank you."

After the dance, Dean and Connie headed home. When they arrived at her house, he opened the car door for her and walked her to her front door.

"I had a nice evening with you." Dean gently took hold of her hand and kissed it.

"I enjoyed my time with you too."

"You have a safe trip to L.A., and don't forget about me when you return."

"Are you sure you don't want to come inside and have a drink?" Connie offered. Dean wanted to come inside, but it was already after ten, and he would be late picking up Dean. He knew he was going to get an earful from his former mother-in-law, complaining about him being late *again*.

"Maybe next time," he gently kissed her cheek. "Have a safe trip to California."

"I will," she hugged him. "Thank you for a nice time."

Neither of them wanted to leave each other. Connie really wanted him to come in. Dean wanted the same, but he didn't want their first time together to feel rushed. He wanted it to be right. For a moment, their eyes danced with each other. They could feel the passion rising within their souls. Dean desperately wanted to kiss her and she wanted him to kiss her, but he wasn't sure if he initiated the first kiss if she would turn him away. As she looked up into his eyes, Connie wanted to know what it would be like to kiss him. She hadn't kissed in months, and hadn't had sex since she conceived Tracey. All those old feelings of longing to touch and be with a man had returned.

"By the way, that was a good choice of song you told me to listen to by Shalamar."

"Well I hope this time around *is* indeed better than the first," Dean's lips curved a flirtatious smile.

"It was." She reached up and gently stroked the side of his face with her leather-gloved hand.

"We'll do this again soon." He blushed from the sensation of her touch.

"For sure."

Connie went inside and tried to catch her breath. Dean was doing a number on her heart. She thought Dean was smooth like Billy Dee Williams when he played in the movie *Mahogany*. She had to tell herself to calm down and remind herself that it was just the first date. She knew May was right. Having a social life again was what she needed. She was definitely looking forward to seeing Dean next time . . .

CHAPTER TWENTY

NETWORKING

While Connie was in California, all she could think about was Dean. Each time her hotel phone rang it was Dean or Tracey calling to talk to her. After attending another business meeting, she went back to her hotel. As soon as she walked in her phone started ringing. Assuming it was Dean, she put on her sexiest voice.

"Hello?" she answered.

"Connie, this is Jet. How are you?"

Connie's mouth dropped. She sat her briefcase on the living room table, and sat down on the sofa.

"Hello? Are you still there?"

"I'm . . . I'm here. I'm just surprised to hear from you after all these years, Jet."

"Well, I was hoping Tracey could spend the Christmas holiday with me next week."

She rested the phone against her shoulder, and crossed her arms. "Are you serious?"

"I've been settled here in Buffalo for quite some time. I need to get to know my daughter, don't you think?"

"What brought all of this on?" Connie questioned.

"A man can't see his child?"

"I didn't say that, but Tracey is six-years-old. Why now?"

"I'm getting married soon Connie, and I want my fiancée Sabrina to meet her."

"Oh, so that's your real reason for wanting to get to know Tracey," Connie was surprised. A part of her thought back to the days when he had promised to marry her. She hadn't been holding her breath on the idea, and knew that in a million years, she would never marry Jet. They weren't compatible. However, she did wonder for a brief moment what made Sabrina marriage material and not her.

"Well, let me think about that. I'll call you when I get back to Chicago."

"That's fine. If your decision is yes, I sent two tickets to your home. You can fly here with Tracey to make sure she gets here safely, and I can introduce you to Sabrina."

"Like I said, I'll call you. This is not official. I need to think it over and see how Tracey feels about it too." Connie had wanted Tracey to meet her father a long time ago. She had only seen him a couple of times as a baby and a toddler, but she didn't remember him without being shown pictures or seeing him play on TV.

After they said good-bye to each other, Connie called May back in Chicago and told her not to give her hotel number to anyone else unless it was an emergency.

Later that day, Connie watched the taping of the Doobie Brothers performing their single *"One by One"* on *Soul Train*. Afterwards, their manager handed her a check in an envelope for her services and promised to do business with her again. Connie ended up staying in L.A. a few days longer than what she had expected, as she solicited her concert promoting business with various record companies.

While visiting one record company, she bumped into Chaka, a fellow Chicagoan whom she had interviewed on WCHI. Chaka invited Connie to see her perform later that night, and Connie dared to turn down a diva like Chaka. Chaka then invited Connie to the after party, where Connie was able to meet several other celebrities and their managers. She casually filled her appointment book so she could talk with them by conference call once she got back to Chicago.

She grinded hard in L.A., but as soon as she got back to Chicago, she had just enough time to hug and kiss Tracey and leave gifts from California before hurrying off to work that night. She tried to prepare herself for the tongue-lashing from Billy, but it was worse than she thought.

"Just who do you think you are?" Billy fussed. "I made you, and if it wasn't for me, you would still be spinning records in the projects!" Billy went on and on, and Connie felt herself shrinking in the chair in front of his desk. "One week vacation means one week, not a week and a half. Now I'm telling you, Cat, you're walking on thin ice around here. If it wasn't for Ray and Smokey telling me not to fire you, then I'd give you your walking papers. You got one more time to mess up and you are out!" he pointed his finger. .

Smokey was no better. "I know what you went out to L.A. to do, and it wasn't a vacation, and you're not slick. If you keep this up, Billy is going to replace you before your contract is over. You need to stop thinking about yourself. At least give me a heads up!"

Connie apologized to Smokey, and later to Billy once he calmed down. However, Connie had no regrets about all the connections she made in L.A., and was prepared to make her conference calls to several famous record companies to work out contract deals.

At the rate things were going, she knew they weren't going to renew her contract. She had already gotten wind from other staff members that Billy and upper management had been interviewing other women to replace her. Whomever they chose to hire would be Smokey's new co-host on "Pillow Talk."

In the meantime, Connie agreed that Tracey could spend the Christmas break with Jet in New York. Tracey was excited, so Connie flew to New York over the weekend. A limousine picked up Connie and Tracey and drove them to the suburbs in Buffalo.

The limo pulled in front of a huge mansion where Jet, his mother, and Sabrina greeted them when they walked through the door. Jet still had the same sleepy bedroom eyes and sandy brown hair, but he had grown a full beard, which made him look older than twenty-five. His voice was deeper, arms more hairy, and he was thicker in stature. He was all man now. Not the boy who used to live in the Cabrini Green Row Houses, and hang out on the corners with his friends.

The more they talked over dinner and wine later that evening, Connie could tell he was still the same arrogant and shallow Jet. He bragged about everything, and after dinner he showed off his house, awards and trophies, basketball court, and swimming pool. He told Connie he had bought a house for his mother who really lived down the road, and houses for his brothers back in Chicago.

". . . And when I said our daughter wouldn't want for nothing, I meant it," he continued, showing Tracey her bedroom. It was twice the size of Connie's living room back at her bungalow home in Chicago. Sure, Connie could afford a bigger house, but timing was everything, and she was trying to get her own business off the ground first so she could maintain her next home.

Connie insisted that Tracey didn't need all of what Jet was offering to her.

"Tracey always wanted you and your time, not things, Jet" Connie reminded him. As the evening wound down, Tracey went to sleep in her room, and Connie sat down and talked with Sabrina and Jet. Sabrina did seem like a nice woman, who had her head on straight. Connie learned Sabrina had insisted that Jet make time for Tracey, because she herself never had a father in her life, and Connie respected her point-of-view.

Together, they worked out a visiting schedule for Jet to get Tracey every other summer, holiday, and every other birthday. Before Connie left, she hugged and kissed her daughter goodbye, and promised she would be back to get her after the holiday break.

On Christmas Day, Connie opened the small box the Jet had given to her as a gift. Inside the box was a beautiful gold bracelet with diamonds with a card that read, *'Thank you for raising my daughter.'*

"*My* daughter?" Connie frowned. "He acts like I was doing *him* a favor."

"Oh Connie lighten up," May said, as she helped Lydia unwrap her gifts.

"Here you can have this one, I don't want it," Connie handed May the bracelet.

"Are you sure you don't want it?" May was already snapping it around her wrist before Connie could change her mind.

"I'm fine. I need to get ready to meet Dean for a quick lunch. The nerve of Jet!" Connie stormed off upstairs.

Connie caught up with Dean on Christmas evening for a quick bite to eat at Leo's Pizza. After small talk, they shared a Chicago Style deep dish pepperoni pizza.

"How is little Dean?" Connie asked, taking a small bite of her pizza.

"He's good. I talked to him last night on the phone. He seems to be having a good time with his cousins at his maternal grandmother's house for the holiday break."

"Tracey is spending her holiday with Jet. I still can't believe he called out of the blue like that."

"Sounds like he's trying to impress Sabrina. Let's just hope if they should break up, that he will still be interested in Tracey."

"I hope so. I can't allow him to come and go as he pleases. That's not healthy for a child. Tracey needs stability regardless of who he may be trying to impress. If things don't work out with him and Sabrina than he should still stick to the schedule we worked out for visitation."

Dean nodded. "I agree."

"So I thought about you while I was in New York, and I got you something," Connie pulled out two wrapped gift boxes from the bag sitting next to her in the booth.

"I was wondering why you brought that bag in here."

"Go on, open them," Connie beamed a bright smile.

Dean wiped his hands and mouth with a napkin, then proceeded to open the boxes.

"Oh this is nice," Dean held up a pair of gloves with a matching scarf and hat. Inside the other box was a pair of earmuffs and long-johns.

"While you're out there in the hawk working your beat, those should keep you nice and warm so you won't catch a cold."

"Perfect timing," Dean grinned. "You know the Big Sting I've been telling you about is about to go down soon. I will need to dress warm when we go out to raid the projects."

"Please be careful Dean. I get so worried when you tell me about things like that. I know it's your job, but those projects are filled with some pretty tough cats that aren't afraid of cops."

"Aw don't worry about it. I didn't just do push-ups and jumping jacks at the Illinois Police Academy for two years you know. I'm trained at this. Trust me, I know what I'm doing," he replied proudly. "Here, I brought something for you too," Dean reached inside his coat pocket and slid a velvet box across the table.

Connie's heart raced with anticipation as to what could be inside. She slowly lifted the lid, and her eyes sparkled at the beautiful pair of gold hoop earrings. "These are beautiful. Thank you Dean!"

"You're welcome. Glad you like them. Listen baby, sorry to be short with our date. But, I gotta' split. I need to take care of some business."

"I understand. It was good to see you again Dean. I missed you."

"I missed you too," Dean leaned across the table and Connie leaned in towards him at the same time until their lips puckered a quick kiss. They both looked forward to the next time . . .

At the Radio Station . . .

One night when Connie arrived at the station, her booth was filled with red roses. She thought it was from a fan, until she read the card that said, *'You are truly something special. I look forward to spending more time with you- Dean.'*

"Tell that cop dude to send flowers to your house next time. I got rose pedals all over my seat, and I can barely sit down in this booth," Smokey complained, turning green with envy. He knew Connie had lots of male fans, but to him, this Dean person seemed like he was turning into someone special, and he didn't like that one bit.

"Ladies, have you ever been in love?" Connie asked her listeners. "Call us here at WCHI and tell us what love song makes you feel like the jones is coming on." The phone lights lit up, but Smokey got upset.

"That's not what tonight's program is about. We're talking about break ups, and you're asking callers if they ever been in love," he argued.

"We have been talking about break ups for the past week, and I'm sick of it!"

Billy barged into the studio. "Answer the damn phones!" he shouted at both of them.

"Just because you and the cop are hittin' it off doesn't mean everybody else is."

"I'm sorry your social life is in the dumps, Smokey."

"Humph, I have a social life, baby; I was just wondering what was taking *you* so long!"

"You're such a jerk!" Connie snapped.

"I said knock it off!" Billy raised his voice. "Now kiss and make up before I send both of you home for acting like two children."

Smokey and Connie glared at each other, and then at the switchboard. There were no more lights lit up. Connie and Smokey burst out laughing. They knew it was stupid to argue. No there were no more callers.

Selena Haskins

CHAPTER TWENTY-ONE

THE BIG STING
January in Chicago . . .

People were screaming and doors opened and slammed. Peaches thought she was hallucinating since she had been up all night "speed balling." She loved the new high she felt from using heroin and cocaine at the same time. As she lay across the bare floor, she shook her head and blinked her eyes, tried to shake off what she thought was hallucination. But, the screams got louder. She crawled up off the floor and looked around her near-empty living room, feeling disoriented by the sounds. She wasn't sure if they were in her head or happening for real until her front door came crashing down.

"Put your hands up in the air right now!" shouted one of the armed police officers. The rest of the SWAT team ran through her apartment with huge guns in their hands, and police dogs ran around to find drugs.

"I DIDN'T DO ANYTHING!" Peaches screamed. Her high took off and ran with her fears.

"GET UP RIGHT NOW!" Dean shouted at her, but she could barely move.

A policeman named Jack, who was part of the SWAT team, grew impatient. He snatched Peaches up by her hair and threw her against the wall. "The officer said get up, so get up, you stinky junkie!"

"Hey, Jack! Take it easy, man!" Dean told him. He read Peaches her rights and handcuffed her.

"I ain't do nothing!" Peaches cried.

"That's what they all say," Dean stated to her.

"Hey Wilson, the dogs found this dope in the bathroom, and syringes. It's about a kilo of heroin," said Parker, another member from the SWAT team.

"That's not mine!" Peaches shouted at Parker.

While Dean collected the evidence, Jack snatched Peaches by the handcuffs and rushed her out the door. When they got to the steps, he

154

looked over his shoulder to make sure Dean didn't see him, and then he kicked Peaches hard in the back with his boot. She fell down the first flight of stairs and busted her nose and mouth. She had to be treated for her wounds outside before she could get into the back of the police car.

"Do you know why you're here?" Detective White asked Peaches in the interrogation room at the precinct. A public defender who'd told Peaches his name was Peter sat down next to her.

"No I don't know why I'm here, but I know ya'll pigs been harassing me!"

"Nobody harassed you, Peaches. Now listen, we found a kilo of heroin in your apartment," Detective White informed her.

"Ain't mine!"

"Then whose is it?" Dean interjected.

Peaches shrugged her shoulders. "Don't know."

"Fifteen to twenty years is what you're looking at. Now we know your boyfriend Poncho is a drug kingpin, so if you testify against him, maybe we can work out a deal," Dean told her.

"Look, I said I don't know!"

"Peaches, you got priors, and you're already on probation for possession of a controlled substance. This kilo of heroin will put you away for a long time, maybe longer than twenty years," Dean reminded her.

"You don't want to miss this, do you?" Detective White slid a small package of heroin across the table in front of Peaches. She shook with anticipation at the thought of using it. Her pupils widened and her arms started to itch, but she couldn't scratch herself because she was handcuffed to the chair.

"Don't taunt her," Peter warned.

"We're not taunting her," Dean replied.

"Peaches, testify against Poncho and we'll protect you," Detective White said.

"How in the hell you expect me to believe that when one of ya'll officers threw me down a flight of stairs?"

"You tell us who bought the kilo, and we will place you in the Witness Protection Program. You won't serve any time in jail at all," Dean stated.

"I ain't telling you pigs nothing. Just gimme my time."

"Are you sure about this?" Peter asked her.

Peaches threw up her head defiantly. "Yep, just give me my time!"

"So are you pleading guilty?" Dean made sure the tape recorder was on.

"I said gimme my time."

"Donna "Peaches" Morris, myself and Detective White are asking if you are pleading guilty to the crime of possessing one kilo of heroin, knowing that you could serve up to twenty years in prison. Do you plead guilty or not guilty?" Dean reiterated.

"Give me my time."

"Are we to understand that as guilt, Ms. Morris?"

"You can understand that I'm not telling ya'll who it belongs to!"

"Well the drugs were in your apartment and they are considered yours unless you tell us who the heroin belongs to."

"I'm done talking," Peaches gritted her teeth.

"Lock her up. She will go before the judge and stand trial; let the judge decide her time," Dean said to the officer standing in the corner of the room.

"Hold up, I need to make a phone call," Peaches said. Naturally, Dean and Detective White were suspicious.

"You can't do that unless we have permission to listen in," White told her.

"Look, I need to call my sister, all right?"

"What's her name?" Dean asked, ready to jot it down on a notepad.

"Connie, Connie Morris. Folks call her Cat these days," Peaches said, twisting her lips. "She works at the radio station. I don't know the number; I was just gonna dial the operator and get it."

"Connie Morris is not your sister," Dean chuckled, assuming she was still high.

"She is my sister, nigga, how you gonna tell me?"

"If Connie Morris is your sister, than Billy Dee Williams is my brother."

"Just because she's light-skinned with long hair and green eyes don't mean she ain't my sister. She got white folk in her blood, that's all, but that don't make her better than me," Peaches grumbled.

"That wasn't what I was going to say." Dean stopped the tape recorder, as this was getting way too personal.

"She got a White Daddy, all right? We don't have the same father, but we came from the same womb, raised in the same damn projects in Cabrini Green," Peaches uttered. "She may be big time now, but we both had to eat cereal from the same damn bowl. That's how poor we were!"

"You're a ghetto drug addict, and no matter what you say, Connie Morris is not your sister. It's just not possible. I don't care about you two not looking alike. It just doesn't make sense for you to be her sister. Connie is a woman with class. She's intelligent, gifted, ambitious, but you . . . you are everything but that!"

Peaches became filled with rage, but could do nothing with her hands cuffed.

"Screw you! You don't know my life!" Peaches spat at Dean, but missed. Dean's reflexes quickly reached out, and before his hand could strike her face, Detective White stopped him.

"Wilson! Wilson! Don't do that!" Detective White shouted. "Listen! Everybody calm down, all right!"

"You are insulting my client!" Peter, the public defender jumped up from his chair.

Dean ignored Detective White and Peter. "You listen to me," he pointed his finger on Peaches' nose. "It is my business. If you say Connie is your sister, I need to know why you're a junkie and she's not. Why would a successful woman like her not reach back and help her own sister? Why? Tell me why right now!"

Peaches blew hot air through her lips and rolled her eyes to the ceiling. "Man, I don't have to tell you nothing, since you think you know everything. Find out for yourself!"

"Dean, go get yourself some water and come back in a minute," Detective White told him.

Dean left the room and walked over to one of the desk of a young rookie cop. "I want you to pull Donna Morris' entire record. I want to know her family history and even her blood type within the next five minutes. I want everything on her family, especially her sister Connie Morris."

"Yes sir," said the young ambitious officer. Dean walked over to the water cooler, gulped down some water, and took a break outside. He wasn't sure what kind of woman Connie was or had been, now that he had met her sister. He wondered if Connie was a former drug-addict.

He thought to himself, *Maybe Connie's got a record; maybe she's got something to hide. Maybe she used to be a junkie like her sister.* By the time he went back to the rookie cop, he handed Dean a thick file folder. It was filled with newspaper clippings, records, and everything.

"Thank you. Good job," Dean patted him on the back. The rookie smiled like Dean was the president. As Dean read the files, his heart began to race. He not only learned that Peaches was in fact Connie's sister, but she was also the sister of Gina "Baby" Morris, whose case he helped solve back in 1972, just eight years ago. "Unbelievable," Dean mumbled to himself and shook his head. "I can't believe this."

"Here, call your sister," Dean said to Peaches when he returned to the interrogation room. He now knew why Connie had looked so familiar to him. He was usually good with names and faces. He questioned himself, *how could I be so desperate? How could I let myself feel so strongly for someone like Connie, who is from the ghetto? No wonder she said when we first met that she didn't like cops.*

Detective White sat the phone in front of Peaches, dialed the phone number, and pressed the speakerphone button.

"Hello?" answered May.

"Who dis?" Peaches asked.

"This is May, who is this?"

"Let me talk to my sister."

"Peaches? Wow, I haven't heard from you in years!"

"Yeah it's Peaches. Let me talk to my sister, I don't have all night!"

"Say please. You don't have to be rude."

"Heifer put my sister on the phone or the next time I see you, I'mma bust your head to the white meat!"

"If she hadn't talked to you in so long, I would hang up the phone."

"Yeah yeah yeah," Peaches said, slouched down in the chair.

"Hello?" answered Connie. Hearing Connie's voice made Dean feel anxious. He wanted to jump in and say right away what was going on and how he felt. Connie had mentioned to him that she had sisters and that one died, but never went into any details. Still, Dean felt they talked often enough for her to have divulged that information.

"Wassup?" Peaches spoke into the phone.

"Peaches? Are you okay? Where are you? I've been worried sick about you!"

"Can't tell. You haven't been looking for me."

"The last we talked, you refused to get help. What was I supposed to do?"

"Well I'm about to get locked up for fifteen to twenty, how about that?"

"What?!"

"I'm not rattin' out nobody. They tryin' to say they can put me in some Witness Protection Program if I drop a dime on my supplier."

"Fifteen to twenty years?" Connie was in shock. "Peaches, BJ will be a grown man. He won't even know you."

"Hell, he doesn't know me now. He's adopted!"

"I think you should reconsider, Peaches," Connie cautioned. "That's a long time in prison."

"Yeah, well keep in touch with my son BJ," Peaches told her. She didn't want to get emotional, so she quickly told the cop to hang up the phone. Dean felt somewhat different about the situation; it seemed Connie did care about her sister after all, but he still felt a bit inadequate about his involvement with Connie. He felt he didn't really know her as well as he thought.

"One more call. Dial my father; see if he care," Peaches pouted. Dean looked up the phone number, and then dialed it. Again the call was put on speakerphone. A woman answered the phone.

"I need to speak to Mason Morris."

"May I ask who is calling, please?" a woman asked.

"His daughter, Peaches."

"Daughter?"

"Yeah I'm his oldest daughter, fool."

"I'm sorry, you must be mistaken. Mason's oldest daughter is Marie, and she's in high school."

"Well, looka here, Miss, I don't know what he told you, but I'm his daughter. He got two daughters; me and Connie Morris. Now I'm about to go to jail, and I figured it's time I tell him how he ruined my life, so put him on the phone, you home wrecker!"

"I beg your pardon!"

"Just put him on the phone!" The woman became afraid, and nearly dropped the phone.

"Hello?" Mason answered. Peaches remembered his mean, stern voice. He sounded exactly the same, only sober.

"What's up, you jive turkey?"

"Come again?" Mason got upset. He wondered who had the guts to call his house and speak that way to him.

"It's your daughter, Peaches. I just called to tell you that we know all about you and your *other* family. It's your fault that Mama and Baby are dead! When Mama wrote you letters begging for help, you turned your back on the family and you killed us. Now I'm going to jail for fifteen to twenty years while your half-white daughter Connie is living the life you *never* wanted her to have." Peaches went on and on as if she had been holding it in. "I'm hooked on the junk 'cause of you. If you care to visit me look me up in Cook County Jail."

"I'm sorry, you got the wrong number and the wrong guy!"

"I doubt that."

"You will pay for this," Mason sneered in a whisper.

"Make me, punk! I dare you! You can't beat me! Not no more, I'm grown!"

CLICK! Mason slammed the phone down.

"Man, come on and lock me up, because I ain't telling on nobody. I ain't afraid of prison, but I'm more scared of bullets," Peaches said.

"Funny, you're afraid of getting shot, but you're not afraid of dying from heroin use. Ironies," Dean said.

"Screw you!" Peaches shouted. "I lived hard, nigga, and I lived rough. Ain't nobody done nothing for me. My Mama kicked me out when I got pregnant, so don't nobody give a damn about Peaches but Peaches!"

"Right, neither does the guy that gave you the dope. He doesn't care either. That's why you should put him in a place where he belongs," Detective White interjected.

"Shut-up and lock me up!"

"Are you sure about this?" Peter asked.

"What do you care, huh? You pencil-head sucker!"

"Call me whatever you want, but this is your last chance. I'm not going to file any appeals for you."

"Screw you! You get a check whether I get locked up or not!"

"Peaches, we want you to sleep on this tonight, because we know you're a bit high," said Dean. A very small part of him felt sorry for her.

"I don't need to sleep on it! Lock me up! Just lock me up!"

Peaches arraignment was Monday morning. Connie sat and listened as Peaches testified not guilty. She refused to accept any plea deal. A trial date was set, and after a one-day trial, the jury deliberated in less than an hour.

"Donna Peaches Morris, the jury has found you guilty. By federal law you shall be sentenced to fifteen years in prison for possession of narcotics without parole. Case dismissed," the judge slammed her gavel.

Connie rushed towards the front of the courtroom from the public galley, into her sister's arms. "Oh Peaches! Oh God, I wish this wasn't happening to you!" Connie cried.

Peaches eyes watered as she blinked back tears.

"You're all I got don't leave me Sis. Please don't leave me!" Connie's chest shivered against Peaches.

"I didn't do this Sis. I didn't," Peaches and Connie locked eyes and Connie could see that deep down Peaches was really telling the truth.

"Can you appeal?" Connie asked her.

"How? These public attorneys don't care about people like me," Peaches griped, as the officers stepped between her and Connie and handcuffed her hands.

"I can get you a lawyer Peaches."

"Connie, I don't need your money. I don't need nothing from nobody. I'm a damn junkie, if I die in here so what! I'm half dead anyway."

"Don't say that," Connie hugged her one last time before the officer told her to step back so they could take Peaches away.

"I love you!" Connie shouted, as the officers escorted Peaches out of the courtroom.

Connie dropped to her knees right there in the courtroom, and cried. She knew by the time Peaches got out of jail it would be 1995. Connie felt sorry for her sister Peaches. And guilty settled in her heart, as tears streamed down her cheeks. She wished her sister could have had a share in her success, but instead she was going to jail. Peaches looked over her shoulders and saw Connie on the floor of the court. Their eyes caught one last glimpse at each other, although the look they gave each other was a goodbye, their hearts would always be connected by the childhood past they once shared.

"Let me give you a hand," Detective White extended his hand to help Connie up off the floor. "I'm sorry about your sister."

"She's all the family I had left," Connie wiped her tears.

Detective White, who had testified in court against Peaches, hugged Connie.

"If Peaches told us whose heroin it was maybe she wouldn't have to spent so much time in jail or any time at all," Detective White explained. "She didn't want to rat out her boyfriend Poncho. Living up to the code of the streets just ain't worth it. Now she's hurt herself, she's hurt you, and she will probably never ever see her poor son again."

"I don't need to hear all this jive you laying on me. You probably just satisfied to see another black person going to jail."

"You got it wrong. I do care. I've cared about you and your family since Baby Gina was murdered and your mother died. I tried to help Peaches I really did."

"Well it didn't work now did it?" Connie sniffed, snatched up her purse and brushed by him.

"I'm really sorry Connie."

"Yeah . . . sure you are."

CHAPTER TWENTY-TWO

CAREER WHOAS

WCHI-93.3 Soul won the National Radio Programming Award for Urban Music, and was invited to Radio City Music Hall to accept the award. For Connie, it felt bittersweet to be accepting an award while her sister was in jail. She hired a new lawyer for Peaches, but Peaches refused her. "Your sister is sick. She needs rehab before anybody can help her with her case," the attorney explained to Connie. "I went to see her and she was so high that I could barely understand what she was saying. I'm sorry, but I can't represent her."

After the ceremony, the staff along with celebrity guests went to Studio 54 that night to celebrate. Connie had one too many drinks. She intentionally tried to drink away her sorrows that she felt for her sister Peaches, but the results were a blasting headache that next morning.

Connie took some Excedrin, and went to meet with Mr. Yancy, a new radio owner in New York who had been shopping Connie for the past few weeks.

"Despite WCHI winning an award for your nighttime show, Pillow Talk, you know Billy has been shopping you," Mr. Yancy said, puffing a cigar behind his desk, as he stared at Connie with his blue eyes.

"I should be surprised but I'm not," Connie replied, crossing one leg over the other.

"I would never treat you the way Billy does or none of those sorry bastards at WCHI. You deserve better, Connie. I've been watching you since you were a rookie in this business, and I'm impressed with how you turned a low-budget and low rated urban radio station like WCHI into a hot award winning station in all of the mid-west," Mr. Yancy explained. "You should be making more money and you should be much bigger than what you are right now. People all over the U.S. should know you."

"I suppose you're next line will be an offer promising the same crap that Billy did."

"I'm not Billy," Mr. Yancy, spun around in his leather chair, glanced out the window at the New York City skyline. "Come over here to this window. Look at how beautiful this city is." Connie walked over and stood next to him.

"New York needs you Connie, Billy wasn't smart enough to make you the face of broadcasting all over Chicago, but I will make you the face in all of New York and not just with your own people. You will be famous with everyone.

"I don't need fame. All I want is to be able to live comfortably and take care of my daughter."

"That's what I like about you Connie. You don't ask for much, but you give a lot. That's why I need you to help me to build a radio station right here in New York City. I will double what WCHI is paying you, I will let you do your own concert promoting on the side, but you must give the station ten percent from your gigs if you advertise on the airways–that's all I ask. You can do commercials, you can act, model, whatever you want. Just bring me listeners all over New York. You make me happy and I will make you happy."

"If I take this deal, it's going to mean a lot to just pack up and move you know."

"I'll give you money to relocate that you don't have to pay it back."

"I don't want to work at night. I want my own morning show so I can spend time with my daughter in the evenings, and I also want a signing bonus."

"Anything else?" he asked, pausing and blowing smoke from his cigar.

"Then I still have to think about it, I have . . . someone . . . a love interest, and–"

"Tell him to move to New York," Mr. Yancy cut her off.

"But, he has his own career too."

Mr. Yancy heaved a long sigh. "Connie, let me give you a piece of advice sweetheart," he plucked ashes from his cigar into an ashtray on his desk. "If it's love, then whatever you decide to do with your life, it will last. Just remember this opportunity is rare. Decide carefully," he said, his voice sounding firm. He stared at her through dark-framed glasses that rested on the bridge of his long big nose. "Besides, WCHI won't be on top forever. We're in the 80's now, and disco is becoming a thing of the past. What will Billy do to stay afloat? See, I always like to stay on top. Always! Think about yourself, Connie, and your daughter. Think about the change in times and music. There is no better place in this country that keeps up with the trends like New York."

Connie felt Mr. Yancy had a point. It was a lot to think about.

"This is a one-time deal sweetheart. I already bought the building and I'm reading to renovate it into a station as quickly as possible. I don't like waiting, so don't take long to get back with me on your answer."

Back to the "Chi"

When Connie returned to Chicago, the first person she wanted to see was Dean. He had seemed a little distant when she told him she was flying out to New York for the awards ceremony. She called him and asked if he wanted to go out to dinner, and he offered her to come to his house instead. They decided to go grocery shopping together, and Dean picked out what he wanted her to fix for dinner. He was really trying to see if she could cook, and Connie threw down in his kitchen.

She baked potatoes stuffed with bacon and cheese, and sour cream. She steamed some broccoli and topped it with a light buttery sauce, and then broiled steaks and finished with gravy and onions. Dean enjoyed the meal so much that he went back for seconds. While eating, the two filled each other in on what had been going on in their lives, and had small talk about things happening in the community. Despite the good meal, Dean still couldn't get past the idea that Peaches and Baby were Connie's sisters. He felt he needed a better understanding to move forward.

". . . And during the big sting, I arrested a woman who I discovered was actually your sister, Peaches," Dean said, casually, trying to feel his way with Connie, to see how she would react.

"Really?"

"I was wondering why you never told me she was sick in that way," Dean finished up his second course and wiped his mouth with a napkin.

"I didn't think our relationship had anything to do with her. Did you?"

"Yes, it would've been good to know. To be honest, knowing that Peaches and Gina were your sisters took me off guard. I felt betrayed, to be honest with you," Dean vented. "Did you know Detective White and I helped solve Gina's case?"

"Really? Wow!"

"And you're so blasé about this, and I don't understand why."

"I'm not blasé. I do find it ironic that you helped solve my sister's case. That part is a bit of a surprise more so than the arrest of my sister. She was out there, unfortunately. It would have been a matter of time before you or another cop had arrested her. I'm just glad she was found alive," Connie explained. "I've been trying to help my sister for years, but she refused my help."

"Connie, honestly, this is not sitting well with me." Dean tossed his napkin on the plate.

"Dean, it's my sister who is sick, not me!" Connie was starting to be a little rattled. "When people are ready to talk about private things, they will tell you. Hell, I never pushed you to tell me about your ex-wife and why you divorced," she reminded him. "I never pushed you to tell me about your brother Johnny, who you told me died when he was young. I'm not going to impose."

"And I would never force your hand either, Connie," Dean argued. "Look, I know that some things aren't everybody's business, and I know it takes time to get to know someone. All I'm saying is that . . .."

"Do you feel different about me now that you know my past? Yes, I'm from Cabrini Green. Yes, I had a sister who was murdered. And yes, I have a sister who is in jail and sick on the junk, but does that change how you feel about *me?*" Connie asked bluntly, cutting him off.

"I would be lying if I said no."

"Dean, everything that you have ever asked me, I told you the truth."

"Yes, but not the whole truth, Connie."

"Well Dean, I'm not an open book, you know. I have some discretion with myself. Some details I was hoping to fill you in on as we continue to get to know each other. What you know should be enough for now."

"Maybe I should go into a little bit more details about me. You see, my ex-wife trapped me into marrying her. The marriage was doomed to fail since the beginning, and—"

"Dean, volunteering your past to me is not going to make me share mine with you. If you feel like you have to go behind my back and pull up whatever files are out there about me or my family in order to find out the truth, then we don't need to see each other anymore."

"Connie, I want you to know my past so that there are no secrets between us."

Connie abruptly got up from the table. In the back of her mind, she thought about what Mr. Yancy had said: *if it is love it can wait.* Suddenly the idea of accepting Mr. Yancy's offer felt closer to a yes than a no.

Dean followed her into the kitchen. "Baby, look, I'm sorry. Let's not have dinner this way. The past should stay where it belongs."

"You know, Dean; this is exactly why I felt reserved about dating you. You think because you're a cop that it entitles you to know every detail about my life. That's unfair." Connie shook her head in disgust as she paused to wrap her unfinished plate with aluminum foil. "I'm not one of your cases."

"I never said you were one of my cases, did I?" Dean attempted to hug her and make things right, but Connie shoved him away.

"I'm going home."

"But Connie—"

She threw up her hand and went for her coat.

"Please don't go, Connie!"

"Goodnight, Dean."

Dean thought about it. He knew there was nothing he could do to calm the situation, so he didn't go after her the way he wanted to.

When Connie got home, she called Tracey, who was in still in Buffalo with her father. She was scheduled to come home that weekend. Jet's mother was coming to Chicago for a visit, and the two would fly in together.

"Mommy, I love Daddy's house. It's bigger than our house. I want to live with Daddy. Mommy, can I?"

"No honey. Chicago is your home, but you can visit with him again soon."

"Aw, Mom!" Tracey sighed. "But Daddy has a swimming pool and we don't."

"One day, we will."

"We will?"

"Yes."

"When?"

"I'm not sure, honey, but do you miss Mommy? I miss you."

"Yeah I miss you, and I miss May and Lydia too."

"Good. I love you, and I'll see you when you come home this weekend."

"Okay. I gotta go. Sabrina just fixed my peanut butter and jelly sandwich."

"Enjoy it, and I'll see you soon. I love you."

"Love you too, bye." Tracey quickly hung up the phone.

Connie was glad Tracey was enjoying herself, but she missed her. A part of her actually felt jealous that Jet could offer Tracey more. On the other hand, Connie knew that Tracey's love could not be bought. She knew she was a good mother to Tracey. She thought maybe she was having self-doubts because of what had happened with her and Dean, and the next day at the station she wanted to talk about trust issues on *Pillow Talk*.

"Chitown, have you ever dated someone, and everything seemed so right between you two, and then one small thing seems to throw a wrench in your mix? Chicago, this is Cat Morris on the *Pillow Talk*. Give me a call and let me know your thoughts," The phone lines immediately started lighting up with callers. She and Smokey couldn't keep up with the calls.

"Thanks so much for your thoughts tonight. We're sorry we can't take any more calls, but I want to leave you with a song called, *I Try* by Angela Bolfill. Sometimes that's all we can do. I'm Cat Morris."

"And I'm Smokey Jay."

"Goodnight, Chicago!"

"You okay?" Smokey asked Connie once they were off the air.

"I'm cool. Let's go grab a drink."

Smokey and Connie hit up one of the nightclubs and sat at the bar to have a few drinks.

"Billy is letting us go," Smokey admitted.

"Us? I thought of all people he was keeping you."

"Billy won't be around much longer, either. The owner wants to change WCHI into a rock station."

"Is this about that disco protest at Comiskey Park during the Chicago White Sox game last year?"

Smokey sighed. "I'm afraid so."

"But we just won that award in New York."

"I know, but the owners want to broaden the audience, move in another direction outside of disco, R&B, and Latino music."

"No wonder Ray told me he's moving to New York next month," Connie thought out loud. "Maybe he could see the ship going down and he jumped off just in time," Connie finished the rest of her Tequila. She thought about telling Smokey about her offer to work in New York, but decided against it, since she hadn't decided to take it yet anyway.

"I got a few record companies who have verbally committed to working with CMP Concert Promotions."

"Good for you. At least you have something lined up when this is over."

Connie's eyes shifted from her empty glass to Smokey's depressing facial expression.

"Despite how much of a jerk you've been Smokey, I think you were right when you said we make a good team."

"So, what are you saying?" Smokey raised a brow.

"I'm saying I can't run a business alone."

"Are you for real or is the alcohol talking?"

"I'm for real."

"I want a full-partnership and we can split the money straight down the middle," Smokey perked up with excitement. "And I want to help call the shots. We work as a team and I will even put some of my money into the company."

"Welcome to CMP!" Connie and Smokey clicked their glasses.

"So uhm . . . you and that cop dude okay? You were having a moment tonight at the station."

"I hope we are."

"Well if he messes up, I would love to take his place," he winked.

"Boy, get outta here!"

"I'm serious."

"Whatever, Smokey!" Connie laughed. "I'm drunk, not stupid."

"At least I tried," Smokey helped Connie put on her leather jacket.

"Come on let's get out of here and you drive," Connie tossed him the keys to her car.

"Good night fellas!" Smokey waved to the bartenders.

"Ya'll have a good night and be careful out there!"

CHAPTER TWENTY-THREE

IT'S BEEN TOO LONG

*M*ay had a new boyfriend named Roscoe, and told Connie they had gotten engaged. Connie barely knew Roscoe and had only met him twice. He barely spoke, and seemed mentally challenged.

"Are you sure you want to marry this guy?" Connie asked.

"Yes. He's sitting on old money, girl, and owns acres of land down in Florida."

"So you're marrying this guy for money?"

"Of course not, I love him," May said matter-of-factly.

"I just think the guy is weird," Connie admitted. "You should be careful. He seems a bit strange."

"Oh, Roscoe is okay. He doesn't talk much with you, but he got lots to say with me, especially in the bedroom.

"Oh, here we go again!"

May laughed. "Don't get jealous because you blew it *again* with Dean."

"Not me. Not this time."

"You two will never get it right, so just bang each other's brains out and move on with your lives."

"*I* am *not* just a bang."

"Well, excuse me."

"You're crazy for marrying a man with an I.Q. of zero."

"Oh, to hell with you!" May hit her playfully, but Connie was serious. She knew May was marrying Roscoe for his money. Roscoe wasn't smart enough to know any better, and she kind of felt sorry for him.

Dean took a long overdue vacation. He and Dean Jr. went to Hawaii, and left the winter hawk of Chicago behind for two weeks. He was able to get plenty of rest, and he was feeling refreshed. He had plenty of time to spend with his son, and he was enjoying the weather. They went on several excursions, ate fine cuisines, and participated in several Luaus. When he returned home, he decided to hook up with his cousin Hank, whom he hadn't seen in a while. The two met up at the pool hall . . .

"So what happened to that radio chick, Cat?" Hank asked, after Dean finished talking about his trip to Hawaii. Hank leaned over the table with his cue stick, aiming at the solid color ball, and shot it.

"Didn't work out," Dean took a swallow of his Colt 45.

"Why not?"

"She wasn't the woman I thought she was."

"What's that supposed to mean?"

"I thought she was one way, but when I got the skinny on her background, turns out she's a chick from the projects with a drug addict sister. Matter of fact, her youngest sister was Gina "Baby"."

"Do you mean, the little girl who was murdered by her classmate?" Hank recalled.

"Yeah, the one I helped solve the case."

"So did she lie and tell you she didn't live in the projects?" Hank asked, shooting the ball. It went directly into the hole, so he took another turn.

"No, she never really elaborated. She just said she grew up in a tough neighborhood and had a sister who died, and that she also lost her mother."

"Oh! So let me get this straight; she's no longer in the projects, but you found this entire thing out anyway. And what else did you find out?"

"Nothing, I just didn't know she was the sister to Gina "Baby" and had a junkie sister."

Hank raised his eyes from the pool table and looked across at his young cousin. "What in the hell does this have to do with the two of you?"

Dean smirked. "I don't know. That's what Connie said."

"So she's from the hood. At least she made it out of there, and even if she didn't, what's that have to do with you hittin' the skins?"

"Man, it's got nothing to do with the skins. Besides, we never got that far."

"Basically, youngblood, what I'm trying to say, is as long as the chick ain't kill nobody before and she's not using or selling drugs herself, I don't see what the problem is." Dean took the next shot since Hank missed his second turn.

"You want a middle-class woman, college degree, church going, somebody you can take home to meet your Mama and Daddy, and ain't nothing wrong with that, except nobody comes in a complete package these days. Besides, you got issues with your father that you still need to work out. Does Connie know why you two barely speak? I mean, did you tell her what happened to your brother Johnny?"

"Not yet, I'll tell her when it's time."

"Oooh," Hank laughed sarcastically. "So it's okay for you to tell her stuff you want her to know when it's time, but it's not okay for her."

Dean thought about it for a moment. *Maybe I was selfish.*

"The way you explained Cat, it sounded like you were madly in love with her, so you can't let something small as that stop you from moving forward if that's what you want," Hank expressed. "Is she who you want?"

"I do, actually."

"Then do what you need to do." Hank took the next shot and won the game. "Yo' check it. I got a new broad from Indiana named Rebecca, a white chick with money galore, and she gave me all this cash. Money is no object with her. I wine and dine her, lay the pipe down on her good, and I get whatever I want. I'm going to use that money and go on a cruise to Jamaica with my main lady, Contessa."

"You better watch yourself, man, your dirt will catch up with you one day," Dean warned.

"Never that brother. I'm too smooth, but you, on the hand, always trying to be a Romeo, but end up losing your Juliet."

"Tease me all you want, but I think I'll go for it this time."

"Before you get too serious, let me meet her and check her out."

"If she takes me back I will. Connie can be pretty tough at times."

"That's on the surface. Every woman got a weak spot, and if Connie is tough like that, it's usually for a reason. She's probably a woman scorned, and all you gots to do is let her know you're sincere. Do right by her and you can tear down those walls around her heart."

"How do you know so much about love, but you never take it seriously yourself?"

"I haven't found the right one yet, but I do know my women. Contessa is a little bit like Connie. I have to win over her heart."

"Yeah, and get what in return, you gigolo!"

"Honestly, I don't want anything from her. It's the first time I ever felt that way."

"Hank is in love!"

"I'm not quick to call it love, but I'm digging the broad, that's for sure."

"That's what your mouth says."

"Trust me, youngblood, it's what I know."

Connie was packing her bags for New York so she could go to discuss her new contract with Mr. Yancy and her lawyers while May, Roscoe, Tracey and Lydia went to see the movie *Superman*. It was early February, and she and Dean hadn't seen each other in a month, so she assumed it was over between them. Connie had planned on taking Tracey with her to New York because May and Roscoe were going house-hunting. Besides, Jet wanted to see Tracey again, so after Connie was scheduled to meet with Mr. Yancy, she would make the trip from NYC to Buffalo. She would be in New York for at least a week, a planned vacation she had gotten approved for. After she packed her bags, she started packing Tracey's when she heard the phone ringing.

"Hello?"

"Hello, how are you?"

"I'm fine, and yourself?"

"Good, now that I hear your voice."

Connie smiled behind the phone. It was so good to hear from Dean.

"I'm wrapping up things on my beat, and I was wondering if I could stop by and bring your favorite ice cream with me."

"You remembered?"

"Oh, come on, it hasn't been that long. Give me some credit."

Connie laughed lightly.

"I'll be there in twenty minutes. Do you need anything else?"

"No thanks."

Connie suddenly felt like a teenager who had been waiting to hear back from her boyfriend. She jumped into the shower, cleaned up, then slipped into a pair of Jordace jeans and a red Charlie's Angels T-shirt. She snatched the giant-sized rollers out of her hair and ran her fingers through the curls. She smiled at herself in the mirror, puckered her red lips, and headed downstairs.

"Strawberry," Connie smiled, kissing Dean's cheek. "You did remember."

"I never forgot." Dean said, as they sat down on the couch.

"Listen, I just want to say I'm really sorry for the way I overreacted when I found out about your family," Dean explained, looking her in the eyes.

"I accept your apology, but I hope it doesn't keep happening so we can get things moving. I feel like things are stop-and-go with us."

"I know, and I apologize," Dean took hold of her hand. "Since my divorce this whole dating thing is new to me. Learning to trust is a big thing with me."

Connie nodded. "I understand."

"I guess what I'm trying to say is, I am going to make mistakes along the way."

"I may be younger than you, but I do know when it comes to relationships, it's a learning process," Connie gently stated. "You have to give me a little rope and trust me too."

"I'll try."

"You want something to drink?" she offered, not wanting to drag out the night talking about the past.

"Sure, I'll take some wine."

Connie put the ice cream in the freezer, told Dean that everyone had gone out to see a movie, and then rejoined him on the sofa with glasses of wine.

"Before you called, I was packing for New York."

"You're moving?" Dean sipped his wine.

"I don't know yet, it depends." She gazed into his eyes.

"I guess that means I'm too late," Dean's voice dropped.

"If things work out between us, I'm sure we can work something out where I can commute to work. People do it all the time."

As they sat back and watched TV for a little while, Dean felt himself getting sleepy while Connie was engaged in an episode of *Knots Landing*. He got up and walked over to Connie's collection of music, thumbed through each album until he came across Barry White, and played one of his old classics.

Dean extended his hand, and Connie turned off the TV and started dancing with Dean. She always loved how good Dean smelled. With her cheek pressed against his chest, she could hear the soft bass thump of his heart beating. Dean started singing Barry White's *"I've Got So Much To Give"* softly in Connie's ear. He didn't sound too bad either, Connie thought as he rubbed her lower back.

When the song ended, they stood in the middle of the living room, staring at each other.

"You got moves," Dean's lips curved a smile. "I like the way you–"

'Muah.' Connie cut him off with a kiss on the lips.

"Wow, I wasn't expecting that."

"Was that too fast?" Connie bashfully covered her mouth.

"Um . . . noooo, but if you're going to kiss me," he stretched out his hands and cupped both her cheeks, "it should be like this." He planted a gentle kiss on her lips. It was so warm and gentle, with just enough tongue for Connie to taste its wine sweetness and slow enough for her to capture his rhythm and follow it. The kiss was good—*almost too good*, Dean thought to himself so he broke the kiss.

"What's wrong?" Connie asked in a whisper, eyes half-closed. She was feeling it.

"I don't want you to do anything you're not ready for, and then I end up apologizing again." He tenderly stroked the side of her face.

"Who says I'm not ready?" Connie's eyes danced with his as she took hold of his hand and led him to her bedroom upstairs. She shut the bedroom door behind them. In seconds, they were all over each other working up an erotic heat as they peeled each other's clothes off.

Connie paused for a moment, stared at Dean's amazing body, and thought *'who knew all of this was under this suit?'* She kissed him all over his chest and his neck as the heat of passion rushed through her soul.

"Take me, Dean," she moaned, and he took control over her breasts with his mouth. "Take me," Connie begged. His every touch filled her with electricity. She could no longer handle the foreplay He slipped on a condom and entered her soul. His movements were slow at first, and then increased to a good rhythm, almost calculated. Connie wrapped her long legs tighter around his waist and dug her nails into his lower back. She shivered slowly as they moaned a blissful orgasm. Afterwards, they fell into a deep sleep, cuddling each other. It had been too long, but the wait was worth it.

In the morning, Dean drove Connie and Tracey to the airport, and they gave each other a long kiss goodbye.

"Ewww!" Tracey frowned at them kissing, and covered her eyes with her gloved hands.

"Wow," Connie blushed as she looked up into his dark piercing eyes. "I am coming back, you know?"

"I just wanted you to remember what you're coming back to," he flirted.

"Oh I'll remember," she assured him. She hadn't stop thinking about last night.

"Well, we better go now. I'll call you when I get back."

"Do that."

CHAPTER TWENTY-FOUR

THE VISIT

Peaches was told she had a visitor. The guards escorted her to the visiting room with her hands and feet in chains. Peaches glanced around the room, not knowing who she was looking for. After a few seconds, she grew impatient as she stood there in the middle of the room in her green jail dress.

"Who in the hell is Beth-Ann? I ain't got all day!" Beth-Ann put down her newspaper and waved for Peaches to come to the table in the back of the visiting room. Peaches slowly walked towards her.

"How is my son?" Peaches asked, pulled out the chair from the table to sit down.

"Excuse me?"

"I said, how is my son, how is Barry Junior, you know, BJ?" Peaches asked, assuming she was BJ's adopted mother.

Beth-Ann shook her head. "I'm sorry. You and I haven't met, at least not in person."

Peaches looked at her with a puzzled expression. "Well, what is this about? I mean, do I know you? What's up?"

"You called my husband, Mason."

Peaches eyes bucked. "Oh, so you're my Pop's side chick?"

"Excuse me?"

"You heard me. Couldn't wait til' the ink dried, could you?"

"I'm Mason's wife. I beg your pardon," Beth-Ann stated, holding on tight to her purse. "I know what you had said over the phone that night was true. I found letters from your mother, Frieda. Now it took me a while to come here, and Mason doesn't know. I snuck away while he was at work because I need to know the truth about you, your sisters, and your mother."

"You got a cigarette?" Peaches asked, skipping the subject.

"No, I don't smoke. I'm a Christian."

"I've seen people who claim to be Christians smoke cigarettes. All of ya'll are heathens," Peaches countered. "Now I needs a smoke, so go on over there to the machine and buy me a pack of Newports, then we talk."

"Here," Beth-Ann slid her a few single dollars across the table. "Go get it yourself."

"Hey, watch it, lady! You can't do that in here. If you want me to have money, you gots to send me money order. Don't ever do that. I ain't trying to go to the hole. The feds may think I'm dealing." Beth Ann didn't understand the prison dialect, so to avoid all the confusion she just got up and bought Peaches the cigarettes.

"Yeah, this is it." Peaches dragged on the cigarettes as if she hadn't smoked one in a long time.

"Listen, Donna, I can't be long. I just need to know if your mother's letter to Mason was true."

Peaches laid her head back and slowly blew smoke into the air. One side of her hair was braided, and the other half was combed out in an Afro. Beth-Ann couldn't tell what look she was going for, and neither did Peaches.

"So, what did the letter say?" Peaches asked between smoke circles.

"She said it's three of you and that you were starving and needed clothing, and she said she was still married to him. Is that true?"

"It *was* true. My Mama dead now, and so is my baby sister Gina," Peaches sat up straight in her chair and blew her smoke into Beth-Ann's face.

"Excuse you!" Beth-Ann quickly fanned the smoke with her hands. "Listen, young lady, I'm sorry about the loss of your mother and your sister, but please don't blow that smoke in my face."

"Whatever!" Peaches sneered. "I need you to tell Mason to send me some money up in this piece, ya dig?"

"I need my questions answered first."

"That's gonna cost you two packs more of cigarettes, and some Twinkies while you at it."

"Now young lady, stop blackmailing me. This is the last time, you understand?" Beth-Ann bought everything Peaches wanted from the machines, and even made two more trips to the vending machines for chips, sodas, and more junk food.

"Listen, I need answers and I need them quickly, if you don't mind."

Peaches shrugged. "What difference does it make? Those letters you read was a long time ago. Ain't nothing else to tell you. They were married, but as soon as my Mama heard about you, she filed for divorce."

"That's good to hear. I'm so glad he's not a polygamist. I was worried he was still married to her."

"So tell me something." Peaches leaned in and stared Beth-Ann straight in the eyes. "Is my father beating on you? Is that why you sneaking out here to get answers from me?" Beth-Ann looked into another direction, feeling ashamed.

"I got nothing else to say to you. Ask Mason if you want to know anything else," Peaches abruptly got up from the table.

"Donna, please don't leave!"

"Tell Mason thanks for turning me into a junkie!" Peaches walked away.

Mason found out about Beth-Ann snooping through his things and he beat her up. He also learned he went to see Peaches in jail. "This is the last time you ever hit me! I'm calling the cops!" Beth-Ann had enough, and the police came and arrested Mason. He spent one night jail, and when he was released he tried to go back to Beth-Ann but she handed him his things that she packed up, and told him he couldn't stay with her anymore. Mason ended up in a motel.

"I'll get them girls for this!" he shouted. "Somebody is gonna pay for taking me away from my family. Somebody is gonna pay!"

CHAPTER TWENTY-FIVE

CMP
1981

"Connie, I think you're in over your head," Smokey said, while having a business meeting with Connie.

"A nightclub called *Gina's Lounge* is a great idea, Smokey. We need a club here in Chicago that's similar to Studio 54."

"No deal."

"You want to be rich, right?" Connie asked Smokey.

"Yeah I want to be rich, but still one thing at a time. We haven't even gotten CMP off the ground yet."

"The time to cash in is now while things are being offered to us," Connie told him. He knew Connie was ambitious, but she had never been over confidant.

"You're serious?"

"Next year by this time, I'll be at the top of my game, and you will be with me. I'm ready to make moves, baby."

"All right. I'm with you," Smokey shook her hand. He definitely wanted to get paid, but he was a little nervous by how fast everything was moving. Their contracts hadn't been renewed, and WCHI had turned into a rock radio station. Connie had signed the deal with Mr. Yancy, and was planning to spend her summer running her new nightclub and concert promotion company. She wouldn't start her new job in New York until the end of the summer, so she needed the income in the meantime. Mr. Yancy had already given her bonus money for signing the contract. She used the bonus money as start-up money for CMP Promotions, and a down payment to lease a building on the Southside to start a nightclub. Since she agreed with Dean that she would commute to New York, Connie felt comfortable setting up shop for CMP in Chicago.

Connie set-up a well-oiled machine for CMP once her realtor found a space for her to run her business. They hired a full staff of administrative supporters, engineers, and contracting graphics and special effects companies. Cheryl (the receptionist from WCHI) was out of a job once the station changed ownership, so Connie hired her to be her secretary and personal assistant.

May joined the staff. She would help with putting together the promotional packages for the celebrity tours, such as making sure they had enough tickets to print, T-shirts, posters, celeb bios, press pamphlets, and etcetera. Since welfare had finally cut her off and was starting to make her pay back all the money she'd embezzled from the government. Roscoe had paid most of it back on May's behalf, but it would take another year or two before everything was totally paid off. Roscoe had paid enough to keep them and the IRS off her back to the point where she only had to small monthly payments. Smokey helped Connie book the venues. He and another assistant would travel to check out the venues in person, and make sure the capacity was right, the stage and lighting were okay, and the sound system. On top of trying to get all the celebrities that she had booked, Connie had meetings all the time, mostly via conference calls to New York, DC, and California.

By summer, CMP was increasing in revenue faster than Connie could keep up with it, so she hired an accountant, an auditor, and new lawyers. Her name was spreading through the music industry at the speed of lightning.

"You can't go wrong with Cat Morris. Get her to book your gigs for your artists," people were saying. Although Connie's first few tries at promoting concerts outside of Chicago had flopped, she recovered so quickly that no one noticed. She learned right away about secondary gigs in states not popular for music at that time- like the Dakotas, Missouri, Montana, and Utah. Still, she and Smokey quickly recouped the money and found other ways to earn a better profit.

"Let's do double night gigs," Connie had said to Smokey after one of their losses.

"Connie, nobody books artists back-to-back at the same venues," Smokey argued.

"We do. If it sold out the first night, then it will sell out the second," Connie insisted, and soon Smokey saw that she was right. They not only recouped what they had lost, but earned even more money.

Connie put together shows for funk and R&B Artists, rock artists, and even country artists. Music was music, and Connie didn't discriminate. If she believed an artist or group could sellout tickets, she booked them. Smokey became more and more amazed by Connie's talent, creativity, and the power that her name began to ring with in the industry. He studied the things she did, and hoped to run things on his own soon.

Connie was conducting interviews and doing photo shoots for *Billboard Magazine, Ebony,* and *Jet.* Local newspapers started printing and rating the concerts she was putting together. Almost every critic gave her concerts four stars, and a few of them gave her five-star ratings. No other concert promoter was doing the things Connie was doing.

Smokey found himself becoming more and more attracted to Connie, not just on a business level. He'd always thought she was beautiful since high school, but Jet had been her boyfriend back then. He wasn't sure about her relationship with Dean, but whatever it was, he decided not to care. He felt it was time enough for him to tell her how he felt.

Smokey decided to fill the office with red roses one day, and Connie smiled, thinking they were from Dean. "These are gorgeous." She and her staff admired them.

"Those are from me to you. Beautiful women deserve beautiful things," Smokey winked, contemplating his next move.

"Aw, thanks Smokey." Connie thought it just a nice gesture.

A week later, Connie received a package at her house, and when she opened it, it was a diamond bracelet. Again, she assumed it was Dean, but when she opened the box and read the note, it said, '*From an admirer, not Dean!*

The gifts continued to come, and they were getting more expensive; Connie began to worry. "Whoever this secret admirer guy is, he's spooking me out," Connie said to Smokey. "Don't be afraid, he just likes you," Smokey said, inching his way closer to her. "You're a beautiful woman."

"Cut it out, Smokey," Connie gave him a light shove. She was looking over artists' contract agreements.

Smokey had leaned over her desk as if he was going to kiss her. "What if I told you the admirer was me?"

"Pah-lease!"

"I'm serious!"

Connie looked up at him as she sat the contracts to the side on her desk. "You can't be serious, Smokey."

"I am."

"But you're like my brother!"

"Aw man, come on Connie, don't say that!"

"Have you really been sending me all these gifts?"

"Yes, I have!"

"I appreciate the gifts, Smokey, but I don't view you in that way."

"This is about Dean, isn't it?"

"He *is* my boyfriend, Smokey," she reminded him. "But, even if we weren't a couple, I would still view you as a very good friend. Now if you keep this up we'll have to part ways."

Smokey shoved his hands in the front pockets of his pants and stared down at the floor. Connie could see that he felt disappointed and embarrassed.

"Are you going to be okay? Do you think we can keep it all business?"

"Yeah, I guess so." His eyes avoided direct contact with hers. "Doesn't seem like I have much of a choice."

"Good. If you can make copies of these contracts, than we can get out of here early for a change. We've done enough for one night." Connie quickly signed each contract, and then she handed him the stack.

"Sure. No problem." Smokey realized he didn't have a chance, but he told himself if Dean ever messed up, he would be right there to take his place.

CHAPTER TWENTY-SIX

MAY

The one thing Connie enjoyed the most besides work was her personal time with Dean. They would talk about everything, laugh, double date with Hank and Contessa, go to the nightclubs and parties together, and they would take their children to parks and beaches. The two had met each other's families, and their children were becoming like big brother and little sister. They were madly in love with each other, and felt like two high school sweethearts who couldn't get enough of each other's attention. Nothing or no one could come between them they felt.

Then, one morning while Dean was taking a shower, he suddenly felt soft hands rubbing his back from behind, and then traveled to his manhood.

"Aw baby, you going to start something you know I can't finish," he moaned with excitement. The movement of the hands continued and stroked him more and more. He slowly began to turn around, figuring he could give Connie a quickie before he left for work. When he opened his eyes . . .

"What the hell are you doing in here?!" Dean jumped out the shower and quickly grabbed his robe off the back of the door to cover himself. "Get away from me! CONNIE!" Dean shouted.

"Shhh . . . she's downstairs cooking us breakfast. She doesn't have to know," May whispered, grabbing hold of Dean's hand.

"Stop, get off me! CONNIE!" Dean fled out of the bathroom, and May tried to beat him down the stairs. Roscoe, who had also stayed the night, was outside working on his car when he heard disturbance coming from inside the house. He dropped his wrench and hurried inside. Lydia and Tracey were in the living room watching *The Smurfs*.

"Connie, May just tried to come on to me in the shower!" Dean approached Connie in the kitchen.

"He is lying!" May contested.

"What?" Connie dropped her cooking spatula and turned off the stove. "What is going on?!"

"Connie, I was in the bathroom, and Dean came in there talking about letting me hit it while Connie's downstairs."

"WHAT?!" Dean wanted to smack May for lying. "Connie, look at me! I was in the shower, and May came in and started putting her hands all over my Johnson. I thought she was you. Please believe me, baby, you know I would never allow another woman to touch me, never!"

"Look, we need to step into the den and talk about this, because the kids don't need to hear this kind of stuff." Connie was marching off angrily to the den when Roscoe walked in, asking what was going on.

"Roscoe, baby, Dean tried to come on to me," May said, rubbing Roscoe's chest.

"He did what?" Roscoe started towards Dean.

"No, Roscoe, don't do it!" May tried to act as if she was holding him back, but she gave little force to stop him.

"Nigga, I'll kill you!" Roscoe started towards Dean.

"NO! STOP IT!" Connie rushed towards them and ended up catching his punch in her mouth. Immediately, Dean and Roscoe went to blows.

"May, help me take the girls upstairs! They don't need to see this!" Connie shouted, pulling a crying Tracey from the scene. May ignored Connie, but Lydia ran upstairs with them, not wanting to be left behind with all the fighting going on. Once Connie got them into their rooms safely, she rushed downstairs to the phone to call the police.

"Cops are on the way, so you better go pack your stuff and get out of here!" Connie said to May.

"I'm not going anywhere!"

"Oh yes you are! Your time has been well-spent here!" Connie argued. "You got some nerve, girl, putting your hands on *my* man!"

"I put money into this house too, and I kept your daughter while you was busy being a slut in order to get ahead!"

"Slut? Did you just call me a slut? I never slept with anyone to get ahead!"

"I ain't stutter." Connie took the phone and hit May over the head with the receiver. May fell to the floor, but got up quickly. The two of them started fighting all over the living room. Roscoe passed out on the floor from Dean's punch. Dean turned towards May and Connie and saw Connie beating the crap out of May. He let Connie get a few extra licks in before he broke them up.

May was crying like a baby when the police arrived. Dean reported it a domestic situation that he was trying to get under control. Meanwhile, Lydia and Tracey stood at the top of the stairs, crying from the whole scene and seeing their mothers and their boyfriends fighting like cats and dogs. The police officers stayed until May had packed all of her belongings and her daughter's and left. Dean had gotten dressed, but stuck around long enough to make sure Connie was calm and that she and Tracey would be okay. He had Connie file a Restraining Order against Roscoe and May in case they tried to retaliate. That didn't change the fact that Connie was still upset with May for her coming onto Dean. She trusted Dean, and believed he was telling the truth.

With May and Lydia now out of the picture, Connie realized that the only reason she kept May and Lydia around for so long because they made her feel like she had a family. They took the loneliness away, but she regretted that things had to end the way it did after so many years of friendship.

A few days later, Jet and his fiancée, Sabrina, picked up Tracey, and they flew back to Buffalo, New York so that Tracey could be a part of their wedding. Afterwards, Jet had Tracey flown to South Carolina by his personal assistant, as per Connie's request. Connie wanted Tracey to spend the rest of her summer with her grandparents Scott and Margaret, who hadn't seen her since she was a toddler. Connie felt it would be a good idea for her to get to know them, especially since she was getting ready to go on a tour leg and would be away for at least two months.

Before leaving for her first tour, Connie visited her new club, Gina's Lounge. She wanted to make sure everything was running smoothly. She and Smokey hired Cheryl's brother Donald to run the club, since he had lots of experience. Mr. Yancy came to Chicago to visit *Gina's* and was so impressed, that he invested some of his own money into the club.

The night before Connie was leaving for California, she and Dean made love for most of the night at her house. Usually, Connie would be relaxed afterwards, but she was finding it hard to unwind. She eased herself out of bed, slipped into her robe, and went downstairs into the kitchen. She looked around for her stash, and finally remembered that she had placed it inside a small canister on her top shelf near the flour and the sugar. She pulled out the small dime bag and Top paper, and then rolled a doobie. The joint brought back memories from high school days when her, Smokey, and Franco would share a joint during parties. She and May would occasionally smoke a joint when they went out, so she always kept a small stash for moments like this to unwind. She took a few long puffs and tried to hurry and finish it before Dean suspected anything. She was trying not to choke from smoking it too fast when Dean called her from upstairs. Connie slowly dragged the joint, filling her lungs with herbal smoke.

"Connie, are you okay?" Dean called again from upstairs.

"Yes . . . (Blowing out smoke) I'm . . . okay," she answered, catching her wind. As she took another puff, she heard Dean's footsteps. She quickly threw the half-smoked joint in the kitchen sink and ran the water and the garbage disposal.

"What are you doing?"

"Nothing." Connie shrugged her shoulders. "Got something sticky on my fingers, that's all."

Dean knew better. He could see the guilt in her face that she was up to something. He sniffed and then sniffed again to make sure what he was smelled was right. His eyes searched the room, shifting from counter to cabinet, and stopped when he spotted a book of matches on the counter near the sink.

"Are you down here getting high?"

"Dean, just for tonight, don't judge me, okay? I need to relax, that's all." She approached him and wrapped her arms around his neck. She stood on her tiptoes to kiss his lips, but Dean turned his head. He could smell the herbs on her breath.

"You don't need to mess with that stuff, Connie."

"It's not what you think."

He rolled his eyes. "Then what is it?"

"I asked you not to judge me, Dean. Not tonight!" she backed away.

"You do realize how much I love you. Don't you?" He shot her a deep look of concern.

"Of course I do, what kind of a question is that?"

"So I'm not judging you. I care about you. You know they say marijuana is the gateway to all other drugs. That's how it starts," he fussed. ". . . And *you* of all people should know that. Just look at your sister!"

Connie's eyes widened. "You know what, Dean? I don't need this tonight. Just pack your things and go home!"

"I'm sorry. I shouldn't have said that about your sister, but I do care about you, Connie. You are a successful Black woman. You don't need drugs. If you can't relax, drink some hot tea, take a hot bath, meditate, but you don't need that stuff!"

"It's not a habit, Dean. I'm not an addict. Everybody smokes a joint occasionally. It's like having a cigarette, only stronger."

"It's either me or the drugs, or I'm done with this relationship, and I mean that. I can't get down like this, and you know it."

"Fine, okay? It won't happen again!" Connie dumped the rest of the bag in the sink and flushed it down the garbage disposal. She would never touch it again. Afterwards, she stormed up the steps and rushed into the bathroom, with Dean trailing behind her.

"What are you doing now?"

"You said if I need to relax then I should take a bath, right?"

"Well . . . yeah . . ."

"Then that's what I'm doing." Connie rolled her eyes as she ran the water and poured the whole bottle of bubble bath in the tub, then forcefully tossed the empty bottle in the waste basket.

"Hey! Stand up a minute." Dean reached out for her hand, seeing how upset she was.

"WHAT?!"

"Calm down, okay? Let's not end a beautiful night together like this, especially when you're going on the road tomorrow. He stared into her green eyes. "Everything will be all right," he whispered in her ear.

"I'm under a lot of pressure, Dean. You need to stop yelling at me like I'm a child."

"I apologize. I'm just surprised you would do something like that that's all."

"I'm stressed out. It's my first leg, and people want me to blow this whole tour so they can boast about this being a man's business. I've been getting dirty looks and hate mail from people who want me to fail in this business."

"Don't worry about them. I believe in you. The tours will be a success." Dean gently removed her robe and guided her into the tub. He turned on the radio on the bathroom rack, and then joined her. They settled in the tub and relaxed for a little while, just lying in each other's arms, listening to music from the radio.

"I always loved the way this song starts off," Dean whispered, as Connie laid her head back against his chest. He wrapped his arms around her, and kissed her cheek, easily forgiving her for what she had done.

"I like the way it starts off, too," Connie replied as The Jones Girls came right in after the melody to sing *"Nights Over Egypt"*.

"How come you never told me what happened to your brother Johnny, Dean?" Connie asked, in between singing the song.

Dean wondered where that came from. He assumed it was her high.

"Well?" Connie looked over her shoulder at Dean as she was lying against him, between his legs. Dean had buried his brother's death a long time ago. It was painful to bring it back up because it forced him to see it all over again. However, he realized that maybe it was time to talk about it. He never talked about it, not even to his ex-wife Phyllis.

He closed his eyes and let his mind drift back to when he was twelve and living down south.

"Johnny and I liked to watch trains from our bedroom window," Dean began. "We would get all excited, and we would name the trains and claim them as our own. So if we saw it again, we would say, '*there goes my train*'," Dean smiled. "One day, me and Johnny came up with the idea to hop the trains, and we did. Maybe it was more my idea than his, but, man, it was so much fun. We would ride them all the way out, as far we could go, and then jump off at the next stop so we wouldn't get caught. Man, those trains were like rollercoasters. Only difference was you could take in the world around you in slow motion."

Connie shut her eyes and listened. She felt like she was watching a movie as he told it. "We had so much fun that summer. Then one day, it just wasn't fun no more," Dean solemnly expressed. His facial expression changed. "One day, me and Johnny was running for the train, and I was able to grab on to the rail. I told Johnny to hurry up and hop on, or he would miss it. Johnny grabbed the rail and . . . it broke."

"Oh no!" Connie gasped, covering her mouth.

"I tried to grab Johnny's other hand while he held on to the rail that was hanging from the train, but I couldn't, so I said, 'Let the rail go, Johnny, and I'll see you when I come back.'

"But Johnny cried, 'No, Dean, don't leave me. Please don't leave me!'

Johnny refused to let go of the rail. The train began to pick up speed, and it took off. I could see the heat from the tracks burning through Johnny's pants. His clothes went flying everywhere. Johnny was hollering, but he wouldn't let go of the rail. After a while, I couldn't hear Johnny screaming because the train engine was so loud, but he was still holding on to the rail as it dragged him down the tracks. I started banging on the train as hard as I could with my fists. I knew the train conductor couldn't hear me if I yelled, but the banging would vibrate and make him hear it, so the conductor finally stopped. I saw his head peep out the window of the front of the train from afar.

"What in the devil is going on?' The conductor asked me.

"Help!' I shouted. "It's my brother Johnny." He was lying on the track in a puddle of his own blood.

"Johnny, are you okay?'

"I'm okay. I thought you were going to leave me," Johnny said, and when he stood up, his legs were bleeding profusely, and suddenly his knees buckled and he collapsed to the ground.

"'What in the devil were you boys doing? We need to get him some help!' the train conductor ran to the train and he called an ambulance. I remember a helicopter came and transported Johnny to the nearest hospital. The medics said he was losing a lot of blood and falling in and out of consciousness. We rushed back to my house and told my mother, and then we rushed to the hospital in her car. Johnny was in and out of consciousness, so by the time my father got there to be with us . . . .Johnny was . . . Johnny had died," Dean choked.

Connie turned around to face him. He was crying.

"It's okay, Dean." Connie wiped his tears from his cheeks gently with her hands.

"He lost too much blood, they said."

"I'm sorry you lost your brother, Dean. I'm so sorry, but you know it's not your fault."

"We shouldn't have been there, Connie. I was the oldest, and I knew better!"

"Is that what your father told you?" Connie wondered. "Is that why he barely says anything to you?"

"My father never had a chance to say goodbye to him, so it was my fault."

"Dean, it was your brother's decision to follow you, and his decision not to let go of the rail. It wasn't your fault. You've been carrying this inside of you for far too long, baby."

"I guess you think I'm a punk now, crying like this." He quickly wiped his eyes, regretting that his woman saw him in such a vulnerable state.

Connie giggled, "You and your ego. You lost your brother, there's nothing *punk* about that. But I do see why you're so anxious to be a hero and save everybody else's lives."

"What are you talking about?"

"That's why you wanted to take on my sister's case."

"Yeah maybe so."

"And that's why you became a cop."

"At least justice was served for your sister. I solved her case."

"It's been solved, but no one can change the fact that I'll never see her again or my mother. I know your pain Dean. I feel like everyone I love leaves," Connie admitted.

"Oh come on, don't think that way. You know I'll never leave you," Dean assured her. "Not unless you give me a reason to."

Connie smiled, accepted his embrace, thinking how good Dean was to her. She laid back in his arms as he sponged her down.

"Thanks for sharing your story with me Dean."

"It's been a while since I talked about it. As a matter of fact, I don't think I ever talked about it to anyone since that day."

Connie gently stroked his arms. She felt special that he shared it with her.

"Connie?"

"Yes?"

"I love you," Dean expressed without reservations. For the first time in his life, he felt it was from his heart.

Connie turned around. She had to see it. She had to look into his eyes and see if he was for real. She stared into his eyes and held his gaze.

"I love you, too," Connie felt her heart opening up for him more, and hoped that he would be careful with it.

Connie's tours were successful. All the music critics gave the concerts great reviews, which contributed to sellout shows. Connie hustled long days, doing early morning rehearsals to make sure the sound, lightning and special effects all worked properly. It was her job to make sure that the companies she hired to do the work were prepared to do a good job, and they did.

Connie's secretary Cheryl created the timelines that all artists had to follow, but not everyone did. Oftentimes, artists were late, especially the headliners, who felt they didn't have to be on time. Other times, Connie had to deal with some celebrities who battled drug addiction, too many groupies, and entourages. This caused problems with their performance, and some artists would back out of a show because they were too high to perform. Connie ended up getting insurance to cover the costs and file lawsuits against those who had breached their contracts.

Connie also missed her daughter and Dean terribly during the tours. Despite talking to them on the phone, it wasn't the same as face time. The good thing about touring, however, it allowed Connie to see places she had never been to. She loved traveling out of the country the most. Europe was good to her, and she felt she could one day live there.

Being on the road with various artists also gave her a chance to get to know them personally. Some artists would complain to her about their bad record deals, mismanagement, family problems, or just vent to Connie about whatever was on their minds. She became a counselor to many, but for some of the male artists, they would take her personal attention the wrong way and would start coming on to her.

Initially, Connie was flattered to have well-known celebrities from certain funk bands coming on to her, but one night a band member went too far. When Connie returned to her hotel room after a show, she found the drummer of one of the bands in her bed naked. Connie screamed for him to get out and never come back again.

"It's cool. Calm down, Mama. I thought I would give you a little something to cap off your night."

Connie called a meeting that next day before continuing the tour. She was furious. "Guys, we need to get serious. This is a business, and I am a businesswoman. If you can't respect me, then the show is over," she told them bluntly. "If the shows end, we all lose money, and I know you don't want that to happen. You're going to respect me, starting right now." Connie didn't have any more problems after setting boundaries.

Once they returned to the states, Connie found that she liked Ohio and Minneapolis the best. They had a lot of big bands and local talent. While in Ohio, she met the OJay's lead singer, Eddie Levert. While she was in Minneapolis, she watched Prince perform at the famous *First Avenue* venue, and knew one day he would be a superstar.

When Connie toured the southern states, she went to see her daughter who was with her parents, and spent every day with her while she was in town. She also had a playground built there, and named it *'Scott's Circle of Fun.'* She wanted to name it after her half-brother Willie, but some of the people in the community were still racist and against naming anything after someone who was black.

The word about Connie building a playground in the South traveled back to Chicago, and many former neighbors of Cabrini Green were upset that Connie never built a playground for them.

"Do you have any comments about that?" a reporter asked. "I tried to have a playground built there, but there was so much red tape about building it that I gave up. If the people of Cabrini really want one, they should speak to the Mayor. He's the one who wouldn't allow it."

Connie assumed her quote would be verbatim until one of her staff members back in Chicago called her from the CMP headquarters. "Ms. Morris the papers here quote you as saying, '*If the people of Cabrini want a playground built they should talk to their Mayor.*'

"That's insane! They left out the part about him not wanting it built there," Connie was upset. It was her first lesson in being careful about what she said to the press.

Back at the office in Chicago, Smokey found out he had gotten two interns pregnant at the same time and paid them money not to tell Connie or his girlfriend Wanda. He was heavy-handed in the way he treated the other staff. Even at Gina's Lounge, Smokey would walk in bragging and bossing people around. He told Donald that in spite of how he kept the club jumping that *he* was still the "HNIC." He sat in the lounge and puffed cigars while women surrounded him as if he was a celebrity.

People didn't like the way Smokey was carrying on, and some of them began to think that Connie had sold the club and her business to Smokey.

Meanwhile, Dean was busy running track again. Connie gave him the inspiration to get back to doing what he loved. Although his days of competing were over with, just being at the track again felt good in his heart. He missed Connie too. Although he and Connie talked every day, he knew nothing could replace her physical presence. He missed everything about her; her cooking, her infectious laughter, and the intellectual conversations they had. Dean loved Connie like he had never loved any other woman before. He spoke highly of her to his friends and family, and kept her picture in his living room, so that anyone who stopped by knew that she was the woman he loved. Weeks had gone by since she had left, and he did everything he could to keep occupied until she returned.

CHAPTER TWENTY-SEVEN

"CHARLIE DID IT"

*T*he phone in Connie's hotel room seemed to be ringing very loudly. Connie had just gotten in from an after-party, and had a lot to drink. Sluggishly she answered the phone on the nightstand, trying to figure out who was calling her at three in the morning.

"Ms. Morris?"

"Yes?" Connie slowly sat up in bed.

"This is Officer Chavis," the stern voice said. "I'm calling because there was a fire at your place of business- CMP Promotions," Officer Chavis began. "I understand you are the owner of the company, and I wanted to let you know that the office was badly damaged."

"Oh no! Was anybody hurt?" Connie turned on the lamp to make sure she was alert.

"No one was injured, but there's a lot of damage that was done. In fact, nearly a total loss," Officer Chavis explained.

Connie broke in, "How did this happen?"

"So far it looks like it was purposely set. We could smell kerosene all through the place, and there was a strange graffiti tag that said 'Charlie did it.'."

"I don't know anyone named Charlie. Have you called my business partner, Smokey? I want him there right now to find out what's going on!"

"We did try to reach him, but we didn't get an answer. We left a message on his answering machine."

"Well I'm in California right now. I can try to take the red eye out tonight," she said, already slipping into a pair of shorts and a top.

"I know you're in California, Ms. Morris, we were able to see your tour schedule from Detective Wilson. He's here at the scene with me, and just went back inside to check on something. He told me to call you right away."

"Let me talk to her."

"Oh, here he is. Hold on a minute." Officer Chavis handed Dean the payphone.

"Hey, baby."

"Dean, what the hell is going on?!"

"We will find out. You know I'm on it."

"Dean, please tell me it's not that bad."

"Truth?"

"Yes, the truth!"

"Um . . ." he hesitated because he knew it would hurt. "You will need to relocate," he told her. Connie burst into tears, and Dean wished he was there to hold her and comfort her.

"I'll throw the book at whoever did this, I promise you."

"Oh Dean, why would anyone want to hurt me like this?" she cried. "All I've done was nice things for people. I even hired people struggling to find jobs! I put people on."

"I know. I know."

"I wonder if somebody got upset about the whole thing about me not building them a playground."

"Stop speculating, baby, and let us do our job. We'll get to the bottom of this," Dean assured her.

"I need to get packing. I'm taking the next flight out."

"Good. I'll see you when you get here."

By the time Connie had arrived in Chicago, Dean had received a call on his police radio that there had been another fire. This time, it was at Connie's house. She and Dean rushed to the scene. Jumping out of Dean's work car, Connie saw hot orange flames shooting through the roof of her house. One fire fighter kicked down her front door, and a gush of hot flames nearly knocked him over. Flames burst through the front living room windows, and bits of ash flew out. Connie froze in devastation, watching everything she worked hard for go up in smoke. It took hours before the firefighters were able to put the fire out.

Tears streamed down Connie's cheeks as Dean and the firefighters carefully escorted her inside to see if there was anything left to salvage. Connie cried when she saw the pictures she had in the living room burnt to pieces, especially the ones of her and her daughter. As she tried to hold it together, she remembered the fireproof safe she kept in the basement of her house, and rushed to check it. The safe contained very important papers—her Living Will, accounting and bankbooks, expensive jewelry, and the gray box her mother had kept that had family photos. The fire had destroyed everything else in the house.

"Whoever set these fires knew you," Dean lamented. "They know where you live and where you work. Whoever it is, I'm gonna get 'em and make them pay." Dean hugged a crying Connie in his arms. "I need to make some calls. I'll be right back." Dean walked to his car to contact the office.

Meanwhile, Smokey showed up in his corvette, with his girlfriend Wanda in the passenger seat. She stayed in the car while Smokey got out to see what was happening at Connie's house.

"Where on earth have you been?" Connie asked him, staring at him suspiciously.

"I was out checking out CMP, and then I went by Gina's Lounge to make sure everything was okay there. I heard there was a fire here."

"Was everything okay at the club?"

"Everything was fine," he assured her. "Aw man, I'm sorry about this!" Smokey looked up at Connie's bungalow.

News reporters arrived at the scene, asking all sorts of questions. The neighbors were hanging out, wondering what was going on as well. "I don't know who did this, but they burned my business, too," Connie said frantically to the newswoman. "I have always done good things for this community, so for someone to do this to me, it just pisses me off!"

"So someone from this community did this?" the newswoman asked.

"I don't know who did it, put it that way, and make sure you print it right this time!"

"Ms. Morris, in spite of these tragic events, I heard your tour has been quiet a success, and your last stop will be here in Chicago. How will these tragic events affect the concerts here?"

"The show will still go on, so people who bought tickets don't have to worry about that. But right now, I'm focused on getting my life back together."

Smokey stepped in front of the camera.

"And who are you, sir?" the newswoman asked.

"Smokey. I'm Connie's business partner, and I just want to let everyone in Chicago know that we care about this city. We love this city, and if you know of anyone who did this to my partner's house and *our* business, please step forward and help the police. The award is one thousand dollars and free concert tickets with backstage passes if you know who did this."

"So there you have it, Chicagoans, free concert tickets and a one thousand dollar reward if you know who did this. Please call the Chicago Police right away. I'm Dorothy Bourke, News 8."

"How dare you do that!" Connie snapped at Smokey after the cameras stopped rolling.

"I was just trying to help." Smokey hated seeing Connie this way. "You want to stay at my place?"

"I'm staying with Dean. I'm headed there after the insurance people get here to check things out."

"Here, take this." Smokey handed her a roll of hundred dollar bills."

"No thanks, Smokey. I'll be just fine. Dean will take care of me."

"Suit yourself." He smirked as he put the money back into the pocket of his jacket.

"Wassup, Smokey?"

Smokey stared Dean up and down. "Well, if it isn't Chicago's finest," he laughed sarcastically.

"Watch yourself, bro," Dean warned.

"I'll see you later, Connie." Smokey winked her and drove off with Wanda.

Dean drove Connie to his house and made sure she got settled before he and Detective White plotted how they would handle the investigation. Since it was now the early morning, they would have to wait until normal hours to start questioning people. First thing the next morning, Dean was on it. Dean interviewed each employee of CMP, and then he went to Connie's former radio station, WCHI. He and White had already questioned people in the neighborhood. They even hunted down May and Roscoe. Dean learned that they had moved to Florida a month ago. Dean also visited Peaches in jail and asked if she had heard anything. She told them she hadn't, but mentioned that Beth-Ann had come to visit her. They went to Beth-Ann's house, but she said she didn't know anything about it. Dean even interrogated Smokey and made him take a lie detector test, which he passed. Smokey was upset and thought Dean was accusing him on purpose, since the two never liked each other, but Dean wanted to make sure. He was just doing his job.

Meanwhile, Connie's father called as soon as he heard the news to see if Connie was okay. She assured him that she was, and asked him to keep Tracey a little while longer until she worked things out. Connie's celebrity friends and artists whose tours she had put together. They also sent her money and gifts. For weeks, Dean's living room was flooded with fan mail, flowers, and gifts of well-wishes. It was amazing to Connie how quickly people found things out, and the support they offered was heartfelt. While Connie was trying to establish some type of order of things in Dean's living room, the phone rang.

"Hello?"

"Connie it's Jet, are you okay?"

"Hi Jet. I'm okay."

"Is Tracey with you or still with your grandfather?"

"She's still with her grandfather."

"Good," Jet sighed with relief. "Sabrina and I just got back from our honeymoon. I called as soon as I heard the fires."

"Thank you."

"I'm not sure how to say this, but I think Tracey should come to live with me."

"I beg your pardon!" Connie snapped. "Tracey is *my* daughter, Jet, and she is going to live with me!"

"Connie, if Tracey moves back there with you, her life will be in danger. Now, I'm willing to get my attorneys to file for full-custody if you won't let her stay here with me."

"Don't threaten me!" Connie shouted in the phone. "Nigga, who do you think you are? I raised Tracey by myself, and now you want to come in all of sudden and be her daddy because you have a wife and money?!"

Jet sighed. "Maybe I'm overrating a bit, so calm down. I apologize."

"If you're through talking, I have better things I need to be doing."

"Is there anything my wife and I can do for you?"

"I'm some charity case Jet. I can take of myself."

"If anything should change, please call us, and we will—"

Connie hung up the phone. She had heard enough. Shortly after her conversation with Jet, Mr. Yancy called, offering his sympathies, and then offered Connie to move to New York right away into a penthouse he owned. "All you have to do is furnish it," Mr. Yancy stated.

"I'll have to think about that Mr. Yancy. If I do decide to take you up on your offer, I'll buy the penthouse from you instead."

"If you like it just let me know and we can work out a deal."

"I will. It's time for me to get out of Chicago."

Over the next couple of days, Connie continued to work with her insurance company, which finally agreed to pay for all the damage to her house and her business. Having to tell her staff at CMP that she was closing shop was going to be her next challenge. They met at a public library on West Hirsch Street in the Humboldt Park community, blocks away from where Connie rented the space for CMP.

"So we're out of a job now since you're moving to New York?" asked one of the interns.

"Unfortunately, yes," Connie replied, ". . . unless you can move to New York."

"Off to New York we go!" Smokey happily said. "You interns weren't getting paid anyway."

"But what about us who aren't interns?" asked Cody, a designer for the promotional flyers. Connie loved his work.

"The opportunity is yours if you want it, Cody, but I can't stay here in Chicago anymore. My goal is to set up shop in New York."

"If you can hang, come along. And if you can't, see ya 'round like a donut!" Smokey laughed.

"How dare you cheer at a time like this?" said Evelyn, one of the female interns with long hair.

"Excuse me?"

"I'm having your baby in five months, and you're leaving me to go to New York?"

"Hey, wait a minute, I'm having his baby, too!" said Marsha, who was short and wore glasses.

Connie looked puzzled. "What is going on here?"

"Finally, the cat is out the hat!" Belinda, the receptionist blurted out.

"Yes, and the truth always comes out in due time!" said Catherine, an administrative assistant. She slapped hi-fives with Belinda.

"What's going on?" Connie turned to Smokey.

"They don't know what they're talking about, Connie."

"Connie, we do know what we're talking about," said Evelyn. "Looks like Smokey have been sleeping with the both of us, and we're both pregnant."

"Smokey!" Connie's mouth dropped. "Have you lost your mind? These girls are barely twenty-one! Besides, you know better than to sleep with staff members. What happened to your girlfriend, Wanda?"

"Wanda? Who is she?" both Evelyn and Marsha asked at the same time.

"Look, ya'll don't be jumping on me at one time," Smokey snapped.

"What else has been going on?" Connie asked. One by one, each staff member complained about Smokey, and Connie had heard enough. She asked to speak with Smokey outside.

Outside of the library, Connie questioned Smokey about what the staff members were saying. He did not deny any of it. In fact, he boasted, "Yeah, so what. I ran the show while you were gone. You made me your partner, so I held it down like a man is supposed to." He popped his collar.

"You don't sleep with staff, Smokey."

"You're just mad I'm not sleeping with you!"

"Oh, don't flatter yourself."

"You're just jealous."

"Smokey, I'm far from jealous," Connie assured him. "What you did was unprofessional, and secondly, there is only one boss around here—and that's me! You don't make decisions about this business without consulting with me. And you better hope we're not brought up on sexual harassment charges."

"I'm not hoping for nothing. What I did was my business."

"You know, I don't like your attitude about this."

"I don't like you getting into what's *my* personal business."

"Let me get this straight," Connie folded her arms. "You don't think that making decisions without consulting your boss first is wrong, and you don't think sleeping with staff members is wrong?" Connie glared at him.

"No I don't, and remember you're not my boss. We're partners."

"We *were* partners. It's over Smokey. We're done!"

Smokey shook his head, "I want my money back. I invested in this company and I want it back."

"You'll get what's owed to you and nothing more."

"Oh yeah? Well you better make sure I get some of that insurance money too because I haven't seen it yet."

"You'll get your share."

Smokey pointed his finger in Connie's face. "You better watch your back."

"I'm not scared of you, Smokey!"

"You better be, woman. If you think whoever set those fires had it coming for you, then you better watch out for me!" he warned. "I'm going to start my own concert-promoting business, and nobody will remember *Cat Morris*."

Connie watched Smokey drive away in his corvette. She wasn't afraid. She remembered in high school when Smokey tried to run his own party promotion company and it failed, and then he came crawling back to her and Franco. This time, if he ever tried to come back, Connie knew in her heart that she would never hire him again, or do any type of business with him. She went back inside the library to inform the staff of the news.

Later that evening . . .

"This whole thing about you moving to New York is not sitting well with me," Dean said to Connie at the dinner table. Connie had told Dean her decision a couple days ago, and Dean hadn't said much about it since. He was trying to digest it all and choose his words wisely. Dean Jr. could feel a deep conversation coming on, so excused himself from the table. He loved Connie staying with them. He ate better meals, and appreciated Connie's motherly company, but whatever was about to go down between her and his Dad, he did not want to hear it. He went upstairs and called Patricia instead.

"I can understand how you feel, Dean, but my mind is made up," Connie stated. She was irritable from a lack of sleep and trying to piece her life back together again. "You know I had to fire Smokey today," she said, skipping the subject.

"Smokey was long overdue for that, but what about us? If you're moving to New York, where does that leave us?"

"Dean, it's only two and half hours away." She didn't see what the big deal was, but the last thing she wanted was an argument with him.

"That's only if I fly out every week to see you."

"We could rotate. Besides, you were cool with me commuting, so what's the difference?"

"You would be here with me, is the difference. Tracey would be here with me and with Dean Jr. I wasn't going to kick you out on the streets. You have a place to stay-right here," Dean protested. "We would be a family."

"Dean, you said someone could be trying to hurt me, and you know what, you may be right. I have to think about my safety and my daughter's. I'm worried, my father is worried, and so is Jet!"

"The same thing could happen in New York, but at least living here I can protect you, Connie!"

"I'll hire a bodyguard, but I'm not staying here anymore. I've got bigger fish to fry in New York."

"You keep chasing every opportunity that's offered to you without thinking about the people who love and care for you. You know, I don't like Smokey, but to his credit, he was right to a certain degree," Dean said, pointing his forkful of roast before stuffing it into his mouth.

"Oh, really?"

"Yes." Dean quickly chewed his food and swallowed it. "You have no loyalty."

"I'm the most loyal person you will ever meet!"

"Sure, until the next big thing is offered to you."

"I put people on."

"Sure, you put people on. You lead people on, too. Then you leave people, people like me, who love you and care about you. People like Billy at WCHI, who gave you your first break, but you had to fight against him so you could start your own concert company. Maybe if you were completely devoted to the station without pursuing your own selfish goals, the station would not have folded. Have you ever thought about that?" Dean argued. "And what about the people here in Chicago who love you for your charitable efforts in the community? You just turn your back on all of that for bigger dollars. Even the people who worked for CMP are out of jobs unless they relocate to New York."

"Dean you don't understand," Connie tried to interrupt.

"I do understand. I can see everything quite clearly now," Dean contested. "You're young and still have a lot of growing up to do. I thought you would be more mature than this. Here I am, putting aside all my other cases to try to find out who set fires to my woman's place of business and her home, even working overtime, and now you tell me that you're leaving me? Yeah, I understand all right!"

Dean got up from the table and left Connie sitting there by herself. She couldn't believe how upset Dean was with her. She had never seen Dean act that way, and she felt he was being selfish and didn't understand her situation.

A week later, Connie had her bags packed. She told her father she would send for Tracey once she got settled in New York. She kissed Dean Jr. on the cheek and told him goodbye while Dean was getting dressed for work. He hadn't said two words to her since their last argument about her leaving to New York.

"Can I get a ride to the airport?" Connie asked Dean, as he stood in front of the mirror checking himself out before work.

"I can't be late for work," he answered bitterly; adjusting his tie to make sure it was straight. "Why don't you call a cab?"

"Fine!" Connie stomped downstairs with her heavy suitcase, filled with new clothes and shoes that she had bought for her and Tracey with the insurance money. Speaking of which, she mailed Smokey his share of the insurance money. Later on, she would hear through others how he blew it on gambling and women.

Finally, Connie was standing on the front steps of Dean's house when the taxi cab pulled up. Dean just stepped out of the house to head out for work. Connie turned around to face him. She looked up into his eyes, searching for a little bit of hope, but couldn't see it.

Dean felt overwhelmed and hurt as Connie placed her arms around his waist to hug him. He loved Connie, but felt there was no consistency in their relationship the way he had wanted it to be. He didn't just want to have a woman; he wanted to be *with* his woman. He felt confused about his feelings for her and questioned whether he was being selfish as her soft lips touched his. He wanted to say something, but a lump formed in his throat as he reluctantly kissed her back.

Connie wanted more affection from him, but there was none. Dean looked down at the ground and then up at the sky to try to keep the tears from escaping his eyes.

"You don't have to say anything, Dean." Tears streamed down her cheeks. This felt almost as awful as when she lost her mother and sister in death. "Maybe it's better if you don't," Connie wiped her tears. The cab driver came up to the steps to take her luggage. Dean was unresponsive, and as Connie got into the cab, she felt that Dean was punishing her more with his silence. The cab driver offered her a tissue and drove her to the Chicago O'Hara. Dean went to work, ready to take out his frustrations on the first person who so much as jaywalked across the street.

CHAPTER TWENTY-EIGHT

A CONFESSION

*P*eaches heard about Connie's house and business being set on fire, so when they told her she had a visitor, she hoped it was Connie. Instead an old man who looked familiar to her stood up from the guest table. He had a shabby beard and was bald. The dark circles under his eyes looked like he hadn't slept in days, and his hands were trembling when Peaches approached him. The closer Peaches got to him the more she recognized him. Poking out her lips and folding her arms, she asked with contempt, "Wassup, chump?"

He pointed his wrinkled, aged finger at her face. "You stay away from my family!" he shouted. He coughed convulsively, spitting into a handkerchief.

"What are you talkin' 'bout, old man?"

"You messed up my family, and you been trying to kill me!"

"Man, ain't nobody trying to kill you, but I wish I could snap your neck right now!" Peaches returned the same evil look he was giving her. She hated his guts for not helping the family, and not attending her mother and sister's funeral. She knew he must have heard about the tragedies.

"Stay away from my family!"

"Nigga, you don't come up in here making threats to me!"

"Be quiet, Charlie is watching." He looked over his shoulder.

"What?" Peaches stared at him like he was crazy.

"You always have to be mindful of your enemies."

"You need to leave that bottle alone, 'cause ya trippin'!"

"Stay away or I'll burn down your boy's house next time. I know where he lives. I got his name." Mason pulled out a wrinkled piece of paper from his plaid shirt pocket. "His name is Barry, folks call him BJ, and he's adopted. I know where he lives. I'll set a fire to him, too, like I did your sister. I know where he lives. Social worker told me his address. I told them, 'I'm his Granddaddy', but they don't know I'll burn him like Charlie burned us. Made us walk on hot stones in the Army."

"You ain't doing nothin' to my son!" Peaches lost control and punched him in the face. He dropped to the floor. The guards immediately rushed over and cuffed Peaches. They told Mason to leave, and then they took Peaches to see the Warden.

"But he threatened to kill my son!" Peaches shouted. "He said he would set his house on fire like he did my sister's, said something about a dude named Charlie burned his feet or something." Peaches tried to explain as she sat cuffed to the chair in front of his Warden's desk.

The Warden raised a brow, stared at Peaches for a moment, said, "Maybe he did threaten you, but that didn't mean you should respond that way. You know those actions can put you in the hole, don't you?"

"Cut me some slack man. I been doing good until that happened. Don't nobody threaten my son. Nobody!"

"I need you to get back to controlling your temper young lady. You can't let *words* cause you to react like that. Now, since you've been composed up to this point, I won't throw you in the hole."

Peaches smirked.. "Thanks Warden."

"But," he pointed. "I am going to put you on cleaning duties of the ladies' room for a month."

"Aw man! I don't wanna clean no pissy bathrooms!"

"It's either that or you go in the hole for a week. Take your pick."

"Just tell me where the mops are."

"In the meantime, because your father did admit he set Cat Morris' house on fire, I need to report it to Detectives Wilson and White. I think they're still working that case. Once I get them in here, would you be willing to go on record as a witness against Mason?"

"Yeah I'll tell them, but what's in it for me? Will my time get cut short?"

"Hold on, slow down," he waved his hands. "That's something you will have to speak with the detectives about."

A few days later, Peaches was called into the interrogation room and she explained to Dean and Detective White what happened.

"Thanks for that information Peaches," Dean put his notepad away. "So how you been holding up?"

"Man, how you think I been holding up?" she barked.

"Well why don't you work on getting yourself cleaned up? I can have Mr. Dudley meet with you. He's a rehab counselor. With good behavior, it could cut your time short . . . maybe," Dean told her.

"Say Wilson," Peaches called as Dean was leaving out of the interrogation room. "How are you and my sister doing, man? What's up?"

He tilted his head, and gave her a look that said, *how do you know?*

"Saw ya'll in a picture together at a concert in one them magazines," Peaches chuckled. "Figured ya'll was boning each other."

Dean smiled for a moment, but it quickly went away. "Yeah, well, it's over between us now."

"My sister never could keep a man. She don't trust them," Peaches laughed. "Either that, or she gets bored with them easily, just like Jet."

"I'm far from boring, believe me."

"Oh, I believe you brother, with your bowlegged self. If you wasn't my sister's ex, I'd take you in that bathroom and show you why they call me Peaches."

He shook his head. *Peaches is a wild woman. Definitely not like her sister.*

"Hey, Wilson, get me a pack of Newport's or something. I mean damn, I did give ya'll some evidence about them fires. I want some cigarettes and some Twinkies up in this piece!"

Dean and Detective White found out that Mason Morris set the fires. Not only did he confess, but also they discovered his fingerprints on one of the Molotov bottle. After undergoing a series of psychiatric evaluations, Mason was diagnosed as a bipolar schizophrenic. The judge ordered him to a psychiatric hospital, where he could finally receive the help he needed.

Dean tried to contact Connie to tell her the news. He got no response. His curiosity about Mason Morris did get the best of him. He wondered about the deeper affects that his mental illness had on Connie, and he sought to investigate Connie's old neighbors in Cabrini Green.

"Mason was very mean," said Ms. Knight. "He would beat on all of them, and I would call the police, but his wife never pressed charges."

"Did you ever see signs of his abuse, especially with the children?" Dean asked another neighbor.

"Yes, especially Connie," the neighbor replied. "We went to school together, and she would come to school with a black-eye or busted lip. I remember that. Yep, and she would say she got into a fight with one of the girls around here in Cabrini, but none of us ever hit her. We teased her for being a redbone n' stuff like that, and we called her "Cat eyes", but we were young and ain't know any better."

"Did Connie have any close friends?" Dean asked another neighbor just across the courts.

"Not as a kid, 'cause her father didn't let her come outside really, but later on, she had a friend named May in high school and a boyfriend, "Jet." Yeah, she got really popular in high school. She was prom queen, She would deejay parties, but all this happened when her mother kicked her father out the house. Not before then."

"Thank you for your time."

Dean continued to try to reach Connie. He wasn't going to tell her what he found out from speaking to people in her old neighborhood, since she'd asked him not to go discovering information about her behind her back, but he wanted to let her know they caught who set the fires. A part of him felt sorry for her. He now understood why she had a hard time trusting others and being loyal to them, especially men. It seemed the only person she'd ever trusted was her mother.

"Connie, if you're there, please pick up. It's important. I got some news about the fires. This is my last time calling."

"What's going on, Dean?" Connie stopped her answering machine and picked up the phone. That's when Dean realized she had been screening her calls. He wanted to be upset with her, because what he had to tell her was not about their relationship.

"Connie, your stepfather, Mason Morris sets those fires. He was arrested and charged with arson, and was admitted to a psychiatric hospital."

"WHAT?!"

"His wife Beth-Ann found out the truth about him having another family and neglecting you guys, so she kicked him out. He's been homeless ever since. That stressful reaction caused his mind to flip, so he set those fires, and threatened to set fire to your nephew BJ's house. If Peaches wasn't locked up, he probably would have done the same thing to her. He felt you guys ruined his family, and this is what he confessed to Peaches when he threatened her during a visit, and later to us. We also found his fingerprints matched the prints on the Molotov bottles."

"That monster!" Connie shouted. "How could do something like that, and then blame us? He's a monster, do you hear me? A monster! I hope he goes straight to hell!" Her hands shoot just thinking about Mason. Tears shimmered in her eyes as she angrily paced the room back and forth.

"I'm sorry this happened to you, Connie. He was diagnosed as a bipolar schizophrenic. He's in a ward now, getting the help he needs."

"Yeah, well . . ." Connie sniffed as she walked over to her bar to pour herself another drink, " . . .thanks for working on this for me." She swallowed a shot of vodka straight, with no chaser.

"It's no problem. If you ever need anything, just—"

"Goodbye, Dean." She cut him off and quickly hung up. Dean stared at the phone from the other end. He wanted to call her back because he knew she was hurting and wanted to console her, but he couldn't find the words to comfort her in a situation like this. The problem was much deeper.

Connie woke up the next morning hoping that last night's news about her stepfather setting those fires had been just a nightmare, but it wasn't. She called to tell her father Scott the news and he insisted she get out of the house and go for a walk to calm down. Connie decided her father was right; the longer she stayed, inside the more she would drink, and she didn't want to end up getting drunk with Tracey around. She and Tracey got dressed and decided to go shopping.

The minute she stepped outside of her penthouse, she was surrounded by the smells and sounds of vendors' foods, people shouting at each other, and cabs blowing horns in the midst of standstill traffic. It was easy to distract herself from her depressing thoughts while in the city. A sense of security came over her; she was worlds away from the things that happened in Chicago. She longed for this change. Still, if Tracey wasn't living with her, she knew she would feel lonely. She still missed Dean terribly, and wished they hadn't broken up the way they did. A part of her felt like they weren't finished, but she couldn't stay on the phone with him because she was afraid all those old emotions would come up.

After she finished shopping and explaining to Tracey that New York was their new "permanent" home, she took her to see the musical *Annie*. It was on its first U.S. tour, and the show's first stop was New York City. Connie was able to buy last-minute tickets from a booster outside of the theater. It was more than the ticket price, but Connie felt she needed to keep her mind occupied. Besides, Tracey had lost everything back in Chicago: her clothes, toys, and even her best friend, Lydia.

"Mom, why did we leave Chicago? Isn't that our home?" Tracey asked, while they were out.

"It was our home," Connie replied. "Maybe one day we'll go back, but right now we're going to live here. I have a new job at the radio station."

"But I miss my friends in Chicago."

"You'll make new friends here in New York."

"What if I don't want any new friends?"

Connie sighed, "Tracey, listen baby," Connie kneeled down in front of her. "I know you miss Chicago and your friends back home. I miss my friends too, but they all understand that I had to take this job."

"Including Mister Dean?"

Connie raised her brow. "Excuse me?"

"Dean, your boyfriend. The one you kissed in the mouth at the airport."

Connie wasn't expected that type of mature response from Tracey. Her mind raced with thoughts as to how to respond.

"Well, you let me worry about Dean, okay? Right now, you and I are going to see *Annie*. Now come on, the show is about to start."

CHAPTER TWENTY-NINE

CAT MORRIS THE CELEBRITY
1983

As time moved on, Connie took New York by storm. Fans loved her so much that the ratings shot up in a year's time and remained on top another year later. *"She tells it like it is,"* people said. She met notables such as Donnie Simpson (from Detroit who started working at BET), Cathy Hughes (from WOL in Washington, DC), and Melvin Lindsey (WHUR) while attending a charity event in Washington, DC, and even ran into her old friend Ray Brown, who was at the event as well.

"Good Morning, New York! Happy Friday! This is Cat Morris on the *Sunnyside Up Morning Show*, waking you up to something new. New York is the place of eclectic taste, so I figured I would let you all hear something new. Let me know what you think. This song is by a new artist who goes by the name MC J-Love. It's called, "Party Hearty". I know that's what you plan to do later tonight, so tune in your ears to this, and call me and let me know what you think," Connie played the rap song as a favor to Ray who had just started his own rap label. Listeners started requesting it every day after played it. Eventually, the song became a national hit, putting Ray's record company, *Rapping Brown Music,* on the map.

Ray invited Connie out to celebrate the success of his new label at *The Roxy*. Ray had all his artists at the Roxy, including MC J-Love, and he invited other celebrity rappers—*Run-DMC, Kurtis Blow,* and *Afrika Bambaataa.* At Ray's party, Connie had the opportunity to meet MC J-Love in person. He introduced himself as Jayson, and he and Connie hit it off right away.

Connie was careful not to let her feelings get in too deep, because she knew how some music artists had a list of women they dated from one state to the next. Jayson was funny, loved going out and having a good time, but there was always some other woman waiting to whisk him away from Connie as soon as they got the opportunity. Soon enough, Jayson felt he could no longer fight off the advances of other women. One night after he and Connie had stayed together, Jayson got up in the middle of the night. Connie heard him sneaking away to make a phone call. When he returned to the room, Connie saw him getting dressed to go back out.

"Jayson, when you come back, I won't be here," Connie told him.

"I'm just going out to help my boy, he caught a flat tire and . . ."

"You don't have to explain. I'm just letting you know I won't be here, and I won't ever come back here again if you leave me to go be with her."

Jayson knew what Connie meant. She was a smart woman, but he also knew he wasn't ready to settle down. He looked over his shoulder and said to her cordially, "At least we had fun, right?"

Ray was upset that Connie had dated Jayson in the first place. He felt Jayson was too young and still had a lot of play in him. Ray decided to express how he felt when the two agreed to have lunch one day.

"Jayson was never your type anyway, and I don't know why you dated someone so whack!"

"Why are you so bitter about who I choose to date?"

"I just expected more from you, Connie."

"Yeah, well, everyone is filled with surprises, aren't they?" Connie smirked. She could tell Ray liked her. She'd always known.

"You want to check out my pad? I don't think you've ever seen it yet."

"Sure."

At Connie's place, she and Ray played records and had a few drinks. Ray smoked some reefer, but Connie didn't. It was still early afternoon. Once their high kicked in, hers from drinking, his from herbs, they started looking at each other differently. A hug led to a kiss, and a kiss led to them sleeping together. For Ray, they had now crossed the lines of friendship, and he was okay with that. He was willing to allow things to go to the next level. For Connie, it was just casual sex.

"You feel better now?" Connie asked Ray, stepping out of her bed and sliding on her satin robe. Ray smiled with excitement, feeling happy that he had made love to her. She was a sex symbol these days, and every man's dream, especially after she posed in *Jet* Magazine as "Beauty of the Week".

Ray lifted a concerning brow. "What do you mean, if I feel better now?"

Connie shrugged. "You were obviously upset about me and Jayson, so I figured I'd make it right." Ray's feelings dropped to his socks.

"This wasn't about getting even or competing with Jayson," Ray declared. He was surprised Connie would think that way. The Connie he once knew was kindhearted and sweet, but he wasn't sleeping with Connie Morris. He had slept with *Cat Morris*, the celebrity, and he felt like her trick instead of her longtime friend from Chicago.

"Sure, you're right, Ray," Connie chuckled. "Just get your clothes and go, all right? I don't need my daughter coming home from school and finding a naked man in my bed. She may think I'm a slut."

Ray quickly got dressed, but before he left, he said to Connie, "This was not cool."

"I hope we can still be friends, Ray," Connie replied, smirking.

"I don't know. I mean . . . I need time to think about that."

"Well, it's your choice, Ray. Either I'll see you later or I won't, but you gotta go," Connie said abruptly. She opened the door for him to leave, and he left. She knew it was easier if Ray left right away, before she allowed herself to feel any hurt or guilt. She was tired of men hurting her; using her, abusing her, not understanding her. Now she felt she was handling business . . .

Cheryl moved to New York, agreeing to become Connie's personal assistant again. Connie helped her to get an apartment in her building several floors below her penthouse. Connie set up shop for CMP after she found a space a few blocks away from WHKY, her new station. Eventually, Connie had a full staff again, and was quick to lay down the rules. Connie decided on a formal atmosphere instead of the casual atmosphere she'd allowed in Chicago. More importantly, she stressed the strict policy of no flirting with fellow coworkers or engaging in intimate relationships.

Once Connie got CMP up and running, she went back to having fun, and decided to give famous R&B singer Kelvin James, a chance to take her out. He had been asking to date her since she had been in New York, and would send her flowers. He made it known publicly that he had a crush on her, and the public wanted to see them together, so Connie gave him a chance.

Kelvin had a velvety singing voice and average looks, but women loved him like he was Luther Vandross. Connie enjoyed his company, because he was very romantic but respectful. He was falling in love with her, but Connie didn't want to take things that far. Enforcing friendship, Connie quickly invited Kelvin to fly with her to Chicago to visit her club, *Gina's Lounge*. "It will be fun!" Connie said, "and you can sing if you want to," she added.

The two flew out to Chicago and partied hard all weekend at *Gina's*, while Tracey stayed with Cheryl back in New York. Kelvin had to leave Chicago to go on a tour in L.A. Before he left, he asked Connie where they stood. "Let's just be friends. I'm not ready another relationship right now," Connie said to him. From then on, Kelvin moved on with his life. Whenever he and Connie ran each other, there were no hard feelings.

Before Connie headed back to New York, she stopped at the Cook County Jail to visit Peaches, and took BJ with her so BJ could finally meet his biological mother. BJ was twelve now, and Connie felt it was time.

The visit was an awkward one; BJ was used to his adoptive parents and family, so Peaches was a stranger to him, and the conversation was dry. He had more to say to Connie, whom he had gotten to know over the years. In fact, he loved his Aunt Connie, who never missed his birthday or Christmas, and called him at least once a month. After sitting silently and saying few words, BJ felt a need to leave the visiting room.

"I want to go home now," BJ said to Connie.

"Why don't you give your mother a hug and kiss goodbye first."

BJ looked at Peaches, and then gazed back at Connie. "No, I don't want to. I just want to go home. If you don't take me home, I'll call my parents. They'll come and get me."

"Connie take the boy home. He don't want to see me no ways," Peaches lit up a cigarette. "Let him go. Don't force him to do what he don't wanna do."

Connie sighed. "Alright, come along BJ." BJ abruptly stood up from the table, and headed for the exit.

"You hang in there," Connie turned to Peaches and gave her a hug.

"I always do. Just make sure you put some money on my books before you leave alright?"

"Is that the way to ask me for something?"

Peaches looked away and blew smoke from her lips.

"I'm not obligated to take care of you, Peaches."

"You don't have to do me no favors," Peaches sneered.

"Fine. See if I put something on your books then."

"Connie wait!"

Connie turned around.

"Just help me out . . . please. I know you good for it, miss celebrity," Peaches cracked a smile.

Connie shook her head. "Girl you are something else."

Connie was scheduled to fly back to New York later that Sunday night, but there was something pulling on her heart. Before she knew it, she had parked her car at a distance from Dean's house, just enough not to be noticed. She spotted a middle-aged looking woman, who was light-skinned and big boned. She wore her hair in a mushroom with a flip-up bang in the front. Dean Jr. trailed behind her; he had grown tall. Connie figured he had to be almost fifteen now. Dean Jr. and the lady were both dressed up, so Connie assumed they had just come from church, perhaps a late service, but there was no sign of Dean Sr. She wanted to know if this woman was Dean's girlfriend or wife, so she thought she would pay Mrs. Wilson a visit and let her know she was just in town and 'wanted to say hello'.

After small talk with Mrs. Wilson over a cup of tea, Connie nosily shifted to questions about Dean.

"I was going to stop by Dean's house, you know, just to say hello because it's been so long . . . but I saw a woman going inside his house with Dean Jr., and I didn't want to intrude," Connie said, sipping the cup of tea Mrs. Wilson had made for her. "Oh, that hussy. I don't care too much for her," Mrs. Wilson admitted. Connie thought, *so he has moved on.*

"Must be pretty serious, since she met you, though, right?"

"I hope not. I think she's too pushy," Mrs. Wilson admitted. "I don't normally meddle in Dean's private life, because I feel like me and his father pushed him to marry his first wife since she became pregnant. So I minds my business now. But, I don't think Angie is much competition, if you know what I mean." She raised her brow at Connie as she took a sip of her own tea.

"Well, unfortunately, Mrs. Wilson, Dean has made it quite clear that he's not interested in a relationship with me anymore, especially not a long distance one. After all, it's been two years."

"Let me tell you something, honey. Love can travel many places, but it never leaves your heart."

Connie wanted to believe Mrs. Wilson's saying about love, but it was obvious to her that Dean's love for her had left his heart for good. *He's moved on, while I am still carrying a torch for him,* Connie thought as she drank a shot of vodka on the rocks. She regretted spying on Dean. Like the old saying her mother used to tell her— *'if you go looking for trouble, you will find it.'* Connie's heart ached more now than before. She wanted to lose herself, get rid of the pain somehow. She felt guilty for still loving Dean, knowing he had moved on. She questioned if things would have been different had she stayed in Chicago, and wondered if they would be married with a child of their own by now. As her plane began to land in New York, she hoped that maybe Mrs. Wilson would tell Dean that she had stopped by and he would call her to see how she was doing. The call never happened.

CHAPTER THIRTY

BIG DADDY HANK

When Hank got the call from *Ebony* Magazine to model in the Fashion Fair Showcase in New York, it sent his ego flying to another planet. He had been modeling for *Sears* and other clothing catalogues for years, and finally his agent landed him a gig in one of the biggest fashion shows of the year.

He decided to take his ladylove Contessa, whom he had been seeing now for four years. He still dated Rebecca on the side and used her for money. Rebecca asked to join him in New York, but Hank told her he would be so busy that he wouldn't want her to be all by herself in the hotel, so she didn't push the issue.

While in New York, he saw Connie and Tracey at the show, and Connie's celebrity friends. They all went out to dinner together and had a good time. Connie felt good about seeing Hank and Contessa again. Being with them reminded her of old times. Hank enjoyed himself too. He missed Connie, and although he didn't tell her, he preferred Connie over Dean's new girlfriend, Angie.

After the show in New York, Hank flew back to Chicago and spent the night with Rebecca at her place.

"Is everything all right in there, baby?" Hank asked Rebecca the next morning from the bedside. She was taking a long time in the bathroom.

"Everything is fine," Rebecca replied in a way that was intentional, but not honest. She wanted this day to be perfect, nothing out of the norm. She searched through her cabinet to find the perfect medicine needed to top off the day.

"What are you doing, did you fall in?" Hank laughed with his hands behind his back, watching TV.

"No, I'll be out in a minute," Rebecca replied. She loved Hank for years from the moment she laid eyes on him. He was handsome, charming, and a perfect gentleman. Rebecca believed in Hank's ambitions, and supported him in his so-called business ventures, especially financially. Money was no object; she had plenty of it, and if she could use it to support her man, why not? But where was this business? Was it being set up in Chicago? Indiana? Wisconsin? Where? Rebecca had had many unanswered questions for far too long, including why she'd never met Hank's family. Besides Dean, she didn't know who his immediate family was, and every time she asked to meet them, Hank always found an excuse. It had been four years, and Hank hadn't even proposed marriage. Her suspicions led her to hire a P.I. because this time, she refused to have her heart broken again. She couldn't bare it. Time was of essence. She wanted marriage and a baby. However, when the P.I. showed her the photos, her dreams became shattered.

"Her name is Contessa Ichiki. She's Hawaiian," the P.I. informed Rebecca. She learned of the news just two days before Hank had returned to Chicago. Rebecca was a chemist, and she loved what she did for a living. She never thought about doing anything that would bring harm to others or harm her career. Things were a little different now since her heart was broken once again. She held on tight to the small bottle of what she figured was the "solution" to her situation. She opened the bathroom door, wearing Hank's oversized shirt, and slowly walked into the room with her hands behind her back. Hank was lying in bed when he noticed her headed towards him. She had somewhat of an unusual grin on her face.

"You never told me about New York," she said as she slowly walked towards him. The covers lay across his lower body while he leaned back against the pillows.

"It was great! The show will be advertised in the next issue of *Ebony*."

"What else did you do?"

"Nothing," he replied. "Say, why you have your hands behind your back? You got a surprise for me?"

"I find it hard to believe that you did nothing in New York, especially while you were with Contessa."

Hank nearly choked. "Wh-who-who you say?"

"Oh, come on Hank. I know all about Contessa, Susan, Leslie, and Marianne." Hank's eyes bucked in shock. He tried to come up with something, but was totally at a loss of words. He was slipping.

"This is for you, you two-timing timing bastard!" Rebecca tossed the small bottle of liquid at his face.

"AAAAH!" Hank felt his skin burning and jumped out of bed, screaming as he tried to make his way to the bathroom. "What did you do to me?!" He felt his skin burning and his left eye losing vision. Whatever it was, it was eating away at his skin as he tried to reach for the bathroom faucet.

"It's acid! Let it burn!" Rebecca hit him over the head with the empty champagne bottle. Hank fell to the floor and blacked out . . .

Dean and Angie jogged around the track at DePaul University. The campus was busy for a Friday evening. Football players practiced on the field, cyclists rode by, and the basketball court was filled with players, including Dean Jr., who just turned sixteen. Dean finally managed to build the stamina, speed, and muscle power in his thirty-six-year-old legs. It took about two years, but he did it. As he and Angie came around the last stretch, he looked up at the skinny and empty bleachers, remembering how the college students back at Loyola University cheered him on for winning one race after another.

"What are you smiling about?" Angie asked, wiping her face with the towel around her neck. She and Dean had met at this very track only a year ago.

"No reason." Dean kept the thoughts to himself.

"You had to be smiling about something," Angie insisted.

"I just had a thought, that's all."

"Remember, you promised to start sharing your feelings with me."

"It's not that important, Angie."

"If you say so," Angie shook her head upset. "Let's go home."

While Angie was preparing dinner, Dean sat in the living room watching TV. For some reason he noticed something was missing from the table in front of him. He remembered it was Connie's picture that used to sit on the table. He assumed that Angie had moved it. He didn't want to ask her about it since Angie was the jealous type. She never liked Connie's picture sitting in the living room. When she asked Dean to remove it once she moved in, he promised he would, but he didn't. He got up and searched the hallway utility closet, and after digging through two boxes he found Connie's picture. He smiled as he remembered their times together. Going dancing at the discos, double-dating with Hank and Contessa, taking their children to the beach and amusement parks, and meeting Connie's parents for the first time. He missed everything about Connie, the she smiled, laughed, smelled. How soft her skin felt against his. The way her beautiful green eyes would stare back into his when they made love. The memories of Connie could sometimes be overwhelming. Some nights he felt tempted to call her, even with Angie lying next to him.

"Dinner will be ready shortly. I'm going to bake a chicken, and cook some rice and greens to go with it," Angie said, walking into the hallway, and Dean quickly shoved the picture of Connie back into the box and turned off the closet light.

"What are you looking for?" Angie asked suspiciously.

"My flashlight."

"It's right there on the top shelf," Angie pointed. "If it was a snake it would bit you," she laughed.

Dean grabbed the flashlight, acted as if he planned to make use for it. "Uhm . . . Angie, we'll just order take out for tonight. Why don't you just relax? Go watch TV or call your folks back in Wisconsin."

"Don't put off today what you may not be able to do tomorrow," she told Dean, and headed back to the kitchen. He shook his head, and gave up on convincing her to rest.

Dean went upstairs and took a shower, and when he came out of the bathroom, the phone was ringing.

When he picked it up, Angie was on the line talking to his father.

"Hello?" Dean interrupted.

"Oh there he is, Dad. I'll hang up now," Angie hung up the other end.

"Dean, your cousin Hank is in the emergency room."

"What? What happened?"

"He's been burned. He's at the Chicago Hospital."

"What happened?"

"Just what I thought would happen," he said stoically. "He got just what he deserved for messing around."

"Spit it out, Dad!"

"A woman he was messing around with burned his face up with a bottle of acid."

"WHAT?!"

"Well, now you know, and what you do with it is your business."

Mr. Wilson quickly hung up the phone.

"Is everything all right?" Angie overheard Dean's reactions to the phone call, and ran upstairs to see what was going on. Dean explained that Hank was badly burned, and hospitalized.

"I'm going with you."

"You can stay here," Dean said, quickly getting dressed to go see Hank.

"Baby," Angie stroked his shoulders gently with her hands. "Let me go with you. The family needs our support."

Dean thought: *The Family? "Our" support? It's my family, not yours.* He was speechless for a moment as he continued to get dressed in the bedroom. He wanted to tell Angie to mind her business, but she seemed so sincere and meant no harm, so he decided to let her tag along.

When Dean went to see him, he looked horrible. The doctors weren't able to save his left eye. He would be permanently without sight. It would take many years of plastic surgery before the left side of Hank's face would look human again, and he would end up wearing a patch over his left eye for the rest of his life. He pressed charges against Rebecca for assault with a deadly weapon, but she pled temporary insanity and would serve only two years in prison. Dean sat with Hank for most of the night. He was glad his cousin survived such a horrible ordeal, but it was a terrible price to pay for playing two women against each other. Dean felt glad that he stopped playing games with women's hearts. As he looked at Hank, he realized he could have easily been in Hank's shoes. He was so glad his player days were over with . . .

CHAPTER THIRTY-ONE

ONE NIGHT

Connie never liked traveling during the winter, which was why she booked most of the concerts during the summer. Winters did give Connie the opportunity to spend quality time with Tracey, however. Together, they built snowmen on the rooftop of her building, shopped downtown, went ice-skating together at Rockefeller Plaza, and attended plays. They played dress up together, and Connie would allow Tracey to invite her friends over for sleepovers, including Tracey's new best friend Keyshia King, whom everyone called Kay-Kay. She would overhear the girls singing to Friday Night Videos whenever Kay-Kay spent the night. They loved when FNV played songs like *P.Y.T.* by Michael Jackson, *The Reflex* by Duran Duran or Madonna's *Lucky Star*. Tracey and Kay-Kay were always having fun together.

Connie was glad that Tracey had someone who was like sisterly company. Both of them attended the same private school, and Connie had gotten to know Kay-Kay's parents. It was also around this time that Connie noticed Tracey really liked acting. She participated in school plays, and Connie allowed her to act in commercials as long as it didn't interfere with school. She wanted Tracey to have as much of a normal childhood as possible.

Connie and Tracey had just returned from the premier of the movie *Staying Alive* when she caught her phone on the last ring. Tracey had been talking about how she wanted to do movies and became a famous actor. She bragged about her latest commercial with her father in a *Big League* chewing gum commercial. Connie tried to convince Tracey that acting was hard work, and no easy walk in the park, but it was hard to get her nine-year-old star-struck daughter to see that.

"Hold that thought, Tracey, let me hurry and answer this phone . . . .hello?" Connie answered. It was Contessa, and she was crying hysterically. Connie thought something bad happened to Dean.

"Contessa please calm down. I can't understand a word of what you're saying." Connie felt nervous behind the phone, and Tracey stood in front of her mother, wondering what was going on too.

"Connie, there's been an accident, not really an accident, but . . . Hank is in the hospital, and it's really bad!"

"What?" Connie held the phone to her ear. Tracey stood near her mother wondering what the call was about. Connie waved her hand for her to go on upstairs to her room.

"This woman named Rebecca, who I found out he was cheating with, threw acid in his face when she found out Hank had been seeing me all these years."

"WHAT? OH NO!"

"Connie, I didn't even know he was cheating on me. Dean didn't even tell me. Did you know about this too?"

"Well, I um . . . I never saw Hank with any other woman," Connie said. It was part of the truth. She hadn't seen Hank with any other woman before, but she had heard about them through Dean.

"Is Hank going to be all right?"

"I don't know. I don't care!"

"Oh yes you do, Contessa. That's why you're crying so hard. I thought somebody died!"

"Why would he cheat on me, Connie? Why?"

"Have you asked Hank that?"

"I haven't been to see him yet. Dean called me and I told him to relay the message that it's over between us." While Contessa vented, Connie held the phone to her ear as she fixed herself a drink.

"Can you go with me to see Hank? I don't think I can do this alone, Connie."

"You do realize I'm in New York, don't you?" Connie thought to herself, *she must be trippin'!*

"I'll pay for you to come here. I just . . . I need some support, Connie, please."

"I need to think this over, Contessa," said Connie, sipping her gin. "The last thing I want is to be put in the middle of somebody else's relationship."

"Connie, I'm pregnant," Contessa blurted out. "I have to find a way to tell Hank. His timing of cheating on me couldn't have been more wrong," she cried. "You know I don't have any family here in Chicago with me, Connie. I'm scared, angry, and confused. Please come to Chicago, even if it's just for one day. I need a friend right now."

Connie could sense the desperation in Contessa's voice. When Connie hung up the phone, she made reservations for a hotel in Chicago for a three night's stay and a roundtrip flight for next weekend so she wouldn't miss work at the station. CMP staff was independent enough to run on Connie's absence, but she always liked to prepare them in advance for her absence.

Dean faithfully went to see Hank every Thursday on his day off. Angie insisted on meeting Dean at the hospital to show his family that she was supportive. Angie and Dean's mother clashed over Angie's persistence to force her way into the family. "Your mother will just have to get used to me," Angie would say. When sucking up to Mrs. Wilson didn't work, she tried Mr. Wilson. "I'm looking for a new church home," she told him. "That's fine, as long as you stop being a heathen by fornicating with my son," Mr. Wilson told her. Mrs. Wilson, a woman who was a good judge in character, questioned everything about Angie's motives. For a lawyer, Angie often hung herself in her own lies, forgetting what she had said last while she was busy trying to impress him. Dean knew his mother would be at the hospital visiting Hank, so he really didn't want Angie to meet him there, but she did anyway. Family dinners turned into arguments so much that Dean stopped inviting Angie.

"Man, I'm so glad you're here, Auntie is about to baptize me in this hospital bed with this Bible reading she doing." Hank tried to smile, but his face hurt.

"Now, you stop mocking the Good Word. Hell ain't full, you know?" Mrs. Wilson hit him playfully.

"Good to see you in good spirits." Dean shook Hank's hand as he sat down in the chair next to his mother, while Angie pulled up an extra chair and sat opposite Dean.

"Oh, I have my days, man," Hank said. "By the way, my folks said hello. You just missed them."

"How are Uncle Henry and Aunt Mary doing these days?"

"They're fine. You know they hit me with *I told you so.*"

"Well you will bounce back soon enough. Just keep a positive spirit and count it as a lesson learned man. That's all you can do," Dean pat his back.

Angie chimed in as usual. "That's right Hank. A positive spirit produces positive results. I can't remember which book I read that in, but Dean is right. Stay positive."

"Humph! Child, pah-lease! I bet you don't read the Bible like you claim." Mrs. Wilson cut Angie a look.

"Mama, be nice now," Dean countered.

The nurse walked into the room. "Excuse me. There are three more people here to see you, Mr. Wilson, but you can only have four guests at a time."

"I'm an injured man. You can let me have my way this time, can't you?" Hank was still putting on the charm. The nurse thought about it. After all that Hank was going through, she figured it couldn't hurt.

"Okay." The nurse blushed as she walked over to fluff Hank's pillows. "But just for a few minutes. My boss will be here shortly, and I don't want to get into any trouble."

When the nurse left the room, she told Contessa it was okay for her to go inside. Everyone was surprised to see Contessa. Dean almost smiled, feeling glad that she wasn't too mad not to come see Hank. Mrs. Wilson had only met Contessa once, so she didn't remember who she was. Hank had so many women that she'd stopped counting. Contessa greeted everyone nervously, and then walked over to Hank. She wasn't sure if she wanted to kiss his bandaged face or punch him in it for cheating on her.

Hank reintroduced Contessa to his Aunt and Angie after thanking Contessa for coming. She whispered in his ear that they needed to talk privately soon. He nodded his head that he understood.

"I thought the nurse said there were three people," Hank questioned.

"It is," Contessa mentioned. "It's me, Connie and Tracey. Connie is in the lobby signing autographs and taking pictures with the staff."

Dean perked up when he heard Contessa say that Connie was there. He almost felt his heart jump out of his chest.

When Connie finally walked in, she looked gorgeous. Gone were the afro wigs, the butterfly collar shirts, and the bell-bottoms. Her long curls bounced off her shoulders like *a Dark & Lovely* commercial. Her make-up and lipstick were flawless, and the scent of her *Chanel No. 5* perfume quickly filled the stale room. Dean couldn't take his eyes off of her and his mouth nearly dropped to the floor. Even Hank's eye widened with amazement at how beautiful she looked.

"Hello everyone," Connie smiled with a beautiful set of pearly whites, and there was a confident glow about her that radiated throughout the room. She looked right past Dean on purpose, kissed his Mom on the cheek, and then hugged and kissed Hank and asked where she and Tracey could put the "Get Well" flowers and balloons.

"Honey, you look so beautiful!" Mrs. Wilson went on and on, complimenting Connie. "You must come over and have dinner while you're in town."

"I wish I had enough time. I'm leaving tomorrow evening after I visit my sister and nephew."

"Aw that's too bad. I need your information before you go so we can keep in touch. I sure miss you, honey."

"I miss you too. I'll give you my number." Connie jotted it down for her so she wouldn't forget.

"And look at Tracey, growing up pretty just like you. Hi, baby! Come give Grandma Wilson a hug," Mrs. Wilson extended her arms and Tracey hugged her.

Dean thought, *Grandma?*

Angie sat with a poker face. She knew about Connie from when she used to host *Pillow Talk* on WCHI-93.3 Soul, but she knew of her better as Dean's ex-girlfriend. Angie sighed heavily, and then whispered to Dean, "Did you invite her here?"

Dean shook his head but kept watching Connie's every move until Angie elbowed him. "Put your tongue back in your mouth," Angie snapped under her breath. "I'm Angie, Dean's *girlfriend*," she stood up and extended her hand to Connie. Connie stared at Angie's hand for a moment, and then hesitantly shook it.

"It's nice to meet you," Angie forced a smile.

"Thank you. People tell me that all that time," Connie replied, then quickly turned to Hank, ignoring Angie altogether. "How are you coming along, baby?"

Mrs. Wilson started laughing. "Oh my, there's going to be trouble in the wateeeers! Yes Lawd! Troubleeees in the wateeeers," she sang and rocked back and forth.

"Mama, cut it out." Dean glared at her.

"Dean, would you like something to drink? I'm going to the vending machine," Angie offered. Dean had started talking to Tracey, asking her how was school and how she liked New York, and Angie felt like she may as well not have been there.

"Dean, would you like something to drink?"

"Oh, no thanks," Dean quickly turned his attention back to Tracey. "Well, I'm glad you like New York."

"So when are you coming to see us?" Tracey asked one hand on her hip. "You know we miss you, and I miss Dean Jr. We had so much fun together. He's like my brother." Dean could tell she was growing up, and obviously spent way too much time around adults by her mannerisms.

"Um . . ." Dean was hesitant to answer.

"Tracey, don't ask grown people questions like that," Connie said to her, still not saying anything to Dean or looking him in the eyes. She was afraid she would see something in them that would spark nostalgia.

"Well, Dean, when *are* you going to New York?" Mrs. Wilson asked Dean.

"Mama!"

"I think it's time we let Contessa spend some alone time with Hank," Connie suggested. Mrs. Wilson and Dean knew she was right.

"Where are you off to, darling?" Mrs. Wilson asked Connie, grabbing her purse and Bible and following Connie out the room.

"Back to our hotel at The Four Seasons." Connie answered loud enough for Dean to hear. He was practically on her heels as they walked down the hallway. "Tracey and I have been running around all day. I'm ready to kick off these heels and relax." When Connie mentioned her heels, Dean looked down at her red patent leather heels and the tight calves of her legs under her short skirt. He remembered how smooth and firm her legs felt when she would wrap them around his neck or his waist. He wanted to touch them now and see if they felt the same.

Connie hugged Mrs. Wilson once they were outside the hospital saying their goodbyes. "It was so good to see you."

"You too, Sugar. Now stop by and see me before you go."

"I'll try, but if I'm not able, I'll call you. I promise."

". . . and I just don't appreciate her being there if she's not with you anymore."

"Angie, knock it off!" Angie exhaled in frustration.

"I'm expressing how I feel, Dean. You know, you weren't helping matters by isolating me and staring at Connie as if she was a Playboy centerfold. That was disrespectful!"

"Don't be so insecure!" Dean parked the car in front of his perfectly manicured lawn. They walked inside the house. Dean stopped briefly to greet Dean Jr., who was playing Atari in his room while holding the phone to his ear. They waved hello to each other.

"I'm going out for a beer," Dean said to Angie as they walked into his bedroom. He changed into a pair of jeans, a cow-neck sweater, leather jacket, and cowboy boots. Angie changed into her pajamas.

"You know there's beer in the fridge."

"I don't want that kind."

"Then I'll go with you." Angie attempted to slide her clothes back on. "I could use a drink myself."

"Angie, I need to be alone right now."

"Then maybe I should go home, since you don't want me to come with you!"

Dean did not feel like another argument, so he replied, "It's your choice."

"Well, on second thought, I'll stay, but make sure you're back at a decent hour."

"The last I checked, I was a grown man."

"I didn't mean it that way, Dean."

"Sure you didn't."

"I'm sorry, I just meant—"

"You meant it, and I'll be back on my own time."

Tracey fell asleep once they got back to the hotel. She and her mother had had a long busy day. Connie always tried to see everyone in Chicago whenever she visited, and poor Tracey was drained. Connie took herself a long, hot bath, then sat on the white plush sofa of the hotel suite in her satin robe and had some champagne. Atlantic Starr was on the radio, singing, *Let's Get Closer.* This used to be her favorite song, and Connie would play it all the time. No other group sang beautiful ballads the way Atlantic Starr did, Connie felt. She watched the snow landing all over the city of Chicago from the hotel window. . Despite her difficult upbringing, she could see that Chicago was still a very beautiful city, especially at night. She only wished she'd had the chance to enjoy what city had to offer when she was growing up, but they were too poor to enjoy most things.

Ding Dong.

"Sorry to disturb you, Ms. Morris," Truck, her bodyguard, entered her room with a secured keycard. "There is a guy by the name of Dean Wilson who would like to see you." Connie was surprised, but not totally. Her lips curved a flirtatious, giddy sort of a grin. It felt so good to have seen Dean earlier that evening and to feel his eyes on her every move. Connie sipped her champagne, and said flirtatiously. "You can let him in."

"Thanks, man." Dean and Truck slapped fives as if they had known each other for years. Truck went back to standing post outside of her hotel room door. Connie stared at Dean over top of her glass, slowly swallowing the rest of her drink. She sat on the sofa, crossing one leg over the other, making sure she revealed just enough thighs to make Dean guess if she was wearing any panties.

"How did you know I was here?" Connie looked at him just as seductively as he was staring at her.

"You told me . . . well . . . not in so many words, but you were quite specific at the hospital."

Connie slowly stood up and walked over to the bar. Her hair had so much body that her curls bounced with each move. "Would you like something to drink?"

"Rum and Coke." Dean removed his leather jacket and tossed it on the chair across from the sofa.

"What if I wasn't here alone?" She fixed both Dean and herself rum and Coke.

"Then you wouldn't have been so detailed about where you were staying."

"Don't think I was hitting on you, Dean. I was just answering your mother's question."

"That's bull."

"No really, I was," she giggled as she handed him the glass, and sat down next to him. Dean took a few sips of his drink and sat it down on the coaster on the table in front of them.

"So how have you been?" His eyes danced with hers.

She crossed her legs. "Fine."

"I see."

"Does *she* know you're here?"

"No. Does Kelvin know I'm here?"

Connie looked puzzled. "Kelvin?"

"Yes, Kelvin James, the singer. I read in the papers you two were dating or something like that," Dean twisted his lips, remembering how jealous he was when he saw it. He stopped listening to Kelvin's music after that.

Connie laughed. "We're good friends, nothing more."

"That's a typical celebrity answer."

"Noooo." Connie shook her head, and sipped her drink. "Kelvin is a good guy, just not for me. We were friends and nothing more."

"I saw you posing in that *Jet* magazine too."

"And did you like it?" She raised a flirtatious eyebrow.

"Was it for me?"

"I did it because I was asked to, Dean."

"Connie, come on now, you know that's not your style to pose half naked in a two-piece bathing suit."

"Maybe I've changed. Besides, why do you care? You're with Angie."

"I'm not with her now." He leaned in and attempted to kiss her, but she turned her head.

"I think you should go now, Dean."

Dean smirked. "You don't mean that."

Connie stood up from the sofa. "I do mean it, Dean. You should go."

"No you don't mean it," Dean rose to his feet and stared down into her eyes. He eased Connie into his arms, and started placing passionate kisses behind her ear and along her neckline.

"Stop it, Dean. I want you to get out!" Connie shoved him, testing him to see how serious he was and how badly he wanted her.

"You don't want me to get out."

"I do because you don't mean *this*."

"I do," he pulled her into his arms. "I really mean it, and if you don't let me show you, I'll have to put you under arrest." In one swift move, he handcuffed one of her hands to his. "No more games. We got some unfinished business." Dean scooped her up easily and carried her off to the bedroom.

In the bedroom, Dean cuffed Connie's hands to the poles of the bedpost. He started loving her from head to toe with warm kisses and tender touches, arousing all the areas of her body that he knew were sensitive. She moaned uncontrollably when he reached her weak spot and stayed there a while. She was still cuffed and feeling vulnerable—not knowing what Dean would do to her next. It drove her crazy.

With passion, she whispered, "You know it's unfair for you to pleasure me like this, and I not having a share in it too." Dean uncuffed her, and she returned all the favors and then some, rolling on top of him and rocking a good harmonious rhythm. The bed shook hard from their intense and passionate lovemaking.

Dean rolled her over. She wrapped her legs around him as her head hung off the side of the bed, and her hair brushed the carpet on the floor. He took control over her body. For almost an hour, they worked up an erotic sweat, until they collapsed with no more energy and no more loving to give. Their bodies felt so relaxed that they fell asleep immediately afterwards, not even realizing that they had actually stopped.

Dean woke up early, mostly out of routine, but also because Connie's hair was sprawled across his face. When Connie felt him move, she woke up and sat up slowly in bed, with the sheets draped across her naked, sex-scented body. Wiping the sleep from her eyes, she asked, "So, what happens next?"

Dean knew that was coming, and that was why he wanted to hurry up and leave. He shrugged his shoulders. "Well, we both got what we wanted, right?"

"And what was that?"

Dean raised a brow. "I think you know, and I don't have to *say* anything."

"I wish you would."

"You worked it last night. Whew, blew my mind baby. It was *really* good."

"I was hoping it meant more than just sex, Dean."

Dean tilted his head. "You know it did, so I don't know why you would even have to ask."

"I'm asking because I need to know where we stand now."

"Connie, let's not go through this again. You live in New York now, and I'm here in Chicago. That *is* where we stand."

"Dean, I told you last night not to do anything you didn't mean."

"I meant it," he said, fastening his belt, and then sliding his sweater over his head. "It wasn't just sex, but you're just looking for answers about our relationship when you know I don't want a long-distance one. Besides, I can't just break Angie's heart."

"You already did."

"Are you saying you plan to tell her about last night?"

"I won't have to tell her anything, Dean. You're going home to her at four o'clock in the morning smelling like my Chanel No. 5 perfume."

"Well, then, I'll just tell her the truth." He shrugged as if it was no big deal, but he really wasn't sure what would happen once he went home. Angie was a lawyer and he knew she would interrogate him.

"And what truth is that?" Connie barked.

Dean gave her a blank stare. He wasn't really sure.

"Fine, it was just *one* night, but I want you to know you will *never* get any more of this!"

"Connie, don't act like you didn't want this to happen."

"So what if I did!" She snapped. "Am I wrong, Dean? Am I wrong for wanting you back? Am I wrong for still being in love with you?"

Dean walked over to the bedside and gently cupped her cheeks with his hands and kissed her forehead. "No, Connie, you're not wrong. Neither one of us is wrong about how we feel about each other. It's just not the right time for us now. You have your career in New York, and I have Angie. It's not fair, but that's the way it is unless something changes."

"Then why do I feel used?"

Dean wiped her tears with the tips of his thumbs. "You shouldn't, because you know I love you. We both wanted last night to happen. I don't regret it, and neither should you."

Connie sniffed. "But you're going back to her."

"And you're going back to New York, so where will that leave me?"

Dean hated having to leave Connie in such an emotional state, and although last night felt good to him, it made him feel more confused about their relationship than ever before. He'd never stopped loving Connie, but now there was Angie.

"I know you said you're a grown man, and I respect that, but it's almost five o'clock in the morning. Where were you? Because I know the bar closes at some point." Angie had a mean poker face. She was cleaning out the oven when Dean walked in, trying to take her mind off worrying about where he was, and who he was with.

"I'm sorry, I should have called."

Angie tossed the scrub sponge down in the sink and yanked off her giant yellow gloves.

"I wasn't born yesterday, Dean. I know that you went to see Connie, didn't you?"

Dean scratched the side of his head. He wanted to lie.

"You could have at least taken a damn shower, because you smell like her perfume!"

Dean shoved his hands in the front pocket of his jeans.

"You had sex with her, didn't you?"

"Yes, but—"

SMACK.

Dean held his cheek. He couldn't believe Angie hit him. No woman had ever hit him before.

"I hate you!"

"No you don't!"

"I do!" she pushed by Dean and ran up the stairs. Dean took a few minutes before he went after her. In that moment, he felt totally off balance and confused. He tried to plan what he would say on the way home, but all of his lies went out the window. For some reason his heart wouldn't allow him to lie. When he finally went upstairs, he stopped in Dean Jr.'s room, and he was still playing video games. It was five o'clock in the morning, and he was talking on the phone again.

"Cut that thing off! You been playing it since yesterday, and tell Patricia to go back to sleep!" Dean ordered him.

"But Dad, it's winter break!"

"Well read a book or something, or go back to sleep!" Dean Jr. sucked his teeth and rolled his eyes, but he did what his father said. He knew what was going on really had nothing to do with him, but everything to do with his father and Angie.

Dean walked into his bedroom to find Angie sitting on the bed, crying. "I knew you were going to see Connie, but the other part of me wanted to trust you and believe that you were really going to a bar for a beer. How could I be so stupid and go against my better judgment?" Dean looked at her for a moment, felt unsure of what to say, and started to get undressed so he could take a shower. His whole body smelled like Connie, and reminded him of how good last night was. He tried to fight off thinking about it. For some reason his mind replayed every scene so clearly he could taste Connie all over again, hear her moaning in his ear, and feel their skin-to-skin touch. He nearly felt himself getting aroused again by thoughts of her.

"Do you still love her?" Angie questioned.

"Let's just try to move on from this, okay?" Dean opened the door to the bathroom and Angie stormed behind him.

"Why can't you answer me, Dean? Are you not sorry for what you done?"

Dean turned around sharply, sick of her pushing him and said, "No, I'm not sorry, Angie, okay? I'm not sorry. Why should I be sorry?"

Angie burst into tears, and Dean rushed into the bathroom and shut the door.

When Dean got out of the shower, Angie was packing her things. "I can't share you, Dean, and I won't share you."

"Connie is going back to New York and she knew I was coming back here to you."

Angie flopped down on the bed with her face buried in her hands. "Dean, I need to know that last night was a complete mistake, and that the next time Connie comes to town, you won't go running back to her. Can you promise that?"

Dean stepped into his boxers, crawled into bed, and got under the covers. He didn't know what else to say. He loved Connie, and he also cared about Angie, but he didn't want to explain his feelings to either one of them. Both had gotten what they wanted from him, he believed. *Now why am I the bad guy?*

"If you can't promise me you won't sleep with Connie next time she's in town, then it's over," Angie said to him. He just looked at her. His thoughts wondered off to last night. He wondered what Connie was doing at that very moment and what her thoughts were, and if she was still hurt. He still regretted leaving her hurt like that.

"You don't have anything to say right now?" Angie questioned him. Dean was tired of arguing with Angie. He knew if he ignored her, she would just keep interrogating him to find answers to help her to solve how *she* felt and what decision *she* needed to make. For Dean, the answer was simple if it bothered her that much.

He sat up in bed and said to her frankly, "If I ask you to stay, you'll always have doubts about me and Connie, and if you leave, you will have doubts about whether or not you should have stayed. I can't promise you that it won't happen again if Connie comes to town, because I don't know the future. But I do know I'm here with you now because I want to be."

"What kind of answer is that?!" Angie shook her head in disgust. "You're just a player like your cousin Hank, and you saw where that got him!" she threw one of the pillows at him. "It's over! I don't have to take this crap from you!" she shouted, tossing her clothes in her suitcase. "I deserve better than this!" She closed her suitcase. Before she left the room, she looked over her shoulder and said, "And by the way, you can tell your mother that she never has to eat my mac n' cheese, because her greens tasted like a jar of pickles!"

Dean tried calling Connie over the next few days in New York, but she purposely ignored his calls. Frustrated, Dean flew to New York to see her, and met her right outside of the radio station after her morning show.

"Dean? What are you doing here?" Connie looked at him, puzzled.

"You wouldn't answer the phone."

Connie chuckled in disbelief for a moment. It was blistering cold, and Connie wore her long black mink coat with matching gloves and hat. They were calling for a blizzard later in the day. The warm winter temperatures they had been experiencing now disappeared. Old Man winter was now in full force.

"Look, I'm sorry for the way things happened, Connie, but I'm here because I'm willing to give a long distance relationship a try," Dean explained, talking over the blistering wind as his lips quivered.

"But for how long? My schedule will not change. When summer comes around, I'll still be doing tours for months at a time, and then the radio station is doing a city-to-city tour this summer as well. I'm going to be busy. Can you handle that?"

Dean was taken aback by the way Connie laid it out for him. He wasn't so sure now. This was supposed to be simple. *Yes, let's do this. I visit you, and you visit me,* he thought.

"Your silence is always your response to tough questions, isn't it, Dean?" Dean's eyes darted in every direction except at her eyes. He felt tongue-tied and dubious about everything he thought he was once sure of.

"You know what I keep playing over and over again in my mind after we made love that night?" Connie asked, rhetorically. "You said you didn't want to break Angie's heart, but you never thought about mine. In fact, I bet the only reason you're here right now is because Angie left you, didn't she?"

Dean twisted his lips, shoved his hands in the front of his pockets, and gave a heavy sigh.

"Yeah, I figured she did, so you come crawling back to me like I'm sloppy seconds? Hell no! I deserve better than that!"

"Connie, why are you acting like this?"

"Acting like what?"

"Cold and distant." Dean thought about it, and he was not going to take all the blame for what happened. "Let's get out the cold and go back to your place and talk about this more reasonably." He stepped in close to her, and pulled her into his arms.

"No!" she gave him a light shove and stepped back. "I can't do this with you anymore, Dean. I'm tired!" She threw up her hands.

"Tired of what?" he was starting to feel defeated. One minute she wanted a relationship, and the next minute she didn't.

"We just keep hurting each other, Dean, and I'm emotionally worn-out. My heart is not a yo-yo."

"Neither is mine!" he retorted. "But I'm willing to sacrifice, having a long-distance relationship with you if it's the only way for us to be together. We don't have to go back and forth anymore."

"When you left me in that hotel and went back to Angie that showed me who you really loved and who you wanted to be with, Dean. So don't say you love me, because you don't!"

"I do love you, Connie, but I didn't know you were going to show up in my life again after two years. You know what," Dean paused, shook his head in frustration. "This is not about me. It's about you not being able to accept that finally here is a guy who truly loves you. Connie, I'm not Jet. I won't ever leave you or abandon you, and I'm not Smokey; I won't betray your trust. And I'm damn sure not your abusive stepfather, Mason!"

"How dare you even bring that up!" Connie's face turned beet red at his mentioning her stepfather, and she quickly turned around and headed to her car.

"I'm sorry, I shouldn't have mentioned him. Wait, don't go!" Dean caught hold of Connie's hand.

"How do you even know about what Mason did to us? Oh, let me guess, you investigated it, right?" Connie snatched her hand back.

"Connie, let's not change the reason why I'm here. Either we're going to do this or we're not."

"Dean, none of this feels right don't you understand?" Connie said. "It doesn't feel right because *we* were wrong. We shouldn't have slept together while you were in a relationship with someone else. Now two women's hearts are broken—mine *and* Angie's."

"So what are you trying to tell me?" Dean asked, searching her eyes for truth. "Are you saying I flew up here for nothing? Are you saying you don't love me anymore or want a relationship with me? What?"

"I'm saying it's over, Dean, and it should have stayed that way." Truck let Connie into the car and shut the door.

"Sorry brother," Truck said to Dean.

"Yeah man, me too," Dean lamented. Truck got in on the driver's seat and drove Connie home. Dean watched them drive away; feeling like a piece of his heart went with them. He turned and walked in the opposite direction, against the cold winds, to haul down a cab. It was going to feel like a long flight back to Chicago.

CHAPTER THIRTY-TWO

ATONEMENT

Peaches was in her fifth week of rehab, and this was her third attempt at trying to get clean. She had been incarcerated for three years now. She went from fighting a heroin addiction to fighting a crack addiction, which she got hooked on right in prison. She was now seeing a different counselor, a man named Mr. Delroy, whom Dean had referred her to.

In fact, Dean told Peaches, "I can get you out of prison, but you have to help yourself first." Peaches wasn't sure how, but for reasons she couldn't explain, she trusted Dean. "Look, you can appeal your case, because Poncho's been busted, and some of the confessions he made during his trial indicates that the heroin found in your apartment was not yours but his. He planned to distribute it," Dean explained to her. "But you can't beat this rap sheet all strung out like this. The judge will take one look at you and throw your case in the slush pile."

Peaches asked Dean, "Why do you care so much about me?"

Dean wasn't exactly sure, but he knew he was sick of seeing innocent people in prison. Besides, Detective White said something to him weeks before Dean had spoken with Peaches. "You have the power to free the only family that Connie has left. So if you can separate what happened between you two personally, you will see that Peaches should not be in prison." Dean felt that Detective White was right.

So there Peaches was, sitting in Mr. Delroy's office lying on his couch, while an officer stood in the corner to make sure Peaches didn't get out of hand. Mr. Delroy talked to her some more and dug into her past. Unlike Peaches' previous counselors, Mr. Delroy had a no-nonsense approach, and he had been well informed about Peaches by Dean and from viewing her files.

". . . .and why do you hate your sister Connie?" Mr. Delroy was asking her.

"I don't hate my sister, but she was always a goody-two-shoe."

"Why do you say that?"

"My mother favored her, and that's what made me not like her."

"I see."

"My father used to beat the crap out of us, but he beat Connie the worse. So my Mom's pampered Connie a lot, you understand. Nobody treated me special like that, though, not my Mama or my father."

"Peaches, you keep pointing fingers at everybody else who has hurt you, but have you ever thought about the hurt you may have caused other people?"

"Man, I ain't never hurt nobody!" Peaches dragged on her cigarette, then released the smoke into the air.

"Oh, I doubt that," Mr. Delroy chuckled. "When you got pregnant at a young age, you don't think your mother was hurt?"

"Hell, she got pregnant young, too, so why judge me?"

"From what you've told me up to this point, it seems you defied her rules."

Peaches thought about it for a minute. *Yeah, I was one defiant little heifer,* she thought to herself.

"Do you think you hurt your son BJ?"

"I don't know. I guess." She shrugged her shoulders.

"Poor BJ. He suffered while you were strung out on drugs, and all he wanted was his mother."

Tears escaped Peaches eyes. "Yeah, he's still hurt. That's why he won't talk to me. He only talks to my sister. He won't even respond to my letters or phone calls."

"You lied to your friends and your neighbors and hustled them out of money for your habit, and you stole goods out of stores, but you don't think you hurt those people either, do you?"

"Yeah I guess I did," She sniffed.

"Connie, your sister, the only family you have left next to your son, chooses to stand by your side through your battles of addiction while you serve time in prison," Mr. Delroy continued. "She could have easily moved on with her fame and riches, but she visits you at every chance she gets, and provides for you. And not only that, she visits your son and gives him whatever he needs and wants, and you think she's just a goody-two-shoe, right?"

"I mean . . . well . . . sometimes," Peaches suddenly felt unsure.

"When Connie sends you care packages, do you send her a thank you letter or a card?" he asked. "How about when she's come to visit you, do you give her a hug and say, '*Sis, thank you for helping me and caring for my son.*' Have you ever done that?"

Peaches choked, "Why are you doing this Mr. Delroy? Why?"

"I just want you to see how your addiction has made you selfish," he explained. "You see, nobody owes us anything, Peaches. Until you understand that, that's the only way you will stop blaming and finger-pointing, and making excuses for your own behavior. Nobody owes us, but we owe ourselves."

"I didn't mean to be selfish."

Mr. Delroy handed her a tissue. "I have a project for you. I want you to write a letter to everyone whom you have ever hurt and apologize to them. Start with your son, and then your sister. They are the only family you have left. If you ever want to get out of prison and start a new life for yourself, perhaps you should reach out to your family and apologize for hurting them."

Peaches wiped her tears. It had been a long time since cried so heavily. "Peaches, you have the power to bring your family back together again and make what's wrong, right. Some people don't get a second chance, but for some reason Detective Wilson and Detective White believe you deserve one. Honestly, I do too, but you must take advantage of this opportunity before it's too late."

Dear Connie,

I hope things are cool with you. I met this cat name Mr. Delroy who is my rehab counselor and he's been bringing some things out in me that I never saw in myself. I been selfish, but I want to change that. You know when we were little girls I was always jealous of you because you were so pretty and so smart. I hated when dudes would bypass me to get to you. I hated how Mama favored you. I was jealous and I want to say I am sorry. I am proud of the woman you turned out to be despite the abuse you suffered from our father. I wish I had your success. I wish I never got high on drugs or gotten pregnant so young. I failed at almost everything in life, Connie, but I'll not fail rehab. I promise! I am going to get my life together for me first, then work on being a better person to everybody else. Thank you, for everything you have done for me, and for BJ. Oh, guess what? I am ten credits away from earning my bachelor's degree in business! They say if I keep good behavior, I can stay in the minimum-security section and get more privileges, like a job working in the library instead of busting suds in the kitchen. I'm on my way baby, so keep praying for your Big Sis! Tell my niece and my son that I love them very much!

Peace and Love,

Peaches

When Connie first read Peaches' letter, she felt happy. She'd waited a long time to hear Peaches apologize. She had also been waiting to hear something good about her getting her life together. Yet, a part of Connie felt guilty, guilty about the way she had started living her own life. She was drinking almost every day now to try to escape her years of pain and heartache.

CHAPTER THIRTY-THREE

TRUTH NEVER HIDES

Dean was more hurt from his breakup with Connie this time than before. He started to harassing people and bullying criminals he arrested to the point of beating them up and denying that he did it. Today was no different, especially when Detective White called him and said, "I got something for you."

"What?" Dean snapped, eager and ready to knock someone upside the head.

"Not *what*, but *who*," Detective White stated. "Calm down. Meet me on 43rd Street ASAP."

Dean quickly got dressed, grabbed his gun and badge and headed out the door until Dean Jr. called for him.

"Dad, where're you going? We have the fishing trip today with Grandpa and the fellas from the church," Dean Jr. approached him at the front door. It was five o'clock in the morning, and they were supposed to meet at seven AM at his father's church and take a camper down to Taylor Lake in Lake County.

"Shoot!" Dean retorted. "Tell your Grandfather to come pick you up. I have some business to take care of now."

"That's messed up, man. You promised, you said—"

"I know what I said, Dean, now just do it!"

"Don't yell at me!" Dean Jr. countered back. "I'm not a little kid, so don't yell at me!" Dean paused for a moment as he stood at the door. He turned around slowly and faced his son. Dean Jr.'s eyes watered with anger and disappointment. Dean placed both his hands on his son's shoulders and looked him in the eyes.

"One day you will understand that what I do is for you too, son."

Dean Jr. knocked his father's hands off his shoulders. "Man, step off! I won't ever understand!"

"Dean, there will be other trips. You say you're not a kid, so quit acting like one. Only punks whine about stuff!"

"I'm not a punk!" Dean Jr. argued. "But a real man is there for his son. Only suckers aren't. So go on to your stupid job, see if I care!" Dean Jr. stormed upstairs, slammed his bedroom door, and starting blasting his music. Dean knew there was no way to change his son's feelings, so he didn't go after him. He opened the door and headed out for work.

"Dean, what you did earlier was dirty," Detective White said, after witnessing Dean beat up a drug dealer in an alley.

"I know, but it felt good, and if I see another buster so much as piss against a wall, I'm gonna bash his head in."

"That's not who you are, Dean. Now, what's eating you?"

"Nothing's eating me!" he yelled.

"Something's eating you, I know it." Detective White left their beat on 43rd Street near the Robert Taylor Homes. He felt they needed a break, and took a scenic route down interstate 90 to 94 towards Lakeshore Drive. He hoped it would break the monotony.

"I'm just doing my job, and I have the right to get pissed off like everybody else!"

"Not like that. You're a rules kind of guy, you always have been."

"Maybe I'm tired of rules. Have you thought about that?"

"There's no harm in bending the rules to get justice, but whatever is eating you, you need to let it out."

"I told you man, it's nothing. Now drop it!"

"Fine, I won't push it."

Dean looked out the window from the passenger seat as they sat at a red light. He spotted a couple kissing on the corner of East Jackson Drive, at the entrance of Grant Park. He thought of Connie, and remembered when they would kiss by the Buckingham Fountain.

"Can't they do that stuff in private?"

"Do what?"

"That couple over there, kissing like that, is what!"

"They're in love. You remember what that was like, right?"

"Don't patronize me, man."

"So, did she break your heart or did you break hers?"

"Both."

"Then either move on or make it right."

"It's not that simple, Gary."

"Why not?"

"She's in New York."

"Oh, you mean Cat Morris. What happened to the lawyer?"

"Gone."

"Gone? Both of them?"

"Yep."

"Well it seems you at least know who you want," White said. "You can always request a transfer and go to New York. I'll miss you as a partner, but I'll get over it."

"I'm not going anywhere, man! Chi-town is my town, you got that?"

"Hey, you don't have to get snappy with me, buddy," White countered. "I'm just saying if you love Cat, don't mess around and be like me. I'm sixty years old, twice divorced with children who hate my guts. It ain't worth it," White continued. "Worse part is, my children are grown and I can't fix how I ruined their lives. The closest I'll ever get to another woman again will be a ten dollar hooker."

Dean didn't know what to say. He just kept looking out the window feeling angry and frustrated.

"Your son, does he love you?" White asked trying to make sure he had Dean's attention, as they rode around downtown. They had been partners for years now and he grew to care about Dean like a son.

"It depends on what day you ask."

"Then you're not doing enough for him. Trust me, I know," White pointed at himself. "I normally don't get all personal, but I'm just telling you not to waste too much time out here trying to solve crimes when what's personal needs solving. I don't have much of a life anymore, so this doesn't matter to me. It's what I do. It keeps me busy. It helps me not to focus on the past, but you don't have to be me. You can be different."

"Oh yeah?" Dean smirked. "In what way, since you got all the answers?"

"Aren't you even listening to me? What do you think I've been saying this whole ride?" White shook his head. "Dean, you're blowing it. The truth is right in your face, it's not hiding. You just need to open your eyes and see it."

"Take me back to my car."

"Do what?"

"I'm supposed to be on a fishing trip with my son."

White looked at his watch. It was ten-thirty in the morning.

"Let's grab a cup of coffee first, and then I'll take you back."

"No, take me back to the station to get my car now!"

"If you say so." White turned the car around and took the ramp to get back on the highway.

"All right man, see you later," Dean told him.

"You made the right decision to be with your son. It's a first start to not being me," White gave him the thumbs up.

When Dean arrived at Taylor Lake County, Dean Jr. was very happy that he came.

Dean Jr. found himself sitting on the church pew, listening to his grandfather preach about forgiveness. He glanced around at the congregation, at people who nodded "amen", hung up on every word his grandfather preached.

"Are you all right?" whispered his grandmother. Dean Jr. nodded. After his grandfather's sermon, the choir sang loud and boisterously, and Dean Jr. and his girlfriend Patricia snuck off to the basement, where they kissed.

"We better go now before we get in trouble," Patricia said, feeling nervous.

"Wait," he grabbed hold of her hand. "Can I get a feel?"

"A what?"

"You know, can I touch your breasts?" Dean Jr. asked anxiously.

Patricia thought about it for a moment. "Dean, I don't think that's a good idea, and especially not here."

"Come over my house tomorrow. My Dad's never home anyway."

"I don't know, Dean."

"Oh come on, we been talking about going all the way for a while now. It's time, baby."

"But we're not married. It will be a sin."

"We can ask for forgiveness later." He gently pulled her into his arms, slid one hand up her blouse, and squeezed. "It's so soft. Feels like a water balloon."

"Stop Dean, don't do that!" She pushed him away.

"WHAT ON EARTH IS GOING ON DOWN HERE?" shouted Mrs. Gray, Patricia's mother, who stood at the top of the stairwell.

Patricia and Dean jumped in shock.

"Patricia, you get your fast tail on up here right now!" Mrs. Gray shouted. "You told me you had to use the restroom over thirty minutes ago. And you, young man, you're in trouble. I'm going to report your promiscuous behavior to Pastor Wilson!"

Back at the house . . .

"What you did was very sinful. Don't you ever carry on like that again in the house of the Lord!" Mr. Wilson scolded his grandson. "That's just being a heathen."

"Only heathen in the church today was you," Dean Jr. rolled his eyes.

"I beg your pardon!" Mr. Wilson's eyes bucked in shock.

"How can you preach about forgiveness when you can't even forgive my Dad? He didn't kill my uncle, you know, and I believe him. Why can't you?"

Suddenly they heard the sound of a plate crashing to the floor in the kitchen.

"Honey, are you okay in there?" Mr. Wilson called out.

"Just fine. I broke a plate. I'm cleaning it up now," Mrs. Wilson said as she swept up the broken pieces.

"Now look-a-here, young man," Mr. Wilson turned his attention back to Dean Jr., who was sitting on the sofa with his arms folded and long legs stretched out before him. "You don't worry about the business I have with your Daddy," Mr. Wilson pointed. "You had no right fooling around with Patricia in the basement of the house of the Lord, period!"

"It may not be my business, but you guys make it mine when half the time you don't even talk to each other like a father and son should. If God talks to his son, why can't you talk to yours?"

"Dean, you are being disrespectful, and I won't have it," he warned.

"Yeah well I'm just telling the truth. When I have my own son one day, I'll make sure I tell him 'Son, I love you no matter what.'"

"Humph, you think it's that simple?"

"It's three words, but everybody act like it's so hard to say. But it's not."

Mr. Wilson thought for a moment about what his grandson had just said to him and realized he had a point. He could see the truth that his relationship with Dean had gotten out of hand for far too long.

"You go on upstairs and wash up for supper. Your father will be here to pick you after dinner."

CHAPTER THIRTY-FOUR

DIPSO

Connie was scheduled for an interview with *Modern Woman* magazine. Cheryl knew she had to get Connie ready for her interview, so she called to make sure she was awake. Connie answered the phone, sounding very sluggish from working the radio studio and CMP. The night before, she went out dancing and got drunk. She was doing more interviews, hosting charity events and award shows, doing speaking engagements, modeling clothing, and doing photo-shoots for hair and make-up products. Cheryl could see that Connie was trying to drown herself in work and in the bottle to bury her pain since the breakup with Dean.

"Connie, about last night," Cheryl mentioned, handing Connie a cup of coffee and a muffin.

"I don't know anything about last night, and neither do you, right? I just had a few drinks, that's all," Connie said, nearly putting the thought into Cheryl's head that what she had heard from Truck didn't actually happen. Truck told Cheryl that he had to carry Connie out the club to her car and drive her home because she had started dancing on top of the tables and acting belligerent.

"Cheryl," Connie called. "I'm not an alcoholic, so don't think that way about me."

"No disrespect, Connie, but it's not about what I think. It's what I see," Cheryl explained. "Some nights you come home drunk and I end up watching Tracey because I try not to let her see you that way."

"Like I said, my drinking is not a problem!" Connie snapped.

"Is there anything else you need from me before your interview?" Cheryl asked, seeing she wasn't getting anywhere on the subject.

Connie thought for a moment, gritted her teeth. "No, take the rest of the day off. As a matter of fact," Connie reached in her purse and handed Cheryl her MasterCard. "Go shopping."

Cheryl looked at the card Connie was holding in her hand, and imaged how wild she could go with it, but decided not to accept the bribe. "Thanks, Connie, but having the day off is good enough for me."

Mr. Yancy threw Connie a huge surprise birthday party at The Waldorf Astoria. The room was packed, and comedian Eddie Murphy opened the event with standup. Connie had been so busy that she forgot it was her birthday. Mr. Yancy surprised her, hiring her old friend DJ Ray to play the music.

Connie apologized to him profusely for the way she had treated him the last time they saw each other. "I accept your apology, and don't worry. You will always be my home girl from the Chi," he said to her. Later on that night, Ray introduced Connie to his new girlfriend. Connie was glad there were no hard feelings.

After a few drinks, Connie danced up a sweat on the dance floor, and Mr. Yancy stepped in to dance with the birthday girl. She laughed at the way he two-stepped through *Candy Man* by the Mary Jane Girls. "Hey, I don't think I did too bad for a white guy," he laughed at himself.

The next day, Connie couldn't even remember all of what happened at the party. She was hung over. Cheryl had seen enough. She wanted to save her friend. Out of concern, Cheryl called Connie's father and told him about Connie's drinking problem. He flew to New York within a few days and had brunch with his daughter. He told Connie that he used to have a drinking problem, and that was how he and his father began to lose the company before they eventually had to sell it.

"If it wasn't for Margaret, I would still be hittin' that bottle, but I gave it up cold turkey," he said to Connie over brunch.

"But I don't have a problem," Connie insisted. There was no talking to Connie. She wasn't listening to anyone.

Connie jumped back into the dating scene after a friend of hers introduced her to millionaire Adolfo Pacelli. Adolfo was a thirty-three-year-old Italian who owned several women's clothing and jewelry stores in the United States, Italy, and Paris, called *Pacelli*. On his first date with Connie, he bought her three hundred different pairs of shoes with matching purses as a belated birthday present. The press was all over it, including *Entertainment Tonight*. Then, after dating for just three months, Adolfo bought Connie a Porsche.

Their faces graced the covers of almost every magazine as Hollywood's new hot interracial couple. Paparazzi followed them around everywhere, and Connie hated it.

Coffee always helped Connie to get over her hangover. Despite partying often, she never missed a day of work.

". . . and I'm Cat Morris from the Sunnyside-Up Morning Show. Thanks for listening to the number one radio station in New York, WHKY-The Beats!"

Connie stood up from her chair and turned around to leave the booth and bumped into a person she least expected.

"What are you doing here?" she forced a smile, as Mr. Yancy stepped into the studio with him.

"Connie, Smokey Johnson is our new program manager." Mr. Yancy smiled and proudly patted Smokey on the back as he puffed his cigar.

"But I don't understand," Connie was perplexed. "What happened to Marty?"

Mr. Yancy replied, "He was dismissed." Connie had never seen Mr. Yancy behave this way before. His easygoing, friendly manner got up and ran somewhere else. "It's time to head in a new direction, Connie," Mr. Yancy stated. "Music is changing, people are changing, and Smokey here is just the right person to help give the station an added spark to make sure we stay afloat."

"Smokey's resume lists a huge body of creative programming that he has done in Chicago, and we could use that here." Connie immediately felt her throat getting tight. Smokey as her new immediate supervisor did not sit too well with her. "I'll be in my office while you two get *reacquainted*."

"Welcome aboard." Connie forced a fake smile and shook his hand, trying to be a professional about things.

Smokey grinned, and then leaned over and whispered in her ear, "You better start kissing my ass if you want to keep your job."

Connie whispered back, "I'm not worried, but if you don't watch it, you'll end up on *your* ass in the end."

Connie was explaining to Adolfo what happened at the radio station while having dinner at her house later that evening.

"Eat your dinner, and leave Smokey away from the table, okay?" Adolfo told her. His long, skinny arms plated her food. Adolfo was the skinniest man Connie had ever dated, and she couldn't understand why, because he loved to cook and eat. He could easily devour a couple of steaks.

"I can't. I can hardly eat because I'm so upset." Connie ran her fingers through her hair in frustration.

"Mmm, this smells good." Tracey sniffed the aroma coming from her plate of food.

"I know you will enjoy it, Tracey, I cooked it especially for you, since you like Italian food." Adolfo smiled as he reached into the pocket of his cream-colored linen pants. He pulled out his cigarette lighter and lit the candles on the table.

"This is called Rigatoni con la Pajata. You ladies will love it!"

"Adolfo, I'm sorry, but I just can't eat this right now," Connie pushed her plate aside. "I need a drink."

"Just quit if it bothers you that much!" Adolfo exclaimed. "I tell you every day to quick the business and let me take care of you. Then you wouldn't have to worry about a douchebag like Smokey," Adolfo said. "The guy's a freakin' schmuck."

That night, Adolfo tried to come on to Connie while they were lying in bed watching TV, but Connie was not in the mood, and didn't want to spend another evening faking it.

"You are so tense, still. I thought maybe your drink would have relaxed you," Adolfo said as he began to massage her shoulders.

"No. I'm still upset."

"Come, give me a kiss." Adolfo gently tried to lure her on top of him.

"I really don't feel like it, Adolfo."

"Once we get started, you will love it. Now come."

"No, Adolfo, I can't," Connie pulled the covers up to her neck. That's when she felt Adolfo sliding his hands between her legs.

"Will you stop it and go to sleep!"

"Connie, I'm only trying to relax you."

"It's not working, and I need you to stop!"

"It usually helps."

"No it doesn't! You're not that good!" the words escaped her mouth without thought. It was true. No other man could please her the way Dean had.

"What did you just say?" Adolfo eased back away from her. The reality of what Connie said made her feel like she had just shattered fine crystal on the floor. She wished she could take it back. Fix it. Make it better.

"I didn't mean that. I'm sorry."

Adolfo stood up and began to get dressed.

"Adolfo, don't leave. Adolfo!"

"Goodnight Connie." he stormed out of the bedroom and rushed down the spiral stairs and out the door.

Connie received a phone call from the Chicago Police. They told her that Gina's Lounge had been shut down for unpaid fines. She hung up and called Donald to ask him what was going on.

"We paid those fines, and yes, there have been fights, but that's typical when you have a club and people are drinking. Gina's is no different from any other club around here," Donald explained.

"I do not understand this. I was just there visiting and you assured me that everything was okay, and everything seemed fine when I checked the books."

"I don't understand it either," was all he could say.

"When were you going to tell me that it was shut down?"

"I'm just finding out from you. I had no idea. I swear."

"So are you just going to just sit on your hands? If the people want Gina's to stay open, then it will. You need to help me get to the bottom of this, and you're in a better position to find out."

"You're right. I'll see what I can do."

"No, don't just *see* what you can do, I need you to act now."

"You're right."

Connie suspected there was more to the story, and she was going to get to the bottom of it. "You know what," she said to him. "Don't even worry about it."

"Connie, I promise you I can fix this."

"You're fired, Donald. You're done."

CLICK'

Connie got on the phone with her lawyer and demanded he hire investigators to find out what was going on with Gina's Lounge. "I'm on it. I'll get back to you."

"Is everything okay?" Cheryl asked Connie, seeing she was upset.

"Your brother was just fired. He allowed Gina's to get shut down."

"What?" Cheryl was surprised.

"Fines for violations, not renewing the liquor license, violence, the whole nine, and he didn't say a word to me about it when I was just there a couple of months ago."

"That's not like my brother."

"Are you and your brother hiding something from me?"

"Of course not!" Cheryl was hurt that she would even ask.

"If I find out you had anything to do with this, Cheryl, you will be fired too." Connie tossed her purse over her shoulder and headed out.

When Connie arrived at the station, Stephanie from the evening show was sitting in Connie's seat inside the booth. She was saying, "Cat's out sick today, so I'm filling in for her."

"Why is she filling in for me?" Connie asked the staff, but no one would say a word. Then Smokey appeared.

"You're late."

"I'm not late. I'm on the set in five minutes."

"You can't come in here with less than five minutes to start and expect to run the show."

"You can't come in here in less than two weeks and tell me that I can't!"

"You're being insubordinate. Be careful. That could get you fired," he said with a devious grin.

"Don't push me," Connie pointed her finger at him. "I'm warning you, you will regret it," Connie spoke through clenched teeth. Everyone looked on, wondering what type of relationship Connie and Smokey had. It was obvious to the staff that they had some kind of a past that was causing a riff.

Eventually, the staff leaked it to the media, and then all of a sudden WHKY was in the news addressing the riff. Mr. Yancy seemed to get a kick out of the publicity, but Connie didn't like it. She felt Mr. Yancy was intentionally playing her and Smokey against each other for ratings, and she hated it.

Connie vented with her good friend Ray Brown over lunch later that day. Ray was operating his own record label these days, and recruiting and producing rap artists.

". . . And the games Smokey is trying to play. I think he's trying to get me fired," Connie was saying to Ray.

"I agree with you. You know after all these years Smokey has been riding your coattail. I think he always wanted to have your success, and since he couldn't have your success, he's trying to sabotage you.

"So what do you think I should do?"

"Honestly, you're much bigger than radio now. I think it's time for you to move on to bigger and better things anyway."

"Like what?"

"Marketing. Go for a marketing gig at a big record company. It's big money in it. It's consistent, and you can still promote concerts if you like."

"I don't know Ray. I love radio, but it seems like a male-dominating business."

"That's just your experience, but I'm telling you you're bigger than radio now. It's time for you to crossover, and you don't need me to convince you. Just look around. You're in every commercial ad, your face is all over the billboards. You're a brand now Connie. Use your name to your advantage."

Connie reached over and hugged him. "Thank you Ray. You always know what to say."

"You're welcome."

"I love you so much."

"I love you too."

CHAPTER THIRTY-FIVE

LETTING GO

Mr. Wilson watched his son Dean run around the track at the University of Chicago. Spring was approaching, and Dean was weeks away from becoming a certified personal trainer. The course was twenty-weeks long, and he aced the written exam and passed several of the exercise tests already. Dean hadn't dated anyone since Angie. In fact, when he saw her a few months after they had broken up; she was already engaged to be married. Angie proudly introduced Dean to her fiancé while they were at the track. Dean simply congratulated the two of them and wished them well. In his mind, he always knew that Angie wanted marriage, and it really didn't matter who the man was.

Blood pumped hard and fast through Dean's veins, while he ran against the warm springy Chicago breeze. He happened to look up and see his father standing in the bleachers. He was holding a timer in his hand and wearing a baseball cap. Mr. Wilson walked down the bleachers towards Dean, who was sweaty and trying to catch his breath. "You were 55.10. I suppose age plays a factor in it now, but that's still pretty darn good for the 400 yard dash in under a minute."

Dean wiped the sweat from his forehead. "I'm trying to get down to 44.10, what I used to run when I went to the Olympics."

"It was 43.86; you tied at number four with some guy named Evans from Mexico City." Dean grabbed his Gatorade and backpack off the bleachers. As Dean gulped down his drink, his father began to talk.

"Dean told me you were here when I stopped by your house this evening," Mr. Wilson mentioned. "You left your timer, so I brought it with me."

"So what's up?"

"I've been doing a lot of thinking lately," Mr. Wilson admitted. He fooled around with the stop-watch in his hands. "There isn't a lot of time left. Life is short, so I want to settle this . . . *thing* between us, and not have to stand before the glory of God condemned to hell for not forgiving you."

"You don't have to preach to me, man, just say what you need to say." Dean finished his drink. He was not interested in hearing about heaven or hell. As far as he was concerned, he saw hell every day on the streets, and heaven was unreachable to some.

"Dean, for years I was angry with you for what happened to your brother, Johnny," he began, trying to choose his words wisely, and praying in his head that he would say the right things. "I felt it was your disobedience that caused his death. Truth is," Mr. Wilson let out a long sigh. "you both were knuckleheads in your own way. I also blamed myself. I figured if I was around more and gave you boys more of my time instead of working and preaching to others, then maybe you wouldn't have been so hardheaded. I recently prayed to God to help me relieve my anger towards you, towards myself, and even towards your mother. I'm just here to say that I'm sorry."

Dean bit down on his bottom lip, not knowing what to do or what to say. He still felt angry, hurt, and uncomfortable just standing in front of his father, who was never a man to apologize for anything.

"Your son needs more attention from you, Dean. He's got one more year in high school before he goes off to college, so don't put your job before him the way I did with you and Johnny," Mr. Wilson cautioned. "Set your family as a priority."

"Yeah, well I've been working on that," Dean cynically replied.

"I know you're trying, and I probably didn't help much by my example." Mr. Wilson looked Dean directly in the eyes. "You know the real reason I never wanted you to be a cop was I feared losing you. If something happened, I would be without two sons," he explained. "You know, your son Dean doesn't have an athletic bone in his scrawny teenage body," he chuckled, skipping the subject a little. "He's tall, but too clumsy for sports. He's more of a brainy teenager, really. He's smart with this new computer stuff and videogames, and he's into these girls, especially Patricia Gray." He laughed lightly. "I just thought you ought to know that so you won't try to force sports on him the way I tried to force religion on you."

"Yeah, well I picked up on it." Dean wiped the sweat from his face with his towel.

"Just so you know, I remembered your numbers in the Olympics because that's how proud I was of you."

"That would have been nice to hear when I was twenty years old, don't you think?" Dean shook his head in dismay. Here it was the spring of 1984 and he was thirty-six.

"Better late than never."

"All right, man, well, I appreciate the small talk, but I need to get going." Mr. Wilson quickly grabbed Dean and wrapped his arms around him.

"Let me go, man. What are you doing?" Dean tried to break loose from the big arms of his father. He was big like a construction worker.

"I love you, son."

"Let me go, man. Come on now, back up!" Mr. Wilson tightened his grip.

"I love you son, and I mean it. I'm sorry for hurting you."

"Let me go . . . let me go." Dean's eyes filled with tears. He knew deep down in his heart that he had always wanted his father to hug him and to show him love and appreciation. He allowed his backpack to drop to the ground, and gave in to hugging his father back.

"I'm sorry Dean. Please forgive me." Mr. Wilson held his son in his arms. Dean was a grown man now, but that little boy inside of him always wanted his father's forgiveness, love and reassurance. Dean's chest shivered and he began to cry uncontrollably on his father's shoulders. All the hurt, all the pain for nearly two decades felt like a heavy burden lifted off his shoulders. Mr. Wilson raised his eyes heavenward and he said, "Thank you, Father."

Peaches sat on a metal cot with her face buried in her hands. Next to her was the plain blue skirt and white top she hoped to wear out of prison if the judge approved her appeal today. She had been living in the boxed cell for the past four years now. Pictures of her son BJ and her niece Tracey hung on the wall. Each photo showed their age progression year after year. She was proud to be thirteen months clean now. She had wasted half of her life on drugs, and now she was anxious to start anew.

"Morris, it's time." One of the officers let her out of her cell and cuffed her hands and feet. He escorted her to a white van waiting outside to carry her and other female inmates to court. She boarded the van wearing her puke green prison dress—a dress she'd always hated. She sat down next to Edna, who had served over thirty years, and was like a mother to the other inmates. She hoped the judge would set her free today, too. As the van crossed over another downtown bridge (one of the Chicago Loops), Peaches looked below at the Chicago River and thought about her sister Gina's poem. It was a poem that Peaches remembered by heart, and she began to recite it. Edna listened as she recited each stanza.

". . . No matter what my troubles, a river keeps flowing by," Peaches smiled at Edna when she was finished.

"I like that," Edna nodded.

"Life goes on, Edna." Peaches finally understood the meaning of the poem. "No matter what happens today, our lives will go on just like a river."

The only drugs Peaches was responsible for was the dope she had shot in her veins. She hoped her appeal in admitting the drugs belonged to Poncho would set her free. Her new lawyer included all the necessary evidence that pointed to Poncho as the violator of the law. She was also able to get two of Poncho's former runners to testify against him in a plea deal. Poncho was already in prison for other charges and serving ten years. Now, if convicted of these new charges, he would have another twenty years added to his current sentence. Peaches no longer feared Poncho or the people he was connected to. She just wanted to be free, and part of being free was telling the truth.

The judge approached the bench, ready to deliberate her final verdict, and the court rose to its feet.

"Case number 455-DRP, Donna Morris verses the State of Illinois, the Court found you guilty of possession of a controlled substance in 1980 under Judge Andrews," said the Judge Jackson. "However, after re-evaluating this case and the new evidence brought forth, the court has found you *not* guilty of the charges as said forth, and therefore overturns your conviction. The Court orders your release effective immediately, and shall remove from your record all charges as so ordered. Furthermore, I recommend that you continue another year of counseling to help you readjust to society. A lot has changed in four years, Ms. Morris, and you will need all the assistance you can get. Case dismissed."

Judge Jackson hit her gavel, stood up, and left the court. Peaches began to cry like a baby as she hugged her lawyer and Mr. Delroy. "I'm free! I am so free!"

While Peaches was hugging Mr. Delroy, she looked over his shoulder and saw Dean standing in the back of the courtroom, smiling. She knew that he'd helped her by telling her about Mr. Delroy. He helped save her life. She moved her lips to say *thank you.*

Dean nodded his head, and left the courtroom. For the first time in his career, he felt like a true hero. Justice was served and a life was saved.

CHAPTER THIRTY-SIX

MY SISTER'S KEEPER

Smokey knocked on Mr. Yancy's office door, then entered when he was invited in. "I'm sorry to disturb you, Mr. Yancy, but there is a matter that needs to be brought to your attention." Mr. Yancy looked up from his newspaper. His office was huge, with a beautiful backdrop of the New York City skyline.

"What is it Smokey?"

"I see you're reading the stock market section of the *Wall Street Journal*," Smokey grinned. "Well, I guess my timing couldn't have been more than perfect. Sir, Gina's Lounge closed due to unpaid fines. I realize you are a man who takes deep interest in the money he invests, and I felt you ought to know, Sir."

"And just where did you hear this information?" Mr. Yancy asked, staring Smokey up and down.

"A good friend sent me this newspaper article from the *Chicago Sun*, and I showed it to Connie. It seems she didn't know that her own club was in shambles. I told her that's bad business practice and that she ought to notify you, since you are one of her investors. I'm assuming she has?"

"No she has not," Mr. Yancy examined the article.

"I'm sorry to be the first, Sir, but I was just concerned."

"I appreciate it, Smokey, but you do know that any business I have outside of this radio station is none of yours, correct?"

"Absolutely."

"On the other hand, I do respect a man who doesn't just look out for his own interest," he mentioned. "Have Connie to come see me after she wraps up her show this morning."

"Yes Sir, would you like me to be present, sir? I just don't want her to accuse me of hearsay."

"No need. I think the article speaks for itself."

When Connie finished her show, Smokey approached her. "Mr. Yancy would like to see you in his office, immediately."

"What's it about?"

He smiled deviously. "Go see for yourself."

"Please have a seat, Connie," Mr. Yancy lit up a cigar. "I just read in the *Chicago Sun* that Gina's Lounge shut down."

"It will reopen in a few weeks."

"You should have informed me about this, Connie. You know it makes me look bad to be an investor of a club that ended up shut down. How will others continue to trust me as a business man if they see I make bad investments?"

"I can understand your concerns, Mr. Yancy, but I was hoping to resolve this before you or any other investors grew concerned. Unfortunately, it's taking a little longer and—"

"I'm withdrawing the money I invested, Connie, and I'll take my earned interest as well."

"But Mr. Yancy—"

"I expect my check by Friday, do you understand?"

"Yes sir."

"Good day, Connie."

Connie was upset about Smokey's latest antics, and needed to talk to someone she could trust. She knew that Ray had gone to California on business, and although she had other friends, she didn't trust them the way she did Ray. She broke down and called Adolfo instead. After apologizing to him, he agreed to meet her for drinks later that evening. She told him everything that happened to her at WHKY.

"Ray was right, you're bigger than radio. So quit that business, and stop worrying about Smokey," Adolfo told her, but quitting wasn't Connie's idea of a solution. She loved radio and enjoyed connecting with people. If she wanted other opportunities, she could have taken advantage a long time ago. "Let's fly to Italy and you can meet my family."

"I can't go to Italy right now. My job at WHKY is on the line right now. Besides, Tracey's in school. It's not summer yet."

"*Bene così sia,*" he threw up his hands, which meant, *fine, so be it.* "Let's have dinner tomorrow night."

"I'm helping my sister move. She's coming to live with us. I have to pick her up from the airport tomorrow."

"Wonderful. I would love to meet your sister."

"That's fine. I'll see you tomorrow."

Peaches was in awe when she stepped into Connie's penthouse. "Wow, man! Look at this pad, it's laid out!" her eyes widened, and then she broke out singing the theme song to *The Jeffersons.* "

Connie and Tracey cracked up laughing. "Girl, you are something else. Let me show you your room," Connie laughed, happy her sister was home. It was time to get to know her all over again.

"So they let you watch *The Jefferson's* in jail, Aunt Peaches?"

"Of course we could watch TV!"

"Did they have color TV's in jail?"

"In my unit they did, but not all of them had color TVs."

"Tracey, stop asking your aunt so many questions."

"Oh hush, Connie! I don't mind," Peaches stated.

"Wow. This ain't a bedroom, it's an apartment!" Peaches had never seen anything like it in her life. Her bedroom was huge, with a high ceiling, king-size bed, floor-model color TV with a VCR, full bathroom, and a walk-in closet. It was one of Connie's guest rooms, but she had it redesigned for her sister.

"Sis, you are rich!" Peaches exclaimed. "I never thought we would be living like this. God is good!" Peaches couldn't believe it as she walked into the bathroom to check it out. "Look, it's a giant bathtub!"

Tracey laughed. "That's not a giant bathtub Aunt Peaches, it's a Jacuzzi bathtub."

"Okay, well, whatever. Just show me how to work it so I can hurry up and get in it. I ain't had a bath in so long, I can't wait to just sit and soak."

"How come they don't have bathtubs in jail, Aunt Peaches?"

"Not enough room, baby. They only have showers."

"Tracey, I'm not going to tell you anymore to watch your mouth!"

"Don't worry about it, Sis, she got it honest. She gets it from me," Peaches winked at Tracey.

Connie showed Peaches where the towels and washcloths were. She also told her about all the building's amenities: the gym, indoor and outdoor swimming pool, and hair salon (though Connie preferred her own hair stylist).

". . . and since you told me your size, I bought you some clothes to get you started," Connie opened the closet door. "If you don't like the selection I chose, we can go shopping for what you really want later on."

"Aw shucks! Guess Jeans, Gucci shoes, Ann Klein shirts, Fila jumpsuits, child, pah-lease!" Peaches smiled, excited to have the latest 80's fashions.

"What would you like to have for dinner?" Connie asked.

"Anything!"

"Let's have some pizza!" Tracey interjected.

"You know what, I would like some pizza. They sell pies here?"

"Unfortunately not, that's a Chi-town thing. Here, they have huge thin-crust slices of pizza, but I miss those pies."

"Girl, me too. Remember we used to stop at Gino's after school?"

"Yes, they made the best pies!" Connie and Peaches slapped fives. "I'll call Cheryl and see if she can find a shop that makes special Chicago-style pizza."

"Girl, pah-lease, you don't have to go through all of that!"

"It's no problem," Connie dialed Cheryl, and when she asked Cheryl to help, Cheryl got right on it.

Ding Dong . . . .

Connie looked at her watch. "Oh shoot! That's Adolfo. He's punctual as usual."

"Who?" Peaches frowned.

"He's my mother's boyfriend," Tracey answered. "He's rich, and he's always buying us stuff and taking us on trips."

"Nah, hold up! Wait a minute. You talking about that slick haired dude that looks like one of those cats from *Miami Vice*?" Peaches asked. "Man, I saw ya'll in a magazine together, but I thought that stuff was a lie! What happened to you and Dean? That brother saved my life. You need to get back with him!" Peaches said, as Connie was leaving out of the room.

Peaches told Connie all about Dean getting Mr. Delroy to help her, and how Dean showed up in court for her appeal, but Connie never said anything about it her and Dean breaking up.

"Hello, darling," Adolfo handed Connie a dozen red roses.

"Beautiful," Connie smiled. *I'm sick of all these damn flowers like it's a funeral* she thought to herself. Adolfo always brought flowers with him each visit. Although they hadn't seen each other in a while, nothing had changed. "You know, you don't have to bring me flowers every time you come over."

"I know, but I really wanted you to have something as pretty as you."

"Thank you. I'll be right back. My sister is here, so I'm helping her get settled. Help yourself to whatever you like." Connie dashed off up the spiral staircase. She only told Adolfo that she had a sister back in Chicago, but she never told Adolfo that Peaches was in Cook County Jail. It was not that she felt embarrassed; she wanted Peaches to start fresh without anyone knowing her personal business unless she cared to share it.

Upstairs, Tracey was showing Peaches how to use the Jacuzzi bathtub. Peaches got the hang of the fancy knobs, and then she got in it. When she was finished bathing, she got dressed in her new clothes. Afterwards, Connie shared their plans for the week, which included a spa treatment and a visit to Connie's hairstylist so Peaches could finally get rid of her 70's Afro.

Connie introduced Peaches to Adolfo and Cheryl. She invited Cheryl to stay, but she and her boyfriend were going out tonight. While eating pizza, Peaches and Connie laughed and talked about old times. Adolfo felt disgusted at the way Peaches chewed loudly and talked with food in her mouth. He didn't find any resemblance between the two of them, and frowned at Peaches each time she asked him a question about himself. Connie noticed Adolfo's disdain, and didn't know that Peaches did too. She didn't like it. Not one bit.

Peaches burped loud, "Excuse me. My fault," she laughed like a kid. "Woo, that burp kind of stunk too."

"Aunt Peaches, you burp like a man!" Tracey laughed.

"So what, that food was good, child." Peaches patted her full stomach. "I guess I should let you two have your alone time," she said to Connie and Adolfo. "I swear I need me a man too." Peaches got up from the dining table, and Tracey followed her up the stairs. She was happy to have company, and she thought her Aunt was funny.

"Whew, I am so tired," Connie twisted her neck around, trying to relieve the tension as she started to clear the dining room table off.

"Let me help you." Adolfo gathered the plates and followed Connie into the kitchen.

"So, who is the oldest between you and Peaches?"

"She is. I'm the middle child."

"You mean to tell me that there are *more* like her?"

"What do you mean, *more* like her?" Connie stopped what she was doing and stared Adolfo up and down.

"Well, I'm going to be honest, Connie. Peaches is what we call a "brutta Donna", and she has no class the way you do. She speaks incorrectly and she behaves like a man. She reminds me of a street person that I give spare change. Was she adopted?"

"You got some nerve to talk about my sister in that way!" Connie knew that *brutta Donna* meant 'ugly woman'.

Adolfo hit himself upside the head. "I am sorry, please forgive me. I did not mean it. All I'm saying is she's not from our world."

"What do you mean, *our* world?"

"Oh come on, Connie, you and me, where we come from."

"You don't know a damn thing about me, do you? I guess I'm your black jungle bunny, huh?"

"Darling, of course not!" Adolfo chuckled. "You're too gorgeous and too classy for that, but Peaches, she's just—"

"Get the hell out!" Connie cut him off. She had heard enough.

"Excuse me?"

"I said get out, you racist bastard!"

"I'm not a racist! I love black women. I just prefer the ones with class."

"Get out!"

"Fine!" Adolfo stomped out the kitchen like a pompous jerk. "There're plenty of women waiting in line to take your place, darling, believe me."

"And you will probably go through the whole line and not satisfy any of them!" Connie tossed him the keys to the Porsche he bought her.

Adolfo tossed them back. "I don't need them. I can buy plenty more of those things." He turned around and left. He already had in mind who he wanted to date next.

Peaches appeared in the kitchen. "Are you okay, Sis?" She'd heard arguing, but didn't know what they had been arguing about.

Connie hugged her sister tight. "We just broke up, that's all."

"Well, damn, I just met the dude."

"Mama said to never let anybody come between this family, and that we should always stick together. I'll never let anybody come between us, Peaches. Never!"

Peaches smiled proudly. "Same here, Sis. Same here."

Connie quickly turned off her anger. "You want some ice cream?"

"Oh yeah!" Peaches rubbed her hands together, feeling excited.

"I'll bring some upstairs to you. Why don't you go find a movie on cable, and I'll bring it up."

"Cool," Peaches replied, sounding almost kid-like, but she couldn't help it. She was gleefully appreciating every little thing about life now.

"Little sis, I'm proud of you. I really am," Peaches said. The movie was playing, but they were focused on each other. "We made it out the projects, man. I never thought we would be living like this, straight up!"

"This life comes with a price at times," Connie was starting to realize that.

"I'm sure it does, but we may as well enjoy it while it lasts!"

Connie knew that Peaches didn't get the full sense of what she was trying to say.

"You know, I never thanked you for that letter you sent to me. Actually, you gave me too much credit. I don't deserve all of that, Peaches."

"Girl, you are trippin'!" Peaches shook her head, disagreeing. "Let me tell you something. The women in prison couldn't believe you was my sister 'til you came to visit me. I got special treatment because of you sometimes, but other times I had to crack a few heads cuz' chicks get jealous. People love you, girl. You saw how people asked for your autograph at the airport. Now that's love. You came a long way from Cabrini. I remember I used to have to beat up chicks in the hood for picking on you, now they begging for your autograph."

Connie modestly waved off the accolades. "The admiration is good, but I try not to let it go to my head."

"Good for you, because a lot of other celebrities do."

"Enough about that. Let me tell you about what's been happening these days . . ."

Peaches and Connie talked into the wee hours of the morning. They laughed and cried together as they reminisced about old times in Chicago. While it felt good to have Peaches back, Connie felt it was more responsibility added on her plate. She knew she had to look after Peaches and show her the ropes. Peaches needed time to adjust to society again, and Connie knew it was going to be a challenge to do that, run her business, raise her daughter, and keep her drinking habits *hidden*.

In the days that followed, Peaches tried to reach out to her son, and she apologized to him for not being the mother she knew she should have been. She understood that their road ahead would be uneasy. "I can't change the past, but I just want you to know that I'm here for you now. I'm just a phone call away," Peaches told BJ by phone.

"I'm glad you're home now. Thanks for calling me," he replied, before hanging up.

Peaches still felt a little hurt by him being short with her, but she understood his resentment and realized the rebuilding process would take some time. She would continue to call him at least once a month, even if he only said two words. She learned from counseling the important thing was taking baby steps and being consistent. The very fact that BJ was taking her calls gave Peaches a small ray of hope . . .

CHAPTER THIRTY-SEVEN

LIFE MATTERS
1985

Dean would write in his book log a list of his daily runs, including new evidence or noted a lack thereof. The names, faces, verdicts, and cases changed from day-to-day, and the pace seemed to remain fast. Phones at the Chicago Police District still rang off the hook, and even more with the new social drug called "crack" being sold in the streets.

Detective Gary White died in his sleep earlier that year, right after he and Dean watched the San Francisco 49ers beat Miami in the Super Bowl at a sports bar. Dean's old partner Stuckey was shot and killed in the line of duty.

It was now June 1985, Dean was sick of losing friends. Dean and his new partner found themselves knocking on more doors, telling people that their loved one was dead. Even Dean's so-called vacations or long runs at the track could not erase the scenes of some of the most horrific crimes he ever saw. Just when he thought he had seen it all, the next scene would be worse. What happened in the streets wasn't any better than what was taking place in the courtrooms. Dean had witnessed public defenders who were so overworked that they didn't care if the person they were defending ended up in jail for life, as long as they could quickly move on to the next case. Dean even witnessed a few public defenders representing their clients drunk, and the judges were no better.

"Guilty! Next case, please!" the judge would state nonchalantly, and another possibly innocent person went to jail. That very same thing had happened to Peaches, and she still would have been serving time if not for Dean. He was responsible for putting her there, and had since apologized for his part in it.

Peaches would tell him over the phone, "No need, my brother, you saved my life. So I'm not going to sue the Chicago Police Department, because I want you to keep your job."

Connie also thanked Dean for helping Peaches by sending him a Bulgari watch. Dean called to thank her, but Connie let him leave a message. She avoided talking with him, knowing her heart still had a soft spot for him.

At any rate, Dean's new boss of the homicide division was pressing Dean to work more cases than ever before. Lieutenant McMann was impressed with Dean's ability to make drug busts. He also liked Dean's detailed paperwork. That was flattering to Dean, except he knew he couldn't take on any more cases. More cases meant more stress and less time with his son, who had just graduated from high school, and would be going off to college in August. In fact, Dean put in requests to transfer to a less stressful department, but was denied.

Despite the milestones Dean achieved as a Detective, the luster of fighting crime was losing its spark. It was just too much. Dean finally realized that no matter how much he tried to '*save the day*', there would always be a new crime to solve. With crime being so prevalent, it was obvious to Dean that people were acting out because they had no hope for the future and the lack of response from the government made them wary of change. Dean realized one thing his father told him when they played golf together a few weeks ago was still true; "the people in this world don't need just you," his father said. "They need God."

"I quit." Dean handed McMann his official resignation papers. Lieutenant McMann looked at the letter without reading it, and then tossed it on top of a slush pile full of unsolved cases.

"I want you to take this new case with Williams." McMann reached in the other slush pile and attempted to hand Dean a new case file.

"It's over, McMann. I quit. You got my papers, I'm done," Dean told him firmly. McMann sighed heavily as he watched Dean set his gun and badge down before him. He was one of Chicago's finest, but this was it.

"You won't make a lot of money doing that silly personal training stuff, you know? And even if you try out for the Olympics again, you won't beat Carl Lewis," he chuckled, his belly jerking up and down behind the desk.

"I appreciate your optimism," Dean replied. He turned to walk out of the office.

"Yeah, sure, whatever," McMann laughed. "You'll be back in six months."

Dean would never return to the force, and he felt very happy with making that decision.

Connie found out that payments for the fines incurred by Gina's Lounge were made, but the checks were never deposited. Two women who worked for the Illinois Board of Licenses kept the checks in their drawers. The two women turned out to be Evelyn and Marsha who used to work for CMP. They were the mothers of Smokey's children. Evelyn and Marsha had no prior criminal records. They would only serve ninety-days in jail for intrusion of payment. In court, they told the judge that Smokey promised them child support payments and extra money if they held back the payments. They tried to bring Smokey down with them, but it was their word against Smokey's in court. The judge did order Smokey to appear in court for his past due child support payments on a later date. Otherwise, Smokey walked out the courtroom free, while his children's mothers were behind bars. Connie tried to hire Donald back after the results of the case, but he felt disrespected by Connie's mistrust and refused to come back. She hired someone else.

When Smokey returned to New York after spending a day in court in Chicago, he returned with the spirit of revenge in his heart . . .

"Let's face it, Mr. Yancy; Cat Morris is not getting any younger. She's thirty-one now. We need fresh young voices," Smokey was saying to Mr. Yancy. "Now Stephanie, she's hot, she's young, and knows what young listeners want to hear."

"You have a point, Smokey. Tell Connie to see me before she goes on the air. Our ratings have dropped five percent, and maybe our morning show does have something to do with that."

When Connie walked into the studio, Smokey told her to see Mr. Yancy, and then blew her a kiss as she walked down the hall to Mr. Yancy's office.

"Good morning, Connie. Please have a seat," Mr. Yancy began, as he poured himself a cup of coffee. "Connie, our ratings have dropped five percent."

"Yes, I read about that, but we'll bounce back."

"I'm not so sure about that, Connie."

"I don't think we should worry at this point. We're still in the top five. With all the work we did with helping the *"We Are the World"* project against apartheid in South Africa, I think we'll always remain in the top."

"I'd prefer to be number one like we used to be, and therefore, I want us to move in another direction so that will happen again," he mentioned, pacing the room and sipping his coffee. "I want Stephanie to host the Sunnyside-Up Morning Show. She's young, fresh out of college, and can connect with our youth."

"I'm very much connected with our youth. It was my idea to start the Teen Enrichment Program, and offer them summer jobs here at the station this summer," Connie explained. "While Stephanie may be younger than I am, she doesn't have the experience I have. I am the one who can bring in celebrity guests for interviews. I am the one who creates community outreach programs on behalf of the station. I'm the one who interviewed Nelson Mandela in prison. I'm the one who interviewed Jesse Jackson about the *Rainbow PUSH Coalition* he started. Stephanie wouldn't have been able to do any of those things because she hasn't even made a name for herself in this industry. I have!"

"I know, but I'm afraid that's not enough."

"So am I being pushed back to evening programming?" Connie asked, concerned.

"Not quite. I have some other business for you off the air. I think there's been enough bad blood between you and Smokey. Maybe you two can patch things up so that you can be his program assistant."

Connie cocked her head to the side. "Program Assistant? I don't think so."

"Connie, I don't want to lose you as an employee."

"I *will not* be Smokey's assistant. We were partners before and it didn't work out."

"I appreciate what you have done for WHKY, Connie. If you want to stay here, you will accept my offer."

"Is that a threat?"

"It's not a threat. It's an ultimatum. Besides, I've done a lot for you, including paying the press not to publicize your drinking problems."

"I'm in control of that now," Connie admitted. She hadn't had a drink since Peaches had been home, and she was able to see things much more clearly than ever before, especially now. She stood up from her seat. "I see why you invested so much money into my club, into CMP, selling me your penthouse, and covering up my habit with the press," she stated angrily. "It wasn't because you were being nice or because you were truly interested in me as a person. It was because you wanted to use me for selfish gain and control me. Now that I've helped build this radio station, you want to throw me out to the dogs. Well, I got news for you," she pointed her finger at him. "You don't have to give me an ultimatum because I quit!" Connie turned around and left his office. She turned off her anger as she grabbed her things out of her office, refusing to give Smokey the satisfaction. She left with a cool and calm demeanor that puzzled Smokey, but inside, she wanted to strangle him for what he had done.

When Connie got to her Porsche, she dialed everyone she knew in the business and told them what Mr. Yancy and Smokey had done to her. In a matter of weeks, the ratings at WHKY dropped thirty-percent. Fans called in to complain about Stephanie being on the air instead of Connie. Whenever they ran into Connie on the streets, they would ask her what happened. Connie would tell everyone the truth, which made WHKY have to fight even harder to earn its ratings again.

As for Smokey, he found himself in the hot seat with Mr. Yancy because of his "brilliant" idea to get rid of Connie. He knew it was just a matter of time before Mr. Yancy would fire him, knowing that he'd deceived him. Smokey shopped his resume around the business, but received one rejection letter after another, even from small town radio stations in the South. Then one night, while sitting in his office at WHKY, he started thinking about what Connie said to him when she told him, *It will be you landing on your ass in the end.* As he pondered over that moment, while staring out the window it finally hit him. "She blackballed me," he said under his breath. "I can't believe Connie blackballed me!"

Connie was still working with CMP despite quitting WHKY. She was still hurt about Smokey, Adolfo, Dean, May, her stepfather Mason, and everyone who had hurt her; and she was back on the bottle again. She would drink when she wasn't around Tracey or Peaches by stopping at bars after work. This one evening was no different. She downed four Kamikazes and asked for a fifth before the bartender told her she had enough.

"I'm outta here, guys!" she waved to the bartender and tipped him well.

"Be safe, Cat, it's raining out there."

"You got it, Babes!" she winked as she slowly stood up from the barstool and tried her best not to let her knees wobble. They buckled for a moment, but she stabilized herself on the chair, and then edged her way out the door.

When she got to her Porsche, she could barely open the door with her unsteady hands. Finally, she got in, and started the car, easing her way down 9th Avenue towards Park Avenue where she lived. The flashes of lightning here and there made her eyes hurt. With so much rain, Connie thought the city had turned into glass, and she had a hard time seeing where she was going.

She turned up the radio to try to keep herself alert, and came across Journey's, *"Who's Crying Now"* on a soft rock station, and started singing along. Connie always loved the song, and she thought about her mother and sister as she sang; she missed them. She also thought about Dean and how she'd lost his love, gained it back, and lost it all over again. She wasn't sure if she would ever meet another man like Dean, and questioned if she wanted to.

In a drunken daze, Connie missed her street, and ended up at Penn Plaza, where WHKY was located. Its neon lights bounced off the slick city streets like the stores next to it. She spotted Smokey and Stephanie coming out of the station arm-in-arm underneath an umbrella.

"You evil bastard! I hate you!" she screamed through clenched teeth and slammed her foot on the gas. The Porsche took off at full-speed, leaving a trail of smoke on the wet streets and flying pass the cars in the left hand lane next to her.

"SMOKEY, WATCH OUT!" Stephanie shouted, jumping out of the way.

BAM!

Connie's Porsche drove straight through the doors of the radio station. Smokey dived out of the way and landed on his ass. The Porsche kept going, crashing down doors and knocking over whatever was in the way. Connie threw up her arms to protect her face as objects crashed through the front windshield. She slammed her foot on the brakes, her head slammed into the stirring wheel, and she blacked out . . .

"Cat Morris survived a terrible car accident, and was treated for a concussion and injuries to her arms and hands. She was released this morning from St. John's Hospital. Morris crashed her Porsche through the studio of WHKY. Some say it was because she had been fired by the station's manager, who had this to say.

'While I am happy that no one was injured in this incident, I only wish Cat had taken my advice and attended AA meetings. Cat's drinking and belligerent behavior has been a problem for the station for years now. It became very difficult for me and the staff to deal with. It doesn't surprise me that she tried to kill one of her very own staff members by trying to run him over with her car. I'm just glad Smokey wasn't hurt. Smokey is a good employee who, like me, tried to help Cat. He had recently taken over responsibilities that she could no longer fulfill because she wasn't sober enough. I pray for her recovery, and I hope she gets the help she needs before someone gets hurt or worse.' That's all the news for today, I'm Brad Miller with News-9."

Peaches turned off the TV and took the newspapers from Connie. She was sick of the bad press her sister was getting, and tired of seeing Connie down in the dumps from watching it or reading about it. "You don't need to keep listening to that stuff," Peaches said to Connie. She was helping Connie around the house with basic tasks, since her hands and arms were healing.

"There's nothing else on TV," Connie spoke from her bedside.

"Yes it is." Peaches flipped the channels and stopped once she came across *The Cosby Show.*

Peaches was doing well for herself. She'd gotten her driver's license and was now finding her way around the city, driving herself to her final days in rehab and to work part-time at CMP. She helped Connie with the budget and finances, since she was very good with numbers and had earned her bachelor's degree in business while in prison. She and Connie had also planned to start a foundation called *Freedom for Frieda* on behalf of their deceased mother. However, now that Connie was down and recovering from the crash, all projects were at a standstill. Peaches didn't mind; she wanted to care for her sister after all she had done for her.

"It's time to change your bandages," Peaches said to Connie. Connie felt miserable, and wished she had died in the crash rather than face all the embarrassment she was dealing with now. Her drinking problem was now public knowledge, thanks to Mr. Yancy, and her so-called friends at the bar added fuel to the fire by telling nosy reporters how often Connie visited there.

On the other hand, she'd received well wishes and support from music artists whose concerts she promoted and put together. A few of them who had become her friends, called her personally to offer words of encouragements. Ray stopped by to visit her, and Dean's mother actually called her when she found out. Dean figured Connie still wanted nothing to do with him anymore, so he decided against calling or sending well wishes. Little did he know, Connie was hoping she heard from him this time.

"The phone is ringing," Connie said to Peaches, as Peaches changed the bandages on her hands.

"Hold on a minute, we're almost done here. You come first, before that crazy phone!" Peaches said to Connie. "I would unplug that damn phone, but since Tracey's at Summer Day Camp for Acting Classes, I won't do it in case something comes up." Peaches finished with Connie and then walked to answer the phone, catching it on the last ring.

"I'm trying to reach Connie Morris. This is Ms. Tyson from the Psychiatric Institute in Chicago," the woman said.

"Connie is tied up at the moment, but this is her sister, Donna. How can I help you?"

"Your father is gravely ill. He was rushed to Medgar's Hospital. We tried to reach your stepmother Beth-Ann, but we didn't get an answer so we've been going down a list of family names. Someone needs to get here to Chicago, and fast!"

When Peaches hung up, she thought about whether she should tell Connie what was going on, since she was already experiencing a lot as it was.

"Well? Who was that?" Connie asked.

"Dad is in the hospital. They said we need to get to Chicago right away," Peaches solemnly replied.

Connie didn't know what to say. She rolled over on her side, turning her back towards Peaches.

"I can fly out to Chicago tonight. You can stay here and recover, so don't worry about it," Peaches suggested.

"Have Cheryl book us arrangements for two nights in Chicago, and have her watch Tracey," Connie stated. "As long as I'm back here in time for my court date, we'll be fine."(Connie had to appear in court for driving drunk, attempted murder charges *per* Smokey and Stephanie, who insisted she tried to kill them by running them over, and Mr. Yancy was suing her for property damages.) When Connie told Cheryl she needed to leave for Chicago to see her ailing stepfather, Cheryl agreed to keep an eye on Tracey without hesitation.

As soon as Connie and Peaches entered the hotel lobby, the media was right there to meet her. Cameras flashed, microphones were shoved to her face, and they bombarded her with questions . . .

"Cat, is it true that you have a drinking problem?"

"Cat how do you think the attempted murder charges will affect your career?"

"Cat, are artists still willing to do business with CMP?"

"Listen," Connie stopped to talk to the news crews out of frustration. The media had flooded the lobby area of the hotel. ". . . What happened with WHKY radio station was not intentional. I regret that it happened. In spite of what's been said about me in the media, I am not a murderer, and would never hurt anyone intentionally. Anyone who truly knows me can vouch for that. I have no further comments about this matter, and I await my date in court to settle this once and for all."

"Okay people, no more questions. Ms. Morris would like to check into her room." Truck stepped in front of the cameras and insisted they back away.

At the hospital . . . .

Connie and Peaches were escorted to Mason's room in the Intensive Care Unit. Inside, a nurse was sitting next to him monitoring him as he fought for his life. He was connected to a breathing machine and a heart monitor, but when he heard footsteps, he opened his eyes to see who was coming into the room. Connie and Peaches slowly approached his bedside. The doctor explained to Connie and Peaches before they went into the room that Mason was suffering from emphysema and kidney failure from heavy drinking and smoking for so many years. Connie stared at the man who used to be big and muscular. He was now scrawny and frail-looking, like he couldn't hurt a fly. He looked so tiny that the bed seemed to engulf him.

Vivid memories of the past seemed to pass before Connie's eyes: all the beatings he gave her, the verbal abuse, and how he set her business and her home on fire. She wondered how this frail man could be capable of such evil things. The longer Connie stared at him, her fear turned to rage. She was not that little girl anymore. She was an adult with a child of her own. Her eyes looked at all the wires connected to him, and she started huffing and puffing as angry emotions began to stir up inside of her.

Peaches watched Connie's face tighten, and her green eyes stared at the cords he was attached to. The thought of pulling the plugs crossed her mind, but she couldn't. It just wasn't in her heart to do it.

Peaches quickly grabbed Connie and pushed her in the opposite direction of the breathing machine. "He's on his way out. He ain't worth it."

Mason's eyes widened as he heard what was happening around him, and his heart began to race with fear when he recognized Connie and Peaches.

"We gotta make peace with this man, Connie. We can do this together." Peaches looked in Connie's eyes. She could see all the pain and hurt that Connie felt.

"I'll go first," Peaches turned to Mason. "Dad, I hate to see you like this, but I hope you made peace with God so he won't condemn you to hell for all of what you put us through. You abused us, and then you abandoned us. You treated us like we never existed, and that wasn't right. Baby was killed, Mama died, I was hooked on the junk and been to jail, and none of that would have happened if you had been a better father to us. That's what I believe, and that's what I'm sticking with." Peaches felt anger building inside, so she took a deep breath before she continued. "The only reason I'm forgiving you is because God forgave me for my own mess, you know. But let this serve as my peace with you." Peaches reluctantly kissed his forehead and stepped away.

"Go on, Connie, say what you need to say," Peaches told her. "We need to hurry up, 'cause I'm feeling some kind of way right now, and I need to get out of here. Don't know if I should cry or be angry with this man or just . . . I don't know, but let's wrap this thing up fast." Peaches walked away from Mason's bedside and looked out the window, tried to turn her attention elsewhere.

Mason slowly raised his eyes as Connie moved in closer to him. He became so afraid that she would do something to him that he wet himself.

"Don't worry, I'm not going to pull the plug," Connie stated angrily. "But the little girl you abused would have if she was given that opportunity. I want to hate you so bad, but I can't, because unlike you, I wasn't made to hate people or treat them evil the way you did me!" Connie fought back her tears. "It would have been better if you had just divorced Mama after she cheated on you, but instead you punished me for years like it was my fault. Did I remind you of Scott, the white boy you hated? Huh? Is that why you practically made me your slave? Or was it to punish me for what Charlie did to you in the army?" Mason shivered in fear. "For years, I felt unwanted and unloved, and I always thought something was wrong with me. But nothing was wrong with me, everything was wrong with *you*. It's because of you that it's hard for me to trust when someone truly loves me, but no matter how hard you tried to destroy me, you couldn't. You could burn all my possessions, but you could never burn my soul!"

Mason began to pant, as if he was trying to catch his breath, despite wearing the oxygen mask. He felt his body getting cold, and his mouth was so dry that his tongue was stuck to the roof of his mouth. His eyes rolled into the back of his head for a moment, then dropped down and focused on Connie.

"What do you have to say for yourself, Mason Morris, huh? What do you have to say?" Connie shouted.

In a weak, raspy voice, he gasped, "I'm . . . I'm sorry."

Connie held his left hand, and Peaches walked over and held his right. He started to nod off and his heart rate slowed down.

"I'm going to go get the doctor," the nurse said.

Mason's hands were turning cold, and Connie and Peaches began to cry.

"I accept your apology Mason," Connie sniffed, wiping her eyes. A very faint smile came over his face as he shut his eyes for good.

'BEEEEEP'-----------------

Mason's funeral was the following week, and Connie was excused from court. She flew back to Chicago for the funeral, but at the last minute, she decided not to attend. Peaches went alone, but at the funeral, she would meet Beth-Ann and her half-siblings for the first time. To her surprise, it was a warm welcome, but Peaches just couldn't accept them as her step-family.

Connie decided to go visit her club, Gina's Lounge, which finally reopened for business. With newer clubs on the scene, the younger generation found themselves hanging out elsewhere besides Gina's.

"Gin and juice, please," Connie told the bartender.

"Anything for the boss lady," the bartender smiled. Connie happened to look up from the glass, and she spotted the picture of Baby hung on the wall behind him. She didn't remember it being there before. She specifically remembered it being in the V.I.P. lounge, not at the bar.

Baby's eyes seemed to be staring at Connie, making her feel nervous and guilty for drinking. *"If I win the cash for the poetry contest, I would buy*

Connie a new record player because I know she loves music," she remembered Baby saying. Connie shut her eyes for a moment and visualized herself in the living room again, teaching Baby how to dance. Then her vision flashed to her mother. *"Live your life, child."* All the memories seemed to be playing in her mind at once. She asked herself if she wanted to end up in a coffin like Mason, with Tracey standing over her dead body, crying.

"Is everything all right, Ms. Morris?" the bartender asked. "Is the drink okay?"

Connie opened her eyes, stared at the glass before her. "I don't need this," she said, and slid it across the counter.

"Okay, would you like something else instead?"

"I'll take a Coke instead."

"Anything for the boss lady."

Connie finished the soda, checked the accounting books, (which only made her feel more depressed since sales were low), and then she went back to her hotel where Peaches told her the details of the funeral. The next morning, they flew back to New York.

Court . . .

Connie returned to New York to face a three-week long trial that the media followed closely. The jury found Connie not guilty of attempted murder, but guilty of drunken driving. The jury believed if Connie had not been under the influence of alcohol, she wouldn't have run her car through the radio station. Connie had a good lawyer who gathered witnesses from the radio station and in the music industry to testify to Connie's character. Cheryl, Ray, Kelvin James, Cody (who used to work for her), were included in the lists of witnesses who talked about Connie's character.

However, the judge ordered Connie to pay a $5,000 fine for driving drunk and added points to her driver's license. He also ordered her to attend one year of AA meetings and perform two hundred hours of community service.

In the civil suit, Mr. Yancy sued her for property damages for $500,000 dollars, and Connie filed a countersuit for defamation of character for his remarks about her in the news for the same amount.

The judge decided that both of them were right in their suits, and decided that each one would pay the other half of the amount they were suing for. The judge ordered both of them to pay the judgment order within ninety-days. Connie didn't want to cough up the bulk of her savings, so she sold Mr. Yancy Gina's Lounge and CMP.

It was a heavy price tag, and Connie's father offered to pay for the property damages, but Connie told said to him, "Dad I love you, but you have to stop saving me. You have been saving me all my life. You don't owe me anything but love. *I* did this, and it's *my* responsibility to get myself out of it."

CHAPTER THIRTY-EIGHT

LOVE IS A FRIEND TOO

Connie told her staff that she had sold the company to Mr. Yancy, and had no plans of starting up another concert promoting company again. Mr. Yancy decided to turn the CMP office into an AM radio station, a spin-off of his FM station that would consist of talk radio, mainly for sports. Connie gave everyone who was on payroll their final checks, nice reference letters to use for their next job, and she wished them well.

Connie didn't know what her next move would be, but she didn't want to be on the road anymore with a concert promoting company. With Tracey getting older, she wanted to be around more. She received many offers from modeling companies, directors who offered her movie and TV roles, and marketing positions for various record companies in the past. However, her recent trial put somewhat of a damper on her image. The opportunities were slowing down, but Connie applied to whatever opportunities were still available. She was thinking that maybe it was time for her to do something different within the industry that wouldn't require her to travel a lot, except on special occasions.

She still loved music and working behind the scenes, so she applied for marketing jobs at different record companies, starting with the ones in New York. Ray offered her work, but she no longer wanted to do business with friends. Although she could live off her savings for at least another year or so, she didn't want to sit out that long without a job. People would forget her name in the industry. Her career uncertainties made her feel more depressed. While she agreed to go to AA, she would show face but then leave. She felt too embarrassed to stay. Too many people knew her and thought better of her. She couldn't bring herself to face anyone in that manner.

One day, while she was going through some of her old things inside her closet, she came across the gray box her mother had used to store old pictures of the family. She sat down on her bed and flipped through family photos, smiling and remembering each one. Her mother used to say *pictures keep your memories alive, child.* She could hear her voice, as loud as if her mother was right in front of her. She wished her mother was there so she could give her advice and tell her what to do with her life now. She wiped a small tear that escaped her eyes as she took out one picture after another. As she continued to look through the box, she came across a picture of her and Dean. "How did this one get in here?" she asked herself, knowing she had kept pictures of them in a photo album, not in her family box of mementos. It was a picture of them hugging outside of her father's ranch in South Carolina when they had gone to visit him one summer. She smiled, recalling how in love they were with each other back then, and how fond her parents were of him.

She wondered how Dean was doing and glanced at her phone, toying around with the idea of calling him. *Call him to say hello,* her mind said. *No, he's probably married now.* Her mind went back and forth, but her heart made her pick up the phone.

Dean caught it on the last ring, and was out of breath trying to get it. "Hello?"

"Hi Dean. It's Connie," She spoke nervously.

Dean smiled behind the phone. "Hey!" he was surprised to hear from her, and felt excited that she had finally called him.

"Did I catch you at a bad time?" she asked, noticing he sounded out of breath.

"Well, I just got in from a run, but I can talk," Dean replied, kicking off his sneakers and pulling off his sweaty jogging suit.

"Thank you for the sympathy card you sent when my stepfather died."

"Sure, anytime."

Silence lingered for a few seconds. Both of them could feel the awkward space between them; it had been so long since they talked. Connie felt so bad for treating him as if he was a stalking fan after all he had done for her. She knew she could have at least returned his phone calls when he called to thank her for the watch, and to give his condolences when her stepfather died.

"Hello?"

"I'm here." Connie walked out onto her balcony with the cordless phone to her ear. She stared at the people below. She had to serve community service for the DUI charge starting next week, which meant cleaning the New York streets. Thoughts of jumping off the balcony crossed her mind just for a split second, but she thought of Tracey and immediately decided against doing that. She just wasn't sure how to get her life back.

"Dean," she cleared her throat. "I'm . . . I'm so sorry for my part in what went wrong between us."

"Me too."

Connie cried on the phone. She couldn't hold back. The floodgates of her soul opened up, and the pit of her pain that she'd been carrying around for so long poured through her tears.

"Do you need me, Connie?" Dean could hear her crying as much as she tried to hide it, he could hear her. Dean knew everything she had gone through. It was written in the papers and on the news. He didn't know how she was handling it all by herself.

"Yes, I need you Dean," she replied without hesitation.

"I'm on my way."

Dean and Dean Jr. arrived in New York at close to eleven o'clock the next morning. Dean Jr. was happy to be in New York because he'd been accepted at NYU, and it would give him and his father an opportunity to check out the campus as well. Patricia was also attending NYU. Dean was majoring in engineering, and Patricia majored in education.

Everyone was excited to see each other, and there were lots of hugs and kisses like a family reunion.

"Peaches, look at you. You look good!" Dean stepped back to look at her. He almost didn't recognize her. Her hair was styled in a trendy 80's hairdo- called a "snatch-back", with full layered curls in the front and long in the back. Her skin looked flawless, and the needle tracks were gone. She wore EK glasses to correct her vision, but they looked nice on her. When she smiled big and wide, feeling happy by his compliments, he noticed the beautiful dental work she had done on her teeth as well. She looked healthy and beautiful.

"Thank you, Dean. It's good to see you, brother. Thanks for all you did for me," she kissed his cheek. He laughed, because when she spoke, she was still Peaches.

"Peaches got a boyfriend," Connie teased.

"We're not there yet, but on our way," Peaches blushed.

"Should I run his prints?" Dean joked.

"He's cool people," Peaches stated, ". . . and he's young, just the way I like them, so I can get 'em sprung!" She twisted her hips, and everyone laughed.

Dean shook his head, laughing. "You haven't changed, girl."

"His name is George. I'm headed out to meet him, so I'll check ya'll out later."

"Mom, I'm going to ask Truck if he can drive me and Dean to see the rappers houses in Queens and in Brooklyn," Tracey said.

"Why don't you call Uncle Ray and see if Run-DMC is in town?"

"Run-DMC?" Dean Jr. got excited.

"Sure, why not. Give Ray a call. He produces rap artists on his new label now. I'm sure he knows Run-DMC."

"Cool!" Tracey and Dean were both excited, and after Tracey called Ray, Ray sent a limo to pick them up. They would not only meet Run-DMC, but also eat White Castle burgers with them in the studio.

When everyone left the house, everything grew quiet as Dean and Connie were standing in front of each other as if they were seeing each other for the first time. Dean gave her a hug, but was careful not to display too much affection towards her. He sensed that all she needed right now was a friend.

"I'm glad you came, Dean," she spoke softly. "Would you like something to eat or to drink?"

"I'm okay. Why don't you come on over and sit down?" Dean led her to the sofa. He thought her penthouse was amazing—a huge upgrade from the bungalow in Chicago that she'd once shared with May. He took it all in for a moment, and then he turned his attention to why he was really there.

For a few seconds, they couldn't stop looking at each other. It had been two years since they saw each other. Connie could tell Dean was still working out a lot. He was wearing a short-sleeve Nike shirt and his arms looked beefy, like he'd been lifting weights. His matching Nike shorts, showed his muscular legs and calves. Gone was the 70's Afro. Dean was sporting a short, faded haircut that was tapered on the sides with a near perfect shape-up in the front. His dark thick eyebrows still had a natural arch, and his dark, piercing eyes still glared at her as if he was reading her soul. He'd always had a mustache, but now he sported a nice, shaped-up goatee with it. Connie couldn't help but notice how handsome he looked. He and Dean Jr. looked like brothers these days.

Dean saw that Connie was still beautiful, but she looked worn out and stressed. Her hair was pulled back into a neat, long ponytail, but her hazel-green eyes looked drained, as if she hadn't slept in days.

"So how have you been?" Dean asked, concerned.

"If I said fine, I would be lying," she took a sip of her Pepsi, wishing it was something stronger in the glass. Peaches had gotten rid of all the alcohol in the house, including the bottles Connie would try to hide.

"Neither one of us will no longer self-medicate anymore!" Peaches had said to Connie.

"What's going on?" Dean slid his arm behind her.

"I'm exhausted from this life. Now I understand why so many celebrities just cut off the world and go into isolation, or worse."

"So this isn't just about your stepfather passing away, from what I'm hearing," Dean sensed. Connie went on to explain everything that had weighed heavily on her heart, starting with the car accident and what led up to the accident. She then worked her way backwards. Dean listened to the words that came from her mouth, but he could hear the feelings behind everything she was saying. He didn't interrupt, except to ask a question here and there for clarity.

". . . And I'm not the same woman you knew in Chicago. As you know, since it's public now, I'm a . . . I'm . . . a drinker," she uttered, but she didn't feel comfortable in saying that. It wasn't the truth. "You know what," Connie thought. "I'm not just a drinker, but I'm an alcoholic. There! I admitted it!" She threw up her hands.

"That's a start," Dean nodded.

"I'm not proud of it, and I'm sure you and other people expect more of me, but everybody has a breaking point."

"Yes we do."

"I started drinking after my stepfather set those fires, but I drunk heavier and frequently when we broke up," she admitted. "I went to pieces, Dean. I just . . . I fell apart. Just knowing you chose Angie over me was a hard pill to swallow."

"Connie, I never chose Angie over you. You left *me*, remember? After two years, I had to move on with my life. I never knew you were going to come back."

"I understand all of that, but I was still hurt, Dean. I was crushed, even for my part in that, so whenever you called I didn't talk to you because I was hurt."

"So what made me you call me now?"

Connie thought about it for a moment, said, "Because despite what we went through, you're the only person I can depend on and trust. I needed you, Dean, and I need you now."

"I appreciate you sharing all of that with me. I knew you were still holding on to the past, which was why I said I was sorry on the phone too, but it's behind us now. You have to let go of the past, too, and not just what happened between us, but with your stepfather and everyone else who has hurt you in some way. Punishing yourself through the bottle won't change the past; it's just going to mess up your future for yourself and Tracey," Dean expressed. "It's time for you to find yourself again, and when you do, you have to learn how to separate *Cat Morris* the celebrity from Connie Morris the human being. Only then can you overcome your addiction to alcohol."

"It's not that simple for me."

"Maybe not, but I know you can do it, Connie. If you put the same energy into it that you used to establish your career, then I know you can get through this. Think about how far you've come already, and I know you don't want to go back to where you used to be."

"Maybe I just need help in believing that."

"We're all here for you." Dean took hold of her hand, and she rested her head against his chest.

"I don't deserve you, Dean."

"Hey." Dean lifted her chin and looked into her eyes. "You don't tell me what you don't deserve. You *do* deserve me. You deserve the same care and love, time and attention, as anybody else. You just have to accept it."

"So where do *we* go from here?"

"Right now, you need to focus on yourself. Make yourself the priority right now."

"But—"

"Shhh . . ." Dean gently placed two fingers over her lips. "No buts. You can do it. I'll be watching you from the sidelines."

Over the next couple of days, Connie, Peaches, and Tracey all had a good time with Dean and Dean Jr. After they visited Dean Jr.'s new campus, they hit up all the tourist spots in New York. Peaches was glad to see her sister smiling again. She knew she was going through something heavy, and Dean was the only person who could bring that smile out of her.

The night before Dean left, he went to Connie's room and stood in the doorway while she was sleep. Connie sensed someone near her and woke up. "Are you okay?" she rubbed sleep from her eyes, bringing Dean into clearer vision.

"You look like an angel."

She blushed. "You want to sleep in here instead of the guest room?" Dean wanted to join her, but he really wanted her to know that she could have a friend without any strings attached.

"I'm enjoying watching you sleep," he winked, and watched Connie get back under the covers. For Connie, just knowing Dean was there made her feel safe and secure in every way. She felt like she had her best friend back. Knowing Dean was willing to support her and help her get through this rough time gave her the boost she needed to piece together her life again.

When Dean got back to Chicago, he had one of his former partners pull Smokey's rap sheet. He knew a person like Smokey wasn't squeaky clean, and sure enough, he owed back payments on child support and had outstanding parking tickets. It wasn't much, but Smokey was out of a job and couldn't pay it, and had a warrant for failing to show up in family court. It was enough to give him six months in jail and a big fine.

When they tracked Smokey down and arrested him, Dean told them. "Put him in the cell with Bubba. He needs a new girlfriend."

"I hate you for this Dean!" Smokey shouted, as the officers threw him inside the cell.

"I just wanted to remind you why I was one Chicago's Finest," Dean said to Smokey on the other side of the bars. "Make sure when you bend over to pick up the soap that Bubba over there won't be watching."

Smokey slowly looked over his shoulders at the big bulky Bubba who was grinning flirtatiously at him.

"AAAAAH! HELP ME!"

Dean Jr.'s going-away party had just ended. When everyone left, Dean called his son into the living room to chat.

"What's up, Dad?"

"We need to talk."

Dean Jr. sat down across from his Dad in a chair while Dean sat on the sofa in the living room.

"I'm proud of you, son. Proud of the man you're turning out to be. I just want you to know that when you go away to school, keep your head in the books and off them girls. Get your degree, get a job, and later for the girls."

"Aw Dad come on now!" Dean griped.

"Listen to me, son. Use them Jim Hats I gave you, 'cause I'm not ready to be a grandfather yet, all right?"

"Yeah," Dean chuckled. "Alright."

"No matter what happens, always be a man, son. Be responsible; do not be ignorant. Do not go away to college, drinking and using drugs, and get caught up with the wrong crowd." Dean Jr. was listening, but he thought his father's timing was off. He was still in a celebration mode.

"Yeah, okay Dad. It's a little late for the birds and the bees talk, don't you think?" Dean chuckled. "I mean, I've had plenty of honeys by now. I know what I'm doing Dad."

"You just make sure you don't get any of those *honeys* pregnant, alright?"

"I know Dad. I know. I got this."

"Patricia on the pill?"

"Come on Dad! You killing me!" Dean laughed in disbelieve. He felt uncomfortable having this type of conversation.

"Well?" Dean folded his arms.

"I don't know. Patricia is a good girl Dad. I haven't hit it yet, but she's the one."

"Don't break her heart son. Be real with her, alright?"

"I won't Dad," Dean got up from the sofa.

"Hold up, I'm not finished."

"Dad! Come on!"

"Look, I know I wasn't always there for you the way I wanted to be, but now that I have resigned, always know that I'm just a phone call away, all right? We cool?" Dean extended his arms.

"Yeah, we're cool, Dad. You did the best you could, so don't sweat it." The two of them embraced. "All right, I need to bounce." Dean Jr. took off running upstairs.

"Yo', and tell Patricia I said hello!" Dean knew his son was running upstairs to call her. Patricia and Dean Jr. had been boyfriend and girlfriend since they were kids. He hoped Dean would do right by her. She was a sweet girl. He sure hoped he wouldn't be a player like his great cousin, who he called "Uncle" Hank.

Speaking of Hank, Dean called him up and asked him to meet him at the bar to watch the Laker vs. Celtics championship game.

At the bar, Hank and Dean had small talk about Dean Jr. going away to college and about his girlfriend Patricia.

"I just hope he won't get that girl pregnant. I hope he stays out of trouble and keep his head in them books," Dean took a swig of his beer.

"Don't expect him to be perfect. You weren't."

"I didn't say anything about being perfect, Hank, but every parent wants what's best for their child. They don't want them to repeat their own mistakes that's all."

"Yeah well, there'll plenty of other fish in the sea. I met this lady named Melanie. She's gonna help me open up a barbershop on 45th Street."

Dean shook his head. "You can't be serious! You back out there taking advantage of another woman again? Look at you; you got a patch over one eye man. What's it gonna take? For a woman to snuff you out?!"

"Lower your voice youngblood. Now listen, Melanie is good people. All she's doing is putting a deposit on the space for me. It's up to me to take care of the rest."

"If you say so man. Whatever you say," Dean couldn't believe it.

"Don't hate the player Dean, hate the game," Hank chuckled.

Dean shook his head in disbelieve, popped some peanuts in his mouth and finished his beer. He was ready to go. For the first time, he felt like he didn't want to be around Hank anymore. His cousin had let him down. After all Hank had been through, Dean expected better of him. He was a father now to a baby girl, and he hoped that for her sake at least he would get himself together. He glared at his cousin and rolled his eyes as he got up and approached one of the waitresses wearing a short mini skirt. She easily gave him her number, and Dean shook his head. He thought to himself, *it's not totally Hank's fault. If women fall for his game that was on them. One day Hank will meet his match. He just needs to find a woman strong enough who won't take his crap. Hopefully, he will be smart enough to treat her right. Next time he may not be so lucky.*

The crowd in the bar cheered as the Lakers redeemed themselves over the Boston Celtics, and Dean got up from the bar to leave.

"I'll catch you later Hank," Dean patted Hank on the back while he chatted with the young lady.

"Later bro!"

Back in New York, Connie developed a new routine. In between attending her AA meetings, she took long walks in Central Park, read self-help books, the Bible, and meditated. She hired a life coach who helped her to work through issues of her past, and to help her to regain confidence. She was also building a positive image for herself by doing speaking engagements at local colleges, schools, and she did a commercial on drunk driving. In the commercials, she admitted the mistake she made from driving drunk, and how serious it was to drink and drive. She partnered with advocacy groups for the cause, and slowly regained the favor of the public.

Connie didn't try to explain what really happened anymore. She ignored all the speculations. Smokey had gone to jail, and would never find another career in radio. Connie thanked Dean for his help. Mr. Yancy's FM station WHKY failed, but his AM station in sports became a success. However, Connie learned recently that Mr. Yancy was headed to court for tax evasion.

After returning from a long walk outside with Tracey in the park, Connie settled on the sofa in her living room, while Tracey went over her friend Kay-Kay's house to hang out. Peaches handed her the mail that arrived.

"Bills, bills, and . . . hold up," Connie ripped open a letter addressed from BigStar Records. She quickly read through it, and with each word her heart began to pound with excitement.

"What is it?" Peaches sat next to her.

Connie beamed a smiled. "This is awesome!"

"What? You won *Publisher's Clearing House* or something?"

"No, but I got it!" Connie hugged Peaches.

"Got what?"

"I got the job at BigStar Records!"

"Congratulations!" Peaches shouted, and then she got serious. "So, who in the hell is BigStar?"

"It's a big record company. I'm going to be the Director of Marketing. They said they tried to reach me but had a bad number. I forgot I still had my old phone number on my resume."

"So how much money we talking?" Peaches folded her arms.

"Don't worry about it, but we do need to start packing," Connie stood up and went into the kitchen, grabbed a *Tab* soda out the frig.

"Pack? What for?"

"The job is in California."

"Yes!" Peaches clasped her hands. "I always wanted to know what California was like. I can't wait to move there and see the palm trees, beaches, and hopefully I get to meet that fine Eddie Murphy!" Peaches shouted with excitement.

The front door opened and Tracey walked in with Kay-Kay.

"Girls, I have great news!" Connie announced.

"What?" Tracey was curious.

"I got a new job," Connie smiled, hugged Tracey.

"That's great Mom."

"We're going to have to start packing soon."

"Packing?" Tracey's jaw dropped. Her initial enthusiasm went out the window. "Why? Where are we going? Are we moving back home to Chicago?"

"Nope. This time we're going somewhere warm."

"Florida?" Kay-Kay asked.

"That's close Kay-Kay."

"Oh Connie just spit it out!" Peaches huffed.

"We're moving to California! Isn't that great?!" Connie looked at Tracey's long face. "Aw don't worry sweetie. You will love California."

"But I don't want to leave New York, Kay-Kay and my Dad lives in Buffalo!" Tracey cried.

"I understand how you feel Tracey but—"

"No you don't!" Tracey pushed Connie's hand off her shoulder.

"We're always moving because of your job. I hate your job. I hate that you always have to work, and I hate California too."

"Kay-Kay, why don't you come back later on so I can talk with Tracey, okay?"

"Okay," Kay nodded. "I'll call you later Tracey."

Tracey rolled her eyes and heaved a long sigh. Connie asked her to sit down on the sofa.

"Baby, I know this is hard on you right now, but one day you will understand that I work so hard because I love you. I don't want to see you suffer the way me and your Aunt Peaches did."

"But we're not suffering Mom. We're doing just fine the last I checked."

"Now young lady, you watch that tone with me. We're moving to California or else I won't have a job and we'll all be out on the streets. Is that what you want?"

Tracey tightened her lips and began to rapidly tap her feet against the floor.

"Then it's settled. We're moving to California."

Tracey got up and stomped her way upstairs to her room.

Ding Dong . . .

"You get the door. I'll go up and talk to my niece," Peaches said.

Peaches knocked on Tracey's door.

"Go away!" Tracey shouted.

Peaches opened the door to find Tracey on the bed crying. "Are you alright niecey?"

"Do I look alright?"

"Hey, you better watch your mouth because I'm not your mother. I'll give you two busted lips in a heartbeat!" Peaches pointed.

Tracey rolled her eyes.

"I black eyes too. If you don't believe me. You should see some of the girls I beat up in jail."

"Yeah well if you hit me that's where you will end up at again. I'll call the cops!"

"Typical brat!" Peaches argued. "So we're moving to California and you don't like it. Well so what! You ought to be happy kiddo. Let me tell you something. There are kids out here who wish they could choose where to live at, but they can't. Some of them are homeless and living out in the streets. Have you ever thought about that?"

Tracey sat up on her bed crossed her arms. "But I'm tired of moving. Doesn't anybody care about how I feel? I have friends here you know? And what about school?" She pouted.

"I know how you feel kid, but getting mad at your mother and showing disrespect like that is not cool. Your mother has been through a lot and she doesn't deserve your funky attitude. You need to apologize."

"Maybe I will and maybe I won't."

"You know what, I was wrong about you," Peaches shook her head in disbelieve.

"Wrong about what?"

"I always thought you were smart and mature for your age, but you're just a big baby."

"Am not!"

"You are! I'm going downstairs I think I heard Cheryl's voice. I like hanging out with mature people who are understanding."

Peaches got up off the bed to leave.

"Wait Aunt Peaches!" Tracey called. "I'll go with you."

"Why? I don't like brats hanging around me."

"What if this brat apologizes to her mother?"

Peaches smiled. "Maybe I'll let her hang."

Tracey hugged her. "I'm sorry Aunt Peaches."

"I'm cool. You just make sure you tell your mother the same."

"Robert proposed," Cheryl announced, holding out her left to Connie, just as Peaches and Tracey came downstairs.

"Oh, the ring is gorgeous!" Connie awed. "Congratulations!"

"That's good to hear Cheryl, does Robert have any older brothers or younger? Don't matter so long as they single," Peaches smiled, gave Cheryl a hug to congratulate her.

"He's an only child," Cheryl replied.

"Dag!"

"What happened with you and George?" Connie asked Peaches.

"Who said I had to just have *one* man?"

"Oh, well excuse me!" Connie and Cheryl laughed.

Connie went on to share her news with Cheryl about California, and then she offered Cheryl to join them.

"Well, Robert and I are going to stay here in New York. I'm moving out of my place next week."

"Oh Cheryl, I'm so happy for you, but I'm going to miss you. You were really a good friend to me and the best assistant I ever had."

"It was nice working for you Connie. Keep in touch when you move to Cali."

"Absolutely. You and Robert should come out to visit."

"We sure will."

Cheryl left shortly after her announcement, and Connie sat on the sofa with her favorite bowl of strawberry ice cream and started watching TV.

"You go be with your mother," Peaches whispered to Tracey. "I'm going out tonight. I'll see you later."

Tracey approached Connie who was sitting on the sofa. "Mommy."

"Yes?"

Tracey sat down next to her. "I'm sorry about earlier."

Connie put her arm around Tracey. "I forgive you."

"I just wish Kay-Kay could come with us, but I'll take Aunt Peaches. She's cool."

Connie smiled. "Yes, she is cool."

"Good night Mom."

"Goodnight."

Connie finally settled in bed that night, after calling and telling her father about California. He was so happy for her. "Oh shoot how I could forget to tell Dean!" Connie realized, just as she had fluffed out her pillows to get comfortable enough to go to sleep. She thought of waiting until tomorrow, but decided not to wait another minute.

"I'm moving to California," Connie said over the phone to Dean. His heart nearly dropped. He thought, *not again.*

"I accepted an offer to work for Big Star Records, and no, I'm not dream chasing again. This time it will be a desk job, and it will be my only job from nine-to-five, no weekends, except for special events. That's what I called to tell you."

"Wow! This is sudden."

"Not really. I had applied for the position after I sold CMP and Gina's Lounge to Mr. Yancy. I'm just now hearing back. I decided to accept the offer."

"Congratulations. I'm really happy for you, and you sound good too," Dean said. They had rebuilt a pretty good friendship over the past few months, and he was feeling pretty good about the way things were going between the two of them. Now his friend was leaving him again, and a part of him already felt lonely. Dean Jr. was away in school, and Connie was moving further away to California. He wondered if there was actually more to life than the big city of Chicago. He loved the city, but the curiosity of being somewhere else was starting to intrigue him as well.

"Well, it's been a long day Dean. I'd better go."

"Have a good night, and thanks for calling."

"Of course. I couldn't forget about you," Connie blushed behind the phone.

"You better not ever forget about me."

Connie giggled. "I won't. Night night."

CHAPTER THIRTY-NINE

TIMING IS EVERYTHING

Connie was busy packing her things one Saturday afternoon when her doorbell rang. It was September, and she would be moving to California to start her new job by October 1st. Meanwhile, she was shipping her stuff out to California, to a new home that she'd bought on her own.

"Get that, please!" she yelled downstairs to Peaches and Tracey, who were packing up their kitchen stuff. Connie planned to move out of the Penthouse by next week, and let her brother Willie rent it while he attended NYU with Dean Jr. The two had only met once, but Connie hoped they would get reacquainted at school.

"Hello," a voice called from behind.

Connie looked over her shoulder, wiping the sweat from her eyes. Whitney Houston was crooning *"Saving All My Love"* in the background from Connie's radio. There he was, standing in the doorway looking like a Calvin Klein jeans ad.

"Dean? What are you doing here?" Connie dropped the box-tape to the floor, and the two rushed into each other's arms and embraced.

"Well, I wanted to see you before you left. Do you need a hand?" he offered.

"Actually, I do. If you can grab some of those boxes over there to take downstairs, that would be great."

"All ten boxes here are shoes?"

Biting down on her pinky finger, Connie smiled and answered in a coyly, girlish voice. "Yeeees."

"Wow! You women are a trip. I have five pairs of shoes, that's it," Dean shook his head, laughing, as he took a few boxes down the steps and sent Dean Jr. upstairs to collect the rest.

The moving truck came and hauled away all the major stuff to ship to California, like her furniture, her Mercedes, and other heavy stuff. Once the movers had left, everyone sat around catching a second wind and gulped down beverages.

"How about we all go get something eat?" Dean offered.

"I'm tired," Peaches yawned. "I'll just make me a choke sandwich and call it a night."

"I'm tired too. I moved too many boxes, and I already broke two fingernails. This is so not cute. I need another manicure." Tracey stared at her fingers. She was twelve, now, going on twenty.

"Same here, I'm too tired." Dean Jr. yawned. "I need to head on back to campus."

Dean turned towards Connie. "I guess that leaves the two of us."

"That's fine. Let's get cleaned up and head out someplace."

"Sounds good," Dean agreed, following her upstairs. He showered in the guest room, and she showered in her own bathroom.

Dean and Connie walked by the Hudson River after dinner. They had taken the Ferry to Liberty Island. It was a warm, beautiful late-summer night in New York.

"She's beautiful," Dean paused in the middle of the walkway to look at the Statue of Liberty.

"Yes she is. You know, I'm going to miss New York. I loved it here. Who knows, I may come back here if I make enough money to live in the Hamptons one day." Connie smiled, thinking of the good memories she had there.

"It's a nice city, but I know I'll miss *you* more than this place," said Dean, looking down into her eyes.

"Are you sure you're going to miss little 'ole me?" Connie flirted.

"Why do you think I came all this way?" he slowly took her into his arms. "You know, the last time I came here, you left me standing out in the cold like a dog with its tail caught between his legs."

"I was at a different place in my life, then," Connie admitted, her eyes dancing with his.

"Seems like you've found your way back to the real you."

"I had God's help and yours."

"You put in the work, too."

"I did. I'm proud to say I haven't had a drink in three months, and I have no desires for one."

Dean smiled. "I'm proud of you. I always knew you could do it."

"It's amazing, isn't it? We've been through so much in our lives and yet here we are," Connie gently stroked the side of his face. "I'm going to miss you, Dean. You are really someone very special to me, and I'll always love you for everything you have done for me. You solved my sister Baby's case, you helped free my sister from jail, and you did so much for me personally."

"Like what?"

"You taught me how to love, and how to accept love."

"And you once said I needed to stop trying to be everyone's hero, and so I learned to be my own. You inspired me to want more for myself and to follow my heart. I've been doing that, thanks to you. You were my motivation."

"I'm proud of you too, Dean. You followed your dreams. I hope that life will continue to bring you everything you ever wished for."

"I hope so too." Dean kneeled down in front of her and got down on one knee. "You got away from me twice, but I won't let you go a third time. If you'll have me, you will make the rest of my dreams come true."

Connie gasped. *Is this really happening? Is this what I think?* Her eyes lit up brighter than the stars in the sky as Dean removed the velvet box from his jacket pocket.

"Connie Marie Morris, will you marry me? Will you have me as your husband?"

Connie's eyes swelled with tears. "Yes! Yes, I'll marry you, Dean!"

Dean slid a beautiful princess-cut diamond ring onto her finger, and they kissed.

"I love you, Connie."

"I love you too. I never stopped."

"You guys can come on out now!" Dean shouted.

Connie turned around. Tracey, Dean Jr., Peaches, Cheryl, and Hank seemed like they had come from nowhere, but they were sitting inside a limo watching the whole time.

"What are you guys doing here? Don't tell me you were all in on this?" Connie shook her head in shock, and was surprised to see they were all dressed up.

"Yep!" Tracey said proudly.

"Dean, how did you have time to plan this?" Connie asked.

"With speed!" Dean wiped the sweat from his forehead. "And, thanks to Cheryl and Peaches for their help as well."

"Peaches, you knew?" Connie asked her.

"Girl, he called me last week and asked what I thought about you two getting married, and I told him I was cool with it. He called your father Scott in South Carolina and got his blessings too."

"So, do I finally get to call you Mom?" Dean Jr. kissed Connie's cheek.

"Yes you can," Connie smiled. "This is the happiest day of my life!"

"Mine too!" Tracey hugged her mother and Dean. "I get to stop calling you Dean, and I can call you Daddy now." Dean kissed Tracey's forehead.

"I'm so happy for you guys. I always knew you were the woman for my cousin." Hank hugged and then kissed Connie.

"I'm proud of you, man," Hank hugged Dean. "Make sure you guys make some babies on that honeymoon."

"Yes, make some beautiful babies," Cheryl agreed.

"You bet we will." Connie planted a kiss on Dean's lips. She couldn't wait to start planning.

"I'm going to make you very happy, Mr. Wilson."

"You already did when you said yes."

EPILOGUE

I Have Seen the River
(A Poem for Baby)
I am a dancing vision of light under the sun
I am a reflection of a rainbow after the storm
I am the clouds that hold the rain
I am the soul that has endured much pain.
I have seen the river because I have seen God
Through my troubled life when times were hard
And now I watch the river with a feeling of tranquility
God has saved my soul and helped me to help many
For what I couldn't see then, I can see now
My reflection in the river waters- I was always God's child
I have seen the river, and I'll keep watching it move
and flow with God's spirit
because I have so much more to prove . . .

~Connie Morris

Riding the Waves
The sequel
Coming Soon!